A HEARTS DESIRE

Valentine's Day—a much awaited holiday filled with long-standing traditions, formal balls, and everlasting love. And these three charming stories by three favorite Zebra Regency authors tell of a Valentine's Day long ago, in an age of strict conventions, proper manners . . . and hidden passion. Smugglers, masquerades, and French lovers are just some of the things you'll read about in these tales of romantic intrigue and secret desire.

So give a gift to the one you love and give a gift to yourself as you join with Karla Hocker, Mary Kingsley, and Anthea Malcolm for three delightful novellas of Valentine's Day love and romance!

D1398788

ELEGANT LOVE STILL FLOURISHES—
Wrap yourself in a Zebra Regency Romance.

A MATCHMAKER'S MATCH   (3783, $3.50/$4.50)
by Nina Porter
To save herself from a loveless marriage, Lady Psyche Veringham pretends to be a bluestocking. Resigned to spinsterhood at twenty-three, Psyche sets her keen mind to snaring a husband for her young charge, Amanda. She sets her cap for long-time bachelor, Justin St. James. This man of the world has had his fill of frothy-headed debutantes and turns the tables on Psyche. Can a bluestocking and a man about town find true love?

FIRES IN THE SNOW   (3809, $3.99/$4.99)
by Janis Laden
Because of an unhappy occurrence, Diana Ruskin knew that a secure marriage was not in her future. She was content to assist her physician father and follow in his footsteps . . . until now. After meeting Adam, Duke of Marchmaine, Diana's precise world is shattered. She would simply have to avoid the temptation of his gentle touch and stunning physique—and by doing so break her own heart!

FIRST SEASON   (3810, $3.50/$4.50)
by Anne Baldwin
When country heiress Laetitia Biddle arrives in London for the Season, she harbors dreams of triumph and applause. Instead, she becomes the laughingstock of drawing rooms and ballrooms, alike. This headstrong miss blames the rakish Lord Wakeford for her miserable debut, and she vows to rise above her many faux pas. Vowing to become an Original, Letty proves that she's more than a match for this eligible, seasoned Lord.

AN UNCOMMON INTRIGUE   (3701, $3.99/$4.99)
by Georgina Devon
Miss Mary Elizabeth Sinclair was rather startled when the British Home Office employed her as a spy. Posing as "Tasha," an exotic fortune-teller, she expected to encounter unforeseen dangers. However, nothing could have prepared her for Lord Eric Stewart, her dashing and infuriating partner. Giving her heart to this haughty rogue would be the most reckless hazard of all.

A MADDENING MINX   (3702, $3.50/$4.50)
by Mary Kingsley
After a curricle accident, Miss Sarah Chadwick is literally thrust into the arms of Philip Thornton. While other women shy away from Thornton's eyepatch and aloof exterior, Sarah finds herself drawn to discover why this man is physically and emotionally scarred.

Available wherever paperbacks are sold, or order direct from the Publisher. Send cover price plus 50¢ per copy for mailing and handling to Zebra Books, Dept. 4471 , 475 Park Avenue South, New York, N.Y. 10016. Residents of New York and Tennessee must include sales tax. DO NOT SEND CASH. For a free Zebra/ Pinnacle catalog please write to the above address.

A
Valentine's Day Delight

Karla Hocker
Mary Kingsley
Anthea Malcolm

ZEBRA BOOKS
KENSINGTON PUBLISHING CORP.

CONTENTS

The Dilatory Groom   7
by Karla Hocker

The Crystal Heart   95
by Mary Kingsley

Fit For A Prince   221
by Anthea Malcolm

The Dilatory Groom
by
Karla Hocker

One

"Wilt thou, Alan Edward Trent, have this woman, Claire Marie Sutherland . . ."

Beautiful words. Blessed ritual. Holding her breath, Claire waited for Alan's response. But when the apse should have resounded with the groom's "I will," silence hung thick and heavy in the flower-scented air.

Claire frowned and gave herself a quick, impatient shake. Daydreams! What a wasted exercise they were. Not even in her imagination could she get Alan to the sticking point.

She collected the basket in which she had carried the Sutherland floral offering for Sunday service and, after a final critical look at the arrangement of catkins and primroses on the altar, left the chill gloom of Thistledown's four-hundred-year-old church. Some day she'd be married here. To Alan.

"Claire, when will you and Alan finally be wed?"

If anyone but Sarah had asked the question, Claire would have raised an eyebrow and said, *"Wed? Alan and me? Great Heavens! Whatever gave you such a notion? Oh, you must have remembered that old tale . . . that we were promised from the cradle. Believe me, dear ma'am, that's a fantasy our parents indulged in but briefly. Alan and I would not suit, and* if Sir Arthur and my father were still alive, they'd be the first to admit it."

However, this was Sarah asking, Claire's twin, and Sarah knew and would not hesitate to point out that "the lady doth protest too much." Indeed, Sarah was well aware that quiet, sensible Claire and restless, daring Alan did not suit—if personality was the one ingredient to make or break a marriage. But Sarah was also aware of her twin's feelings for Alan Trent, feelings innocently awakened with a simple kiss goodbye when Alan went off to war as an eighteen-year-old cornet. Claire had been thirteen.

In the intervening seven years Claire had seen Alan only when he was home on leave, once when Alan's father died, and about half a dozen times when his injuries demanded more care than could be provided by army surgeons and orderlies.

The previous November, Alan had finally sold out. Claire, now twenty years old, still suffered a breathless excitement and pulse-quickening eagerness whenever she faced Alan. And, Sarah knew, Claire was determined to fulfill the ancient cradle promise made by the late Sir Arthur Trent and the late Harold Sutherland—no matter how impetuously Claire denied this when questioned by anyone other than her twin.

The sisters were sitting on the windowseats in the large bay of the vicarage parlor, two young ladies as alike as two peas in a pod. Both had wide gray eyes that could light with amusement at the most unexpected moment; they had identical straight, slender noses, and thick medium-brown hair with a deplorable tendency to escape confining ribbons and hairpins; and each showed a dimple at the left corner of her mouth when she smiled. But now, for the first time in twenty years, they could easily be told apart even by a casual acquaintance. Sarah, the younger by thirty-five minutes, had been married two years and was expecting her first child.

Sarah was knitting, her eyes on her work, and gave no sign that she eagerly awaited Claire's answer. After an almost intolerably long silence, her reticence was rewarded.

"I'm beginning to doubt that Alan will ever settle down."

Claire absently fingered the soft wool Sarah was knitting into a baby blanket. "Let alone marry."

"Humbug! Years of fighting the bloodiest battles the world ever saw . . . catching bullets, getting cut up by sabers and bayonets . . . it must be enough to make the most adventuresome man wish for a quiet life."

"Not Alan." Wistfulness struggled with pride in Claire's voice. "He'll always be dashing and daring. A little wild and reckless. And, well, splendid! And I wouldn't want him any different."

"Then, what *do* you want? If you've changed your mind about marrying Alan, you should have accepted Admiral Seymore's nephew."

"I have not changed my mind. And I wouldn't accept Roger Seymore if he were dipped in gold. All I want is for Alan to realize that being a husband—*my* husband—does not mean he must also be a staid and stodgy country squire."

"Then it's up to you to convince him. Should be a simple undertaking for someone who persuaded the admiral to host the Valentine's Day Ball this year."

Claire rolled her eyes at the memory of her uphill battle with the crusty old tar. The admiral enjoyed parties, but not at his house. He claimed his niece, Lucinda, was too young and too flighty to play hostess. In truth, he didn't like his household turned upside-down with preparations. But the Sutherlands, who usually hosted the Valentine's Day festivities, were giving a birthday ball for Anne, the youngest Sutherland daughter, just two nights earlier. Thus Claire had taken it upon herself to volunteer Admiral Seymore for Valentine's Day.

She reached over and waggled one of her sister's knitting needles. "You tell me how I can convince Alan of anything! He avoids me."

Sarah dropped a stitch and, what was more unusual, ignored it. "How can you say that! He's forever at your side. Even Lady Abercrombie noticed—as shortsighted as she is—and made some sly remark about Alan sitting in your pocket."

"Hmm, yes. When faced with a choice between Lucinda

Seymore and me as a conversational partner, Alan definitely prefers me."

"Goose. Of course he prefers you. Lucinda is but a pretty widgeon, and Alan never could abide a featherbrain."

"Precisely, slow-top." The warm laughter in Claire's eyes took the sting out of her words. "That's why Alan's attentions to me don't mean anything. The point is, I have not had a private word with him since his return."

Sarah held the baby blanket high to catch the light from the narrow mullioned panes in the bay window. When she had recovered the dropped stitch, she said, "Patience, dear. It has been only three months."

For Claire the three months had stretched like years.

"You're not timid," said Sarah. "But you're too cautious and reserved in your approach. How is Alan supposed to know that you love him? During his leaves, you concealed your feelings all too well."

"What are you saying? That I should moon and swoon over him? Wear my heart upon my sleeve? Sarah, I'm not that ill-bred."

"Of course not. But how will you ever find out whether he's the marrying kind if you make no push to be alone with him? Would I be married now if I had allowed George to set the pace of his courtship?"

"No, but this is hardly the same situation. You knew that George loved you."

Sarah waved the argument aside. "Listen to me, Claire! Don't sit around waiting for Alan to ask you to go riding or whatever. *You* do the asking. What you need, dear, is a smidgen of resolution."

"Not resolution. I have that." The dimple at the corner of Claire's mouth peeped as she gave Sarah a quick smile. "What I need is a share of the daring you and Alan have so abundantly. But, in truth, I fear he already regrets leaving the Duke of Wellington's staff. And how can I blame him? Life in Thistledown is so very dull."

"And Paris is so very gay and exciting, especially for the

conquerors. You don't suppose—" Sarah hesitated. "Claire, could Alan have formed an attachment in Paris?"

An attachment in Paris . . .

The window, Sarah, the low table between them, everything spun around Claire in a dizzying circle. Her fingers dug into the seat cushion. It hadn't occurred to her that Alan might find someone else. Lucinda Seymore could be no rival; but a sophisticated Parisienne?

"Oh, my dear, I am so sorry." Clumsily, Sarah moved her increasing form closer and wrapped an arm around her sister. "My wretched tongue!"

Claire took a deep breath as equilibrium and confidence returned.

"It's all right, Sarah. I'm in no danger of swooning or having an attack of the vapors. I was merely taken by surprise."

Sarah squeezed Claire's shoulders. "It was just a thought that popped into my head. Stupid of me to have spoken it aloud. I don't really believe Alan lost his heart in Paris."

"Neither do I. If Alan were in love with some other woman, I would know."

At half past three, Claire shut the stout vicarage door behind her. While she visited with Sarah, the sky had turned leaden with the threat of snow, and the cold, moist February wind had picked up. It caught her cloak, whipping the heavy cloth as if it were a sail waiting to be filled.

Quickly, Claire flipped up her hood and fastened it before retrieving the empty flower basket from the stoop. She wished that George, her brother-in-law, could take her home in the vicarage gig; but Saturday afternoons he was out and about on parish business which might occupy him till evening. Thistledown was but a middling village of some ninety-odd cottages and a dozen substantial brick houses, of which the vicarage with five bedrooms was the smallest. The parish, however, was far spread and encompassed the neighboring village of Snuffton, several freehold farms, and three large estates with their manor houses and tenant farms.

Passing the bay window, Claire waved to Sarah, then turned her back on the vicarage. She hurried past the bakery, the smithy, the Thistledown Inn. She shouldn't have stayed so long. A snowfall seemed imminent, and on foot it would take her the better part of an hour to reach Sutherland Hall.

Basket swinging from one hand, thick folds of cloak and gown clasped in the other, Claire ran across the common, where the wind howled and patches of old gray snow and ice clung to the frozen ground. Only when she reached the woods separating village and manor houses did she slow down.

Here, where the previous days' feeble sun had been filtered by tall oak and beech trees, snow still lay thick and clean, glistening with a thin crust of ice. The lane, bordered by frozen wheel ruts, was trampled hard and slick by horses' hooves and booted feet—the smugglers again, if the whispers in Sutherland Hall's kitchen could be believed. Drat the rascals! They passed far too often lately, and their tracks did not make for comfortable walking; but at least she was sheltered from the biting wind.

Claire could not have been in the woods longer than a quarter hour when the first snowflakes tumbled through the tree branches. Heavy and wet, the size of tuppence pieces, they smacked against her face, spurring her to lengthen her stride. A grave mistake, for which she paid instantly with a very sore backside and a dented basket. Dotted with new snow, the icy patches in the lane had turned treacherous; unless she wished to invite further tumbles, she would have to plod through the deep snow beneath the trees.

Grumbling about a certain inconsiderate brother who had selfishly appropriated the carriage just when his sister needed it most, Claire waded into the snow. She couldn't afford a sprained or broken ankle. Not if she wanted to attend Anne's birthday ball on Monday, or Lady Abercrombie's dinner on Tuesday night. Or the Valentine's Day Ball on Wednesday!

Functions the dashing Sir Alan Trent had promised to grace with his presence.

After a few steps Claire abandoned the basket and used both hands to hitch her skirts. Even so, the hems of cloak and gown grew sodden and heavy in the back. Worse, the tops of her calf-length boots began to fill with snow and ice crystals she kicked up.

In general, she enjoyed a walk in the snow as much as the next person, but this walk had ceased to be fun. The trees no longer offered shelter from the wind as it tore around thick, unyielding trunks and tried its best to knock her down. The snow fell faster, a curtain of cold, wet whiteness that kept slapping at her face. The temperature, nothing to boast of at noon, when her brother had set her down at the church, had plummeted several degrees, and daylight was fading fast.

Claire struggled on, concentrating on staying upright and putting one icy-cold foot in its sopping wet boot before the other. Just a few more steps . . . a hundred paces at the most . . . and she would reach the small clearing where the lane forked three ways. Straight ahead, nearly two miles to Sutherland Hall, her home. Left, one mile to Trafalgar, Admiral Seymore's estate. Right, a bare quarter mile to the sprawling brick Tudor house commonly known as the Manor. Alan's house.

A gleam lit in her eyes. Naturally, someone caught in a snowstorm would seek refuge at the closest shelter. There was hope yet that this wasn't a totally miserable day.

On the other hand, she need not have been miserable at all if she and Alan were married. Alan Trent's carriage house, unlike the one at Sutherland Hall, held more than one roadworthy vehicle. As his wife, she would not be reduced to walking in a snowstorm.

But as his wife, she'd gladly walk for miles. In a blizzard. In a hurricane. As Alan's wife . . .

And what a goose she was! Dreaming again when she should be giving thought to a meeting with Alan. A private meeting.

Claire couldn't see for the thick, swirling mass of snow, but she suspected she had reached the fork in the lane when the wind, which had been blowing more or less straight at her, suddenly whirled all about her as it often does in an open space.

The next step confirmed her suspicion. One foot stumbled into a rut, the other encountered a patch of ice, and her backside once more made painful contact with a stretch of hard lane. A steep but worthwhile price to pay for a visit which, during a veritable blizzard, Alan could hardly cut short with the excuse of having promised a friend to go rabbit shooting.

Claire had just scrambled up and regained a firm foothold in the snow accumulation along the right-hand fork when she heard above the howl of the wind a different kind of howl. An animal howl. An instant later, she was knocked down in the embrace of a huge hound. A hot, wet tongue licked her face.

"Rufus." Winded and exasperated, she could barely whisper. Neither did it help that her heart was beating in her throat. For where Rufus was, Alan would not be far behind.

"Get off, Rufus. You're squashing me."

Ordinarily the most obedient of dogs, Rufus ignored her. He raised his sleek head and howled, again louder than the fierce wind.

A horse whinnied. A man swore. A dark shape, a bat the size of a door, swooped down on Claire and dog and dumped into the snow mere inches from them. One of the wings hit her in the face. But of course, it wasn't a bat wing.

"What the devil!" That was Alan's voice, deep and resonant even in irritation; a voice that always struck a chord inside her.

Claire brushed the fold of cold, damp, horse-smelling cloak off her face. Rufus, after giving her an affectionate lick, bounded off. She could finally sit up—and found herself eye-to-eye with Alan, on his knees beside her. Snow clung to his

16

dark hair and his clothing. His lean face was reddened from the wind and the cold.

"Claire? What are you about, walking in this weather?" His voice held no irritation now, only incredulity and a hint of censure. "And unaccompanied, I suppose."

"Lud, yes! I haven't taken a maid or a groom in years. None of them can keep pace with me. Help me up, will you, Alan?"

He got to his feet in one smooth movement, drawing her with him. "Are you hurt?"

"Not at all." She'd hardly complain about soreness in a certain part of her anatomy. "And I owe my good fortune to Rufus, I suspect. He knocked me down before you could ride me down. You were riding, weren't you? I heard a horse just before you landed beside me."

"Yes, I was riding." His voice turned rueful. "And, thanks to Rufus's howl, I was thrown!"

She laughed, snow and cold forgotten in the sheer pleasure of his presence. "Poor Alan. The ignominy of it! And you won't be able to hide your shame, since horse and hound will reach the stables long before you do. Your grooms will dine out on the story for a twelvemonth."

"Serves me right. I couldn't see, and I was pressing Beelzebub harder than I should have." He cupped her chin in his gauntleted hand. "Are you certain you're all right, love?"

"I'm fine."

But she wasn't. His touch, his nearness took her breath away, and the way he addressed her as "love" turned her knees to jelly. It meant nothing; he addressed every female under twenty-five in that carelessly caressing manner. But awareness did not equate with immunity.

She forced a brisk tone. "If we stand around much longer, though, we'll both turn into icicles."

He chuckled. "That's my Claire. Delightfully prosaic and practical."

"Speaking of practical, will you please help me with my hood?"

Alan obligingly shook out the hood, which had slipped off during Rufus's loving assault and was filled with snow.

He said, "Many a time I wished for your calm voice and common sense advice when we were plagued by the elements during a campaign. I'm sure you would have known how to deal with dust and grit in our provisions, and rain and mud soaking our bedding."

"Would I?" she said faintly. He had thought of her those long years abroad! But, alas, it was her common sense he had missed.

"All set, love?"

Snow had also somehow worked its way inside the neckline of her cloak and melted along her throat and down her back in icy trickles, but that couldn't be helped now.

Shivering, she urged, "Let's go!"

Alan placed an arm around her shoulders and turned her toward the Manor. At least, she hoped it was the direction of the Manor. What with the tumbles, Alan's sudden appearance, and the twirling, whirling snow, she had lost all sense of direction.

Claire had not forgotten or dismissed her wish for a prolonged tête-à-tête with Alan, but even with his arm around her she had no desire to walk in circles in the icy wind. Or to stumble into a snowdrift. Or to trudge all the way to Sutherland Hall. And if this meant that she lacked romantic spirit, so be it. She still intended to marry Alan. He had spirit enough for the two of them.

Meanwhile, she stamped bravely at his side, determined not to drag or lag or be a nuisance in any way. Walking did seem easier with his support, and the elements less punishing with his solid form pressing close. She could almost wish . . .

Nonsense! She did not wish to get lost merely to prolong the walk. She had no breath for speech, and besides, her heels were beginning to blister.

When a familiar brick gatepost and the blurred outline of a high stone wall suddenly materialized out of the swirling white mass, Claire was heartily and most unromantically glad that very soon Alan would deposit her in the motherly care of his housekeeper.

Then, warm and dry, she would snatch her opportunity with Alan.

Two

Bathed and changed, Sir Alan Trent awaited his unexpected guest in the library, where a generous mound of glowing coal spread comforting warmth. If his mother were in residence, a fire would have been laid in the front parlor and in one or two of the upstairs sitting rooms as well. Lady Trent, however, had finally, a sennight ago, submitted to her physician's and friends' urging and departed for southern Italy with her companion. And Alan had given most of the staff a holiday.

A bachelor's existence, he had decided then and there, and the absence of housekeeper, maids, butler, and footmen, would suit him for more reasons than one. But he hadn't counted on a visit from Claire.

Sipping brandy, Alan paced in front of the fireplace. After a few moments, he stalked to the windows and closed the heavy velvet drapes against the wind and snow whirling outside. He lit more candles. He plucked a couple of books off a chair and restored them to their shelves. He collected used glasses from various repositories and stashed them in the credenza. He picked a rumpled cravat off the blotter on his desk, scowled at it, then tossed it back.

The deuce! He was not embarrassed by his slovenly housekeeping, and he was definitely not nervous about spending an hour or so alone with Claire Sutherland.

Alan remembered her—or, rather, *them*—as pigtailed little

girls of five or six: Sarah, the younger by half an hour, always a length ahead of the more cautious Claire; and Claire ever on the alert to keep her twin from harm or to rescue her from a scrape, which often had its origin in a dare posed by Alan and the girls' older brother, Stuart.

The pigtailed little girls had grown and gained the coltish long-legged grace of adolescence. Alan remembered the year they let down their hair and skirts. Sarah at thirteen already knew how to flirt. Claire was reserved and shy. Painfully shy. Nothing could have been more agonizing—for Claire or for Alan—than the bright crimson burning her face when he kissed her goodbye before taking himself off to war.

He had kissed Sarah first—she was still always a few steps ahead of her twin—and Sarah had cried a little and told him to return safe and sound. She had kissed him back, making him feel quite the man of the world. Then he had turned to Claire. And Claire was embarrassed.

Devil a bit! There was nothing like a blushing, shrinking damsel to dampen a man's spirits, especially when he was a man only in his dreams and in reality was a mere stripling with more swagger than savoir faire.

Chuckling at the memory, Alan poured a second brandy. According to his friends, he still had swagger and more daring than was good for him. He had also, however, acquired a good deal of polish. As had Claire. Strange, then, that he should now remember that awkward scene rather than some other, later meeting when he was home on leave.

Overnight, or so it seemed to him on his first visit two years after his leavetaking, Claire had acquired poise and serenity, qualities Sarah had not been able to match until she was *enceinte*. Claire was still quiet, but no longer shy. She still had the habit of rescuing a younger sister, although, since Sarah's marriage, that service applied solely to Anne, the baby of the family, who would be seventeen in a day or so.

Why flirtatious, giggly Sarah had turned into a respectably married matron ahead of the practical, sensible Claire was more than Alan could understand. Except, of course, that

Sarah had always been ahead of Claire. But the vicar's wife? Devil a bit! If one of the Sutherland girls must marry into the vicarage, Claire would have best suited the studious, conscientious George Melton.

And even if Claire didn't want George, she should have been married by now. She was going on one-and-twenty, which must be considered long in the tooth. Claire was pretty, of good family; she was pleasant . . . dashed good company, in fact. So, why wasn't she married?

Unbidden, a snatch of gossip came to mind, something Alan had overheard at the dinner his mother hosted in honor of his safe return from the wars. Some old dame, the dowager Lady Abercrombie, if he recollected correctly, had confided to another that Claire was waiting for *him*, Alan; that Claire considered herself promised. The second beturbaned matron had nodded and whispered something Alan could not hear. Then Admiral Seymore, who *had*, apparently, heard the whispers, gave a snort of disgust and said it was all a humdudgeon; that young people were not so mawkish as to set store by some tomfoolery their sires had cooked up years ago.

With that pronouncement Alan wholeheartedly agreed. And he was quite certain that Claire was not a mawkish sort of girl; most likely she had all but forgotten the ancient promise, as had Alan until that night.

Or *was* he as certain of Claire's good sense as he'd like to be? He would not acknowledge that he was uneasy about being alone with her. That would be ridiculous in a man who'd had as many as five horses shot from under him in the course of a single day's work and lived to deliver the dispatches entrusted to him by the Duke of Wellington at Waterloo.

On the other hand, Alan was forced to admit, he had made no effort since his return or, rather, since his mother's dinner party, to reestablish the easy relationship he and Claire had enjoyed when he was home on leave. He had neither invited her to go riding or ice skating, nor had he challenged her to a game of chess or piquet.

And, devil a bit, he missed her companionship.

Absorbed in thought, Alan had absently shelved another few books and poured a third brandy when the door opened and Claire joined him in the library. The sight of her in a most unsuitable emerald silk dinner gown designed for a much larger woman brought a grin to his face.

"Don't you dare laugh, Alan Trent!" She caught a toe in the dragging hem and quickly adjusted her clutch on the skirt before advancing to the nearest chair.

"I'm not laughing at you, love. Merely at my own fancy." He set his glass on the mantelshelf. "I'd just been thinking what an admirable vicar's wife you'd have made, and there you come traipsing in, clad in a gown with a décolletage more revealing than Princess Caroline's."

Her hands fluttered, but she did not raise them to tug at the drooping neckline. Only her chin rose a little higher.

"A vicar's wife? You do spout the barmiest nonsense, Alan."

"And, I blush to see, you're barefoot." He stood in front of her and inspected the toes and elegantly arched instep peeping out beneath folds of silk. "If that's a gown my sister refused for her trousseau, there should have been a pair of slippers to go with it. Agnes always had matching slippers for her gowns."

"I lost the dratted things on the stairs, because, unfortunately, not only Agnes's figure but also her feet are shaped more generously than mine. And if you're blushing, why is it that you don't turn red?"

"A good question. Why aren't you succumbing to a maidenly blush in the presence of a gentleman?"

"Because I know you for the shameless tease you are. You don't give a fig whether I display a bit of bosom or my bare feet."

"But *such* a bosom," he murmured.

She could not miss the glint in his eyes and spoke with some asperity. "I'll be dashed if I let you put me out of countenance! Now stop teasing, Alan, and fetch me one of your coats. I'm still cold in this gown, but there's no shawl and your wretched valet refuses to invade your wardrobe without your permission. He is as disobliging as ever and leaves me in no doubt that he cannot wait to see the last of me."

"A wretch, indeed. I'll have his hide."

"Bah! More likely, you'll give him a medal. And," she added on a softer note, "I cannot say that I blame you. I'd give him one myself."

He cocked a brow. "Because Meyer doesn't approve of your intrusion into a bachelor's household?"

"Because he saved your life."

Their eyes held and, for a moment, neither spoke. Alan indeed owed his life to Meyer, the lanky, gruff German who had been with the French troops when they advanced on the English-Portuguese army defending Busaco Ridge. During the skirmish, Alan had suffered saber cuts in his thigh and left side. Then his horse was killed. But for Meyer, who dragged Alan from the melee of plunging hooves and thrusting bayonets and sabers, the British stand at Busaco Ridge would have been the end of Alan Trent, newly promoted lieutenant.

Since then, the autumn of 1810, Meyer had served as Alan's self-appointed guardian, his batman, as surgeon and orderly when the ferociousness of battle made a visit to the field hospital impossible, and now he acted as Alan's valet.

Alan turned away. "I'll fetch that coat. And a rug wouldn't come amiss either. But first let me pour you a drop of medicinal brandy."

"I'd prefer tea, if it isn't too much trouble."

"I'll tell Meyer."

"Where are the rest of the staff? Surely your mother did not take Mrs. Simpson and the maids to Italy? Or the footmen and the butler?"

"I gave them a holiday."

She stared at him, then looked about her, saw the evidence of a week's neglect on the once glossy tabletop, and compressed her mouth.

"Dash it, Alan! The house will fall to rack and ruin in no time at all, and your poor mother will suffer an immediate setback when she returns. Why on earth did you let everyone go at once?"

He glanced at the cravat on his desk, and shrugged. "Everything will be put to rights long before Mother even starts to think of returning. And you wrong me. I did not let everyone go on holiday at once. I kept Louis, Meyer, and three grooms."

She dismissed the presence of grooms, a valet, and a French chef with a flick of her hand.

"It's harebrained, Alan. Your lovely home will be spoiled by soot, ashes, dust . . . and mud, when the thaw sets in! Why did you do it?"

"*Why?* Because, love, I want to savor a carefree bachelor's life to the fullest."

From the door, he gave her an exaggerated bow and spoke in a fair imitation of the absent butler's supercilious tone. "I shan't be long, madam. Pray make yourself at home."

"And Meyer will tell you to go to the dickens when you ask him to serve tea," she said, but the door had already closed behind him.

She gripped the arms of her chair. "A carefree bachelor's life! Bah!"

There was no reply to her expression of disgust, either, and for a moment she allowed her imagination free rein. She pictured scarlet ladies in diaphanous gowns flitting through the Tudor hall . . . reclining on cushions in the splendidly paneled and carpeted drawing rooms . . . champagne bubbling in crystal glasses. She pictured Alan, his arms around—

Rubbish! If Alan wanted orgies, he'd have taken chambers in town.

Drawing her bare feet onto the chair, Claire tucked them into the voluminous folds of her borrowed gown. She relaxed against the chair back but almost immediately sat straight up.

Her eyes narrowed. If not for the purpose of conducting orgies, why, then, did Alan want the Manor cleared of its staff?

* * *

Tea was served by Meyer, his craggy face set in lines of deepest disapproval, which made him look more like eighty than like the fifty years he had admitted when pressed by Lady Trent. That had been the previous March, when Alan was home to recover from a persistently festering bullet wound in the shoulder, a memento from the battle at New Orleans, in America. Alan had healed in time to join his old comrades in Brussels a week before the allied armies faced the French troops at Waterloo.

"The wind," Meyer announced in his harsh, guttural accent, "has much slowed down. And the snow also. We can now make the carriage ready."

"Not until Miss Claire's gown and cloak are dry," said Alan.

"I will tell the chef that he must put the clothing of Miss Claire into the warming oven."

Claire frowned. With one of Alan's coats—a wellworn, soft velvet that had retained the heady scent of spice and sandalwood by which she always remembered him—draped around her shoulders, her feet snug under a tartan rug, the first cup of hot, sweet tea inside her, she was finally beginning to feel quite comfortable and in a frame of mind to tackle a delicate subject with Alan. She wasn't about to let the opportunity slip.

She held out her cup to be filled again. "You do that, Meyer," she said pleasantly, "and I'll be here twice as long as it takes to dry the garments in a more suitable manner. You see, my gown and cloak are made of wool."

Pale blue eyes regarded her fixedly. "They shrink?"

"They'd shrivel so they wouldn't fit a doll. And then you'd have to send someone to Sutherland Hall for a change of clothing."

Meyer acknowledged defeat with a nod. "Then it is better that they lie on the bench, where Louis has spread them out. They are already almost dry. Also the boots."

He set the teapot on a drum table, which he positioned carefully within Claire's reach before removing himself to the door. There he stood with his arms folded across his chest, his gaze fixed stonily on a point at the far end of the room.

Alan raised a brow. "That will be all, Meyer."

"Major. Sir!" The valet snapped to attention. "I will stay and chaperone."

Alan looked astonished, then pensive, and Claire saw the opportunity for a private talk diminish rapidly.

She said, "If you fear for my virtue, Meyer, you needn't. I absolve your master from any intent to ravish me."

"The major does not ravish, miss." Emotion strengthened the valet's accent. "What I fear is the treachery of woman."

Silence followed Meyer's doom-laden utterance. Alan was inured to the man's crotchets and preserved his countenance— albeit with difficulty. Claire, all too aware of her designs on Alan, suffered a stab of irritation generously blended with mortification.

She gave the valet a withering stare. "I assure you, Meyer, Sir Alan is perfectly safe in my company. I do not ravish, either."

A choking sound from Alan drew her attention. "Pray *what* is so funny?"

"I don't think that was precisely what Meyer meant." Alan's face was straight, but the dark eyes gleamed. "That you would ravish me."

"Oh, no?" An answering gleam lit in Claire's eyes as her sense of the ridiculous asserted itself. "Does he believe a lady incapable of ravishing a gentleman?"

"I cannot answer for him. But let me tell you that I believed *you* incapable of such brazen banter."

"You don't know me very well, Alan. You see, one of my flaws is a tendency to levity at the most unexpected moment."

"Indeed." He turned his chair for a better view of her. "Tell me more. What other flaws do you have?"

"Alas! I am, at times, cautious to the extent of being considered dull."

"Cautious, yes. I remember *you* never got caught snatching sweetmeats or got treed by that sanguinous bull my father prized so highly. But you were not dull." His eyes narrowed speculatively. "An interesting, not to say unusual, combination. Levity and caution."

"I'd call it a painful combination." Claire's tone was wry. "The struggles that can writhe in me!"

"And which side scores the most points?"

Claire thought a moment. "I'm not sure I can tell you that."

"My slender share of caution generally loses any struggle it might put up."

"That I believe. In you, caution is not a flaw but a virtue that ought to be tenderly coaxed and encouraged to grow. But I doubt very much that it is. You, Alan, are an adventurer and a daredevil."

"It seems you know me very well, even if I don't know as much about you as I thought I did."

Alan looked at Meyer, still standing sentry by the door. "You say the snow has let up? Then you had best ride over to Sutherland Hall. They must be in a stew about Miss Claire."

"If," she murmured, "they noticed my absence."

Alan, recalling that Mrs. Sutherland was more interested in nurturing her orchids than her daughters, thought it quite likely that Claire had not been missed. But curiosity gripped him about Claire and what she called her flaws, and Meyer as chaperone would only hamper further interrogation.

"Assure Mrs. Sutherland that her daughter is safe and sound, Meyer, and that I shall bring her home in a little while."

With obvious reluctance the valet turned to leave. As he opened the door, he said, "A woman spells danger. Remember her that got me drunk, Major, then sold me to the French!"

"Be easy, Meyer. At present, the French are in no position to purchase cannon fodder. And besides, Miss Claire is a friend and a true lady. She doesn't deal in dirty tricks."

Claire did not dare look at Alan. She was almost certain that he had hesitated before answering Meyer. Was there more to his words than simple assurance for the self-appointed chaperone? It couldn't be! Alan could not possibly know her intentions. In any case, she had no dirty trick up her sleeve; merely a great deal of resolve.

She said, "Is that how you came to be with the French army, Meyer? Betrayal? I had wondered about it."

"I did not go from my own free will, miss. That is for quite certain."

"Who was the woman?"

Meyer gave her a cold look. "My wife."

With deliberate care he opened the door as fully as the hinges allowed and left it thus as he departed, his firm tread ringing on the flagstone floor of the Great Hall.

"If that is true, I don't wonder he is a misogynist," said Claire. "But truly, Alan, there was no need to send him to Sutherland Hall."

Indeed, Alan was already asking himself what mischief had driven him when he decided to be rid of Meyer.

"You're quite right. I should have sent a groom."

"That's not what I meant."

"I know. But, believe me, someone had to go. Even if your mother did not notice your absence, Stuart and his wife might. Or Anne. They might be combing the woods for you even now."

"Not at all. You see, Anne is at Trafalgar, helping Lucinda Seymore with silk flowers and garlands for the Valentine's Day Ball. My brother has gone up to London, and Charlotte . . ."

Claire realized she could not be certain about her sister-in-law, whose interest in her husband's siblings waxed and waned with the tides of her mood.

But there was the staff. Her maid knew she had left the house. And the gardener knew. It was probably just as well Alan had sent a message.

She touched the thick earthenware teapot—no doubt the silver pot was tarnished after a week's neglect—and, finding the sides still satisfactorily hot, poured for Alan and herself.

And all the while, her mind was busily seeking a subtle way of broaching the subject dear to her heart. If the old

29

sourpuss Meyer was correct and her cloak and gown were almost dry, she did not have much time.

"Alan," she said. "Do you ever think about marriage?"

Three

"Marriage?" Alan shot out of his chair as if the seat had suddenly sprouted red-hot nails.

"Yes, marriage."

Striving for an expression of guilelessness and serenity, Claire met Alan's alarmed look. There was no point in deploring the unpremeditated burst of bluntness which, in truth, had startled her no less than it had Alan. The difference was that Claire was quite adept at hiding emotion.

"Surely my question is not so very unusual," she said. "After all, you're approaching six-and-twenty, an age when a fair number of gentlemen turn their minds to matrimony."

"Not I."

"Why not?"

Alan deserted his teacup for the brandy glass on the mantelshelf. As a soldier and a member of the Duke of Wellington's staff, he had learned that to trust his instinct and immediately act on it could mean the difference between life and death. This afternoon, he had made a fatal mistake. Out of sheer vanity, he had denied a distinct feeling of unease.

"Aren't you going to answer me, Alan? If you can speculate about me as a hypothetical vicar's wife—"

"That annoyed you, did it? I wonder why?"

She ignored the interpolation. "Then, surely, I may venture

the question why you won't at least give a passing thought to marriage."

"Dash it, Claire! A moment ago you acknowledged I'm an adventurer. Can you see me dragging a wife along to China?"

She blinked. "What does China have to do with anything?"

"I've applied to go with Lord Amherst, who's supposed to visit the Emperor of China."

"But—" Discarding velvet coat and tartan rug, Claire rose, too. "Why, Alan?"

"I don't know all the specifics of the expedition, but I believe Amherst is supposed to talk the emperor into better commercial relations or some such thing."

"That's not what I meant, and you know it!"

Claire's stormy look unaccountably had a relaxing effect on Alan. Perhaps teasing her would get him out of a tight spot.

"Don't box my ears, love. I daresay you want to know why I applied to accompany our ambassador extraordinary?"

"Yes, very much. And there's no need to tell me it's none of my business. I'm well aware of that."

"Then, of course, I shan't say so."

Again he encountered a stormy flash in her eyes, which made him speculate whether quiet Claire could not, with due provocation, be tempted to give rein to a burst of temper.

He waited while she took several quick, impetuous steps away from him, stood looking for a moment at one of the portraits on the wall, then slowly turned and retraced her steps.

No burst of temper. Her face was calm, her voice patient and reasonable.

"Alan, I know you did not like to sell out and did it only because your mama was ill and begged you to come home. And I know you must regret no longer being part of the Duke of Wellington's staff—his family, isn't that what all his dashing aides are called? And the duke expected you to accompany him to the French Court and to balls and the theater—"

"If you think I miss *that* part of my old life, you're mistaken."

"Well, you *cannot* be disappointed that the fighting is over and Napoleon safely put away. Alan, say you're not!"

"Don't be a goose. Of course I'm not disappointed about that."

"But you're not happy, either."

He no longer wished to provoke her. It suddenly was important to try to explain, to try to make Claire understand.

"I am very glad the war is over. The carnage, the——" Alan caught himself. There was no need for gruesome details. "I never want to see a battle again. But, Claire, I do miss the exhilaration that comes from living under constant threat of danger. I miss camp life, the camaraderie, the hustle and bustle when the duke decided to make a move."

He started to pace. "I miss the feeling of adventure evoked by living in foreign places. In short, love, I am plain restless."

"I saw that when you first got home. But then, after New Year, you seemed . . . well, if not precisely enthusiastic about staying here, you gave at least the appearance of being content."

"Should I have moped and let my mother see that I'm not as happy about selling out as she's convinced herself I must be? What a selfish, rag-mannered son you must think me!"

"Oh, no. Certainly not rag-mannered."

Alan narrowed his eyes. "But selfish?"

Encountering her quizzical look, he turned away slightly.

"I suppose," he said after a moment, "the unselfish thing to have done would've been to sell out when my father died. But, dash it, Claire! I was two-and-twenty. I couldn't possibly have settled down to the humdrum life of a country squire. Besides, I have nothing to do here. Ponsonby is an extremely competent estate manager."

"Whether you manage your own estate or not, life here doesn't need to be boring. And now that you're older——"

"And wiser?" he cut in, facing her again. "You sound like my sister. Next, you'll be telling me that I must realize where my duty lies, namely in the setting up of my nursery!"

"May I suggest marriage *before* you start setting up your nursery?"

She looked demure, but Alan could tell by the dimple at the corner of her mouth that she was stifling laughter. By George! She did have a hitherto unsuspected streak of levity, the minx. This, however, was a most unsuitable occasion to indulge that particular flaw.

"Your brother," he said severely, "is a perfect example of a man who did his duty to family and the continuity of his name."

"Yes?" she said encouragingly.

"And see where it got him!" Alan gave a shudder that left no doubt about his feelings. "If it isn't Charlotte henpecking him, it's his offspring squalling at him. Often both at the same time!"

"That is frequently the case with twins. One starts and the other immediately chimes in. But Maggy and Penny don't cry all the time. They're really rather sweet, and Stuart adores them."

"Indeed? Then why does he spend more time in London than in his nursery?"

Since this was a question that lately puzzled the entire Sutherland household, including Charlotte, Stuart's wife, Claire made no reply.

"Twins!" said Alan. "And girls at that. I don't see why Stuart could not have been satisfied with one child. A boy, preferably. Surely he hasn't forgotten how much trouble you and Sarah were."

Claire drew herself up. "Sarah and I *never* caused any trouble whatsoever."

Alan choked on a sip of his brandy, and she waited politely until the fit of coughing ceased.

"Further, I should like to suggest that quite possibly Stuart had no choice in either the quantity or the gender of his children."

"Well, he should have known," said Alan. "The Sutherlands have a whole line of twins dangling from their family tree, so they're bound to crop up time and again. And if he had sought my opinion, I'd have told him to remain a bachelor. It's what I'd have done in his shoes, at least for as long as possible. In a pinch he could always have relied on a cousin to carry on the name."

For the second time within moments, Claire found herself unable to make a retort. She had known there were difficulties ahead, but it had not occurred to her that being a Sutherland and a twin might be a handicap. Now it looked as if her status would be a major obstacle.

Someone of a less than tenacious nature might feel daunted and give up at this point. Not so Claire. In fact, Claire had it on good authority that she could be downright *pertinacious,* the meaning of which she had looked up at age eight in the fat Dixionary the governess kept in the schoolroom. Claire's father had used the phrase "demmed pertinacious brat" in connection with her efforts to ride his stallion, and Mr. Sutherland's tone had not been complimentary.

Now, recalling that she had mastered the stallion eventually, Claire drew courage from the fact that she had a third character flaw. She was not merely tenacious, but stubbornly so; she was resolute, even obstinate, in the adherence to a purpose or design.

"Stumped, love?" asked Alan.

She smiled and shook her head. "Just wondering whether I ought to confess to a third flaw."

"And will you?"

Again she shook her head, and Alan found himself fascinated by a stray curl that dipped and bounced and finally came to rest in the curve of neck and shoulder lavishly exposed by the ridiculously large gown.

"I am more interested," she said, "in learning how you contrived to divert me from the subject at hand. I promise you, *I* never intended to bring Stuart's babies into the conversation."

"Didn't you?"

"I was talking about your settling down at the Manor."

Alan tore his gaze from rich brown hair and skin that showed a golden glow in the soft light shed from the wall sconces. Claire had a lovely neck and shoulders. And the tantalizing swell of her breasts—

He took a step away from the fireplace, which was giving off rather more heat than he appreciated at present and found himself standing quite close to Claire.

"Ah, yes. You noticed a certain contentment—wasn't that the word you used?"

"I don't remember. But was I wrong, Alan? You see, I thought that perhaps you had discovered our smugglers and were happily engaged in chasing them."

This surprised a bark of laughter from him.

"Oh." Disappointment flattened her voice. "I was wrong."

"Not at all. You're rather too perspicacious. Awake upon every suit. Dash it, Claire! How can you know me so well?"

"How can I *not* know you? You haven't changed a bit in the years you were gone."

"I cannot say the same about you."

Alan caught and held her gaze. He had always thought of her as a pretty girl and realized with a slight jolt that she was more than pretty. She was lovely. Truly lovely. He had met countless attractive women during his years abroad, some quite stunningly beautiful, but he had never found it difficult to resist temptation, if resistance was advisable.

Until he looked at Claire just now.

The deuce! He was not an impressionable youth, to be bowled over by a pretty face, but he might as well attempt to stop the earth from spinning as try to stop himself touching that slender neck.

Slowly, he raised his hand. He knew he was a fool, and if he depended on Claire to put him in his place, he was twice a fool. She stood quite still as his fingers touched her cheek, slid down her throat until he felt the flutter of her pulse.

He stepped closer, one hand moving along the gentle slope

36

of her shoulder as far as the wide neckline of her gown allowed, the other hand cupping her chin.

She still did not move but looked at him with an unmistakable invitation in her eyes. He had forgotten, or not paid attention to just how wide her eyes were, and what an intriguing color. A very light gray, with a narrow charcoal rim circling the iris.

First his fingertip, then his mouth brushed her lips, soft and warm and trembling just the slightest bit. Another invitation he had no desire to resist.

But before he could follow through and kiss her as a temptress ought to be kissed, a howl and the scrabble of sharp nails on the flagstones in the Great Hall saved him from committing the ultimate folly.

He had time only to brace himself and tighten his grip on Claire's shoulder before Rufus bounded through the wide open door and flung his not inconsiderable weight at them.

"Down, Rufus!"

The dog complied instantly, and Alan released Claire. "I apologize."

He did not elaborate what the apology was for. And he himself hardly knew. He could not be sorry that the hound had extricated him from a situation gone out of hand. But neither could he regret what had gone before.

And Claire?

Alan watched her closely but saw no sign of embarrassment—she had indeed changed from a blushing, shrinking miss. Neither could he detect annoyance or regret in her steady look. Only a slight smile, impossible to interpret, struck a vaguely disquieting note.

"I daresay Louis sent the dog," Claire said calmly. She bent to scratch Rufus beneath a pendulous ear. "My cloak and gown must be dry."

"Yes, that must be it. I'll get the carriage ready while you change."

* * *

Having duly deposited Claire at Sutherland Hall, Alan returned to the comforts of his library to reflect on his narrow escape.

"But, escape from *what?*" he asked Rufus, who was waiting for his master to settle in a chair.

Alan obligingly sat down and stretched out his legs so the dog could rest forepaws and head on the soft leather of his Hessian boots.

"I was only going to kiss her, Rufus, not propose to her. So why the devil do I feel as if I had just outrun a regiment of French cavalry?"

Rufus raised his sleek tan and black head and gave Alan an unblinking stare.

"You think I'm making a mountain out of a molehill, don't you?"

Rufus's mien did not alter.

"Well, I'm not, old boy. No matter how firm my resolve not to get caught in parson's mousetrap, if I had kissed Claire—properly kissed her—quite likely I'd have been obliged to offer for her."

It seemed to Alan that the hound's drooping ears pricked a little.

"Chivalry, you know. For one thing, Claire is not the kind of young lady one can kiss and then ignore. And for another, there's that mutton-headed promise our sires made. Not that I feel bound by it, mind you! But if I don't watch my step, Claire may just get the notion I'm dangling after her."

Panting, Rufus displayed his fangs.

"Aye, you may grin, you old rake. You do more than kiss your ladies, then leave them to their fate. Without compunction, too. And nary a one bringing you to account, you rascal!"

Alan lapsed into a pensive silence.

Rufus yawned cavernously, then once more propped his jaw on the Hessians and contentedly closed his eyes. It wasn't long, however, before his master's sudden shift from a relaxed slouch to a stiffly upright position jerked Rufus from his slumber. The hound stood, alert and watchful, tail pointing upward and twitching slightly, head cocked in the expectation of a command.

But Alan had no command for his dog. A thought, a notion so unexpected and astonishing that it startled him, had crossed his mind. It was the realization that, when he would finally resign himself to settle down at the Manor some distant year in the future, the only woman he could picture at his side was Claire Sutherland.

Alan was staggered, flabbergasted, to say the least, but had no time to ponder what might have triggered cognition of this astounding truth. His attention was caught by Rufus, growling deep in his throat and staring toward the door.

A moment later, Meyer ushered in a tall, broad-shouldered individual swathed in a heavy frieze overcoat. A muffler that wrapped several times around the man's neck covered his chin, mouth, and most of his nose. A knitted cap pulled low hid the rest of his face, except for the eyes, which were of an even lighter blue than Meyer's pale ones.

"Higgins! I didn't expect you until midnight. When did you leave Pevensey?"

"Not half an hour after you did." Tugging at the muffler, Jack Higgins displayed a nose that had been broken at least twice and an unkempt dark beard. "Would've been here earlier if that blizzard hadn't blowed up. As nasty a bit o' storm as ever I saw. Damned cold, too."

"Meyer will fix you a mug of grog. Unless you'd rather have brandy?"

A wide grin bared uneven but amazingly white teeth. "Brandy's me trade, sir. But grog's me drink, thank you kindly."

"Come to the fire, then, and tell me the news."

A wary eye on Rufus, Higgins stepped closer to the warmth of the fireplace. When the hound paid him no further attention, he removed his frieze coat and knitted cap, then made a great business of rubbing his hands above the glowing coals.

Alan stared for a moment at the broad back.

"Out with it, Higgins. You've kept me in suspense long enough.

Jack Higgins turned, and again the flash of teeth showed in the scrub of dark beard.

"Aye, sir. But then, it's news worth waiting for."

Alan knew a moment of satisfaction. "The delivery! You've got the date. Well done, Higgins."

Four

"Now, Miss Claire, will you sit still!" The middle-aged woman, who had originally been engaged as nurse to the Sutherland children, but had later slipped into the role of personal maid to the three girls, did not hide her exasperation. "How do you expect me to dress your hair when you keep bouncing up and down?"

"I'm sorry, Nana."

"You haven't been yourself since you got caught in that blizzard on Saturday. One moment you're jumpy as a cat on a hot bakestone and the next you wouldn't notice fireworks go off under your nose. Are you coming down with a cold after all, Miss Claire?"

"No, I'm just a little . . . restless." Like Alan, thought Claire.

"Because if you are coming down with something, I'd best fetch you a dose of Dr. James's powders."

"I don't need dosing. Truly, Nana, I'm fine, and I promise to sit still."

"I should hope so. Now, I can understand that Miss Anne fidgets and squirms, which, I tell you, she did no end when I helped her dress."

"I would have thought she'd be too exhausted to fidget any more. All that dashing from window to window all day long to make sure it truly wasn't snowing again. I swear I felt tired merely watching her."

"Well, she's got a right to be excited, has Miss Anne. What with turning seventeen and having a ball in her honor *and* expecting to have her betrothal announced all in the same day!"

"Betrothal? What nonsense is this?" Claire held out a spray of orchids to be fastened in her hair. "Anne is far too young!"

"A girl's never too young to be thinking of a husband and marriage."

Indeed. Claire frowned at the woman's smooth-cheeked, round face reflected in the dressing mirror.

"It's impossible, Nana. Not Anne. Especially not if the suitor is Lawrence Bellingham. Why, he's still tied to his mama's apron strings!"

"That may be so and may be not."

"Is it Lawrence? Was he here today?"

"Can you tell me a day when he doesn't call on Miss Anne?"

"But did he see Stuart? Oh, Nana, what rubbish! Stuart was preoccupied today, I admit. But that, I'm sure, had to do with his London visit. Not with Anne. Stuart would *not* be so silly and give his permission to a betrothal!"

The woman stood back to cast a critical look at her handiwork. "Will it do, Miss Claire? Or do you want me to pull the curls higher?"

"It's lovely. Thank you," said Claire, without so much as a glance at the cluster of curls cascading from the crown of her head to her shoulders.

"Stuart would have told me. Or Anne. She can never keep anything to herself." A tiny groove appeared on Claire's brow. True, Anne was a prattlebox, but she was no fool. Anne knew that her older sister regarded Lawrence as a ninnyhammer.

"Orchids in your hair!" said Nana. She would never do anything so unrefined as sniff, but her pursed mouth and the shake of her head were eloquent enough. "Whoever heard of it? They'll wilt before the ball is half started. Could've knocked me over with a feather when Mrs. Sutherland cut her precious blooms for you girls."

Claire wasn't interested in the orchids her mother raised with such enthusiasm and loving care, except to note that the white blossoms with their pink and mauve edging went well with her ballgown of shot silk.

"Nana, don't tease me!" Claire rose from the dressing table. "Anne is such a baby. Tell me it's not true!"

"And why shouldn't it be, Miss Claire? Miss Sarah wasn't much older when she made up her mind to have our good vicar."

"But George wasn't as young as Lawrence is. Gracious! George had already been a full-fledged vicar for three years when he proposed to Sarah, while Lawrence—well, the least said the soonest mended. Getting himself sent down from Oxford! Nana, you can't deny he's a silly cawker."

"I'm not one to deny the truth," the woman said, unperturbed. "But Miss Anne is determined to have young Mr. Bellingham. And your brother said they might pledge their troth and make the announcement tonight, provided they wait a year before they set the wedding date."

"The devil, he did!"

"Miss Claire!" The former nurse drew herself up. Arms akimbo, she employed the tone of voice she had used when Claire misbehaved as a child. "You know I don't hold with such language from a lady, and I should hope I taught you better than that."

"I'm sorry. But it is too vexatious for milder words!"

"Then you had better not say anything at all, Miss Claire."

Turning on her heel, Nana went to work on the jumble of brushes, combs, hairpins, and ribbons on the dressing table. Claire stood lost in thought for a moment, then busied herself with a pair of long silk gloves, absently smoothing them over her hands and arms.

Having completed her task, Nana gave her young mistress a searching look. Her face softened.

"I know you're feeling put out, Miss Claire. But there's no reason to let Miss Anne's betrothal spoil a fine ball for you.

43

You're a very pretty girl, and you've got no cause to think you'll be left on the shelf."

And with these heartening words, Nana took herself off before Claire had collected her wits sufficiently to make a retort.

Her eyes on the door that had so firmly closed behind the older woman, Claire sank down on the edge of her bed. She had no thought for the easily crushed silk of her ballgown; she could think only that Nana believed her jealous.

And the shocking part was that, far from being wrong, Nana had pointed out nothing but the truth.

Claire was, indeed, jealous. She was mortified. The oldest of the Sutherland girls, and the only one not betrothed or married.

She had not minded when Sarah, half an hour younger, got married two years ago. Except, of course, that Sarah's leaving Sutherland Hall made Claire feel horribly lonely. But it wasn't that she was jealous of her twin; she merely didn't know at first how to go on without Sarah. And when Alan's sister, Agnes, married a little later, Claire had not been envious either. She had regretted only that Alan could not be present at the celebrations.

The following spring, Claire and her two best friends were presented in London. Claire turned down three very edifying proposals of marriage while her friends announced their engagements and that autumn walked down the aisle. At those two weddings Claire did, indeed, shed a secret tear of self-pity.

She was nineteen then and had just refused Roger Seymore, the admiral's nephew, for the second time. Moreover, she had said farewell to Alan, who spent six weeks at home to recover from a debilitating fever, and Claire was feeling quite hopeless about Alan ever seeing her as more than a childhood friend upon whom he could rely to while away the tedium of convalescence.

Roger Seymore had since proposed twice more and still did not believe that she would not change her mind, but Claire did not wish to marry Roger Seymore. No one but Alan would do for her, and Alan still showed no inclination to settle down. He had sold out a scarce three-months ago, and already he had signed up to go on an expedition to China.

China! He'd be gone a year. More likely, *two* long years.

Surely, no one could marvel that Claire, rapidly approaching her twenty-first birthday, was jealous of Anne, who was about to announce her betrothal on the day she turned seventeen.

Claire scowled so ferociously that Nana, had she seen it, would immediately have pointed out the dangers of premature wrinkling. But Nana was not present and did not see, either, that the scowl gradually lightened as Claire allowed herself to dwell on a certain significant moment in the library of the Manor, just before Rufus had burst in upon her and Alan.

Two days had passed, but Claire recalled that moment as clearly as if it had happened a mere instant ago. Never would she forget how Alan had looked at her.

As if he saw her for the first time. As if what he saw struck a spark in him. As if he wanted to kiss her. Not to place the casual fraternal kiss on the forehead he occasionally bestowed on her, but properly kiss her. The way a man kissed a woman he desired.

And never would she forget the sweetness of that moment when Alan's touch, however light and brief, had drawn her under his spell.

Claire slid off the bed. She gathered stole, fan, and reticule for the dinner and ball celebrating Anne's birthday. Anne might announce her betrothal that night, but Claire would be wed long before her little sister was allowed to settle on a wedding date.

She would be wed to Alan.

Yes, indeed, she would.

Even if it meant she must do something drastic to get him to pop the question.

"Claire. I say, Claire! Will you slow down and give a fellow a chance?"

Claire turned to face the gentleman pursuing her to the corner of the ballroom where punch and champagne were served. This was by no means the first time she had encountered Roger Seymore that evening, but still she was caught off guard when the full splendor of his attire burst upon her.

There were several dandies among the county's younger set but none so splendid as Roger in white pantaloons shot with silver thread, wasp-waisted midnight-blue coat, and pale-blue satin waistcoat hung with numerous silver fobs and seals. Silver stars glinted in the folds of his cravat, the fullness of which was designed to hide a rather weak chin. Silver lace fell gracefully from his wrists to the knuckles of his hands.

"Roger, each time I look at you, I'm dazzled speechless."

He puffed his chest. "Yes, I believe the touch of silver is a cut above the ordinary. My own design, you know."

"Yes." Dryly. "I thought as much."

She handed her champagne glass to a passing footman. Turning slightly so she could see the open double-winged ballroom door, she said, "But you didn't stop me just to gather compliments, did you?"

"Well, no." He bowed. "May I have the honor of this dance?"

"We have danced twice, Roger. Tongues would start wagging if I stood up with you again."

"Let them wag. We'll confound everyone with an announcement of our betrothal."

Intent on keeping an eye on the doorway, all but hidden by the couples on the dance floor, Claire impatiently tapped her fan against her wrist.

"Don't be tiresome, Roger. How many times must I tell you that I shan't marry you?"

"A great many more times. And even then I wouldn't believe you."

Roger Seymore looked complacent, a man certain of his own worth and his position as the heir to Admiral Seymore's estate. When Claire did not reply, he coaxed, "Come now, Claire. I've heard whispers that Stuart will make an interesting announcement about Anne before supper. Surely you, as the elder sister, must wish to take precedence!"

Claire opened her fan with a snap. "Well, you're wrong!"

She did not dislike Roger and generally had no difficulty overlooking his smug air of self-importance. But not this night.

Not after Nana's unfortunate remark.

And not when Claire had built up such hopes of dancing with Alan and convincing him that truly he did wish to get married, and then must face the fact that Alan had slipped away after dinner and two hours later still had not made an appearance in the ballroom.

Claire gave Roger a cold look. "And if all you plan to do is hurl insults at me, you had better go away."

"I didn't mean—Nothing further from my mind—" stammered Roger, for the first time in Claire's experience showing signs of discomposure.

He raised a hand as if he would rake his fingers through his immaculately brushed and pomaded blond locks, but at the last moment thought better of it and brought out a handkerchief to dab his brow.

"Claire, I apologize if I said aught to upset you. You must know I didn't mean to do so."

"Very well, Roger. I accept your apology."

"Am I forgiven, then?"

"Yes, yes. Of course you are. Just let's not talk about it any more."

"And you will give me another dance?"

Claire might have snapped at him again, but in the relative quiet while the musicians rested between dance numbers she faintly caught the sounds of a commotion just outside the ballroom door. And whenever there was a commotion, Alan Trent could generally be found at the center of it.

Catching the half-train of her gown, she started for the doorway as fast as decorum and the throng of guests permitted.

"Or go for a stroll with me?" said Roger, his hopes on the rise.

Claire ignored him, her focus centered on the subdued sound of voices outside the door and the necessity of weaving around clusters of gossiping matrons, giggling young ladies, or hunt-talking gentlemen.

All of the neighboring notables had shown up for Anne's birthday celebration, despite the snowfall on Saturday, and despite the fact that the ball was held on a night when only a sliver of a moon, and that sliver obscured by clouds most of the time, would supplement the feeble light of carriage lanterns. It had been a long, boring winter; and besides, the Sutherlands were great favorites among the gentry and nobility of the county.

"Claire, where are we going?" It went against the grain with Roger Seymore to move at a speed faster than a leisurely stroll, but he stuck tenaciously to Claire's side. "Do you wish to take a turn in the gardens?"

"In February? Don't be daft, Roger."

Claire had finally reached the door just as the musicians struck up the next tune. She swept into the hallway—and came to an abrupt stop at the sight that met her eyes.

There was her brother, looking flustered and harassed as only a host could look when he feared a disaster in the midst of a night's entertainment. She saw George Melton, her brother-in-law, his expression even graver than was his habit; Admiral Seymore, brows beetling and color high, protesting in his booming fo'c'sle voice that something or other was utter rubbish and quite impossible; some young officer in an unfamiliar blue and white uniform facing the admiral; and a half dozen dragoons looking as if they wished themselves elsewhere.

And, of course, there was Alan.

Alan, splendid and dashing in a long-tailed coat of dark-blue superfine and champagne-colored pantaloons, the pristine whiteness of shirt points and cravat a striking contrast to his dark complexion.

And Rufus.

Rufus, at heel, acknowledged Claire's presence with a thump of his tail. No one else noticed her, least of all Alan, who stood with long, elegant legs planted apart, one hand on his hip, and, in contrast to the other men, showing his most carefree grin.

Claire let out her breath on a sigh of exasperation. In the past she had been only too familiar with that cocky stance whenever Alan was caught in some mischief or other.

What sort of scrape he could have gotten himself into during her sister's ball she had not the slightest notion. Or, how Rufus had gained entrance at Sutherland Hall. But that Alan was in a scrape, or worse, Claire did not doubt for an instant.

She cast another quick look at the unknown officer, now contradicting Admiral Seymore in measured but firm tones, and with great presence of mind told the footmen at the door to step inside the ballroom and to close the two panels after them. Roger, unfortunately, had already joined her in the hallway.

"I assure you, sir," Claire heard the officer say as the doors clicked shut, "we made no mistake. Sir Alan Trent is the head of a smuggling gang."

Five

Alan? A smuggler?

Claire stood transfixed, her heart hammering as if it were determined to break through her ribs.

Unlike Admiral Seymore and her brother, who joined the old tar in his vigorous protest, she could not be certain that the allegation was "utter rubbish," or a "tomfool notion," much less a "libelous defamation."

Only two days ago, the day of the snowstorm, she had mentioned the smugglers to Alan. She had expressed the hope that he was keeping boredom at bay and his lust for adventure satisfied by chasing the gang that trekked through Thistledown Woods with contraband from the coast to an inland destination.

And Alan had burst into laughter!

Laughter which suddenly took on a sinister meaning.

But surely Alan had not allowed boredom to drive him into such an outrageous venture. It was one thing to close one's eyes to smuggling or to stock one's cellar with run goods, but quite another to participate in free-trading activities. Especially now, when the government was stepping up the war against smuggling.

It could not be denied, however, that Alan looked—at least to her experienced eye—as if he was in some dreadful scrape.

Neither could it be denied that a Customs officer was involved.

Claire tried to recall what precisely Alan had said that day she mentioned the smugglers to him—something about her knowing him too well—but her brother and the men with him, including a sergeant of the dragoons, were arguing all at once, and Roger Seymore's excited falsetto right beside her all but pierced her eardrum.

Lud! She couldn't think straight in the hubbub. And then again, it hardly mattered what she thought, whether Alan was chasing smugglers or leading them. That could be settled later.

At present, it mattered only that Alan should not be arrested by that stiff young officer and his band of armed dragoons. And for that purpose her help was quite obviously needed, since the gentlemen, including her quiet clerical brother-in-law, stood in imminent danger of starting a common brawl.

Claire swept forward.

"Gentlemen!"

Instantly, she was the cynosure of all eyes. In the sudden hush the lilting strains of a waltz, the chatter and laughter in the ballroom, rang unnaturally loud.

"Stuart, I am surprised at you. If you must conduct some horrid, noisy business on the night of Anne's ball, you should at least have retired to the study."

If Claire had hoped her brother would be gratified by the diversion, she was disappointed. He turned a look upon her which reminded her forcefully of her late father when in a huff, an impression that was strengthened when Stuart drew up his stocky figure and balanced on the balls of his feet.

"Don't meddle, Claire. Be a good girl and go back to the dancing. Yes, and take Roger with you. There are already too many of us here."

"Precisely, dear brother."

A brow raised in question, Claire advanced on the officer. "Sir, I do not know who you are . . . ?"

"Lieutenant Bradshaw, ma'am." Voice and bow were stiff. "Riding officer in Customs service. I've come to—"

"I understand perfectly," she cut in. "You have a need of my brother's services in his capacity of justice of the peace. But you must see, Lieutenant, that he cannot possibly help you tonight. Please be good enough to come back tomorrow."

"I'm sorry, ma'am. That's impossible. I have orders—"

"Nonsense, Lieutenant!" Claire frowned at Alan, whose shameless grin was broader than ever. "The only thing impossible is that you remain here! In a very few moments our guests will wish to retire to the supper room, and you must realize how awkward that would be with dragoons cluttering up the hallway."

"Aye!" said Admiral Seymore. "Damned awkward. And your behavior is a disgrace, Lieutenant!"

Bradshaw's color rose. "Ma'am, I shall disrupt your ball as little as possible."

"Thank you," Claire said absently, her attention once more on Alan, who was pointing first at her, then at Rufus. Did he want her to take the dog away? But Rufus was on his best behavior.

The lieutenant addressed her in his stiff, correct manner. "I don't need a justice of the peace for the execution of my duty, ma'am. Thus your brother is quite at liberty to return to his guests. In fact, I don't need anyone but Sir Alan Trent. I am duly empowered by the Board—"

"Lieutenant, I don't doubt your authority or your efficiency. But kindly execute your duty someplace else."

"Claire," said Alan. "If you'll just confirm to the lieutenant—"

Whatever it was he wanted her to confirm was drowned by Admiral Seymore and George Melton, both offering to see the lieutenant out the front door or, if he got rid of the dragoons, to accompany him and Alan to the study so that Stuart might, with a clear conscience, resume his duties as host.

Stuart ran a hand through his unruly brown hair. "I'll see this settled first. Dash it! Alan's my friend. And this is *my* house. I'll not have him arrested on some trumped-up charge."

"But I won't be arrested," said Alan. "As I tried to tell Lieutenant Bradshaw earlier, I went to the Manor only to—"

"You were at home," Bradshaw interrupted. "Don't try to pull the wool over my eyes by asserting you were elsewhere. We had the house under observation for an hour before you left it and we followed you here."

"I was there briefly, but—"

"You met at the Manor with one or more of the smugglers. Denial is useless, sir. We pursued the men and their pack ponies all the way from the Martello tower at Pevensey."

Alan raised a brow and shrugged. "If you say so. But I fail to understand why you should think they came to see me at the Manor."

"Pevensey, Lieutenant?" Stuart, looking startled, seemed about to question the Customs officer more closely when one wing of the ballroom door swung open, spilling into the hallway four ladies and a young gentleman almost as splendidly attired as Roger Seymore. Three of the ladies immediately besieged Stuart.

"My love, *please* hurry!" Face pink, voice breathless, Charlotte Sutherland wrung her hands imploringly. "The toast, Stuart! The announcement. You cannot have forgotten, dearest!"

"You said you'd make the announcement *before* supper." Anne, a little taller and darker than Sarah and Claire, clutched her brother's arm and tugged impetuously. "Come along, Stuart! When the music stops it'll be too late. Everyone will want to rush off to the supper room."

"Yes, indeed. So embarrassing," lisped Anne's friend, Lucinda Seymore, a very pretty girl with guinea-golden ringlets and china-blue eyes. "No one will be there to hear the good news if we don't hurry."

The fourth lady, the dowager Mrs. Sutherland, paid no attention to anyone, but drifted along the hallway in her usual vague manner. She would undoubtedly have gone off to visit her orchids if Claire had not caught her and deposited her in the charge of young Lawrence Bellingham, the exquisite who was soon to be a member of the family.

53

"Claire," Lawrence whispered, his boyish face taut with suppressed excitement. "That's a Customs man over there! A preventive. And he's brought dragoons! What's going on? And how the deuce did Sir Alan's hound get here? Is there a chase?"

"Hush!" she said fiercely. "We'll talk later."

It did not escape her notice that the lieutenant was clenching his teeth as well as his hands in frustrated impatience. To have him blurt out his accusation in front of more witnesses was the last thing she desired.

She maneuvered Lawrence and her mother toward the ballroom. "Mama, I know you're bored and cannot wait to get away from all the chatter and noise. But promise me you'll stay at least until Stuart has made the betrothal announcement."

Mrs. Sutherland, as slender and dark as Anne and looking outrageously youthful for a mother of four grown children, gave Claire a reproachful look. "Naughty girl. As though I would miss toasting your betrothal."

"Mama—"

Claire bit off a denial and allowed her mother to drift away on Lawrence's arm. This was not the time to try to correct the misconception, and later, perhaps, it might not be necessary if, for once, Mrs. Sutherland paid attention to her son's speech.

More shaken than she cared to admit by her mother's assumption that it was *her* betrothal, Claire cast a self-conscious look at Alan and just as quickly looked away again. Alan might be engaged in a sotto voce argument with Stuart, but his hearing was extremely keen and his eyes had definitely been on her, not on Stuart.

Perish the thought that he had heard her mother!

And she was a fool to waste a single thought on a possible embarrassment when she needed her wits about her to extricate Alan from a tight spot. And rescue him she must. She would hardly be able to further her own schemes if he ended up languishing in gaol.

She noted that Stuart, exhorted by Charlotte, Anne, and Lucinda, finally allowed himself to be propelled into the ball-room. Thank goodness.

She whisked her brother-in-law aside. "George, you'll want to be with Sarah now. Do me a favor. Please? Take Roger with you!"

He gave her a sharp look but nodded. "It would seem odd if so many of us were absent during the betrothal announcement."

That left on one side Claire, Alan, and the admiral, whose thunderous expression indicated that nothing would induce him to leave. And for the opposition, the riding officer and the dragoons.

The admiral fixed Lieutenant Bradshaw with a steely eye. "Those dragoons! Whatever your purpose, you won't need them. Order them to wait outside!"

The admiral's tone was so menacing that Rufus raised his head. He started to growl, but quieted at a touch of Alan's hand.

The Customs officer hesitated only briefly. He nodded to the sergeant, and immediately the dragoons turned about-face. By ironic yet quite fitting coincidence, or so it seemed to Claire, the company assembled in the ballroom broke into cheers and applause just as the men trooped off.

Claire measured the three remaining gentlemen, especially Alan, with a stern look. Alan should be apprehensive but, on the contrary, had a certain buoyant air which, past experience had taught her, portended mischief brewing.

Uneasily she conceded that it might not be such a good idea after all to persuade Alan to settle down at the Manor. China seemed more and more desirable. She would certainly prefer to accompany Alan on a government mission to some foreign place than join him in New South Wales as a convict's wife.

"Gentlemen!" Another severe look. "If you'll kindly follow me to the study, we will settle the matter once and for all."

"Well done," Alan murmured, when he caught up with her on the sweep of stairs leading to the ground floor. "Wellington himself couldn't have done better choosing his ground and his troops for a battle."

High praise from Alan, but the glow of warmth evoked by his words did not suffice to melt the tense knot twisting inside Claire.

Six

Lieutenant Bradshaw stood stiffly by the closed study door. As if, thought Claire, he was afraid Alan would try to escape.

But Alan gave no sign of wishing himself elsewhere. Hip braced against the right-hand corner of the massive oak desk that all but filled the small chamber, Rufus stretched out at his feet, he appeared quite at his ease.

The admiral, still wearing a thunderous scowl, sat behind the desk. Claire occupied the only other seat, a ladderbacked chair just to the left of the desk, near the window. It was not a comfortable chair, but Claire noticed neither the roughness of the cane seat nor the hardness of the wood slats at her back.

Her attention was on Alan, the one person in the study who was calm and relaxed. Maddeningly so.

"Before I present the warrant," said Lieutenant Bradshaw, his voice as hard as the look in his eyes, "I'd like to make it clear that we've had a certain smuggling gang under observation since early December. We know smuggled goods are dropped in a cove below Pevensey, then stored in the Martello tower until mules and pack ponies can be assembled for the overland journey."

He paused, looking straight at Alan. "And this evening we followed the pack train from the tower to the Trent estate. *Your* estate, sir."

Claire, too, was looking at Alan, but he did not appear unduly affected by the disclosure.

"Go on, Lieutenant," he said. "I'm sure that's not all you have to say, and we may as well hear the rest."

"One of the men guiding the train, a fellow known to us for some time by the name of Black Jack, has been observed in your company, sir. Specifically, on five different occasions, at the Sea Gull in Pevensey."

Claire, watching Alan closely, did not miss the brief lowering of his lids. She did not think anyone else had noticed or knew Alan's idiosyncrasies as well as she did; but her heart sank. No matter what would be the outcome of this meeting, she now knew for certain that Alan did indeed have some traffic with the smugglers. And she also knew that he was not quite as calm and unconcerned as he appeared to be.

Alan perched himself on the desk corner. "I admit to having stopped at the Sea Gull. It's a public inn, after all. And I daresay I stood one or two of the other customers—locals, all of them—a pint once in a while. I cannot say, though, that I was ever interested enough to inquire their names."

"I, too, have stopped at the Sea Gull, sir. *Not* the sort of establishment to lure a gentleman on a three-hour ride just for a tankard of ale."

The admiral leaned forward in his chair. "Not ale, no. But the innkeeper brews a devilish fine punch! I've tasted it more than once. Perhaps, Lieutenant, you'd like to include me in that accusation of trafficking with smugglers?"

"No, sir. Admiral! You were never seen at the public bar or in the snug, hobnobbing with the locals. You've always ordered a private room, and you've always had a legitimate reason for a visit to Pevensey. Your yacht is moored at the boatyards, isn't it?"

"Stap me!" Planting his hands on the desk, the admiral heaved himself out of the chair. "You've had me watched, you impudent young dog. I'll have you keelhauled."

He sank down heavily. "Demme if I don't!"

Lieutenant Bradshaw turned to Alan.

"You don't own a yacht, sir."

"No."

"In fact, there's no reason at all why you should visit Pevensey, or anyplace on the coast, for that matter, during the winter months."

Claire saw the flash of anger in Alan's dark eyes, and Rufus, sensing his master's response to the Customs officer, rose and growled at Lieutenant Bradshaw.

"Quiet!" said Alan, and Rufus subsided immediately.

Claire had sat as quiet as a mouse, had scarcely even breathed, so as not to attract attention before she learned all the particulars of the charge leveled against Alan, but now she leaned toward the dog and held out her hand.

"Come here, Rufus."

When the hound joined her in the drafty corner by the window, she rewarded him by scratching all his favorite spots, a pastime that helped greatly to distract her from a mounting anxiety over the depth of Alan's involvement with the smugglers.

Brief as the disruption had been, it had served to soothe Alan's temper. "No, Lieutenant," he drawled. "I have no particular reason to visit Pevensey or any other place on the coast, except that occasionally I fancy doing so. Not that it's any business of yours, but I get dashed bored sitting at home. You'll find me careening all over the countryside. I don't see, however, why that should give you cause to accost me tonight."

"Sir, I have a warrant, duly issued by the Customs Board—"

"That's another thing!" the admiral broke in. "Smuggling is a naval concern now. The Board of Customs ain't in charge any longer. Even the revenue cutters will be transferred to the Admiralty in a matter of weeks. So how the devil do you think you can accomplish anything with a warrant from Customs? Eh, Lieutenant, will you tell me that?"

"You forget, sir," said Alan, "it's the Waterguard that's been placed under naval control. The lieutenant is a riding officer in the Landguard, which is still controlled by Customs. No, I don't question the power of the warrant." He paused, idly swinging one long leg. "It's my name on it that I object to."

Claire watched that elegant, muscular leg with irritation. How could Alan be so dashed casual under the circumstances!

Tearing her gaze away, she addressed the Customs officer.

"Lieutenant, I'm confused. You say Sir Alan was seen at an inn frequented by a certain smuggler. Surely that is no crime? You said *you* have visited the Sea Gull. Does that place *you* under suspicion?"

"Sir Alan Trent and the man called Black Jack were seen *conferring,* ma'am. Hatching plans."

"How do you know? Did you listen to their conversation?"

The Customs officer stared at her.

"Well? Did you?"

He shifted uncomfortably. "Not precisely, ma'am. It was obvious from their manner that they were scheming something."

"Obvious! Pish-tosh! Is that all the cause you have to charge Sir Alan with leading a smuggling gang?"

"This is getting worse and worse," said Admiral Seymore. "And it all comes from putting some young, overzealous whippersnapper in command. So eager to make an arrest that he doesn't bother with evidence! I warn you, Lieutenant, I may be retired, but I still have some influence at the Admiralty. Landguard or not, I'll see to it you face your court-martial over this affair."

A sheen of moisture appeared on Bradshaw's forehead. "I may have been premature when I asserted that Sir Alan is the head of the smuggling gang, since it isn't proven. *Yet.*"

His chin jutted belligerently. "But there's the pack train! I never lost sight of it from the moment it left the Martello tower till it entered the gates of the Manor. I have a warrant to search the premises, and when I find the goods, I'll have all the proof I need."

Claire plied her fan. "We all have smugglers enter our gates once in a while. That doesn't mean we're involved in the trade. Why, even my brother—a justice of the peace!—has occasionally found contraband in one of his barns. It's there one night, and the next it is gone."

"A question, Lieutenant," said Alan, his indifferent tone strangely at odds with the keen look in his eyes. "Why didn't you come to the house, demand to see me then and there, as soon as you saw the smugglers inside the estate walls? Since you had a warrant, I could hardly have refused permission to have the grounds searched."

"Because," Bradshaw retorted sharply, "I did search the grounds. And no matter what the admiral says about my not bothering with evidence, I knew I had to wait for you to join the smugglers. Had to wait to catch you red-handed with them and the contraband."

Alan's voice was silky. "But I did not go out to inspect any contraband. And I did not join the smugglers you *say* were on my property."

"No, you didn't, did you?" Bradshaw let anger and hostility show quite openly now. "While I waited and had the dragoons spread out and station themselves at strategic points, the smugglers, mules, ponies, and all, disappeared without a trace."

"Ha!" The admiral's voice rang out. "And so you lost your temper and what little wits you had and picked out Sir Alan as your scapegoat. I was right! You're an overzealous incompetent."

Bradshaw ignored this. He glared at Alan. "And the next thing I know, *you* leave the house with your dog, jump into the curricle you had waiting at the door, and race off as if the devil were after you."

"That's not unusual." Nothing in Claire's demeanor betrayed the turmoil inside her. What on earth was Alan up to? And how had a mule train disappeared in his yard? "Sir Alan always drives as if the devil were after him."

"That may be true in the daytime," said Alan, smiling at her. "At night I don't usually spring my horses, except that this evening I was in a hurry to return to the ball and claim the waltzes promised me."

She had never been immune to Alan's smile, and it was too late now to try to do something about her susceptibility. Besides, she could not deny the fact that his name was penciled against the two last waltzes in her dance programme; but she did not flatter herself that she had been the cause of Alan's haste. That, however, was not something to confide to the Customs officer.

Lieutenant Bradshaw once more stood stiffly correct, his face expressionless. "Are you saying, sir, that you had not been home all evening but were, in fact, at the ball, *left it,* and then returned?"

Admiral Seymore's fist crashed onto the desk. *"I* am saying, Lieutenant, you had better take yourself off before you make an even greater fool of yourself than you already have!"

Neither Bradshaw nor Alan so much as glanced at the admiral.

Alan was still looking at Claire and did not take his eyes off her when he responded to the Customs officer's question.

"As I tried to tell you earlier, Lieutenant, I was here at Sutherland Hall during dinner, then left, and returned shortly before midnight."

Bradshaw's eyes narrowed to slits; his voice cut. "And no doubt you had a very good reason for such—dare I say it—gauche behavior? *Sir?"*

"Impertinent upstart!" muttered the admiral.

Claire did not entirely blame the lieutenant for his sarcasm and suspicion. She herself did not trust Alan in this strange, cooperative, almost conciliatory mood he had displayed throughout the encounter with the Customs officer. It would have been so much more natural for him to take a high-handed tone.

Unless Alan had learned wisdom and diplomacy as a member of the Duke of Wellington's staff . . . Then again, a wise man would hardly join up with a band of smugglers, which, undoubtedly, Alan had done.

If only she could have a moment's quiet reflection. But it was impossible now, especially since Alan still held her captive with his compelling look, a look that demanded attention and put her on the alert.

Responding with an almost imperceptible nod, she steeled herself for the outrageous fib she *knew* he was about to tell. Undoubtedly, too, Alan expected her to support him in that fib.

Botheration! If they were alone, she would be hard pressed not to box his ears.

Finally, Alan turned his attention to Bradshaw. "Yes, Lieutenant, I had a very good reason for leaving Sutherland Hall after dinner."

"Do you mind sharing it with me?" Lieutenant Bradshaw said between clenched teeth.

"Not at all. In fact, I tried to explain earlier. Unfortunately, you wouldn't let me speak. You were so certain you knew my movements this evening better than I, how could I convince you to the contrary without appearing to brangle in the most common way?"

Alan was so obviously enjoying himself at Bradshaw's expense that Claire felt obliged to intervene.

"Stop teasing, Alan! You're not helping by drawing this ridiculous situation out."

"You're a fine one for scolding." He gave her a wicked grin. "If you're in such a hurry to have the matter cleared up, why didn't *you* tell Lieutenant Bradshaw that you sent me home to fetch Rufus?"

Claire did not bat an eye. There it was, the fib she had expected, although she had not supposed Alan would involve her quite so directly. But she should have known it would involve Rufus.

"Yes, indeed," she murmured, feeling as if she had been thrust on stage to act in a play when no one had remembered to give her the script. "I should, perhaps, have mentioned it, shouldn't I?"

The Customs officer exploded. "Fetch the hound? Do you take me for a fool?"

Admiral Seymore sputtered unintelligibly; but the width of

Alan's grin more than compensated for the admiral's lack of eloquence.

Claire plunged into the breech, forestalling whatever disastrous reply Alan might have made. "No, indeed, Lieutenant! And I must beg your pardon for not speaking up sooner. I would have, too, if I hadn't been so distracted. But to put the matter in a nutshell, there's this mouse, you see. Oh, dear! How embarrassing this is."

In the sudden silence, when she could think of nothing else to say, Alan spoke up helpfully.

"Miss Sutherland is afraid of mice, Lieutenant. She heard one in the wainscoting of her chamber when she was dressing for the ball."

"Yes, I did," said Claire, favoring Alan with a dark look. Afraid of mice, indeed! And why had she said "mouse" instead of . . . whatever? A pox on Alan and the dreadful rappers he dreamed up! What reason could she possibly have had for asking him to fetch the hound on the night of a ball?

The officer was very close to exploding again. "Use a hound to catch a mouse! What tomfoolery is this?"

"Tomfoolery? Oh, no!" Claire's voice quavered. Madness it was, a nerve-wracking, bloodcurdling, hair-raising dare.

"Ma'am, I don't believe a word of this—this ridiculous tale!"

"This is the last straw!" shouted Admiral Seymore. "How dare you question Miss Sutherland's word!"

Alan got off the desk.

"Lieutenant!" Threatening. "If you were a gentleman, I'd ask you to name your friends. But you're no gentleman and deserve only to be whipped."

Bradshaw blanched, his hand reaching for the short sword at his side.

Claire, too, felt the blood drain from her face. For pity's sake! How far did Alan plan to go with this farce?

She slid from her chair and knelt beside Rufus, who showed signs of wanting to emulate his master's menacing stance.

Wrapping her arms around the dog's neck, she hid her face and an incipient attack of hysterics in Rufus's sleek coat.

She choked out, "Hush, Alan! The lieutenant meant no insult, I'm sure. He does not know your dog. Indeed, how could he?"

She peeked over her shoulder at the stony-faced riding officer and at Alan, still in his outraged-gentleman stance. No, much better to keep her attention on the squirming dog.

She held him firmly. "Rufus is such a wonderful mouser. Aren't you, my good fellow?"

The intelligent hound gave a furious bark.

"And so, you see, Lieutenant," said Claire, quaking in her satin slippers, yet committing herself unhesitatingly and irrevocably to Alan's disgraceful cause, "I asked Sir Alan at dinner to fetch the dog right away. I must have that mouse caught before I go to bed, else I shan't sleep a wink."

Seven

"We did it, love!" Alan's eyes held the glint of excitement and triumph. "We put the good lieutenant to rout. And you were marvelous."

"Hush!"

Claire pressed an ear against the solid wood of the study door, which had closed but a few moments earlier behind a disgruntled Lieutenant Bradshaw and the admiral, determined to see the Customs officer personally out the front door. She stood thus, breath suspended, until she no longer heard their footsteps echoing in the long tiled corridor leading to the foyer.

"It's safe now. They're gone."

Alan stood by the window and watched her, his mouth twitching.

"Cautious Claire! What does it matter whether Bradshaw can hear me or not? He knows he cannot arrest me and must be satisfied with a renewed search of the Manor grounds."

But her mind still could not quite take in that Alan was no longer in danger of arrest—at least, not immediately—and his carefree attitude chafed her. Neither did it help that he called her Cautious Claire, the ingrate!

"I don't see what's wrong with a bit of caution under the circumstances!"

"Do I detect a note of pique?"

"Censure, Alan. A show of appreciation on your part would be more appropriate than calling me by a detestable childhood nickname."

"I apologize. I am truly grateful to you, love. You make the best conspirator. But how could I resist? I had not thought of it till I saw you with your ear against the door, but that's what we used to call you, Stuart and I. Cautious Claire."

"*That* was pique! Listening for Cook's footsteps saved me from getting caught snatching sweetmeats, while you"—she pointed the closed fan in her hand the way Cook had accusingly pointed a wooden spoon—"you and Stuart, were always caught red-handed."

"We knew you had the better strategy, but we couldn't admit that of a girl, could we, now?"

She did not want to dignify such nonsense with a reply but could not resist a very speaking look, which he countered with one of supreme blandness.

"Just so. And it used to drive us wild as hornets when you refused to follow our lead and were forever questioning our wisdom."

"You couldn't have been half as furious as I was when you called me 'Cautious Claire' in that odious tone you used!"

He cast a sapient eye over her heated countenance. "It still rankles, does it? Poor Claire. But if you hated being teased so much, why didn't you, at least occasionally, join us in our more daring exploits?"

"Because someone had to be in a position to pull you out of the scrapes you tumbled into, especially when you dragged Sarah with you."

He went toward her. "And you're still pulling me out of scrapes."

"*Not* this time, because I was too cautious to follow your ill-judged lead!"

She took a quick, agitated turn about the small chamber. "Devil a bit, Alan—and don't you dare say a lady mustn't use such language! Assisting you in that stupid fib was the most incautious thing I ever did. Lud! I rushed my fences. Blindly!"

He chuckled. "Rufus, a mouser! I'm surprised I kept a straight face."

"What was I supposed to say? That I sent you to fetch Rufus so he could waltz with me?"

The hound had heard his name and came trotting from behind the desk, where he had sniffed the rug occasionally occupied by Stuart's spaniel.

Alan scratched Rufus's head. "A fox in the henhouse would have done the trick. A poacher? Rufus is far too high in the instep to go chasing after mice. Aren't you, old boy?"

"And I," Claire said stiffly, "am far too sensible to be afraid of them."

"I know you are. But did you see the lieutenant's face when I told that bouncer?"

Their eyes met and suddenly, without warning, they both burst out laughing, which made Rufus sit on his haunches and cock his head, his eyes wide and puzzled.

With every ripple of laughter, Claire felt better. Knots of tension she hadn't been aware of dissolved in her neck and shoulders and her tightly controlled facial muscles. It was marvelous how light and happy a bit of laughter could make one feel, and she wondered if Alan experienced the same sense of release.

"This is more like it." Alan drew a deep breath. "Almost as good as having escaped Boney's men. Dash it, Claire! You can have no notion how we used to laugh and celebrate!"

"Living under the threat of danger," said Claire, sobering. "Yes, you told me that's what you're missing most of your former life."

"Then you do understand? You know why I cannot live the dull life of a country squire?"

"Indeed. But don't you see, Alan? Wherever you are, life wouldn't be dull. You draw excitement and adventure as a lodestone draws metal."

68

"You may be right. But I tell you this! If adventure does not find me, I go out and seek it."

"As if I didn't know!"

She watched his lean, expressive face and realized with a start that, if she were to marry Alan, whether they lived at the Manor or roamed the wide world, adventure, hair-raising excitement, would inevitably be a part of her life, too. And that, for her, would mean living in a state of perpetual apprehension.

A daunting prospect.

What was it she told Sarah not long ago? That Alan was dashing and daring, a little wild and reckless, and simply splendid. And that she did not wish him any other way.

This was still true. She did not wish Alan changed. A staid Alan was as impossible to imagine as dry rain or cold fire. But what had also been impossible to imagine until this night was the effect his wilder exploits would have on her if she shared his life.

"After the Valentine's Day Ball," said Alan, "I'll be off to London to see Castlereagh at the Foreign Office. It's time to do something about the assignment to Amherst's China expedition."

Dismay struck her silent. The Valentine's Day Ball was on Wednesday, two nights hence. If the assignment was confirmed, there was no telling whether Alan would return to the Manor at all before he sailed.

"Claire, we had best make an appearance in the ballroom."

He moved past her, toward the door. "If Lady Luck favors me, I may still get one or both of the waltzes you promised me. Which reminds me—will you give me the supper dance on Valentine's Day?"

"And be stood up if you decide to join the smugglers again?"

Alan was about to open the study door, but at Claire's words he turned quickly to face her.

She could not help but feel gratified at his startled expression. It was a rare occurrence when Alan was caught off guard.

69

And quizzing him about his activities would take her mind off the untimely doubts besetting her.

"Lud, Alan! Did you think I wouldn't demand the truth after telling such a rapper for you? Like it or not, I am now embroiled in your affairs to such a degree that I'll be sharing the hold of a prison transport with you and your free-trading friends if you're caught."

"Devil a bit! You cannot believe I'm in cahoots with a bunch of smugglers!"

"Can I not? Perhaps I'll also not believe that you left the ball?"

"Oh, *that!* I can explain."

"Don't bother unless you wish to tell me how those smugglers, ponies, mules, and all, could disappear under Lieutenant Bradshaw's watchful eye."

"Claire, you wound me. I hoped you were teasing, but you do believe I'm involved with the smugglers!"

She met his reproachful look quite steadily. "The sad truth is, Alan Trent, that I can believe almost anything of you."

"Claire!"

Retreating a few steps, Alan leaned heavily against the desk. His shoulders slumped.

Rufus cocked his head again, his eyes moving from Alan to Claire and back to Alan when he heard his master's mournful voice.

"I know you think me an adventurer, and I don't deny that I am. But a smuggler? That you would believe me without honor! Claire, this is indeed a blow."

"I am also convinced that you are the greatest play-actor off the London stage. A scoundrel, moreover, who stoops to such a low trick as trying to make me feel a . . . *a worm* just so I won't pursue the subject of the smugglers."

His face turned red. He choked out, "Claire, no! A *worm?*"

If only she could believe he was embarrassed. But it was much more like him to choke on a laugh.

She swept toward him. "Cut out the flimflammery, Alan. I *saw* that Lieutenant Bradshaw hit a nerve when he mentioned your meetings with that smuggler Black Jack in the Sea Gull."

Alan gave her a long look.

"How did I give myself away?"

No playacting for him now. He was as serious as could be.

"The way you quickly lowered your lids, wiping out any expression your eyes might betray."

"You do know me too well."

He gripped her waist, and before she knew it, she was sitting on the desk, her eyes level with his.

"Claire, do you trust me?"

"Yes, of course."

The taut vertical lines by his mouth disappeared. "That's a relief. After your damning statement that you can believe *anything* of me, I hardly dared hope for trust."

"What does one have to do with the other? I do believe you capable of any kind of reckless folly. But that does not diminish my trust in you."

"Claire." Huskily. "Thank you. For your trust. And your help."

"You're very welcome."

Her voice was almost as husky as Alan's, but then his nearness always affected her. He was so close she could see the tiny scar high on his cheekbone where a fish hook had caught him years ago. Stuart's doing. He was showing off and casting so wildly that the line wrapped itself around Claire, half a dozen paces away, and the hook cut Alan as he leaped for it, trying to snatch the sharp wire before it could hurt her.

She was eight then, mostly exasperated and angry with Alan for leading her siblings astray. Even Anne, barely five years old, had started to follow him. Alan grandly permitted the little girl to tag along; but it was Claire who had to carry her home when she tired, since nothing could induce Stuart to carry a screaming child. Truly, the young Claire considered all boys a nuisance, but especially Alan Trent.

In the secret depths of her heart, however, Claire had

thought of the tall, dark boy with the evil genius for falling into scrapes as a hero to be admired for his daring.

She became aware that Alan was not speaking but was watching her intently. Dash it! He ought to be busily explaining his misdeeds.

Claire scooted back a little on the desk, away from him. She squared her shoulders and raised her chin by several degrees.

"Trusting you doesn't mean I won't ask questions. Alan, what have you to do with the smugglers?"

"Very well." Sudden mischief lurked in his eyes. "I *am* the head of the Pevensey smuggling gang. Temporary head."

"Alan, why?"

"Dash it! If ever I knew a girl for asking why, it's you. Why I won't settle down. Why I won't marry. Why I want to go to China."

"Don't change the subject. If you were bored or craved excitement, you could have chased and caught a smuggler or two. You know they've become a veritable plague since so many discharged soldiers and sailors joined the free-traders."

"Naturally I chased them first. How else would I have discovered them?" Placing a hand on either side of her on the desk, he leaned close. "And I captured them with some assistance from Meyer and my grooms."

It was Claire who felt captured, blocked in by his arms. But it was sweet captivity and robbed her earlier doubts of substance. If she could be with Alan, she would gladly bear a life fraught with adventure and excitement.

Wouldn't she?

It took resolve to steer her mind to the matter at hand. "And then you joined the smugglers?"

"I bargained with them. Which is the reason I had to deceive Bradshaw. You wouldn't believe the jealousy between the various branches of government, Claire! And Bradshaw, under orders from Customs, would never have agreed to let a whole smugglers gang go free, which is what I promised the men. Their release and honest work at the Manor in return for a bit of work for the Foreign Office."

"The Foreign Office!" Breathless. "I should have known!"

She flung her arms around his neck and kissed him. It was an impulsive act, born of relief, and no doubt she would have speedily come to her senses and released him. But she was not called upon to prove her admirable common sense. Just as suddenly as she embraced him, Alan closed his arms around her. Crushed against his breast, she was kissed with a ruthlessness and thoroughness that melted her bones and had her cling to the only available support—Alan himself.

Loud barking, rapidly deteriorating to a mournful howl, and the desperate scrabble of nails against the desk finally caught her attention. Rufus. Again!

Alan, too, became aware of his faithful hound's displeasure, and loosened his tight hold just enough so he and Claire could draw a much-needed breath, and a cold nose and long, sleek head could push between their bodies.

He reached up and tucked a stray curl behind her ear. "If ever I decide to marry, you'll be the one I ask."

Her breath caught at the warmth in his gaze. He was serious. And here she was, struck dumb!

Even if she had been able to make a retort, she was not given the chance. Rufus was not the only one who had caught them kissing. Stuart had entered unnoticed. He shut the door with a distinct slam.

"Damn it, Alan! If you must kiss my sister, do it without that blasted dog around. Get the beast off my desk, will you? He's tearing up the wood."

"Sorry about that."

Alan smoothly lifted Claire off the desk, then snapped his fingers at Rufus, who instantly jumped down and prostrated himself at his master's feet.

Claire faced her brother. She did not fear his wrath at having caught her in a compromising situation. Stuart could bellow and shout as much as he pleased—later, when they were

73

private. What she feared was that he might say something to force Alan's hand. That she could not bear.

If Alan must be convinced that he did not want to wait for some vague, distant day in the future to propose marriage to her, she was the only one entitled to use persuasion. She had already resolved earlier that night to resort to drastic measures, if need be. And the need was clearly there. All she had to do was hit upon a specific drastic measure.

"Stuart—"

He cut her off. "And what was that I heard as I walked in? Something about the smugglers and the Foreign Office? I meant to ask Bradshaw about those Pevensey men when Charlotte and Anne dragged me off."

"I had a letter from Castlereagh a fortnight ago," said Alan. "About a particularly nefarious bit of smuggling from a stretch of coast just south of us to France."

"Ha!" Hands clasped behind his back, Stuart balanced on the balls of his feet. "I wonder if that's the same bit of smuggling the Home Office asked me to look into?"

Diverted, Claire asked, "Is that where you went in London? The Home Office?"

"Not that it's any of your business, miss, but yes, I attended several meetings at the Home Office." Stuart favored her with critical look. "You look as if you'd been dragged backward through the briars. Dress crushed, hair a mess. Better fix it before you go."

"I'm not going anywhere until I know what this is all about. And dash it, Stuart! You should have told Charlotte what you were doing in London. She asked me if I thought you kept a mistress in town!"

"I'll worry about Charlotte. *You* are going upstairs." Stuart firmly pushed her toward the door. "The guests are beginning to leave, and Lady Abercrombie wants a word with you. That's why I came to find you."

"Oh, very well."

It was unthinkable not to do Lady Abercrombie's bidding, but Claire still hesitated. She looked from one man to the other. There was little danger now that Stuart would discuss anything but the smuggling business with Alan. Once her brother's mind was occupied with one thought he never bothered about a second issue. And come to think of it, Stuart probably found it more worrisome that Rufus had scratched his desk than that his sister was compromised by his best friend.

No, it wasn't her brother she was reluctant to leave. It was Alan. She dreaded leaving him and becoming prey once more to those disturbing doubts. And just when things had begun to look downright promising. If only she could have had a few moments longer alone with Alan . . .

Absently she fastened a loose hairpin. "I warn you, Alan! I'll not rest until you tell me the whole story about smuggling and striking bargains with smugglers. And working for the Foreign Office and, well, *everything*. So do not try to hide from me!"

Perhaps it was her imagination, but it seemed to her that Alan hesitated before he replied.

"Not tonight. I really ought to follow Bradshaw to make certain Meyer doesn't obstruct the search."

"You gave the lieutenant a letter of authorization!"

"Yes, but there's no telling whether Meyer will choose to read English. Tell you what, Claire. I'll fetch you in the morning. The tale is best told at the Manor, where you can see the results of my hard labor as a smuggler."

Eight

Wrapped in multiple layers of shawls and scarves, Lady Abercrombie waited for Claire on one of the gilt chairs just outside the ballroom. With peacock feathers nodding on her head, wisps of brownish-gray hair sticking out from beneath her turban like the ruffled feathers of a sparrow, and a nose resembling a parrot's curved beak, the sprightly octogenarian reminded Claire of nothing so much as some strange, exotic bird.

Claire smiled at her fondly. "Good evening, Lady Abercrombie."

"Well, Claire! Where have you been? I meant to ask how you enjoyed the ball, but that's to no purpose. You haven't been next or nigh the ballroom since *before* your brother made that ridiculous announcement about Anne and Lawrence Bellingham. And neither was Alan Trent here. So, young lady, what have you to say for yourself?"

Claire suppressed a sigh. The dowager Lady Abercrombie was notorious not only for a sharp tongue but also for short-sightedness. Yet nothing ever escaped her notice.

"I am sorry if I neglected you, ma'am. I promise it won't happen again."

"Hmm. Not telling, are you? Well, you're wise. Keep your own council until you've got everything settled."

Claire, preoccupied with thoughts of Alan, said nothing.

"Sit down, gal." Lady Abercrombie jabbed a bony finger at the chair next to her. When Claire had complied, she said, "You're a sensible girl. Always were, always will be. Even if you're foolish enough to set your heart on a restless scamp like Alan Trent. And don't try to deny it! I've known you from the cradle, child. You can't pull the wool over my eyes."

Indeed. Claire was very much aware that the old lady had known her from the cradle. She had been told often enough. Usually Lady Abercrombie added that it entitled her to plain speaking.

Plain speaking . . . Yes, Claire would have to take a leaf from Lady Abercrombie's book when she met with Alan on the morrow. But perhaps tomorrow would best be left to clearing up the smuggling business. And then, on Valentine's Day, a day most fitting for personal concerns, she would—

In truth, she did not know what she would do.

"I shan't waste my breath telling you to forget about him." Lady Abercrombie pursed her mouth. "Know it won't do any good. And besides, he might just be the right one for you. You're certainly old enough to know your mind."

"Thank you," said Claire for lack of anything better to say. She remembered suddenly that Alan had not said *when* he would come for her in the morning.

"But there's one thing I will do. And I'll do it quick because I should have been in my bed hours ago. I'm not as young as I used to be, and why I asked you all to dinner tomorrow when I know I'll be exhausted after gadding about here all night is more than I can tell."

"You're giving the dinner," Claire reminded her, "because Mrs. Sedgewicke in Snuffton is giving one and you want to show her—"

"That'll do, miss! Impertinence doesn't become you. Leave that to Louisa Sedgewicke and her ilk. But mark my words! She has realized by now how foolish she was to insist on town hours. Six o'clock sharp we'll sit down at *my* house, and everybody home betimes to rest up for the Valentine's Day Ball the day after. Now listen sharp, Claire."

"Yes, ma'am."

Valentine's Day. It struck Claire that she never did promise Alan the supper dance. But then, Alan was the kind of man who took assent for granted once he asked for something. Just as he probably took for granted that she would wait years longer for a proposal.

The old lady craned her neck as she looked around for anyone who might be eavesdropping. Satisfied that no one was, she leaned closer to Claire.

"I'll help you get him. That scamp Alan Trent."

She finally had Claire's undivided attention.

"How, Lady Abercrombie?"

"Do you realize what year this is?"

Claire gave her a puzzled look. "1816."

"It's the leap year, gal!"

"I know, but what—"

"Ha! Knew you wouldn't have thought of it. Young people today! Don't see what's before their noses if it bites them!"

"Yes, it's lamentable. But, Lady Abercrombie, *what* should I have seen?"

"In a leap year, gal, *the woman* has the right to choose her man and make him a proposal of marriage."

The woman's right to propose to the man of her choice! Surely, this was the specific drastic measure Claire had been looking for.

So simple a solution to her problem. And yet—

Claire thought about it until she fell asleep some time around four in the morning, and again from the moment she rose at seven until ten o'clock, when Alan finally drove up in his curricle. She was still mulling it over when she sat beside him, a carriage robe over her knees, her feet against a hot brick, and her hands tucked into a fur muff.

It wasn't that she questioned the wisdom of the step she was contemplating. After careful consideration she had come to the conclusion that, adventure, excitement, and apprehension notwithstanding, she still, more than ever, wanted to marry Alan. And since she did not know how much time she had before he sailed to China, the only way to ensure fulfillment of her dream would be to propose to him.

Lady Abercrombie said that the bridegroom-to-be was expected to accept the lady's proposal, unless he could show he was already betrothed to another. He could also choose to buy himself free—or was that the part pertaining to some ancient Scottish law? Lady Abercrombie hadn't been too clear on that point and, in truth, Claire considered it unimportant. She was quite certain that Alan would not refuse her once she spoke her piece and proposed to him.

But there was the rub. Would she have the nerve, the daring, to do it?

Two days to test her mettle. She was glad now that she had decided to devote this morning with Alan to the smuggling business. The cautious streak in her rebelled against something so unorthodox as making a marriage proposal, even if it was her right. But it was unusual. Claire did not know of any lady in her circle who had proposed to her husband-to-be, but then, the number of her female acquaintances was rather restricted, since she had had only one season in town.

Claire thought of her twin. Sarah would not have hesitated. She had quite openly and shamelessly encouraged the young vicar of Thistledown. And if it had been a leap year, Sarah would have plunged, without a doubt or hesitation, into a proposal of marriage.

So deep in her thoughts was Claire, she did not realize that Alan, too, was unusually silent during the half-hour drive until he reined in his pair of matched bays and came to a stop in front of the Manor.

If she did not know him so well, she might have supposed that the business of guiding a high-spirited pair on snow-covered lanes had demanded all his concentration. But Alan was a notable whip, more than capable of driving in worse conditions than they had faced this sunny February morning.

She waited until he had handed the reins to a groom and assisted her from the curricle.

"Is something wrong, Alan? Did Lieutenant Bradshaw find the smuggled goods on your property after all?"

His face relaxed. "Is that what kept you so quiet? Worry? Well, you needn't have fretted. In the grounds, stables, and barns, Bradshaw and his men discovered not a single keg or an animal that doesn't belong here. And in the house, where the good lieutenant suspected hidden smugglers, he found no one but my staff."

As Alan preceded her to open the heavy studded oak door to the Great Hall, Claire's eyes followed the long sweep of the drive to the main gate, barely visible in the distance, and the shorter stretch leading off to the stables. True, there was cover of a sort, lilac and rhododendron bushes lining the carriageway, but even in the dark it would be difficult to miss a pack train of mules and ponies moving behind the bare branches.

"Alan, how did the pack train disappear?"

"Don't you remember the small pedestrian gate about a hundred paces to the left of the main gate?"

"I do. Don't tell me—" Her breath caught on a choke of laughter. "Alan, how did you dare set up something so audacious? So risky!"

"Yes, but don't you see? It was the audaciousness of the plan that made it foolproof. We knew Bradshaw was watching the Martello tower, and it was a foregone conclusion that he'd follow the mule train. But not in his wildest dreams would Bradshaw have expected that the smugglers he pursued all the way from Pevensey would enter the Manor grounds by one gate only to double back by the next, while he and his dragoons tried to tiptoe up the carriageway."

"I cannot deny that it worked, and the smugglers got away with their contraband." Claire frowned at Alan. "But that isn't all, is it? What else was going on while your friends the free-traders led the Customs officer on a wild-goose chase?"

"Nothing much." The gleam in his eyes said otherwise. "It

just so happened that the smugglers managed to lose four of their people here on the grounds."

"Don't be so tiresomely cryptic! Are you saying you have smugglers hidden after all?"

"Not hidden. They're walking around, for anyone to see."

"Ah! When I visited you on Saturday, only two members of the house staff were present. But I daresay, when Lieutenant Bradshaw finally had the opportunity to search your house, he found six?"

"Come and meet them." Alan flung the door wide. "Meyer will have them waiting in the library."

"But, Alan! Why are they here? What do you need them for?"

"See for yourself."

Alan took Claire's cloak and gloves, depositing them with his driving coat and gauntlets on one of the carved wooden settles placed liberally throughout the vast hall, then led her across the flagstone floor to the book-lined room where she had startled him with the question "Alan, do you ever think about marriage?"

His life hadn't been the same since then. His peace of mind was shattered, the future he had envisioned suddenly questionable.

He shot a sidelong look at her as he opened the library door. She was smiling a little, showing the enchanting dimple at the corner of her mouth. Was she thinking about the last time they were in the library? The tentative embrace Rufus disrupted?

Twice now he had held her in his arms. Twice they were interrupted. He had not been able to tell what she had felt that first time; but the second time she had responded with as much enthusiasm as any man could wish. Did that mean she now considered herself courted? For all he knew, she was an accomplished flirt and kissed a great many men.

He almost laughed aloud. Claire was no more a flirt than he was a staid, sober country squire.

No, there was no doubt about it. Claire had kissed him the way a woman kissed the man she loved.

The kiss had shaken him, and like a coxcomb he told her she was the woman he'd ask *when he decided to marry*.

"Alan? Are you dreaming?"

"Sorry, love."

Devil a bit, if his face wasn't growing hot! Not only a coxcomb, but an oaf and a poltroon as well. Today he couldn't do a damn thing about it, though. There was still business to take care of.

"Claire, I want you to meet my new staff. Temporary, of course." He indicated the man and three young women who had hastily risen from seats by the fire. "First there's Higgins, footman."

"Footmen are called by their given names, Alan."

"Jack, then."

"Black Jack!" Her eyes sparkled. "Mr. Black Jack Higgins, I am delighted to make your acquaintance."

"Madam."

Higgins, his muscular frame displayed to advantage in footman's livery, bowed deeply. The only marring note in an otherwise dignified appearance was the wide grin, showing white, slightly uneven teeth.

Or *was* it the grin that struck the false note? Frowning a little, Claire stepped closer to the man.

"You shaved off a beard recently, didn't you?"

Higgins chuckled. "Aye, miss. I mean, yes, madam."

Alan said, "By George, Claire! I'm dashed glad you're not in Customs service."

Claire looked at the three young women. Girls, really, since none of them could be much older than sixteen. They were neat and tidy, even if the gray stuff gowns always worn by the Manor housemaids seemed a bit large. Their caps and aprons were immaculate, their curtsies just right. Two of the girls met Claire's gaze boldly; the third hung her head, her face crimson in embarrassment or shyness.

"Yes, Alan, I believe you have every reason to be glad."

Claire faced him. "I wish you had brought me into this mad scheme of yours much sooner. If you brushed by Lieutenant Bradshaw last night, it was because he is not as observant as he should be. Dash it, Alan! You bungled badly."

"What's wrong now?"

"These girls! When you told me the smugglers left behind four of their people, I had no notion that three of them were female."

"What difference does it make?"

"They're supposed to be maids. But with your mother and housekeeper gone, and no female cook on the premises to fill in for the housekeeper, a respectable maid would not stay here. And if Bradshaw has any sense at all, he knows it, too."

Alan, speechless, wondered if the riding officer was already on his way back to the Manor. The previous night Bradshaw had been too frustrated and angry, furious with himself for overstepping his authority, to notice what Claire had seen at a glance. But by now Bradshaw should have cooled down sufficiently to collect his wits.

One of the girls huddled down on the hearth rug and started to cry into her apron.

"What you should've done, sir," said Jack Higgins, "is hired Miss Claire as your aide."

Alan stared at the young lady he had known all his life and yet never ceased to amaze him.

Yes, indeed. She'd make an excellent aide-de-camp.

"Alan," she said. "Whoever these girls are—smugglers' daughters, sweethearts—can you not release them? Surely you don't require hostages?"

"They're no hostages. Claire, you don't understand. These girls are the goods supposed to be smuggled into France."

Her eyes widened. "Lud, Alan! The nefarious bit of smuggling you spoke of, it's—" She swallowed. "It's *white slavery.*"

"I dunno nuffink about slavery," said one of the bold-eyed girls. "But iffen I'm gonna ply me trade, I'll do it in Lunnon an' not in some furrin place. An' I'll set the runners on them as bashed me on the noggin an' carted me off wiffout so much as a by-yer-leave."

The crying girl stammered between sobs that she wanted to go home to her mum and her da in Kensington.

"And you will go back to London," said Alan. "All three of you. But for now, you'll just have to wait until I catch the men who kidnapped you."

Claire noted that Alan, the dashing, daring Major Sir Alan Trent, was looking slightly flustered.

"They had better come with me to Sutherland Hall, Alan." Claire smiled encouragingly at the girls. "My brother is a justice of the peace. You'll be quite safe."

"Thank you, love." Alan was his old insouciant self. "And I'll take care of Higgins. If Bradshaw returns, Meyer will tell him that the footman and three maids have been dismissed."

"Only the footman was dismissed," Claire corrected him. "For immoral behavior. The girls were fetched home by their outraged fathers."

When Claire, shepherding the young girls, returned to Sutherland Hall an hour later, she was in full possession of the facts known so far about girls and young women kidnapped in London and taken to the old Martello tower near Penvensey, where they were picked up by a French boat.

Stuart had told Alan the previous night that the Home Office was alarmed by the increasing complaints from respectable tradesmen and merchants whose daughters had disappeared. The Foreign Office, on the other hand, had learned of a growing number of young Englishwomen, some of them minors, many of them drugged, in Paris brothels. Letters from the Foreign Office requesting the French government to look into the situation had been ignored.

The Home Office and the Foreign Office had conferred and shared information, but then, apparently, acted independently and without consulting each other. The Home Office alerted the magistrate of the Bow Street Court in London and justices of the peace in the general vicinity of Pevensey, including Stuart Sutherland, while Lord Castlereagh at the Foreign Office turned to Sir Alan Trent, whose courage and daring had often been mentioned in dispatches from the Duke of Wellington.

On Saturday, the day of the snowstorm, Alan learned from Black Jack Higgins that a French boat was expected on Tuesday night. However, three girls were discovered in the Martello tower at dawn on Monday already, watched by one guard. It was unthinkable for a man of Alan's stamp to let three helpless females languish in a drafty stone tower for a night and a day until he could capture the rest of the kidnappers when they appeared to supervise the girls' transfer to the French vessel and to receive payment.

Thus Alan and his free-trading friends overpowered the guard and rescued the girls. Alan returned home in time to attend the dinner at Sutherland Hall, while the smugglers, as usual, waited for the early dusk before they left with the pack mules and ponies—and the girls. Above all, Alan wanted to avoid the white slavers being alerted by any unusual happenings around the tower shared by smugglers and kidnappers, though never before at the same time.

And now, after taking Claire home and sending an apology to Lady Abercrombie for having to miss her dinner party that night, Alan, accompanied by Black Jack Higgins, was on his way back to Pevensey to set a trap for the dastardly men who dealt in white slavery.

Nine

Claire did not know how she made it through Lady Abercrombie's dinner party without fidgeting or committing some major gaffe, but apparently she did fine. No one gave her dark looks or lodged a complaint when the Sutherlands took their leave shortly after ten o'clock that night.

Alan had warned her not to expect word from him before noon the following day, but when the better part of the morning passed without a message or visit from him, she began to feel decidedly unwell. Even Mrs. Sutherland noticed her daughter's pallor and lack of appetite at luncheon.

"Claire, dearest, would you like to help me in the orchid house? I must record the results of experiments I conducted on several species of *Pleurothallis.*"

Claire could not help but smile. Her mother much preferred to have the orchid house to herself and extended an invitation to assist her—a very special treat, in her view—only when she believed one of her children in dire need of coddling.

"Thank you, Mama. But truly, there's nothing wrong with me that a brisk walk wouldn't cure."

"Are you certain, dear?" Mrs. Sutherland rose from the table. "I thought that perhaps you needed a distraction. Time passes so much quicker, you know, when one is occupied."

Claire stared at her mother. She had, naturally, told Stuart the truth about the three girls she brought from the Manor and about Alan's quest to capture the white slavers. But even if Stuart had passed the information on to the rest of the family, their absentminded mother would hardly conclude from those sparse facts that her daughter was pining for news of the gallant rescuer.

Mrs. Sutherland raised a delicate brow. "You look staggered, dear. Did you think I had forgotten it's Valentine's Day?"

"Ah . . . no, Mama."

"I thought you might be waiting for a posy. That's why I said time will fly if you keep occupied."

When Mrs. Sutherland had drifted off, Claire still wasn't sure how much her mother understood about her feelings. But she did follow her advice and occupied herself. She took her protégées, Selina, Peg, and Mary, on a tour of stables and barns and into the dairy.

The excursion could not be considered an unqualified success. London bred, the girls took exception to the swishing tails when they wanted to pet the cows, to the slobber dripping on their hands when Claire encouraged them to feed bits of apple to the horses. They did not like the noisy pigs and were afraid of dogs, which, thought Claire, accounted for Rufus's absence in the Manor library.

Only the dairy, with its clean tiled floor and scrubbed tables, appealed to them. They sampled clotted cream and milk— "Whole and quite fresh, like in Green Park!" exclaimed Mary, the shy one who had cried for her mum and her da. They admired the large wooden butter churns and watched how butter was shaped into golden slabs of a size they had never seen in their own homes.

For that brief hour, while she acted as guide and mentor to the three young girls, Claire was too busy to worry about Alan and why she hadn't heard from him. But as soon as she sent them off to the servants' hall for their dinner, anxiety returned with renewed force.

She did not believe the kidnappers would give themselves up without a fight, and had said as much to Alan.

He, of course, had laughed at her worries.

"Devil a bit, Claire!" he said cheerfully. "Do you think this will be the first time I face a pistol or a knife? Don't you fret. I can take care of myself. Yes, and I can take care of Higgins and his men, too."

It could not be said that Alan's assurances had a calming effect on Claire.

And if everything had gone according to plan, Alan should have returned well before noon. But now it was past three o'clock. Surely he knew she would be waiting to hear from him! Surely he would at least send Meyer with a message.

She consulted with Stuart, who promptly told her not to be a silly widgeon.

"What do you expect, Claire? That Alan will come galloping just to tell you he's fine?"

Yes, she did.

She searched her brother's face. "You're truly not worried, Stuart? The kidnappers would have been at the tower late last night because they'd expect to put the girls aboard the French boat well before dawn. If Alan caught them—"

"Of course he caught them! And he handed the rotters over to the Pevensey magistrate, and now he's home and fast asleep. Dash it, Claire! The man must be tired after romping about most of Monday night, and then all of last night."

"You had word from him! Why didn't you tell me?"

"No, miss! I haven't heard from Alan. And I don't expect to. Alan is his own man, working for the Foreign Office. He doesn't owe me—or you—a report. But no doubt," Stuart added, slightly less exasperated, "we'll hear all about it tonight at Trafalgar. Alan told me he'd be at the Valentine's Day Ball for sure."

Claire's fears were not laid to rest, but Stuart's attitude had a bracing effect. It was true, she had no claim on Alan, no right to expect an immediate report.

Not yet. But as his wife, she would have every right.

Just let Alan make an appearance at the Valentine's Day

88

Ball, and if she couldn't pluck up the courage to propose, then she wasn't the right kind of wife for him.

The ballroom at Trafalgar, Admiral Seymore's home, had been lovingly decorated by Lucinda and Anne in pink, red, and white. The admiral, standing just inside the ballroom door to greet his guests, had a pained look on his face and winced every time someone praised the prettiness of the garlands or the striking color coordination.

If it had been any other occasion, Claire would have teased the older man, the way she knew he enjoyed being teased by a young lady, that he was turning into a regular curmudgeon. But not this night. Not when she was hoping and dreading that at any moment she would see Alan.

And if he did not arrive soon, she would be in no shape at all to speak to him.

Alan entered the ballroom just as Claire was about to step onto the dance floor with Roger Seymore. She saw him immediately, and she also saw that his left arm reposed interestingly in a black silk sling.

Her heart raced. Alan. Thank God! Daring, dashing, and oh, so splendid!

And, judging by the way he greeted Stuart with a thump on the back and the admiral with a bow and a hearty handshake, he was enjoying himself hugely and was none the worse for his encounter with the white slavers. Despite the ostentatious sling.

With a murmured excuse she left Roger Seymore and unceremoniously interrupted the three gentlemen.

"Alan!" Breathless. "I want a word with you."

"My pleasure."

Dark eyes gleaming, Alan offered his right arm and whisked her out of the ballroom, down the corridor a little ways, and into a small antechamber.

The room was dimly lit by a slender lamp on the mantelshelf, and the furniture consisted only of a few chairs and a small table. But Claire was not looking for comfort. What she needed was pluck. Nerve. The kind of daring Alan had in abundance.

Taking a quick turn about the room, she caught a glimpse of a wicked smile, but when she faced him, he was as serious as she could wish.

He said, "No doubt you're agog to know what happened last night with the kidnappers?"

"Later, Alan. I have something more important on my mind."

"You're worried about my injury." He indicated the arm resting in its handsome silk sling.

"I am not."

"Claire!"

She did not wish to be distracted, but how could she not laugh at his outrage?

She primmed her mouth. "Don't playact again! I have something serious to discuss with you."

"Then let me set your mind at ease first and assure you that it is but a minor scratch."

"As if I hadn't known the moment I set eyes on you! How can I believe you seriously injured when you strut in like a knight who slew his dragon and now expects his reward?"

"Ah, but that's the question, isn't it? Will I receive my reward?"

She thought of the assignment to the China expedition. "I daresay you will. I don't know of an instance when you did not get what you wanted."

Even in the dim light, the gleam in his eyes was unmistakable. "I am relieved to hear it, love. Now, what is it you need to discuss with me?"

Pluck, Claire!

"Marriage."

An arrested look crossed his face. "A fitting subject for Valentine's Day."

"Yes. Alan, do you remember that I asked you once before whether you had thought about marriage?"

"Do I remember! You quite cut up my peace of mind! Haven't been able *not* to think about it since you brought it up.

"But don't you see, Alan? With all the adventuring you do, a wife could only be of benefit. You cannot have missed that a woman's touch is invaluable when it comes to outwitting someone."

"The way you dealt with Bradshaw. Yes, I see." Alan frowned. "But could I expect that of my wife?"

"Of course. *And* your wife would help plan your strategy so you wouldn't bungle again as you did with the girls."

He groaned. "A low hit, Claire."

"But justified."

"Indeed. Bradshaw did come back. Meyer told him what you said, footman dismissed and girls taken away by their fathers, and Bradshaw had no choice but to leave again."

"It proves my point. You need someone to help you out in a pinch." She warmed to the theme. "When you were in the army, I daresay you could count on your friends to pull you out of scrapes. And whenever you were home, you had me to perform the office. But who will do it in China? Or Africa, South America? Who knows where you'll want to go next? I tell you, Alan, you *need* someone with you to pull you out of scrapes, because you're forever tumbling into them."

"But must it be a wife?" It was Alan now who took an agitated turn about the small chamber. "I have it! Claire, you could speak to Meyer. Give him a hint or two what to watch out for."

"No." Uncompromising. "A servant can leave you anytime. You must have a wife."

He stood with his back to her, the set of his shoulders and the tilt of his head showing grim resolve.

"In that case, I had better look about me fast. The orders for the China assignment may come through any day. If only I could be certain my wife would wish to accompany me."

"She would if she knew you at all. How else can she help you if you fall afoul of the emperor or some old mandarin? Besides, she might wish to have a bit of an adventure herself."

He turned to face her. "Yes. You're right, of course. She must be someone who knows me well."

Claire swallowed. This was it. The moment to toss her heart over the fence.

"Alan, are you aware that in a leap year a woman has the right to choose her man?"

"And she can propose to him. Yes, I know. I heard Lady Abercrombie tell your mother at Anne's dinner."

"Oh!"

His shameless, wicked grin blazing, he reached her in two long strides.

"But I'll be damned, my own sweet love, if I allow you to beat me to it. That's not why I hustled and tussled with some ornery magistrate all morning and part of the afternoon just so I could be rid of the kidnappers in time to see you at the ball."

Claire heard only the important part of his speech.

"Your own . . ." She felt her knees shake and clutched at his lapels for support. "Sweet love?"

His good arm went around her. "I love you, Claire. I think I have done so for a long time but never realized it. And then, when I thought about the years I'd be wasting—years without you while I would be roaming the world—Dash it, Claire! It wasn't to be borne."

Recovering, she gave him a saucy look. "You always were a bit slow. *I* knew years ago that no one but you would do for me. Alan, will you marry me?"

He tossed off the sling with an impatient exclamation. Then, both arms holding her captive, he kissed her. And this time, Rufus was safely away, dozing in front of the library fire at the Manor.

"Alan," Claire said after a while, a long while, "shouldn't you return that arm to the sling?"

"I told you." His mouth explored a path from her ear to the curve of her neck. "It's nothing but a scratch."

She tilted her head to provide him better access to the hollow at the base of her throat. "What happened?"

"Bradshaw got carried away. Fired his pistol blindly when one of the kidnappers made a dash for freedom. Didn't see I was already after the bounder."

"Bradshaw!" Claire resolutely pushed Alan away. "How does he come into it?"

"He followed Higgins and me."

"You didn't know?"

Alan made a show of replacing the sling. "Not at first. But when I did catch sight of him, I decided I might as well enlist his help. And a good thing I did!"

The black silk positioned to his satisfaction, he placed his good arm once more around Claire and drew her close.

"There were just the two of us, love. Higgins and I. The other smugglers were still delivering their goods. But there were six kidnappers. And they had five more girls with them!"

"And the French boat?"

"Drawing close but still far enough away not to give us any trouble. And pretty soon they turned about and sailed back to France. But it was bad enough without them underfoot. Lud, Claire! What a ruckus those girls set up when we jumped their captors. I hope I never have to rescue females again."

"You'll have me to help you now."

Once again, Claire clutched his lapels. "You will, that is, if you'll ever get around to accepting my proposal. Or are you having second thoughts? Are you remembering what you said about twins?"

"Twins?" Understanding dawned. "You mean our children? Do you think there's a chance we'll have a rascally pair like you and Sarah were? I'd like it above anything."

"Then you had better answer quickly. Alan, will you marry me?"

"I, Alan Edward Trent, take thee, Claire Marie Sutherland, to be my wedded Wife, to have and to hold from this day forward . . ."

The apse of Thistledown Church resounded with the deep, rich tones of the bridegroom's voice. The scent of flowers plundered from every succession house in the county filled the air. Smiling, Claire blinked away a tear.

Her dream come true.

The Crystal Heart
by
Mary Kingsley

One

The four young men gathered around the fire in the Cocoa Tree in London that snowy evening had long ago passed the point of inebriation. They were beyond drinking, beyond gambling, beyond doing much of anything. Certainly they were beyond attending any of the various balls and routs being held during this brief Christmas season, for it was nearer to dawn than midnight. They were, quite simply, sated with life in the social world of the *ton,* and yet none had the energy to bestir himself to do anything else.

John Charles Winston, the Viscount Kirkwood, was bored. It was a failing he'd recognized in himself before, though he doubted anyone else would consider it such. After all, ennui was fashionable. He, however, did not like it one bit.

Lord knew why he should be bored, he thought, staring into the embers of the dying fire, late at night in dark, cold January. He had everything he could want, money, title, position. He was well liked and sought-after. And hadn't he just spent an agreeable evening roistering with his friends? He cast a quick look around the fireside at them, and his mouth quirked with amusement. Danbury was sunk so low in his chair that he was nearly prone; the young Earl of Monkford, recently come into his title, leaned his head on his hand; and Edward Radcliffe occasionally made a noise that sounded suspiciously like a snore. No wonder. After the evening they had had and

97

the wine they had consumed, it was a wonder any of them was still alive.

John sat upright, his elbows resting on his knees and a lock of hair falling over his forehead. He was the most foxed of all, having disposed of several bottles of the finest burgundy without help, and yet his mind worked with a clarity rare even for him. Not for him, the gift of drowning one's sorrows in drink. All alcohol seemed to do for him was make him see them more clearly. What he saw now was his life stretching ahead of him, very much like this, days spent in idle entertainment, nights spent wenching, gambling, and drinking much too much. Eventually, of course, his father would pass on, and then he would be the Marquess of Ware. Things would change then. He'd have to do everything his father wanted him to do now: manage his estates, choose a suitable bride, set up his nursery. The thought was so repugnant that he snorted.

Danbury raised his head. "What?" he said, staring at John blearily.

"I'm bored."

"Can't be." Danbury let his head fall back. "With us for company, old man?"

John grinned. "Such as it is."

"It's the wine." He yawned widely. "It will pass."

"I'm not so sure." Rising, John stretched, and went to stand by the mantel, staring down into the flames. "Don't you ever get tired of it, Evan? We see the same people day after day, go to the same places night after night."

"Heard of a new gaming hell, over in Piccadilly—"

John's hand shot out in a gesture of disdain. "It's just more of the same. One gaming hell is much like another."

"Huh. Next thing you know, you'll be telling us one woman is much like another." John shrugged, and Danbury stared at him, his gaze sharper now. "You don't mean that. Lud, you do!" He sat up straight, shaking his head to clear it. "You are in bad case, my friend. Monkford."

He reached over and pulled at Monkford's arm. Suddenly

98

deprived of its support, Monkford's head jerked up, and he glared at Danbury with astonishment. "I say. Can't a man sleep in peace?"

"Not now. Radcliffe." Danbury gave Mr. Radcliffe similarly rough treatment, until he, too, roused. "Wake up. Kirkwood needs us."

"Lord help me," John said, but he was smiling. "What kind of advice are you preparing to give me, Evan?"

"Needs us? What?" Radcliffe sputtered, his mouth hanging open and his eyes blank. "John don't need anybody."

"Kirkwood has just informed me that he is bored."

At this pronouncement, three pairs of eyes turned to John.

"Well, I am," he said, mildly.

"How can you be?" Danbury sat forward, wide awake now. "I know town is thin of company this time of year, but that's all to the good, you ask me. All the mamas are safe in the country with their marriageable daughters." He shuddered. "Won't catch me in parson's mousetrap."

"Lud, no," Monkford agreed, fervently. "But there's plenty of the other sort around. Saw the way you looked at that opera dancer at the ballet this evening, Kirkwood. Thinking of setting her up as your mistress?"

John's smile was faint. "Perhaps."

"Well, if you don't, I will. Pretty little thing. And willing, I'll wager."

"Aren't they all?" John reached for the one remaining bottle of burgundy, upended it, and was rewarded by only a few drops splashing into his glass. With a shrug, he tossed them down. "That's the problem."

"I don't understand any of this," Mr. Radcliffe said, plaintively. "Why is John bored? Why isn't there any wine left?"

"We drank it, you fool." Danbury remained watching John. "As to why he's bored, don't see why he should be. Capital mill at Gentleman Jackson's today. Handy with your fives, John. The gentleman himself said you were made for the ring."

"And I've the bruises to show for it," Monkford said, gingerly touching his chin. "Danbury's right. Plenty to do. Damned cold out, but there's enough to do within doors. Gaming, don't you know. You were prodigious lucky tonight, curse your eyes." He sank back into his chair, his face gloomy. "Probably the opera dancer will favor you, too. That'll make it three times in one day I've lost to you."

"You can have her," John said, and the others stared at him. "I mean it."

"Lud! There really *is* something wrong with you, isn't there?"

"I'm bored." John left the fireplace and began to prowl the room. "Don't you ever think, sometimes, that there has to be more than this?"

"What more can we ask?" Danbury said. "We've got everything we need, and then some."

"I know. Lord, I know, and I'm not complaining. But it doesn't seem enough, somehow." He stared down into the fire again. "Sometimes I think I should do as my father asks and learn how to manage the estates."

Danbury hooted with laughter. "You? Actually working? You wouldn't last a week."

"I think I would."

"Gammon. You'd be back in town so fast your head would spin. This is where you belong, old man. Not holed up in the country, grubbing in the dirt."

"Care to wager on that?"

"On what? On your going home?"

"No. On my working. Say, for six months."

Danbury stared at him. "You're serious."

"I am."

"Then damned if I won't take you on. My new phaeton against your team of grays."

"I'll take a piece of that." Monkford sat up. "I'll wager the opera dancer."

"You can't wager a person," Mr. Radcliffe protested. "It ain't done."

"What would you wager? Your poetry?" Monkford jeered.

100

Mr. Radcliffe's face got very red. "My poetry's dashed good! Everyone says so. No, I'll wager—well, dash it, I don't know what, but I'm in on this, too!"

"Accepted," John said, and the four young men grinned at each other. Gaming was one thing; a wager of this sort was something else altogether. "Call for the betting book, and we'll write it down proper."

"You'll be back in town within a fortnight," Danbury predicted, as the porter came in, bearing the club's betting book.

"We shall see." John inscribed his name and the terms of the wager, and the others followed suit. "There. Done." He grinned. "Shake hands with me, gentlemen. I'm off on an adventure."

"Or folly. I've always coveted those grays," Danbury said, but he held out his hand. "Best of luck to you, John."

"I don't expect I'll need it." He snapped his fingers at the porter, who came up with his greatcoat and hat. "I'm for bed. If I'm to find a position, I'll have to start immediately. Good night, gentlemen." Sketching a brief bow, John turned, and left the room.

The three remaining men looked at each other. "Easiest wager I've ever made," Danbury said. "He won't last a week."

"Care to wager on that?" Monkford said.

"Capital idea. Porter!" he bellowed. "The betting book, if you will. And more wine." He grinned. "This is capital."

One week later, John would not have agreed with that assessment. As he alighted from the public stage before a coaching inn in Dorset, of all places, he ruminated again on the folly that had brought him to such a pass. What had possessed him to make such a wager? To be shut up in the wilds of the country for six months—six months!—working for his keep, surpassed all bounds. He was a viscount, for God's sake. Viscounts did not ride on public stages, rubbing elbows with farmers and tradesmen and who knew what other manner of people. No. Viscounts traveled in well-sprung private carriages, upholstered in leather and velvet, and did not have to cater to the whims and tyrannies of the coachman. But damned if he'd give in, now, at the beginning of the wager. He wouldn't let Danbury have the satisfaction.

The stage rumbled away in a cloud of dust. Frowning, John brushed off his greatcoat, picked up his valise, and strode into the inn. Impatiently he pounded on the counter, and the innkeeper, a thin, bent man, came out from the taproom, wiping his hands on a dirty apron. "A private parlor, my good man. And luncheon. Dashed cold out there."

The innkeeper continued wiping his hands, all the time studying John. At least, John thought he was. One of the man's eyes had a cast in it, so that it was hard to guess exactly where he was looking. "And who might you be?"

"I am Kirk—er, Mr. Winston." Just in time he remembered one of the terms of the wager. He was to secure his position on his own, with no help from either his title or his connections. Nor was he to reveal to anyone during the six months who he was. Damned inconvenient.

"Winston, eh? Him that's to work up at the big house?"

"Yes. I am waiting, man. Your best private parlor, if you please."

The man cackled. "Hee, hee. Hear that? Best private parlor, he says. You can wait there." He jerked a thumb over her shoulder. "With her. Carriage will be along for you presently." With that, he turned and lurched back into the taproom. "Best private parlor. Hee, hee! For the likes of him."

"I say!" John exclaimed, staring after him, his hands on his hips. "Of all the rude, ignorant fools—"

"You may as well sit," an amused voice said, and he turned. For the first time he realized there was a female in the hall, sitting on a bench set against the wall. In the dim light he could see little of her; she was cloaked in a cape of gray wool, with a bonnet to match upon her head. The clearest impression he had of her was her voice, serene and cultured, and her eyes. They were dancing with amusement. "You won't get more out of Mr. Horton."

"He is a damned, rude—excuse me. Dashed." With an inward sigh, John picked up his valise and crossed the hall to the bench. So this was what life was like for those not of noble blood. He didn't like it one bit. "May I sit?"

The female shifted on the bench to make room for him. "Of course. I realize we haven't been properly introduced, but under the circumstances I think that's not necessary. I am Miss Alana Sterling."

John held out his hand. "Kirk—er, Mr. John Winston, ma'am." He settled himself next to her, entirely disgruntled. First the unspeakable ride on the stage, then the innkeeper's rudeness, and now this. Stuck with a female of indeterminate age and appearance. Why had he ever left London?

"Well, Kirk Mr. Winston." Her eyes danced. "You are to be employed at Heart's Ease as well?"

"If you mean by the Valentine family, yes, I am," he said, stiffly. What right had she to laugh at him? "I've been hired as the new librarian."

"Ah. I see."

He moved on the bench. This female annoyed him more and more. "And you?"

"I'm to be companion to Lady Honoria Valentine."

Somehow, he wasn't surprised. "Is this your first post?"

"Oh, heavens, no. My third, actually. When one is a companion, one's employers have a lamentable habit of dying on one."

What manner of woman was this? John turned to stare at her, and was caught by her eyes. They were the green of spring leaves, and alive, so alive. Mischief lurked in them, along with a hint of ridicule, and more than a little bit of intelligence. Wise eyes, which was perhaps why he had thought she was elderly herself. This close, he could see that she wasn't. Her creamy skin was fresh and smooth, unmarred by wrinkles, with just a touch of color to her cheeks. Natural color, he'd wager, just as the glossy chestnut of her hair was natural. Good God. She was a beauty. Suddenly, his situation seemed more tolerable.

"Well?" Her voice held that amused note. "Do I pass muster?"

"Your eyes," he said, and was annoyed to hear himself stammer. "I could write sonnets to your eyes."

"Could you, indeed." Miss Sterling straightened. "How nice for you."

"What is someone like you doing, working as a companion?"

"Making my way in the world. As are you."

"But surely you could find other ways." He turned toward her, moving just a bit closer. "A beautiful woman like you must have any number of men interested in her."

Miss Sterling edged away. "What is your meaning, sir?"

Marriage, of course. Why hadn't this woman married? Beautiful as she was, most men would be willing to overlook her defects of position and fortune. Not that he wanted to marry her, or anyone. Still, her presence at Heart's Ease might make life more tolerable. "I believe once we reach our destination, ma'am, we might become friends."

"Indeed," she said, with all the hauteur of a duchess.

"Yes. I mean no offense, ma'am."

"But, sir, I find you extremely offensive," she said, so gently that it was a moment before he realized he'd just received one of the most blistering setdowns of his life.

"I beg your—" he began, and stopped, speechless for the first time in all his long experience with women. Dash it, he was the Viscount Kirkwood! She should consider herself honored that he was even talking with her. Any other woman would. Except that this woman saw him only as a penniless scholar. He couldn't set her straight; to do so would be to forfeit the wager, and that he wasn't ready to do. His fists clenched on his knees. Dash it, he was destined to be stuck at a ridiculously named house in some remote corner of the world, with a woman whose disdain of him was obvious. Was any wager worth this?

The door to the inn opened, and a coachman stuck his head in. "You, there. Are you for Heart's Ease?"

Miss Sterling rose gracefully to her feet. "Thank you, yes, we are."

"You took your time in arriving, my good man," John rising as well. "My bags are there."

"Huh. Will you listen to that?" The coachman grinned at Miss Sterling, who was handing him her own bags. "His bags are there. Well, carry them himself, I says."

"I say," John began, and stopped, brought up short again by the reminder of what lay ahead of him. He would repay his friends for this. Imagining their laughter, were they to hear of this day's events, he picked up his valise and trudged behind the coachman, out to where an old, shabby carriage stood. Handing the coachman his bags, to store them in the boot, he began to climb in.

"You, there!" the coachman called. "What do you think you're doing?"

John paused on the stair, holding onto the doorframe to support himself. "Getting into the carriage. What do you think?"

"No room in there." The coachman slammed the lid of the boot and walked forward, grinning. "Got the new maids from the village in there already. It's up on top for you."

John glanced in, and saw that there were, indeed, several young females crammed inside. Sitting among them was Miss Sterling. He could swear he saw a gleam of amusement in her eyes, before she turned away.

"I'll get you for this, Danbury," he muttered. "I'll get you." Climbing to the top of the coach, he resigned himself to a long, cold ride in the drizzle. And thus began John Charles Winston's new life.

Two

"Ooh, that must be it now!" one of the maids exclaimed, and they all crowded to the coach window, looking out. Alana, squeezed into a corner, had just a glimpse of a large, pink, heart-shaped sign lettered in Old English, before the coach swept past into the drive. Above there was a thump and a shuffling sound, and she looked up toward the roof, smiling faintly. Poor Mr. Winston. Odious he might be, but even he didn't deserve to ride atop a coach on a gray, drizzly day. Especially when it was so clearly something he wasn't accustomed to. Come down in the world, had Mr. Winston, she surmised. She well knew what a shock it was, when one confronted the realities of life for the first time.

As she had since boarding the coach at the inn, she let her thoughts drift back to him. Heaven knew why. He had been quite insulting, implying that she might enjoy a dalliance with him. It was too bad of him, because he appeared to be charming. He was certainly handsome enough, with that lock of dark hair falling over his forehead, and his clear hazel eyes, looking just a little bewildered. What had happened to him to bring him down in the world? His clothes, well cut and of good material, were not the clothes of a working man, nor were his hands, though they looked strong enough. Perhaps he had lost money gaming, she mused. Or perhaps he was a poor relative who needed to marry well. Alana's mouth tightened. She'd known enough men like that in her time. If that were Mr. Winston's problem, then she'd thank him to stay well away from her.

The coach jolted to a stop, and the maids, excited, tumbled out. Flinching as they jostled past her, Alana finally descended more sedately and stood in the drive, surveying her new home. It was much like other houses she'd seen, originally Elizabethan, half-timbered and gabled, save in one detail. The plaster was not white. Rather, it was pink. Not an unattractive shade, really, a pastel color that would look well in a gown, but ludicrous on a house. Over the door was a heart-shaped plaque similar to the sign she had seen on the drive. "Heart's Ease," she murmured.

"Good God," a voice muttered beside her, and she looked up to see Mr. Winston, looking decidedly the worse for wear. His hair stood up in unruly curls, and his neckcloth was limp. "What the hell have I got myself into?"

Alana's mouth tilted in amusement and reluctant sympathy. "Did you enjoy the ride, Mr. Winston? Dorset is said to be an attractive place."

He shot her a sour look as they walked into the house. "You must know I didn't. I—good God," he said again, and this time, Alana was tempted to echo the sentiment. "It's pink."

"So it is." Her mouth tilted again as she looked about the hall. In keeping with the style of the house, she had expected to see a traditional hall, which would originally have been the center of the house. Perhaps it had been, once, but at some point someone had decided to embellish it. The walls were colored the same tint as the plaster outside, and on them hung brightly colored romantic paintings, of shepherds and shepherdesses frolicking, or bewigged ladies and gentlemen dancing the minuet, all with heavily gilded frames. Over the doorways twined gilded vines and leaves; surmounting these was another painting, this one of a plump and florid Cupid, apparently aiming his bow at anyone who passed beneath. Nor were the furnishings, few though they were, any less startling.

107

Several armchairs in crimson brocade stood against one wall, while what had probably once been a handsome oak refectory table was in the center of the room, its top and legs painted gold. What wasn't pink in the room was crimson; what wasn't crimson was gilded. Alana looked up at John, and saw her astonishment mirrored in his eyes. "It is pink," she agreed, and for the first time saw amusement come into his face.

"I see you are admiring my hall." A tall, stout woman paced into the room, her fading blond hair piled in ringlets atop her head. Her gown, Alana noted, was mauve rather than pink. But she had no doubt as to who had decorated the hall. "Mrs. Waverly, please see to the new maids," she said, and the plump woman behind her, dressed in black bombazine, took charge of the giggling girls, bustling them out of the room. "I am Lady Pamela Valentine. You must be Mr. Winston? Ah, yes. And you are Miss Sterling. Do you like my hall?"

John and Alana glanced at each other again, and then hastily looked away. "It is, ah, unique," Alana said, managing somehow to keep her composure.

"So it is. I do not believe there is another room like it in the whole of England."

"I hope not," John muttered.

"Who did the paintings?" Alana said quickly, praying that Lady Pamela had not heard.

"I did. Are they not charming? So in keeping with the rest of the house. Heart's Ease." She beamed about the room. "You have come at just the right time. We quite enjoy celebrating Valentine's Day, and this year we plan a masquerade. Of course you will help."

"Of course."

"Dashed if I—" John began, and Alana kicked his foot. "Ahem. Dashed if I wouldn't enjoy that, ma'am."

"Excellent. Sir Ronald, my husband, will see to you, Mr. Winston, and explain your duties to you. You do know we expect you to chronicle the family's history, as well as catalogue our library? Good. And I will take you up to Lady Honoria myself, Miss Sterling. She has been waiting for you."

"Thank you, ma'am." Alana gathered her skirts and followed Lady Pamela up the stairs, the railings festooned with more gilded vines and leaves. The last glimpse she had of Mr. Winston, as she turned of the landing, was of him staring, open-mouthed, about the hall. She could almost feel sympathy for him. Almost.

"I am glad you are here, Miss Sterling," Lady Pamela went on as they ascended the stairs. "I must tell you, in strictest confidence, of course, that Lady Honoria has been something of a trial to me these past weeks, since her last companion left. Why, she does not even wish to celebrate Valentine's Day this year, and she has always enjoyed it. Can you credit it?"

"No, ma'am. Is Lady Honoria well?"

Lady Pamela's mouth tightened. "She'll outlive us all, if you ask me. But, there, I wouldn't want you to think we wish otherwise. We all adore Lady Honoria. A woman could not ask for a better mama-in-law."

"Yes, ma'am." Alana's mouth tilted again. So Lady Honoria was a bit of a dragon, and Lady Pamela did not get along with her at all. Well, it was no more than she'd expected. She'd dealt with crotchety old ladies before. She would manage this time, as well. "I cannot help noticing the coincidence of the family name, and the name of the house. Is there a story behind that, ma'am?"

"Yes, it is the most amazing thing." Lady Pamela stopped in the hall and turned, her eyes shining. "This house used to belong to a family called Hart. Last century, it passed to the Valentine family, through marriage, you see. It was a very happy marriage, I've been told, and that is why the house is named as it is. And that is when celebrating Valentine's Day became a family tradition. It was a very plain house, though, when I came here. I decorated it suitably."

Alana bit the inside of her lips. "Yes, ma'am."

"And of course, there is the ghost."

Alana stopped. "The ghost, ma'am?"

"Oh, heavens, don't tell me you are frightened? 'Tis only a legend, after all. And so romantic, too. You see, this house was built by the Follett family. Sir Gabriel, the last of the family to live here, died on Valentine's Day. Ever since, it is said he haunts the house. I haven't seen him, though," she added, and Alana thought she sounded disappointed.

"I see." Alana followed. Well, it wouldn't be the first time she had lived in a haunted house. Grandfather's home had ghosts to spare, not the least of which was the memory of her own mother. But that was something she would not think about.

"Here we are." Lady Pamela opened a door, to a room furnished in good English oak and faded chintz. Sitting in a chair near a window was a stout old woman, wearing sensible gray and a cap upon her head. No frills or furbelows here, Alana noted with relief. "Mother Valentine, here is your new companion. Miss Sterling."

"Don't call me that ridiculous name," the old lady grumbled. "What is that you have on, Pammy?"

"My new gown." Lady Pamela turned. "Do you like it?"

"Hmph. Well, at least it is not pink. Come over into the light, girl." She beckoned to Alana with an imperious finger. "I can't see you over there."

"Now, Mother Valentine, don't you scare her her first day here."

"Hmph. If she's scared of me she's a ninnyhammer."

"I'm not frightened of you, ma'am," Alana said, calmly.

"You aren't? And why not? I've been told I'm frightening enough."

"Nevertheless, I am not frightened."

"Hmph." Lady Honoria glared at her, and Alana made herself meet her gaze. It would not do to back down now. "You'll do, I suppose. Leave us, Pammy."

"But, Mother Valentine—"

"I said, leave us!" She glared at Lady Pamela, and then her eyes softened. "Leave us, now, Pammy, there's a good girl."

"Yes, Mother," Lady Pamela murmured, and went out, her shoulders just a bit slumped. Alana wondered which bothered her more: being dismissed so summarily, or being called "Pammy." She suspected the latter.

"Well, sit down, sit down," Lady Honoria said crossly. "Can't talk to you with you towering over me."

"Yes, ma'am," Alana said, and drew a footstool over, to begin the difficult task of getting to know her new employer.

Alana encountered John that evening, as she was making her way to the kitchen to fetch her tray. "Good evening, Miss Sterling," he said, falling into step with her as she went through the green baize door that led to the kitchen, in the back of the house. Apparently he was in the same position as she, not quite a servant, but definitely not part of the family, either.

"Good evening, sir. How are you finding your work?"

John grimaced. "Difficult. There are hundreds of books to be catalogued. Do you know, some have not even been opened? I had to cut the leaves as I went through them. Criminal waste."

"You sound as if you really care," Alana said, surprised.

"I like books. There is also a great quantity of papers for me to sort. They want me to write some sort of family history."

"Is it interesting?"

"Not that I've noticed, no."

"Lady Pamela told me a bit this afternoon. About the Hart family, and how the house came by its name."

"Yes. Have you ever seen the like of this place?"

"No, I can't say I've had the privilege."

"Privilege. Hah. Not what I'm accustomed to."

"Not what most people are accustomed to, I should think." She paused as he held the door to the kitchen open for her. "Where were you raised, sir?"

"Here and there." He avoided her eyes. "I say. Was anything said to you about a ghost?"

"Yes. A Sir Gabriel Follett, I believe."

111

"That's what I was told, too. This is a rum go. If I hadn't made that dashed wage—promise, I'd be in London."

"What promise?" she asked, intrigued more by what he hadn't said than what he had. A wager? Could a poor scholar afford such a thing? There was a mystery about Mr. Winston.

"Er, I promised my cousin I'd stay in one place this time." He averted his eyes as he stepped over to the table, where two trays stood waiting. "I say, is this our dinner?"

"It must be. Have you had trouble keeping positions, too?"

"Yes. But not because people die on me." He smiled at her suddenly, and in spite of her distrust of him, Alana smiled back. "My, er, cousin put me through school, you see, and I have been trying to pay him back ever since."

"Admirable of you."

"Thank you. I say." He stopped, holding his tray. "I plan to eat in the library. Care to join me?"

"Thank you, no. I'm a trifle fatigued. I thought I would eat in my room, and then go to sleep."

"Oh."

He looked so crestfallen that Alana momentarily regretted her coolness. The worst part of her working was that she was often lonely. The servants, with their strict sense of propriety, felt uneasy if she tried to socialize with them, and her employers considered her beneath them. Having someone in the house who was in the same position was rare. It would be nice to have a friend, she thought, if only he weren't so flirtatious. "So you promised your cousin you would stay here."

"Yes. For six months, anyway. Well, I don't think he should have to go on supporting me, do you?"

"Many people wouldn't feel that way." Alana lifted her tray, and together they left the kitchen. "Who is your cousin, sir?"

John opened the door and glanced back, as if to see if anyone were listening. "The Marquess of Ware."

"Oh. I see." That explained why his name was familiar. The marquess and her grandfather were acquainted, and she had met several members of the Winston family. Not that she wanted him to know that, however. Let him think she was

112

plain Miss Sterling. "Well, I do hope you will be able to stick it here," she said, as they reached the main floor. "Good evening."

"Miss Sterling," he said, and she paused near the back stairs. "Won't you reconsider and dine with me?"

His smile was so winning that, in spite of herself, Alana responded, smiling as well. "I thank you, sir, but no. Good evening," she said again, and this time turned, climbing the stairs to her room.

In her room, she sank down at the writing table, sighing in relief and tiredness. There, she'd made it through the day, and supper, she saw, lifting the napkin from the tray, looked palatable. Lady Honoria was difficult, but she was confident she could get manage that in time. The strangeness of the Valentine family was another matter. Good heavens, this house was hideous! Fortunately, though, Lady Honoria didn't ascribe to the Valentine mania, and fortunately, her own room had not been touched. Here was the oak paneling, the dark tester bed and worn velvet hangings she had expected to see in the rest of the house. Altogether a most sumptuous room for a mere companion, and on the same floor with the family, too. Unusual, but she wouldn't question it. Spreading her napkin on her lap, she began to eat her dinner.

Sometime later, her head jerked forward with a start. Heavens, she must have dozed, and with the dirty dishes still on her writing table. No wonder she was tired. It had been a very long day. Rising, she stretched, and was bending to pick up the tray, when she noticed a glow near one wall. Had she lighted a candle and left it there? she wondered, rubbing her eyes. No, there was no candle, but the glow remained. Suddenly apprehensive, she backed up against the writing table, as the glow began to solidify, assume a shape. It began at the bottom, swirling into feet shod in high-heeled slippers, leading upward to silk-hosed legs and leather breeches. Over this was a long coat, of the style worn over a century before, with foaming lace at the deep cuffs. Alana was aware of the shallowness of her breathing as her gaze rose to where the head

113

must appear. She encountered twinkling eyes set in a handsome, vaguely familiar face, framed by long, luxuriant curls cascading down his shoulders and surmounted by a huge hat with a feather plume. Good heavens. Was this the ghost? "You—you—"

"Good evening, madam." His voice was pleasantly deep, not at all sepulchral, as she had half-expected. "Forgive me for appearing before you like this. I trust I have not frightened you?"

Alana pressed back against the writing table as he crossed the room. "You—you're—"

"Sir Gabriel Follett, madam." He swept off his hat, bowing low. "At your service."

"Sir Gabriel Follett," she repeated, dazed. And, though she had never in her life been the least missish, Alana fainted.

Three

The sharp aroma of smelling salts filled Alana's nostrils, making her jerk her head up and back. "Oh! Get that nasty stuff away from me."

The man bending over her, his face creased with concern, pulled back. "I am sorry, dear lady. I did not mean to frighten you."

"Well, you did," Alana said crossly, scuttling back and rising, a good distance away. "Who in the world are you, and how did you get into my room?"

"Did I not introduce myself? Ah, yes, I did, and then you fainted."

"I never faint."

"Forgive me, dear lady, but you did. I am Sir Gabriel Follett." And he executed that sweeping bow again, bending low.

"Oh, do get up." Alana crossed the room, circling as far from him as possible, and went to the wall where she had first seen the glow appear. "Sir Gabriel Follett is dead."

"Well I know it."

"There must be a door here." She moved her hands over the oak paneling. "I know old houses such as this often have secret doors. My grandfather's does."

"Who is your grandfather, dear lady?"

"He is the—never mind! There must be a door."

"There isn't. I know this house well. I have been trapped here for a hundred fifty years, waiting for the right person."

That made Alana turn. The man looked woebegone, somehow, standing in the center of the room with his hat held before him, even its jaunty plume hanging limp. "You really believe what you are saying, don't you?"

"I assure you, madam, I am not romancing you. I do not lie." With a flick of the wrist, he sent the hat sailing across the room to land on the bed. "But I can understand if you do not believe me. Shall I show you?"

"Show me what?"

"This." The arm he held outstretched began to fade, the hand first, then the lace-covered wrist, higher and higher, until it was gone. "Shall I go on?"

Alana abruptly sank onto a chair. "No," she said weakly. She could see no way he might be playing such a trick, unless he really were who he said he was. "You really are Sir Gabriel."

He bowed, briefly this time. "At your service, dear lady."

"Good God." Alana passed a shaky hand over her brow. "There are supposed to be ghosts at grandfather's, but I never encountered one."

"I am sorry if I frightened you, but I need your help." He paused. "May I sit down?"

The humor of the situation suddenly struck Alana. Here she was, her first day in her new position, entertaining a courteous ghost. She must be dreaming. "Of course. How may I help you, sir?"

"It is a long story. If I may impose upon you?"

"Of course," she said again, her lips tilting upward. Definitely a dream. "I should pinch myself."

"I beg your pardon?"

"To make certain I'm awake."

"I fear you are, dear lady. Or would you wish me to prove myself to you again?"

"No, don't! Please." She strove to appear calm. "Is there something I can do for you?"

"You have heard of the legend of this house? My legend?"

116

"Not really. Lady Pamela mentioned a ghost—you—but she seems more concerned with the Valentine family legend."

He snorted and rose, pacing the room. "Foolish woman. Quite pretty once, but she's faded. Ah, but that's beside the point." The long skirts of his coat swirled around him as he turned. She couldn't have imagined this, Alana thought. Her dreams tended to be much more prosaic. "I have had a hundred fifty years to repent, and to consider the wrongs I did. I hurt someone very badly once."

Alana crossed her arms and surreptitiously pinched the inside of her elbow. It hurt. She was awake, then. "Everyone has hurt someone at some time in their lives."

"Ah, but not like this. I was married, you see, to the sweetest, loveliest lady. Madeleine. She was French. Petite, dark, with snapping dark eyes. You remind me of her."

"Me? But she sounds nothing like me."

"Not in looks, perhaps, but in spirit. I've been watching you, you see."

Somehow, that alarmed Alana more than anything else he had said. "Watching me?"

"As I watch everyone who comes into the house." He turned toward her, a gleam in his eyes. "You are most attractive, you know, though you pretend not to be."

Good heavens, he was flirting with her! Alana hastily glanced away, biting the inside of her lips. How was she to deal with an amorous ghost? "Go on, sir. I would like to hear more of your lady."

"Ah, yes. Madeleine. I treated her shabbily, I fear, sought, shall we say, other distractions elsewhere."

"You gambled, wenched, and drank."

He stared at her. "And how does a young lady like you know of such things?"

"Men haven't changed, sir. I wonder your lady wife put up with it."

"She didn't. She had a temper, my Madeleine." A smile touched his lips. "Threw any number of things at me, here in this room."

117

"Here?" Alana looked around, alarmed.

"This was our chamber."

"Oh." That explained why she had been given this room. No one in the family would wish to occupy it. "Did you frighten off the last companion, sir?"

He snorted. "She was a foolish woman. Wasn't doing Honoria any good. You'll be better for her. But, dear lady." He went down on one knee before her, and she drew back. "You don't believe I intend to frighten you?"

"I don't know what you intend, sir." Alana held herself steady. "I think, though, that if you wished me harm, you would have done so already."

"I am not a cruel man." He got to his feet, frowning. "I may be a ghost, but by the lord Harry, I am not cruel. The damned woman had the nerve to try to conjure me up."

"She did? How?"

"She fancied herself a witch. Used to conduct rituals in here, intoning my name. Nearly set the room afire, burning her herbs. Dreadful stench. Couldn't have that."

"No, of course not," Alana murmured. She had gone mad, that was what it was. There could be no other explanation for this. "So, tell me, sir. Why do you not try to frighten me?"

"As I have told you, I need your help. My Madeleine—" He stopped. "I was a fool. Even when she begged me to stop what I was doing, I didn't. She threatened to leave me, and I wouldn't stop. She was only a woman, after all, and it was my life. But, by the lord Harry, I loved her." He stood still, his hand to his mouth. "We had a new parlormaid. I—well, I meant nothing by it! Just a kiss. But Madeleine saw us."

"If you ask me, sir, you deserve anything she did to repay you."

"Yes. That I did. Didn't think so then, though. Was relieved when she didn't even so much as yell. She just looked at me. Thought everything was all right, but when I came home the next day, she was gone."

"Gone?"

"Gone. She left me. I thought it was a ruse at first, but

then I saw she took everything she had brought with her to our marriage, and nothing more. That was when I realized she was gone, and I'd been a fool." Agitatedly, he paced around the room. "I was bored, you see. Not with her, but with life. So I kept seeking newer things, hoping to find something to make my life worthwhile, and all the while it was here, waiting for me."

"Madeleine," Alana said, caught up in his tale in spite of herself.

"It was Valentine's Day. We had the custom of exchanging tokens on the day, no matter if we'd been arguing. Valentine's Day, and she left me."

"What did you have for her, sir?"

"A heart. A crystal heart on a chain. It was nothing, just trumpery, but when I knew she'd left, I realized it was my heart I was giving her. I had to get her back."

"Where had she gone?"

"To my sister's house, a few miles distant. It does not matter. It didn't, then. I would have gone to the ends of the earth to get her back. I called to have my horse saddled and I rode out of the stables at a furious pace. It was raining. I remember that well. The hard, driving kind of rain that soaks through your clothes and lowers your spirit. I think I must have been a little mad that day. I didn't care about the rain, or my mount. I spurred him on, faster and faster. And—"

"And?"

"As we came around the corner of the stables, he slipped on the cobblestones. He righted himself immediately, but I wasn't paying attention to what I was doing. I took a header."

"Oh, no!"

"Dear lady, do not distress yourself. I assure you, I felt nothing. I was beyond feeling anything. I was dying, you see." He leaned forward. "And as I lay there, the rain in my face, I vowed that someday the damage I had caused would be undone, if not by me, by one of my descendants. I vowed that he would learn, as I did, but in time, to give up his roistering

119

ways for what really mattered. As proof, he would give his true love a crystal heart, on Valentine's Day. And then—"

"Then?"

"Then I found myself here," he said, simply. "I have been here since."

Alana rose, turning away and wiping at her eyes. In spite of herself, she was touched by his story, and by his plight. "It is a very sad tale," she said, when she had her voice under control. "I am sorry for it. But I do not see what I can do to help you."

"You can help me fulfill the vow." He leaned forward and his hair fell about his face. Again Alana saw a vague resemblance to someone, and then it was gone. "I have been waiting all these years for you."

"Help you? How? I'm not one of your descendants, and I do not lead a roistering life, I assure you."

"No, no, I didn't say you did. And I don't know why you are the one. I simply know that you are."

Alana stared at him. Stranger and stranger. But then, what could be stranger than sitting and talking with a man who professed to be a ghost, and believing him? "Well, I certainly never have been the chosen one before," she said, her good humor reasserting itself, "but I will help you, if I can. If it means I will have peace in my own room."

Sir Gabriel drew back. "Dear lady, you don't think I would bother you, do I?"

"Heavens, I hope not!" The thought hadn't occurred to her before, but now she remembered that roguish gleam in his eyes. Ghost or not, she wasn't sure she entirely trusted him. "What can I do to help?"

"I've lost track of my family." He rose and began pacing again. "After I passed over, the house was sold, and Madeleine moved away. I heard she had a child." He stood, his back to her. "I never saw him. But I know there are Folletts somewhere. I just don't know where."

"And you cannot leave the house to search."

"No. It is my doom to stay here, until the vow is fulfilled."

120

"Hm." She looked thoughtful. "Tracing your family shouldn't be too hard. I could write to—no. That I cannot. But there are ways to find out. What, though, do we do then?"

"We give him the crystal heart."

"You have it, sir?"

"No, it's disappeared as well. That is the other thing I need you to do. To find it."

"I see. So. We find your descendant, give him the crystal heart, and tell him to mend his ways." She laughed. "It's madness! Why should he listen to me, whoever he is?"

"Not you. I will tell him."

That caused her to laugh harder. "How am I to get him here to talk with you? No." She shook her head. "It is a farce. He'll never believe it. I'm not sure I do," she added, to herself.

"Madam, I assure you I am real!" he roared. The glow about him intensified, and then abruptly faded, as his upper half disappeared.

Alana jumped up, her chair clattering back and her hand to her throat. "Don't do that! If you are going to try such tricks with me, I will not help you, I assure you of that!"

Sir Gabriel rematerialized as quickly as he had disappeared. "Damme, but you have a temper!"

"I mean it. You can do what you will, but I will not help you if you insist upon throwing tantrums."

"Tantrums!"

"Well, what would you call it?"

He stared at her for a moment, and then smiled, slowly. "By the lord Harry, you do remind me of Madeleine."

"My misfortune. I will help you find your descendants and the crystal heart, but only if you behave yourself: What happens after that is something I cannot control. Have we a bargain, sir?"

He looked at her consideringly. "I believe we do. If you will help me, I promise I will not do what ghosts are generally supposed to do."

"Thank you. I think."

"Thank you, dear lady. It relieves my mind, knowing you

are here." He bowed again. "I will leave you now. Good night."

Absurdly, Alana found herself curtsying. "Good night to you, sir." She rose. "Sir Gabriel," she began, and stopped. He was gone.

All the strength left her legs, making her sink into the chair again. Good heavens, what had just happened here? Had this happened to anyone else, she would have insisted it was a dream, but it hadn't. Sir Gabriel Follett had stood there, looking as real as a man could look, and she had carried on that mad conversation with him. Worse, she had agreed to help him, whatever that entailed. Madness. She would end up in Bedlam, if she continued with this delusion. For that was all it could be. Everyone knew there were no such things as ghosts.

Suddenly weary, she passed a shuddering hand over her brow and rose. It had been a very long and eventful day. Time for her to be abed. Pulling her nightshift from a dresser drawer, she began to unlace her gown, only to stop and look around. The room was empty. At least, she thought it was, but then, she had no way of knowing where Sir Gabriel was. Quickly, feeling foolish, she snuffed the candle, and continued disrobing in the dark. Her last thought, as she slipped under the covers and succumbed to sleep, was that it all must have been a product of her overtired mind.

John had just fetched his tray for luncheon when the door to the kitchen opened and Alana walked in. She looked tired, he thought, and a little harried, which was no wonder, from what he'd heard about Lady Honoria. She couldn't be easy to work for. He supposed he should feel sympathy for her, but he didn't. Not after the way she had acted yesterday, giving him setdowns, as if she considered him inferior. When he was the viscount—but she didn't know that, of course. He wondered how she would react if she did. Like every other silly female did, he supposed, bedazzled by the title and the prospect of making a good catch. He was rather surprised to find that he was glad she didn't know.

"Miss Sterling," he said, nodding as he passed her.

"Mr. Winston," she replied, stopping. "Might I have a word with you?"

He stopped, too, staring at her with one eyebrow raised, in unconscious imitation of his father's mannerism. "Are you sure it is me you wish, ma'am?"

She brushed at a strand of hair that had come loose from her chignon. Long, glossy hair, he noted. "Yes, I am sure. If you will wait until I get my tray?"

"Of course." He glanced over at the cook, who was watching them with open interest, and gave her a wink. "Luncheon looks excellent, Mrs. D."

"Glad I am of that," the cook replied, beaming at him. "Like to see a man enjoy his food, that I do."

"Well, I enjoy yours." He grinned as the cook turned pink.

"Shall we go, sir?" Alana said from behind him, and he turned. The smile faded. She was eyeing him with distinct censure. It was new in his experience, and it rankled.

"Of course." He held the door open for her. "Thank you, Mrs. D. And behave yourself."

The door closed behind them to the sound of the cook's chuckles. "What did you call her, sir?"

"Mrs. Doolittle? Mrs. D."

"Why?"

"She seems to like it."

"Most improper, sir."

He shrugged. "Perhaps." Standing back, he held open the green baize door for her, and they stepped into the main part of the house. "What did you wish to see me about, ma'am?"

For the first time in their acquaintance, Alana looked a bit self-conscious. "I was wondering if we could take luncheon together, sir. In the library."

John's eyebrow rose again. Hadn't he asked her this very thing last evening, and been rebuffed? "Certainly. I'm honored."

"Well, don't be." She sounded cross as she walked into the library and set her tray down onto the table. "What I need to ask you concerns your work."

"Oh?" He sat across from her, lifting the napkin from his tray. "Ah. Look what Mrs. D. has made for us. Baked ham with raisins, and I do believe that is trifle."

"So it is. Tell me, sir." She set her hands on the table. "In your work, have you come across any mention of the Follett family?"

John glanced back at his work table, piled with books and papers. "I've hardly begun. Fascinating work, though."

"You sound surprised."

"No, no." Truth to tell, though, his enjoyment in this morning's work did come as a surprise to him, it was so different from what he was accustomed to. But then, he always had enjoyed this kind of work when he was at school. "Is there anything in particular you need to know?"

"Well—I was wondering if you'd look for any mention of where the family went after they sold the house."

"I suppose I could." He smiled. "What do I get in return?"

Alana set down her fork with a clatter. "Pray do not be so odious!"

"And pray do not be so condescending," he shot back. "You earn your employment here, just like me."

"You flirt too much, sir."

"Is that bad?"

"In my experience, yes."

"Pity." He leaned back. "Someone as pretty as you, behaving like a dried-up spinster."

"I am not dried up, sir!"

"Never said you were." He reached for the plain pewter tankard set on the tray and found it filled with cider. Simple fare, but delicious. "Why do you want to know about the Folletts?"

Alana took a moment to answer. "I'm curious," she said, averting her eyes.

John leaned forward. "There's more to it than that. Now tell me, or I won't tell you what you wish to know."

She stared at him, her brow crinkled. "I can't."

"What do you mean, you can't?"

"You wouldn't believe me."

"Why? Are you a long-lost connection of the Folletts', perhaps?"

"No, not quite." She threw her napkin down and rose, stepping away and then whirling to face him. "Very well. I shall tell you. Last night I met Sir Gabriel Follett."

"Who?"

"Sir Gabriel Follett." She paused. "The ghost."

Four

John stared at her for a moment, and then let out a laugh. "You're joking," he said.

Alana touched her napkin to her lips. "No, Mr. Winston. I only wish I were."

"A ghost? You can't seriously expect me to believe that." He stared at her as she continued eating, as calmly as if she had said nothing unusual. "You are serious."

"Yes."

He laughed again. "Then, Miss Sterling, you must have windmills in your head. Ghosts don't exist."

Alana took a bite of ham. "I assure you, sir, I am not insane. And, before you accuse me of being foxed, let me also assure you that I never touch spirits." A smile tilted her lips. "At least, not spirits of the liquid variety."

"Miss Sterling—"

"I am no more sure than you of what happened," she went on. "I do know I was not dreaming, but other than that, I cannot say for certain that I really saw anything." She paused. "Except that he certainly seemed real."

"I am real, madam," a voice said behind her, and she started, turning, to see Sir Gabriel.

"Heavens!" Her hand flew to her heart. "You startled me."

"What are you talking about?" John asked.

"Tell him I am here," Sir Gabriel commanded.

"Heavens." Alana turned back. "Sir Gabriel is here."

"What? Where?"

"Standing behind me."

John peered past her. "I don't see anything."

"I assure you, he is there." She turned. "Will you show yourself to Mr. Winston?"

"That Jack-a-dandy? No.

"Then do please go away, sir. I cannot talk with you hanging over my shoulder."

"Oh, very well," Sir Gabriel grumbled, and faded.

Alana turned to see John regarding her with a strange look on his face. "If he had to do that, I wish he had appeared to you as well."

"You really believe you see him."

"Indeed, sir, I do. Oh, I know it sounds absurd!" She set her fork down. "If I were you, I wouldn't believe it, either. It's a ridiculous story."

"So it is." He stared at her. Miss Sterling baffled him. Yesterday she had given him a severe setdown, and yet today she had actively sought him out. "Assume for a moment that what you are saying is true. What do you expect me to do about it?"

"His story intrigued me. I thought if anyone could tell me about it, it would be you. After all, you are the family historian."

"Of one day's standing. You'd do better to ask Lady Honoria."

She shook her head. "Not when I'm trying to gain her confidence. She'd be convinced I'm as henwitted as her last companion." John gave her a look, which she appeared to ignore. "And I suppose I wanted to talk to someone about it, though why I chose you—do you think you could verify his story?"

"Actually, I came across something about him this morning. He was thrown from his horse on Valentine's Day."

"Yes!" She leaned forward. "Was there any mention of a crystal heart?"

"I beg your pardon?"

"A crystal heart," she repeated, and went on to tell him the remainder of the story, leaving out no detail. When she was finished, John was staring at her with both eyebrows lowered in a frown.

"So you are to find some Follett descendant and make him see the error of his ways? How do you plan to do that?"

"I don't know! I only thought, if perhaps you came across some mention of the family, or the heart, you would tell me."

He looked down at his tray for a moment without seeing it, and then pushed it away. "I could do that. Sounds more interesting than listing the various Hart and Valentine marriages. Yes, Miss Sterling." He smiled at her. "I'll see what I can find."

"Oh, thank you. I must admit, I'm curious about this."

"Mm." He continued to gaze at her, and, to his amusement, she looked away. "Though you really didn't need such a ruse, you know."

That made her look at him. "I beg your pardon."

"Come, Miss Sterling—what is your given name?"

"Alana," she said, and then frowned. "What has that to say to anything?"

"Alana." He tested it on his tongue. "Unusual. I like it."

"How nice for you. If you'll excuse me, sir, I've taken up enough of your time—"

"Alana." He reached out and caught her wrist. "Come, don't leave like this. I know we got off to a bad start, but we needn't be at daggers drawn, do we?"

Alana looked down at his hand, and he suddenly felt impertinent for having dared to touch her. Yet her skin was soft, silky, under his fingers, and he could feel her pulse race. "Please let me go," she said, in a voice that was meant to sound commanding, but which cracked.

"Are you sure that is what you want?"

"Yes. Yes!" She twisted free, snatching her arm back and cradling it in her other one, as if it were injured. "How dare you, sir?"

John rose and grinned at her, unrepentant. "I dare because I believe it is what you want, as well."

"What I—! You have a high opinion of yourself, sir."

"Yes."

That seemed to stop her. She stared at him, mouth agape. "Well, it is not an opinion I share!" she exclaimed, and spun around.

"Alana," he said, as she reached the door, and her shoulders stiffened. "This isn't finished, you know."

"It most certainly is, sir!" And, with that, she flounced out of the library, leaving John still grinning. These next six months promised to be far more interesting than he had ever expected.

Alana stormed into her room, pulling her cap from her head and throwing it down onto her dressing table. "Of all the arrogant, insolent—it was something I wanted. I wanted? Only a man would dare say something like that—ooh! If I could get my hands on him—"

"Dear lady, what has happened to upset you so?"

Alana spun around at the unexpected voice, her hand to her heart, to see Sir Gabriel standing there, his hat held before him and a concerned frown upon his face. "Must you continue to sneak up upon me, sir?"

For the first time, something approaching a smile appeared on his face. "Would you rather I knocked? I am sorry, dear lady. Quite an impossibility."

"Oh." This last was too much. Suddenly tired from her encounter with the odious Mr. Winston, she sank down onto her chair. "Why are you bothering me? And why did you come to the library? You made me look quite the fool."

"Dear lady, I am sorry." He stood before her, looking impossibly solid. Yet, if she reached out to touch him, would she feel anything? "If there were any other way, I would leave you in peace."

"I know." She rubbed at her temples. "At least, I think so.

Oh, I don't know what to believe anymore! Yesterday my life was quite sane, and now, between you and Mr. Winston—"

"I do not trust that man." Sir Gabriel frowned as he prowled the room. "Looks like a lightweight to me."

"He's no such thing!" Alana exclaimed, wondering at the same time why she was bothering to defend the man. "He is working for his bread, rather than battening on his family."

"Mm. Nevertheless, I do wish you had asked someone else for help."

"You stayed?"

"Little goes on in this house that escapes my notice."

"Oh." Not for the first time, Alana wondered at the nature of this man's existence, if such it could be called. "What must it be like for you?"

He shot her a look. "Pray do not worry about me. I am more concerned for you, consorting with that ruffian in the library."

"He is not a ruffian. Merely rather taken with himself. Heaven knows I met many such during my season."

Sir Gabriel stopped pacing and fixed her with a look. "You had a season?"

"No, I merely meant, when I was in London during the season, with my last employer—"

"You had a season," he repeated. "You were a success. You received, ah, five offers, I believe."

Alana stared at him. "How in the world do you know that?"

"It is one of the few benefits of my position. I see things."

"You see things." Alana crossed her arms and turned away. "This is absurd. Here I sit, discussing second sight with a ghost! A ghost."

"I am real, madam. Or do you wish me to demonstrate—"

"No! Please do not fade on me again. Oh, fustian." Resting her head on her hands, she gazed into her mirror. Only her own image was reflected there. "I had hoped I had imagined you, from being tired. You have vastly complicated my life, sir."

"I am sorry. But it is your own fault, you know. At your age, a woman should be married."

A smile curved Alana's lips. "You make me sound quite ancient, sir."

"No, dear lady, I do not mean—"

"Not one of those five offers came from the heart. All they could see was my position."

He shrugged. "That is the way of the world."

"Is it?" She turned to face him. "When you have existed as you have for so long, because of love?"

Sir Gabriel glanced away. "Point taken. But, by the lord Harry, it is different for a man! Why did not your father make you accept one of those offers?"

"My father is dead."

"My sympathies," he said, after a moment. "And your mother, as well. What of your grandfather? No, 'tis not the sight this time. You mentioned him last evening."

"So I did." Alana set her cap on her head and rose, bending to check her appearance in the mirror one last time. "I must go, sir. Lady Honoria will be expecting me."

"He doesn't approve of what you are doing."

"He doesn't know." Alana looked at Sir Gabriel, standing in the middle of the floor and looking as solid as she. "You are not going to let me go until I tell you, are you?"

"You are troubled. You behave as if you are not, but you are. You miss your grandfather."

"That cantankerous, overbearing old man—yes." She passed a hand over her brow. "I do miss him. Oh, very well." She sat again. "You may as well know. My grandfather is the Duke of Grafton."

"A duke! By thunder, girl, what are you doing working as a paid companion?"

Alana's jaw jutted out. " 'Tis my own wish. He is a stubborn old man who will not see sense—"

"Exactly like you, you mean."

Alana stared at him, and then let out a laugh. "Yes, I sup-

131

pose I am a lot like him, and that is why we quarrel so much. We never have agreed on much."

"But this, girl. Working for someone else, when you could have anything you wanted. I do not understand."

"Mm." Alana gazed at her reflection without seeing it. "I wasn't raised that way. I was raised to believe in other values besides fortune and position. My father was a vicar, you see. My grandfather never forgave my mother for marrying him."

"And quite right, too. He was quite beneath her."

"My father was beneath no man! He was good, and strong, and brave, and he taught me always to look beyond the surface in a person. He and Mama were so happy together." She sighed. "It was a true love match."

"What happened to them, madam?"

"There was a fever in the village, and both succumbed. I escaped. I was in London at the time." Her voice took on a bitter tinge. "Grandfather never forgave my mother, but he did unbend enough to offer to pay for a season for me. Mama thought it was a wonderful opportunity. I was young enough that I thought so, too. I soon learned." She paused. "Once it became known who I was, the offers came pouring in. Not for me, you understand, but because of who I was, and my dowry. 'Tis quite substantial."

"Your grandfather should have seen to it that you married."

"He tried. Oh, he tried, but I fought him on every one. Especially—well, never mind. Then, when I had the news of my parents—" She broke off, and there was silence for a moment. "I went to live with Grandfather, but it was difficult. I couldn't be what he wanted me to be. I couldn't be my mother."

"My dear lady—"

"So I left. I went to London, managed to procure a post as a companion, and here I am. To my knowledge, Grandfather does not know where I am, and I prefer to keep it that way. I do not want him ordering my life."

"But surely marriage would be better than this."

"Would it?" Her smile was sad. "After seeing my parents' marriage, how could I settle for anything less? Surely you, of all people, understand that."

"I do," Sir Gabriel said, after a moment. "Very well, then, dear lady. I will not tease you about this anymore. But I do wonder what is wrong with the men nowadays. Have they not eyes?"

Alana looked up at that to see him gazing at her, a definite twinkle in his eye. She could feel her face growing pink. Heavens! He was a most flirtatious ghost. "Fustian," she said crisply. "You must excuse me now, sir. Lady Honoria will be waiting for me."

"Of course, dear lady." Sir Gabriel bent low in a bow, sweeping his hat before him, and straightened only when she had left the room. Today's men must indeed be blind, he mused, because Miss Sterling was a most attractive young woman. If he were alive, she was just the type he would have—well, it were better perhaps that she didn't know that. She would be devilishly difficult to deal with, much like his Madeleine. He couldn't afford to offend her. She was his only hope of fulfilling his vow.

And he could help her. His position had advantages that he usually took for granted. He had lost the ability to touch things; he could no longer enjoy a good meal or a fine cigar, and the real pleasure of his life, the company of women, was forever lost to him. Food no longer mattered, however; nor did the fleeting pleasures of the flesh. Too late he had learned what was really important, something Alana already knew. Be a pity if she kept herself shut away from life forever, and thus lost her chance at true happiness. Perhaps he, with his heightened powers of perception, could help her. 'Twould be criminal if a woman such as she remained unwed.

His energy was flagging. It took great concentration for him to reveal himself like this, a force of will he could not maintain for long. He was fading, fading, and there was little he could do about it. His resolution remained, however. Before he faded completely away, he smiled, a smile that would have made Alana most suspicious. God willing, she would find her match. He would have to see what he could do.

Five

Life settled into a routine at Heart's Ease. Alana spent most of her time with Lady Honoria; John was closeted in the library, working. Occasionally they saw each other, when they met in the kitchen to pick up their trays for dinner or luncheon, but rarely did anything more pass between them. John no longer invited her to eat with him, nor did she ask. It was, John thought, just as well. Someone who believed in ghosts was best avoided, no matter how attractive she might be.

The only thing to disturb the even tenor of his days was the approach of Valentine's Day, still some weeks distant. It was hard to believe that Lady Pamela could decorate the house even more than she had, but she did. Hearts of red satin or frilly white lace appeared in the strangest places, on walls and picture frames and hanging from doorways. John closeted himself in the library, ignoring the decorations and reminding himself that the day would soon pass. When red paper Cupids began to appear in the library, however, he knew something had to be done. An appeal to Sir Ronald soon solved that problem. How was a man supposed to work in such a frivolous atmosphere?

John crouched in front of the fireplace in the library on this chilly winter morning, carefully adding logs and rubbing his hands together. There, he had the fire going. Devilish cold place, Dorset, with the dampness from the sea seeping into one's bones. He was rising from the hearth when the door opened. "Mr. Winston," Lady Pamela said, sailing into the room. "A word with you, if you please."

"Ma'am." John glanced toward his work table, piled high with papers. He was planning to start going through the family's journals today, and he was impatient to begin. Strange, this eagerness for what he had thought would be a dull job. It was far more interesting than he could ever have predicted. He could not, however, command Lady Pamela to leave him in peace. She was his employer. John was beginning to learn that there were certain things one couldn't do, when one worked for a living. "Is there something I can do for you?"

"Yes. Do sit down." Frowning, she dusted off the seat of a leather armchair, before sitting. "Such a musty, dusty place this is. I wonder you can stand it, Mr. Winston."

"I rather like it, ma'am." John sat at his table. He did like this room. If Danbury and his other friends could see him now, they would laugh themselves to death.

"Now. You know, of course, that we will be having a masquerade on Valentine's Day."

How could he not know it? "Yes, ma'am."

"I have had the most wonderful idea. Sir Ronald and I have decided that we don't wish to appear in just any costume. This must be special. Sir Ronald is going to appear as Sir Roger Valentine, and I will be Miss Camilla Hart."

"I see," John said, mystified and amused. He knew enough of the family history to recognize the names. From their union descended the current branch of the Valentine family, and with it all the unfortunate associations with the trappings of romance. Miss Hart, he had gleaned from some letters he had read, had been tall, thin, and irredeemably plain, undoubtedly past her last prayers and without a hope in the world of making a match, except for her substantial dowry. Sir Roger, on the other hand, had been a widower, short and portly, who had died just a few years later from an apoplexy. Not the stuff from which grand romances are made. Nor would he have cast either Lady Pamela or Sir Ronald in their roles. "I assume you wish to know more about them, then. Let me see what I can find—"

"There is nothing you can tell me that I don't already know, sir."

"My apologies, ma'am."

"I should think so. No. What I need from you, sir, is an idea of what I should say."

"What you should say?"

"Yes. We are going to have a play, you see, about the first meeting between Sir Roger and Camilla. Oh, how romantic it must have been! Can you not see it, sir?"

The corners of John's mouth twitched. "Er, yes, ma'am, I can."

"Excellent. I told Sir Ronald that you could write a scene for us."

"What? Me?"

"Yes. A short one, you understand. Sir Ronald would have it that you wouldn't wish to do it, but I know better. It must be an honor for you, to be associated with this."

John's lips twitched again. "Er, yes. But, ma'am, I've never actually written a play before."

"You'll do splendidly. I'd like to see it by the end of the week."

John rose as she did. "Ma'am, I don't think I can—"

"No, no, no need to thank me. Consider this a privilege of your position. I'll leave you to it. Good day, sir."

"Good day, ma'am," John said, dazed, and watched as she sailed out again. Outflanked and outmaneuvered, by God! When it came to getting people to do things, Lady Pamela could show even his father a thing or two. A play, by God! As if he didn't have enough other work to do, work that intrigued him far more. Yet he had to do it, or risk losing his post. That, he was not prepared to do. If nothing else, he was determined to win the wager.

Sinking down at the table again, he let his gaze roam around the room. So much to be done. There were hundreds of books, some, he had found from a quick examination, old and rare, and all in dire need of being catalogued. The family papers were extensive as well, ranging from estate accounts to letters to journals. All in all, there was enough work to keep him busy far beyond six months. Depressing thought. He had no intention of staying in this madhouse a moment longer than necessary. The only things to hold him here were the work itself, and a certain young woman. Alana.

Frowning, John yanked a leather bound volume toward him and began to read it, without quite comprehending what it said. He'd been deprived of female companionship for too long, that was what it was. Why else would he be thinking about a tart-tongued spinster who claimed to believe in ghosts? When the six months were up and he returned to London, he doubted he'd ever think about her again.

Forget about her, he commanded himself, and began to pay stricter attention to the journal. By chance, he had chosen the very volume he needed, the diary kept by Camilla Hart before she was married. If he had to write some sort of insipid play, he might as well get it over with. Frowning over the spidery, faded handwriting, he began to read, and soon was engrossed in the details of life as it had been lived over a century earlier. Whatever else Camilla's faults may have been, she had been a keen observer, and her comments on life were sharp and amusing. Trying to imagine Lady Pamela saying such things, he grinned. He'd have to tone down Camilla for her, and keep his enjoyment of the journal to himself. He thought he would have enjoyed Camilla's company.

The morning sped past. By noon, his shoulders ached from his being hunched over, and his eyes burned. He stretched, glanced about the room, and then back at the journal. One more entry, he thought. Then he'd get up to fetch his luncheon. Unfortunately, the entry detailed spring cleaning, and was of no interest to him. He was about to push the journal away, to return to it when he was fresher, when a sentence caught his eye. "Found today a curious thing in the blue bedroom. When Libby and I moved the wardrobe to clean behind it, we found a heart pendant."

John sat up straighter, and read on. The heart, Camilla had written, had a note attached to it by a ribbon, a note which read simply, "To Madeleine." Deducing that it must once have belonged to Lady Madeleine Follett, whose husband had met such an unfortunate death, Camilla had wrapped it carefully and sent it to the Folletts. She could, she added with her typical honesty, do no less, even if she had been tempted to keep it.

A heart pendant. The crystal heart. Camilla hadn't written that it was made of crystal, but what else could it have been? A chill ran down John's spine. Until now, he hadn't really believed Alana's story. Finding confirmation of it, and in such an unlikely place, was eerie. But a ghost? No, that he would not believe.

There was a knock on the door, making him lift his head. "Come in," he called, and received another shock. Alana walked in, as if she knew he had been thinking about her. Again that chill raced down his spine. "Miss Sterling."

"Mr. Winston," she replied. "I was hoping to catch you before luncheon. I've so much to do this afternoon, I wouldn't have time today, and I do need to speak with you."

"And I with you."

"Oh?" Alana took the same leather armchair Lady Pamela had earlier sat in, not bothering to worry about dust. "Something important?"

"Maybe. I found—but what did you wish to see me about?"

She grimaced. "This bloody masquerade. Forgive my language, sir, but that is how I've come to think of it."

John was grinning. "There's to be a play, you know."

"Oh, don't I! Lady Pamela was going on and on about it this morning, until Lady Honoria told her to be quiet." Her eyes sparkled. "She calls her Pammy. It works like a charm."

"Are you finding working for Lady Honoria difficult?"

"Oh, no. She and I understand each other. However, the rest of the family . . ."

John grinned again. "I know what you mean. Is it always like this, working for someone?"

"Is this your first position, sir?"

"Yes." Damn, he hadn't meant to let that out. She thought little enough of him as it was. Though why that should matter to him, he didn't know. "What did you want to see me about?"

"The masquerade. I do wonder how they managed without us. You're writing a play, and I not only have to write out invitations, but I'm to find the appropriate costumes, too."

"They're overworking you."

She shrugged. "I'd far rather be busy. I'm not complaining, sir, except that it is rather silly, isn't it?"

"I've seen worse."

"Yes, in London, but . . ." Again her voice trailed off, and this time she glanced away.

"You've been to London?"

"Yes. Now, what I wished to see you about concerns the costumes. Have you an idea what you'll be writing?"

So, the very proper Miss Sterling apparently had her secrets, as well. When had she been in London, and why? It hadn't been as a companion that she had spoken just now. "Yes. Lady Pamela wishes to do the first meeting between Camilla Hart and Roger Valentine."

"Oh, perfect. She should find that most romantic."

"Yes, except that Camilla doesn't seem to have had a romantic bone in her body. This is her journal."

"Oh?" Alana leaned forward, looking at the volume. "How fascinating. Have you found anything of interest?"

"Yes. A reference to a heart pendant."

"What?" Alana grabbed at the journal and pulled it toward her. "Why didn't you tell me?"

"I planned to. Here, read it. Right there." He pointed to the passage, and his fingertip brushed against her hand. She looked up, and he pulled away, feeling an odd sensation in his fingers. Static electricity, his science-minded grandfather had once told him, whatever that was. Such sensations weren't uncommon in wintertime.

" 'Found today a curious thing in the blue bedroom,' " she read aloud, and then ceased, reading with such concentration that a little line appeared between her eyes. Her elbows rested on the table; her face was propped on her hands and her hair tumbled forward from her cap, making her look young and very pretty. Again John felt that odd sensation, though this time he wasn't touching her. "Good heavens!" She looked up. "It must have been the crystal heart!"

"Maybe," he said, and his eyes met hers, shining like the crystal she spoke of. For the life of him he could not look away, but was held instead by emerald depths flecked with gold, a sun-washed sea. Willingly he would drown in it, in her depths. She was unlike any woman he had ever known, not concerned with parties or gossip or her appearance, but with things that mattered far more. If only she weren't a paid companion . . .

John reared back, horrified at the turn his thoughts had taken. Good God, was he really such a snob? Did it matter what she did to make ends meet? There was no shame in working for a living, as he himself was learning, no shame in earning one's pay by honest toil. The only people who might think so were just the sort of shallow people in society he despised, the sort he had been not so very long ago. That, and his own father. What would he think if John brought home as his bride a woman who had worked for a living?

"It has to be the crystal heart," Alana said, breaking into his thoughts. "What else could it be?"

"It doesn't say it's crystal." His bride? Good God. The last thing he wanted to do was marry. If he did, he would choose someone far more docile and pliable than Miss Sterling, no matter her other attractions.

"No, but I doubt there were two heart pendants meant for Lady Madeleine. We know where it went, now."

"Where?"

"To the Folletts, of course."

"And how do you propose we find them?"

"Hmm." Alana leaned forward, again propping her chin on her hand. "You haven't found any mention of them yet?"

John waved a hand around the room, indicating the multi-

141

tude of books and papers. "In all this? I've hardly had time. And now," his lips twitched, "I'm supposed to write a play."

"Oh, that is nothing." She rose. "I must go. There's so much to do."

"Wait." He stood up, his words catching her just as she reached the door. He didn't want her to go. "You must eat. Why don't we take luncheon together, and discuss this?"

"Thank you, but no. I must see if I can find Sir Gabriel and tell him about this." She smiled. "Thank you for your work. I know he'll be pleased," she said, and whisked herself out the door.

"To hell with Sir Gabriel!" John roared, but she was gone, the door already closed behind her. What sort of woman was she, to prefer to spend time with a ghost, rather than with him? Bah. There were no such things as ghosts, and so there was no reason for him to feel this way, angry and frustrated at being deserted. And for what? Some figment of her imagination, some chimera. He was not used to being treated this way, he, the Viscount Kirkwood. Most women buzzed around him like bees to honey. Not her. But then, she didn't know who he was. How would she react if she did?

Unsettling thought. He didn't know her well enough to predict her behavior, but he very much feared that she would act much as other women did. And why not? She had to work for a living. One could not blame her if she chose a man who could support her in style. Yet he would be disappointed in her if she did. He couldn't explain why it mattered, but it did. He wanted her to be different from the others.

His stomach growled, and for the first time John became aware of how hungry he was. Alana wasn't the only one with a great deal of work to do this afternoon. Besides that bloody play—he smiled to himself, thinking of Alana's ladylike voice saying that word—there were all the tasks he'd been hired to do, all the tasks he was coming to enjoy. Not like him, he thought, heading for the kitchen, but then, much of what he was thinking and doing lately wasn't like him at all. Or, at least, like the person he had been. That man would have scorned the work he was doing, and scorned Miss Sterling as well. That man would have known how to attract her.

He smiled and flirted with Mrs. Doolittle and the kitchen maids, as he always did, and retrieved his luncheon tray from the kitchen. If the Viscount Kirkwood knew how to attract women, how would plain Mr. Winston go about it? Climbing the stairs back to the library, he pondered that thought. So far he hadn't managed to impress Alana, but what if he tried? Because there was no question that he was attracted to her, unlikely though that was. He would not be here beyond six months, and after that would likely never see her again, but what would be the harm in conducting a brief flirtation? A little romance, to make their time here more pleasant. So long as he made it clear in the beginning that he was in no position to think of anything more, it should be possible. Of course it would. He was passably attractive, after all, and he knew how to be charming. In the past, however, those tools hadn't been enough. It wasn't his looks or manner that attracted women. It was who he was.

The question remained, then. Could he attract someone without using the lure of his name? Grinning, he set to his luncheon with relish. He didn't know, but he intended to find out. Miss Sterling had best be on her guard.

Six

When Alana came in, Sir Gabriel was pacing the floor of her room, making her come to an abrupt stop. "What are you doing here? 'Tis still daylight," she said, recovering, and crossing the room with her luncheon tray.

"That doesn't matter. You found the heart."

Alana looked up in surprise as she sat at her writing table. "Were you there again?"

"This is still my house." He took a turn about the floor. "Now. Tell that young popinjay to find my family."

"He's not a popinjay." Alana toyed with her food. "And he only found a reference to the heart. We still don't know where it is."

"We will. If that young—man—will keep his mind on business, and not seduction."

"Seduction!" She laughed. "That was the last thing on his mind."

"Ha."

"Oh, I might have known you'd think that way! He and I are merely pleasant to each other. After all, we are working on this problem together. Your problem, I might add." She took a bite of beef, chewing furiously. "I cannot believe that you were there. Do you often spy on me?"

"It is my fate we are discussing."

"And I've already told you I will do all I can. I do not need a ghost as a chaperone."

" 'Pon my eyes, by the way he was looking at you, you do."

Alana looked up again. "How was he looking at me?"

"By the lord Harry, girl, don't you realize how close he came to kissing you?"

"No!" Alana dropped her fork with a clatter. "He has no interest in me. You were imagining things."

"Was I? I know well the way a man looks when he's attracted to a woman."

"I imagine it's a look you've practiced a great deal," she said, tartly, annoyed to feel color seeping into her cheeks. John hadn't really been about to kiss her, had he?

"To my shame, yes."

"You should be ashamed." She glared at him, hands on hips, but her annoyance fled at the look on his face. He meant it. "I'm sorry," she said, softly. "I didn't mean to upset you."

He waved a hand in dismissal. " 'Tis all in the past, now, and there's no undoing it."

"No." She regarded him. "How did you meet your wife?"

"My Madeleine?" He smiled. " 'Twas in France, after that disaster at Worcester."

Alana sat up straight. "You were at the battle of Worcester? With King Charles when he faced Oliver Cromwell, and had to flee?"

"Indeed, madam."

"Then you must have been one of the men who went to France with him."

"Yes. 'Twas there I met Madeleine. We returned here when Charles was restored to the throne."

"Of course." What a remarkable man he must have been. Oh, he'd had his faults, but he'd proved his loyalty, both to the Stuart king's seemingly hopeless cause, and to a love that had endured beyond the grave. There were not many such like him today. "How brave of you."

"Do not make me out as more than I was. I enjoyed my time in France."

"I'm sure you did," she said, her voice tart again. "With all the willing French women you must have met."

"You know nothing of the matter, madam."

Alana's hand flew to her mouth. "Oh, I'm sorry. I didn't mean—"

"Never mind, madam." His shoulders were stiff, his expression wooden. "I will leave you in peace," he said, and faded.

"Sir Gabriel!" Alana called, half-rising, and then sank back into her chair. He was gone, and he was angry at her. Well, she deserved it, she thought ruefully, for what she had said. Of course, she was still a little angry herself. The idea of his being in the library this morning, watching the encounter between her and John, made her squirm. And when had she begun to think of Mr. Winston by his first name? Most inappropriate. She was employed in this house. She had no right to indulge in flirtations.

But he was attracted to her. She smiled to herself, absent-mindedly picking at her luncheon. She didn't need Sir Gabriel to tell her that; she'd seen it for herself. Oh, she remembered well that moment when she had looked up from the journal and their eyes had caught. Deep hazel eyes, far more attractive than shallow blue, with a sincerity to them she'd never noticed before. Lord help her, but she'd been unable to look away. If John hadn't taken control of the situation, who knew where it might have led? Because if he had tried to kiss her, she didn't think she would have protested.

It couldn't come to anything, of course. They were both employed here, and any misconduct would mean losing their positions. For her, that wouldn't be disastrous; she could always return to her grandfather, much though she didn't want to. For John, though, the consequences would be more severe. He needed this position. Proud he might be, and obviously unused to working, but she had to admit that he had pitched in with a will. She was not going to be the cause of his finding himself out on the street, with no character and thus

146

no prospects of finding another position. She liked him too much for that.

And when had that happened? she asked herself, rising and taking her tray to return it to the kitchen. He was exactly the kind of man she disliked. Or, he had been. She paused at the green baize door that led to the kitchen, looking toward the library door. The type of men she had known in London would never even have thought to look for a position, let alone settle in as well as John had. He wasn't playing at working; he was actually doing it. There was more to him than she had first thought.

Thoughtful now, Alana trudged up to the attic, a capacious apron wrapped around her dress and a mobcap covering her hair. If she was to see to the costumes for this ridiculous masquerade, she might as well begin. Now was a good time, while Lady Honoria took the nap she insisted she didn't need. But, heavens, where to begin? Standing under the gabled roof, Alana surveyed the vast expanse of attic, hands on her hips. In the dusty, uncertain light she could see row after row of boxes and trunks, piled atop each other in haphazard fashion. Apparently no one had thought to clean up here in an age; everything was furred with dust that flew out in clouds at the slightest motion. Returning to Grandfather's house and submitting to his edicts suddenly no longer looked quite so distasteful, she thought, and turned toward the nearest trunk.

She had nearly finished sorting through the contents of the trunk when she heard footsteps on the attic stairs. More recent things were likely piled upon the older; the first trunk had contained clothing some twenty years out of date. Fascinating, the brocaded gowns she had found, with their panniers and frills, but not appropriate for her needs. After giving the gown she held, pink satin trimmed with lace, another look, she set it down and turned. "John! I mean, Mr. Winston."

"Alana." He grinned at her, and she glanced away, acutely self-conscious at her mistake. "It's foolish for us to be so formal with each other. It's not as if we're in a London drawing room, after all."

Startled, she looked at him. There was something in the way he'd said that, as if he knew more than he possibly could. "I do not think it wise, sir," she said coolly, carefully folding the gown and replacing it in the trunk. "And I did not give you leave to use my name."

"Alana." He said it thoughtfully. "Pretty name. Are you named for someone?"

"No." In spite of herself, she smiled. "My mother was a dedicated romantic. She named me after a character in a novel."

"As romantic as Lady Pamela?"

"No. She didn't need hearts and Cupids to show her love. There." She shut the trunk and turned, dusting her fingers together. "Is there something you require?"

He opened his mouth as if to answer, and then shook his head. Not before, however, Alana had seen the gleam in his eye. Now what was he thinking? "No. Lady Pamela has sent me to help you with the costumes. She says," his tone became dry, "it may inspire me in writing my play."

Alana laughed in spite of herself. "Poor John. Is she giving you a very hard time?"

"Lud, if I'd known, when I took this position . . ." He ran a hand over his hair. "Never mind. Have you found anything?"

"Not yet. I suspect the older clothes are in the trunks back there. I'm glad you're here."

John, engaged in looking about the attic, stopped, and turned to her. "Are you?" he said, a slow smile spreading across his face.

"Yes. I need someone to shift the trunks. Now, if you'll just move this one out of the way—"

"Lady, you wound me. Is that all you see in me, a strong back?"

"None of your nonsense," Alana said, but she was smiling. "Come, we haven't all day. Shall we get to work?"

"You are a difficult woman," he grumbled, but he set to,

shifting the trunks in front to give them access to the others. "Lud, what's in these things? Bricks?"

"Let me help you—"

"No. I can do it." He let the trunk drop with a resounding thud. "I hope the rest aren't so heavy."

"Just like a man to refuse help."

"Just like a woman, to save everything."

"Ha." She opened the trunk, biting back her smile. He was flirting with her, and she was flirting back. She shouldn't be enjoying it. She was. "This is hardly a woman's, sir," she said, lifting a coat from the trunk. It was the match to the gown she had earlier taken out.

John grimaced. "Thank God styles have changed. Can you imagine wearing that?"

"Or this."

Alana took something round and furry from the trunk and tossed it at him. He recoiled as it hit his chest and then dropped. "Good God! What is it?"

"Your language, sir. 'Tis a wig." She began to laugh. "Did you think it was alive?"

"Yes, I—no, of course not." He retrieved the wig from the floor. A man's white wig, with two rolls of hair on either side, and a queue in back. "I remember my father wearing something like this. I think he still regrets that powder went out of use."

"You speak as if your father is alive."

"He is."

"Then why do you work, sir?"

"I should think that would be obvious." He set the wig on his head. "How do I look?"

"Dashing," she said after a moment, looking away. He had shed his coat because of the dust, and the sight of him clad in waistcoat and loose shirt, the sleeves rolled up to reveal muscular forearms, affected her in a way she had never expected, or experienced. There was a hollow feeling in the pit of her stomach, a strange giddiness in her veins.

"Dashed hot." He took the coat from her and held it up. "Do you think Sir Ronald—no. I can't quite see him in pink."

"Wrong time period. We'll need to move more trunks."

"Spare me," he groaned, but set to work, moving trunks as she commanded and never once losing his temper. It was a revelation. By now she and Grandfather would have been engaged in a shouting match. Instead John, his face smudged with dirt, seemed cheerful and at ease. There was something to be said for a frivolous man. "How many more trunks are there?"

"Too many." She glanced about the attic again, and brushed her hair off her forehead with the back of her arm. It had been cool earlier, but the exertion had made her warm. She felt dusty, dirty, and decidedly unkempt, with her hair coming loose from the mobcap, and nothing she could do about it. "They must have saved everything over the years. Just think, if these clothes could talk, the tales they'd tell."

"Most of them boring." John grimaced as he shifted a trunk they had already explored. "The Valentines seem to have been a dull bunch, in spite of their name. Camilla's the only one who appears to have had any life. Can't think why she married Roger Valentine."

Alana held up a tiny, and well-worn, baby's gown, not hearing him for a moment. "She was probably tired of being alone."

John glanced up. "Why have you not married?"

"I haven't found anyone I'd want to spend the rest of my life with," she answered, tucking away the baby's gown, and with it, her dreams.

He snorted. "Don't tell me you believe in love."

"Yes."

"Then you're either touched in your upper works, or this house has affected you."

"Neither. I saw what my parents had. I don't think I could settle for anything less. What are you doing?"

"It fits." John grinned at the green riding hat he had placed upon her head. "Quite becoming. Matches your eyes."

Alana pulled the hat off, looked at it, and then dropped it onto her head again. "Come, this is getting us nowhere—"

"And what of this?" He leaned over and, before she could elude him, placed a lace ruff, yellowed with age, around her neck.

"John," she protested, laughing in spite of herself. "Stop it—"

"If I have to wear a wig, then you should do likewise." Atop the hat went a lady's wig, looped high, and with traces of powder still clinging to it. "By Jove, the very thing."

"Oh, no, it's slipping off." She rearranged the wig, placing the battered riding hat atop it. "Oh, dear, yours is crooked." Without thinking, she reached out to straighten his wig, and her fingers brushed his cheek in the process. His hand instantly came up, gripping hers, holding her there. Her laughter died. "John—"

"You have pretty eyes, Alana. Did I tell you that?"

"N-no, you didn't." His eyes held hers in as strong a grip as his fingers held her hand, just as they had that morning in the library. She could free herself from neither; nor did she want to. "John, I think—"

"Hello," a voice called from the stairs. "Miss Sterling? Mr. Winston? Are you here?"

"It's Miss Valentine. Let me go," Alana said in a furious whisper.

"If we don't answer her, she'll go away," he whispered back.

"Hello?" the voice called again.

Alana pulled back. She was not going to be caught in a compromising situation. "We're here, behind the trunks, miss," she called.

"Coward," John said in a low voice, releasing her hand.

"Where—oh!" Susan Valentine, the daughter of the house, who would be making her come-out in the spring, came around the corner formed by the trunks and stopped. "Oh! How silly you look. What is that on your heads?"

"Wigs." Alana rose to her feet, removing the wig. "We were wondering how they would do for costumes."

"Oh. How would one wear something like that, without getting a headache?"

"I'm sure I don't know, miss. Is there something we can do for you?"

Susan held back. She was a sweetly pretty girl, with pale blond hair teased into ringlets, and wide blue eyes. Alana thought she showed promise of one day resembling her mother. "I thought—well, it is a rainy day, and I thought I could help with the costumes."

"Of course. There are enough trunks to go through."

"I remember coming up here when I was little, to find things to play with." She looked around the attic with wide-eyed wonder. "Where do we start?"

John snatched the wig from his head and dropped it onto Susan's. "Well, first, Miss Valentine, you must get into the spirit of things."

"Oh, Mr. Winston!" She giggled. "I must look a sight."

"No, no, I assure you. It is most becoming."

Alana abruptly turned away, the joy of the afternoon gone. What had been a special moment to her apparently meant little to him. His teasing, his flirtatiousness, hadn't been directed at her specifically. Any female would have served. "If you will excuse me, I must see if Lady Honoria is awake."

"Alana," John protested, coming toward her. "We need your help."

Alana looked from him to Susan, standing with her hands clasped behind her back and one toe turning inward, a sweet, uncertain smile trembling on her lips. "You've Miss Valentine to help you. I'm needed elsewhere."

"Alana," he said again, but she was gone, speeding down the attic stairs and heading for sanctuary, though she had never before thought of Lady Honoria's tart, demanding presence in such a way. "Alana, wait."

Alana hastened her steps as she heard John pounding down the stairs behind her. "I've things to do—"

"Alana, dash it, listen to me!" John grabbed her arm and spun her to face him. His grip was surprisingly strong for a scholar, but then, she'd seen for herself how muscular his arms were. "I need your help."

"Do you?" She looked up at him, cool and calm now, as she usually was in the face of someone else's anger. "But you have Miss Valentine to help you."

"Miss Valentine is going on and on about her own costume," he said, biting his words off. "And I must say, this is damned—dashed—rude of you, to run off in such a way."

"Rude? How dare you accuse me of such a thing when you—you—let me go!" She twisted her arm free, uncaring of any bruises his grip might leave, and spun away.

"Dash it, Alana, what's got into you?" He followed close behind her, and she was glad that this floor contained mostly servants' quarters and thus was deserted this time of day. "You're usually so sensible—"

"Sensible. Yes, that's me." She whirled around to face him, no longer caring that he was less than a footstep away. "Plain, sensible Miss Sterling, companion to elderly ladies, someone to flirt with until someone prettier comes along—"

"Ah." His eyes lit up. "I see. You're jealous."

"I most certainly am not! If you prefer a woman's fortune over who she really is, why should that matter to me?"

"Dash it, I'm not a fortune hunter."

"Of course you are. A penniless scholar, who could blame you if you're interested in Miss Valentine?"

"I'm not."

That stopped her. "You're not?"

"No."

"Oh. I see." She took a deep breath. "I should have realized. I've met men like you before. Heartless men who flirt and flirt and mean nothing by it. They don't care how one feels, who one really is. All they care about is one's position, one's fortune—"

"Damn it, Alana, I don't know who you're angry at, but it's not me!" he exclaimed, and, hauling her into his arms, kissed her soundly.

Seven

Mmph!" Alana struggled as John's arms came around her, stunned by this sudden assault upon her senses. But, oh, it felt so good to be held this way, so right. Her arms, held captive at her sides by his embrace, nevertheless rose to clutch him about the waist, and her head angled just a little bit. Alana had been kissed before, but never like this. She had never felt a man's lips possess her so masterfully, never felt the urge to succumb, to lose herself. Enthusiastically she returned the kiss, giving herself up to it. Who she was no longer mattered, nor the fact that she didn't quite trust this man. All that did matter was the strength of his arms and the passion of his kiss, evoking a similar, unfamiliar passion within her.

"Mr. Winston? Miss Sterling?" an uncertain voice called. It broke into Alana's daze, but for a moment she didn't wish to heed it. For a moment, all she desired was to stay as she was, lost to the world. "Mr. Winston? Are you down there?"

John lifted his lips the merest whisper from hers. "Oh, bother," he muttered.

"Mr. Winston." This time, footsteps accompanied the voice. It was enough to jolt Alana at last from her reverie. She jerked her head back and stared at John. His gaze met hers, and in his eyes she saw the same surprised confusion that she felt. She could spare no time to think about that, however. She had to escape. "Miss Sterling?"

John turned his head. Before he could react, Alana pulled away, taking advantage of his momentary distraction, and ran down the hallway. "Alana!"

"Mr. Winston! You are there," Alana heard Susan's breathless, little-girl voice say just as she reached the stairs. "But where is Miss Sterling?"

John's answer was lost to her, lost to distance and her own rising panic. She had escaped him, and yet she was not free. In those few moments, something had happened to change her. She would never be the same again.

Valentine's Day drew nearer. John shut himself up in the library, sometimes working on the play, sometimes on the family's history, and assiduously avoiding any research on the Folletts, or a certain crystal heart. He wasn't quite sure what had happened in the attic the other day with Alana, and he didn't like that at all. Nor did he like the fact that she had run from him. He liked being in control, dash it! When he was with her, however, that control fled. When he was with her, he found himself doing silly things, such as wearing an old, motheaten wig, or suddenly kissing her. Where that impulse had come from, he couldn't say, except that the urge to kiss her had been overwhelming, unlike anything he had ever felt. Strange. He didn't think he even liked her that much. She certainly wasn't in his usual style. Miss Valentine was the type of young woman he usually preferred, sweet, young, pretty. There was no depth to her eyes, though; there were no surprises in her conversation. Alana, with her smudged face and untidy hair, had drawn him; she drew him still. It was Alana he still very much wanted to kiss.

John emerged from his self-imposed exile only on Lady Pamela's orders. Miss Sterling was still searching the attic, and there wasn't a footman to be spared to help her. John was to stop whatever he was doing and concentrate on finding appropriate costumes. Time was fleeting, and she needed to have her costume soon, to make any necessary adjustments.

Of course, with her figure, that shouldn't be difficult. John, ever the gentleman, swallowed the retort that came to mind as he considered Lady Pamela's abundant shape, and acquiesced. Feeling rather put upon and very much like a servant, he trudged up the stairs to the attic.

Alana rose abruptly when he reached there, her eyes wide and startled. "Mr. Winston! I didn't expect to see you."

So they were back to formalities. "Lady Pamela's doing. You do need help moving the trunks, do you not?"

"Yes." She turned away, but not before he saw a hint of uncertainty, of nervousness in her eyes. So she hadn't forgotten their last encounter, either. He found that strangely encouraging.

For the most part they worked in silence, expressing only disappointment when the trunks continued to yield clothing from the wrong time period, or opinions that this or that article might serve. Neither appeared the least bit tempted to try any of the clothing themselves; hats and wigs and other items lay discarded in piles and ignored. John was beginning to think their search would be fruitless, when Alana opened a trunk and lifted out a man's hat. "Ah," she said, holding it up. Broad-brimmed, with a relatively flat crown, it was trimmed with a feather broken near the base, so that it hung crookedly. "This is more like it. Much like the hat Sir Gabriel wears."

John shot her a look. "You really believe in him, don't you?"

"Indeed, I do. This may do for Sir Ronald." She placed the hat to one side, relieved to have found something at last. It was difficult, being here with John, remembering the last time they had been together. Remembering that kiss. Alana's fingers flew to her lips, tingling at the memory, before she snatched them away. A hasty, guilty glance at John showed that he was paying her no mind, but instead was delving into the trunk. It was a relief. Wasn't it? "What else is in there?"

Together they rummaged through the contents of the trunk, declaring some items suitable and others unusable. At the bottom of the trunk was a man's coat, long and full-skirted, trimmed with tattered gold braid. "What do you think of this for Sir Ronald? I think it would fit him," John said, holding it up.

"I cannot quite picture him in mulberry velvet—what is that?" Alana pounced on a small, tissue-wrapped object which had fallen from the folds of the coat, landing with a thunk on the floor. "It must be a piece of jewelry," she said, unwrapping it. "I wonder—good heavens!"

John turned. "What is it?"

"Look what I found." Alana held the object up. From a long, tarnished silver chain hung a crystal heart.

For a moment they stared at each other, and then John reached out to touch it. "By God, then it was real."

"Yes." Alana stared, mesmerized, at the heart dangling from her fingers. It *was* real. And yet, it wasn't quite what she had expected. Smaller, for one thing. Nor did the crystal sparkle the way she had imagined. It could just be from disuse, she thought, polishing it on her apron, and held it up again. No, the crystal was decidedly cloudy, and its facets seemed clumsily cut. "He said it was trumpery," she murmured. "I didn't think it really was."

"Hardly a symbol of true love," John drawled, and her eyes met his. Did he believe in love? Or had that mad moment in his arms been nothing more than simple lust?

Quickly, she glanced away. "Not what I expected, no. But this must be it, don't you think?"

"I imagine so. So it was in the house all this time. I'm surprised the ghost didn't know." His lips pursed. "Unless . . ."

"Unless what?"

"Unless there is no ghost. Unless this is something you wanted to find for your own reasons."

"Why on earth would I want to do that?"

"Perhaps it is valuable."

Alana reared back in shock. "Is that what you think of me? That I'm a thief?"

"No, no, of course not. But a woman in your position, having to earn her living—it must be a temptation."

"You take it, then!" She threw the heart at him, catching him square on the chest. "You're as penniless as I!"

"Dash it, Alana." He retrieved the pendant from the floor, where it had fallen. "I'm sorry. I didn't mean to insult you."

"Well, you did. Do you think women are without honor, sir?"

"Sometimes, yes. But not you," he added hastily. "I am sorry. I don't know why I said that. Here. You take it."

Alana hesitated, and then reached out her hand for the heart. "I imagine we're both a little tired, and thus might say things we don't mean."

"Probably. And you're right. It doesn't look particularly valuable."

"No. Only to the person who treasures it." She rose. "I must find Sir Gabriel and tell him."

"Dash it, Alana." He clattered down the stairs after her. "It seems all I do is follow you down these stairs."

Alana stopped. Into her mind, unbidden, came the memory of the last time she had done so, and with it the awareness of him she had tried so hard to subdue. In his eyes she saw the same memory. "Sir Gabriel will want to know."

"Drat Sir Gabriel." He reached out to grasp her arm. "He can wait. We have things yet to do."

"We've time. We'll see to them later."

"I hardly have any time with you as it is, everyone in this house keeps you so busy. Now you prefer to run off to some figment of your imagination."

"Figment—" Alana at last raised her eyes, a smile dawning on her face. "You're jealous."

John took a step back. "Fustian. I'm angry that you're leaving me alone with all the work."

"No, you're not." The smile blossomed. "You cannot bear it that someone might prefer another man over you," she said, and whirled away.

"Alana! Dash it." He ran after her, catching again at her arm. "Do you? Prefer him?"

"A figment of my imagination?"

"Alana—"

"I must go." She slipped from his grasp and turned. "Lady Honoria will be waking soon. She'll want me."

"Oh. Then you're not—dash it, I must look every kind of a fool." His smile was sheepish. "I thought you were serious."

"I am," she said, from the top of the stairs, enjoying again the startled annoyance in his eyes. "Oh, and John?"

"Yes?"

"I do find Sir Gabriel rather attractive," she said, and ran down the stairs.

At the bottom of the flight, when she was certain John hadn't pursued her, Alana stopped, hand to her mouth to muffle her laughter. Oh, that had been unworthy of her! But he had looked the very picture of masculine pique, so outraged, so—jealous.

Her hand dropped; her laughter stilled. Jealous. Was he really? Oh, no, it was absurd. She was a plain little dab of a woman, certainly past her last prayers, with little to recommend her but her fortune. John didn't know about that. How would he react, if he did? Thoughtful, she began to walk toward her room. She feared she knew the answer to that, too well. He was, after all, a penniless scholar, apparently of good family. There must be times when his position galled him. Yet he worked for his living, rather than batten off a relation. That showed him to be a man of pride and honor. Perhaps he wouldn't rise to the bait of her fortune, if he knew. She had no way of knowing, however, unless she asked him, and that she was reluctant to do. If he proved to be a fortune hunter, she would be hurt again. Better not to take the chance. Better to go to Sir Gabriel, as she had planned, and much, much safer.

"Sir Gabriel?" she said to the empty air in her room. "Are you here? I've something to show you."

"What is it?" his voice boomed behind her.

Alana spun around, her hand to her heart. "Heavens, I do wish you wouldn't do that! Oh, never mind. Wait until you see what we found."

"What are you doing with that young man, madam?"

Alana paused in the act of pulling the crystal heart, again wrapped in tissue, from her pocket. "What do you mean? We were looking for costumes."

"Ha. Called it something else in my day."

"What are you insinuating?" she demanded. "And what gives you the right to do so?"

"Pray do not play the innocent with me. I am thinking only of your best interest. I do not trust a man like that."

"Like what?"

Sir Gabriel removed his hat. "Like me," he admitted, not meeting her eyes.

"Like you!"

"Aye. You do not see it?"

"He's flirtatious, I'll grant you—"

"Watch out for him, Alana. I know his sort too well."

She frowned. "You've been watching me, haven't you?"

"For your own good."

"My own good! With your history, you've the nerve to say that?"

"A lady would not point out such a thing."

"This lady is tired of your spying on me!" How much had he seen? Had he witnessed that kiss the other day? Just the thought of it made her want to squirm. "You've no right."

"Someone needs must watch over you, madam."

"Pray cease at once." Her voice was icy. "I will not help you fulfill your vow, unless you do."

Alarm flared in his eyes. "You gave me your word."

So she had, and she had no intention of going back on it. To think of his following her and watching her every move was intolerable, however. "And I am now asking for yours."

"Damme, but you have a temper!" He strode a few steps away and turned. "Tell me this, Alana. Do you love him?"

"Of course not. But I will live my life as I please, sir, without any interference from you."

"Not every man is like your grandfather, Alana."

That hit closer than she cared to admit. "Your word, sir?"

"Oh, very well. My word I will not spy on you."

"Thank you." Turning away to check her appearance before she went to Lady Honoria, she shoved her hands into her apron pockets. Her fingers encountered the lump of tissue. "Oh! I completely forgot. I did not come in here to brangle with you," she said, smiling. He returned the courtesy by inclining his head. "I've something to show you."

"What?"

"We found the crystal heart."

"What? You found mention of it?"

"No." She withdrew it from her pocket. "We found it."

He frowned. "Here? But I understood it was gone from the house."

"You understood wrong." She held it out to him. "Here. Look at it."

"I cannot, dear lady." His smile was wistful. "I no longer have the power of touch."

"Oh." She stared at him. "I am sorry."

"It is of no moment. Hold it up for me to see, if you please."

"Of course." Fumbling at the tissue, she unwrapped the heart and held it, dangling from her fingertips.

Sir Gabriel leaned forward, his eyes at first bright, eager; and then, to her surprise, dull. "That is not it."

"What?" Alana stared at him. "But it must be. We found it in a chest with clothes from the right time, and—"

"It is trumpery! I would never have given my love such a thing. Silver instead of gold—bah."

Deep inside, Alana felt a curious relief. "I didn't think so," she said, tentatively.

"Tell me this. Does it have anything engraved upon the clasp?"

Alana squinted at the chain. "No. No, it doesn't."

"Then it is not *my* heart. Our initials were writ upon it."

Alana looked at the heart again, and then back up at Sir Gabriel. He stood proud, aloof, and looking somehow very lonely. "I am sorry."

He shrugged. "A mere setback. I have every confidence in you." He reached out as if to touch the heart, and then abruptly faded. "Do not let that Jack-a-dandy seduce you," his voice floated back.

"Sir Gabriel!" Alana exclaimed, though his voice had been almost more imagined than heard. As if there were any danger of that! John was handsome, she'd grant that, but he was a flirt. She knew better than to allow herself to become involved with his sort.

Still. She sighed, scooping the heart up from her writing table, where she had dropped it. He would have to know, so that they could continue the search. A hopeless thing that was beginning to look, too, she thought, leaving her room. Time was growing short. She doubted very much that Sir Gabriel's vow would be fulfilled this Valentine's Day.

Camilla Hart's journals and letters were spread out on the table before him, detailing the mundane events of life more than a century ago, in a wry prose that ordinarily delighted him. This afternoon, however, John could not seem to interest himself in them. For all her fascination, Camilla was long dead. Alana, however, was very much alive, and very much on his mind. Strange. In town he'd not have given her a second glance. Here, he thought about her constantly. He liked her, dash it! He couldn't remember ever feeling that way about any other woman, but it was true. He liked her.

Maybe that was why he'd got so angry when she walked away from him in the attic. Certainly no woman had ever done that before, leaving him for some other man. No matter if that man were the product of her imagination; it was annoying. Of course there was no truth to her accusation. Jealous of a ghost? He snorted. Ridiculous. This churning, baffled lost feeling wasn't jealousy. It was anger.

At the knock on the door, he raised his head. "Come in," he called, and rose as Alana walked in. "Alana."

"I've come to return this." With little ceremony, she dropped the heart upon the table. "It isn't the heart."

"Of course it is. What else would it be?"

"It isn't. Sir Gabriel's had a gold chain with his initials engraved on the clasp. He was rather disappointed."

"Alana." He made his voice patient. "There is no Sir Gabriel. When will you admit that?"

"I know you don't believe me." Her fingers toyed with the silver chain. "I wish you would."

"I can't."

She looked up at him, then, her eyes clear and direct. "Do you still believe I wish it for my own gain?"

"No. That was a stupid thing for me to say. You're no adventuress."

"How do you know? I might be very clever."

"I think you would choose something of greater value. Greater apparent value, that is. Besides, I've met adventuresses in my time."

Alana opened her mouth, as if to ask where, and then closed it again. "Oh."

"I think you should have this, though." He lifted the chain, stepping around the table. "Clean the chain and polish the heart, and it's a pretty thing."

"But it's not mine, sir. It belongs to the family."

"Just for now."

"John," she protested, and then her voice trailed off, as he reached around her to fasten the chain at the nape of her neck. This close to her, he was acutely aware of everything about her: the softness of her skin; the tendrils of hair that had come loose from her cap; her sweet, feminine scent. To no one else would he ever have given this heart. No one else would have deserved it so.

"It suits you, I think," he said, his voice husky.

Alana looked down at the heart, sparkling against her bosom, and then back up at him. "It is pretty."

"So it is. Alana." His fingers, still at the nape of her neck, shifted, pressing just a little harder, slipping into her hair. Her eyes, huge, luminous, never left his as he bent his head. "You are pretty," he said, and slowly brought his mouth down on hers. And, in the moment when their lips met, he knew that what he felt for her went far beyond mere liking.

Eight

Three hours later, Alana was still thinking about that kiss. Strange, for it had been brief and rather sweet, not like the kiss they had shared the other day when they had quarreled about his flirtatiousness. That had been born of anger and possessiveness. This was—this was more like affection. Lightly she touched her lips, smiling to herself. She could still feel the touch of his mouth, demanding in its gentleness. Demanding what, though? She did not know.

"You are paying me no heed, miss," a testy voice said, and Alana straightened.

"My apologies, ma'am." She bowed her head in acknowledgment of Lady Honoria's rebuke. "I fear I was woolgathering."

"Hmph. That is the problem with you young people nowadays. You're flighty, do you hear?"

"Yes, ma'am."

"Hmph." Lady Honoria shifted in her chair, her expression so cross that Alana suspected her rheumatism was bothering her. "It is a young man, is it not?"

"Ma'am?"

"That foolish look on your face. Only a young man could have put it there."

"Oh, no, ma'am! I promise you, I was merely daydreaming."

"Of Mr. Winston?" Lady Honoria's smile was sly. "Handsome devil, ain't he?"

"Oh, no! I mean, yes, he is handsome, but I wasn't thinking of him."

"Hmph. Say what you wish, miss, but I know the signs. You're carrying on a flirtation with him."

"No!" Alana eyed her with alarm. "Please, you must believe we are not. I do not want to lose this position."

"Fond of me, are you?"

"Actually, yes."

Lady Honoria cackled. "You lie exceedingly well, miss. Very well, I'll keep your secret."

"Yes, ma'am." Alana looked down at her hands to hide her expression of relief. She was fond of Lady Honoria, though she knew better than to say so again. Her feelings for John, however, were more mixed. She couldn't say exactly what she felt. He exasperated her; annoyed her with his roving eye; and then would do something such as giving her the heart. Even if it wasn't his to give.

Her fingers reached up to touch the heart, and Lady Honoria's eyes sharpened. "What is that you have there?"

Alana started. "This? Oh." She reached behind her to unfasten the clasp. " 'Tis something I found while looking for costumes. I meant to ask you if you remembered it."

"Let me see it." Lady Honoria held out an imperious hand, and Alana placed the heart in it, watching anxiously. Without it she felt lost, bereft, which was ridiculous. It meant nothing to her. "Now, let me see—ah." Lady Honoria held the heart up. "I remember this."

Alana leaned forward. "Do you, ma'am?"

"Oh, yes, very well." The old lady's eyes were soft with memory. "So long ago. I was young. Yes, I was young once, and don't you doubt it."

"I wouldn't dare," Alana murmured.

Lady Honoria chuckled. "I like you, girl. You've got spirit. That daughter-in-law of mine. Bah. Thinks she's the first one ever to celebrate Valentine's Day in this house. I'll have you know, miss, that that is a tradition that goes back many years. We have even had masquerades before. But we never painted the house pink."

"No, ma'am."

"Ah, me." She sighed. "So many parties, and so long ago."

"Tell me about it, ma'am," Alana coaxed. "Was this your heart?"

"Sir Cedric gave it to me. My husband, you know, though he wasn't at the time. 'Twas at a masque, right in this house. A Valentine's Day Ball token, it was. It was the first time I knew he had feelings for me. We were married the following summer."

"What a lovely story, ma'am," Alana said, after a moment.

"I haven't thought about that for years. Or this." She looked at the heart. "When he passed on, I put it away and forgot about it. To see it now . . ."

"Oh, ma'am, I'm sorry if it's brought back painful memories."

"Not painful, girl. Pleasant ones. When one has lived as long as I have, one learns to treasure the pleasant memories. Ah, me." She sighed again, and then her eyes sharpened. "How came you to be wearing it?"

Alana felt her face color. "I, ah, thought I would see how it looked. Forgive my presumption, ma'am."

"Pish! He gave it to you, didn't he? Young Mr. Winston?"

"Ma'am—"

"I thought as much. Here." She thrust the heart back at Alana. "Take it."

Alana recoiled. "Ma'am, I cannot—"

"Take it, I say! It is mine to give, is it not? Take it."

Alana stayed still. "It wouldn't be right."

"Right. Hah." Lady Honoria reached out and grasped Alana's hand, placing the heart in it. "I'll decide that. What would be wrong is for me to hold onto the past. My day is over, girl. Yours is just beginning."

Alana glanced down at the heart, and then nodded. "Thank you, ma'am. I shall treasure it."

"And well you should, if a handsome young man gave it to you."

"Ma'am—"

"Listen to me, girl." Lady Honoria leaned forward. "Life passes very quickly, and sometimes we haven't a second chance at what we want most. Don't make that mistake."

"No, ma'am, I'll try not to."

"Good." She leaned back, closing her eyes. "I am tired. Leave me now."

"Yes, ma'am." Alana rose, settling the knitted blanket more comfortably around the old lady's knees. "Sleep well, and I'll come when you need me."

"You're a good girl. Alana?"

Alana turned from the door. "Yes, ma'am?"

"Remember this always. Follow your heart. Always follow your heart."

"Yes, ma'am," Alana said, and went out, mystified not only by the old lady's advice, but by her own feelings. For, if she followed her heart, where would it lead her?

Daylight was fading. John's eyes burned from deciphering the old, faded handwriting in the letters spread before him. Interesting though they were, he doubted his mind would absorb much more tonight. One more letter, and then he would stop for the day. Then he would be free to seek out Alana. No. Better not. Not when his mind, and his heart, were in such turmoil. He turned his attention determinedly to the letter.

Unusually for her, Camilla had written volubly and pleasantly of a long-ago wedding held at the village church, though she hadn't known the young couple. The bride, however, had a connection to this house; her grandparents had once lived here, and she had chosen to marry in this church for sentimental reasons. Her name was Belinda Follett, and she had married a Mr. Alfred Carstairs.

It took a moment for that to penetrate into John's tired

168

brain, but when it did, he bolted upright. Sir Gabriel had left descendants, after all. This was the first mention John had found of them. It was not the bride's name that riveted him, however, but the groom's. Alfred Carstairs. It was the name of John's great-grandfather on his mother's side.

Good God. John let the letter fall, staring into space. Good God. Could he possibly be descended from Sir Gabriel?

Nine

"Good God!" John jumped up from his chair. No, it couldn't be. It was stretching fate too much, to think that he had come here, by chance, at the very time when he was needed by Sir Gabriel. And that, he still refused to believe. He didn't know why Alana persisted in her story, or why she insisted they search for both the Folletts and that damned crystal heart. He only knew he was being manipulated in some way, and that he didn't like it at all.

Damn it! Without stopping to think, he tore out of the library and headed for the gallery. Here were all the portraits of the Hart and Valentine families, including one of Camilla he'd grown fond of. Here, too, was a replica of the portraits of both Sir Gabriel and his wife, which John hadn't before paid much heed to. He strode toward Sir Gabriel's portrait now, however, his lip curling as he stared at the picture of a man with luxuriant long locks of hair, wearing foaming lace and what appeared to be a coat of burgundy velvet. Damned man-milliner. John would like to have him here, just once. He'd set matters straight then.

"What do you want of me?" he demanded of the portrait. "Damned if I'll believe you brought me here somehow, to fulfill some stupid prophecy. Damned if I'll believe I'm your descendant! If it weren't for the wager I'd leave right now, and you could go hang. Come on, show yourself." He stood with his hands balled into fists on his hips, chin thrust forward. "If I'm your chosen tool, reveal yourself to me. Or are you only brave enough to appear to women?"

"I'm no coward, sirrah!" a voice boomed behind him, and John spun around.

"Good God! Who the devil are you?"

"Sir Gabriel Follett, sirrah." Sir Gabriel swept off his plumed hat and bowed briefly. "If you do not know me, I, sir, know you." He sneered. "And a more frivolous lightweight I've never seen in my life."

"Danbury put you up to this, didn't he?" John challenged. "I'll pay him back for this."

"Your friend knows nothing about me, sirrah. I am who I say. I wouldn't mention the wager to Miss Sterling, were I you. She seems to think you a man of some worth." Sir Gabriel's gaze flicked over him. "God knows why."

This couldn't be happening, and yet it was. "What do you want of me? Do you know I may be your descendant?"

"Is this a flam, sirrah?" Sir Gabriel demanded. "God help me, if this is what the family has come to."

"I'm no more pleased about it than you, sir. Good God." John took a turn about the gallery. "Good God, you are real, aren't you? Alana didn't imagine you."

Sir Gabriel inclined his head. "As you see. You are my descendant, you say?"

"It's a possibility." John paused. "You didn't know?"

"No. Though you've the look of me, boy, in my salad days. Hmm. Perhaps you'll serve, after all."

"Not for you. I'll not dance to your tune, sir. Find someone else."

"You love her, do you not?"

"I beg your pardon?"

"You love Miss Sterling."

"No! I do not love anyone."

Sir Gabriel snorted. "Ha. In my day a man went after what he wanted, and to the devil with the consequences."

"That's what got you into this fix," John retorted.

"I learned, sirrah, I learned. Do not scorn love when it is offered you."

"I don't love her," John repeated.

"Think of a lifetime without her, then."

"I—" John began, and stopped. A life without Alana in it somewhere? A truly horrifying prospect. "Good God." He did love her.

"I was right, was I not? Question now is, what do you intend to do about it?"

"I won't be manipulated by you, sir, because of some long-ago vow." John's voice was stronger as he faced his rival. "This is my choice, not yours."

"Damme, I care not about the vow! But I do care about Miss Sterling. Let her go, and you'll be making a mistake you'll both regret."

"I'll have to think about it."

"You're a popinjay." Sir Gabriel set his hat back on his head. "Remember this, then, boy. Do not take too long in deciding what to do. Hearts are like crystal. They can shatter," he said, and faded.

"Wait!" John exclaimed, and started forward into emptiness. Sir Gabriel was gone, if he had even really been there. He passed a hand over his brow, noticing with detachment that it shook a bit. Good God. There was a ghost in the house, a ghost who had made him see what he had tried to ignore. He loved Alana. What he would do about it, however, was another matter. The confrontation with Sir Gabriel hadn't solved a thing. It had, instead, left him more confused than ever.

The crystal heart swung lazily back and forth, back and forth. Elbows propped on her writing table, Alana gazed at the heart as it dangled from her fingers. She had polished the chain, washed the crystal, and now it shone in the candlelight, catching flame and refracting it. A crystal heart, on fire. That was rather how she felt, afire, and yet as if she might shatter

172

at any moment. When she had taken this position at Heart's Ease, she had not bargained on this.

"Cleans up rather well, doesn't it?" a deep voice rumbled, and she looked up without surprise to see Sir Gabriel.

"Good day, sir. I haven't seen you for a time."

He shrugged and began pacing the room. "I thought perhaps I could hurry things along, but . . ."

She turned. "How?"

"It matters not." He shrugged again and turned toward her. "I begin to see how difficult a task I've set you."

"There's time yet, before Valentine's Day."

"Very little. I fear we're doomed to failure, my dear."

"Do not say that! I've not given up, and neither has John."

"John, is it?"

"Mr. Winston. I will admit it's proving difficult to find any trace of the Folletts. They seem to have disappeared. Even Lady Honoria has no idea where they went."

"Nor the heart."

"No." She glanced back at her own crystal heart, and a slight smile appeared on her face. "Lady Honoria is allowing me to keep this."

"Ah. She gave it you, then?"

A blush stained Alana's cheeks, and she studiously avoided looking at him. "Yes."

"And before her?"

"It doesn't signify."

"It came from Mr. Winston."

"And if it did?"

"He cares about you, girl."

"Fustian. He is a flirt."

"Aye. I misdoubt, however, that he would give a heart to simply anyone."

Alana looked up at that. "You think—?"

"Aye. I do."

"It doesn't mean anything," she said, more to herself than to him.

"Marry him, girl. You know 'tis what you want."

"Marry!" The chain slipped from her fingers, and it was only by quick action that she saved it. "I cannot marry him."

"Why not?"

"My grandfather would not approve."

He stared at her. "And that matters to you?"

"Yes, it matters." In one smooth movement, she laid down the heart, folded her arms upon the writing table, and put her head down. "It is all so confused."

"Tell me, then. Perhaps we can make sense of it."

"I don't know how." She raised her head. "Very well. If I marry before I reach twenty-five without my grandfather's consent, I forfeit my inheritance."

"That is a problem." He paced about. "Are you so certain, though, that he would disapprove of Mr. Winston?"

"I disapprove of Mr. Winston! He is exactly the kind of man I dislike."

"I think not."

"How would you know?"

"Has he ever given you any reason to distrust him?"

"He flirts—"

"Aye. Mostly with you."

"And Miss Valentine, and the cook, and—I could go on! How could I ever be certain he's serious? I've known so many men like him."

"The men you knew worked for their bread?"

"Well, no—"

"Would they have helped you on a search for something they're not even certain exists?"

"No, but—"

"No. They would not. At least be honest with yourself, girl. He's not like anyone you've known, and it scares you."

"Yes," Alana said, after a moment. "It does. Oh, Sir Gabriel, you're right! He is different. But what if I tell him of my fortune?"

"What of it? If money comes along with the love, what is so wrong with that?"

"How will I ever be certain that it's me he wants, and not the fortune?"

Sir Gabriel snorted. "Does he know of your fortune now?"

"No, but—"

"How will he feel when you tell him? Don't you think he'll wonder why you kept it from him?"

"But it has nothing to do with him! At least, it didn't." She groaned, sinking her head into her hands. "Oh, Lord, what a coil."

"Tell him, girl," he urged. "Tell him, and then write to your grandfather."

She raised her head. "Do you really think I should?"

"Aye. You'll not know until you do."

"No." She rose, carefully placing the heart in a drawer in the table. "I couldn't bear it if he wants me only for my money." She looked away. "It wouldn't be the first time."

Sir Gabriel's gaze sharpened. "One of your five proposals?"

"Yes. The last one. I loved him, you see." She gripped her hands together. "And then I overheard him telling a friend that, now he was marrying an heiress, he could afford to set his mistress up in her own house. I broke the engagement that evening." She looked down at her hands. "I could not bear to go through that again."

"Dear lady, I am sorry," he said, after a moment.

"Thank you."

"But just because he was a cad does not mean every man is." Sir Gabriel held her gaze with his own. "You have to find out, girl. Don't let love slip away from you. 'Tis a mistake you'll regret forever."

Alana glanced away. "I'll think about it."

"Do that, girl." Sweeping his hat off, he bowed and faded, leaving behind not a trace of his presence, leaving Alana alone and confused. Vastly confused.

Did she love John? She didn't know, and she could see no way of learning if he loved her without revealing herself. Nor could she approach her grandfather. He wouldn't approve her marrying a penniless scholar, and there would go her inheritance. She could live without that. What she couldn't face was his towering anger, or being estranged from him, as her mother had been. Grandfather was the only family she had left. In spite of everything, she loved him.

Oh, her thoughts were all in a muddle! She sank her head into her hands, trying to see her way through this dilemma, and failing. It was a terrible coil. How could she possibly marry John?

How could he possibly marry her?

John sat hunched over the papers on his work table, looking at them without seeing them. Not that he needed to. The words were forever engraved upon his mind. A Follett had married into his family. He had little doubt of that, even without confirmation. The ramifications of that, and of his presence here in this house at the crucial time, were stunning. It was as if fate had stepped in and directed all his movements, even to his ridiculous wager. Already he had fulfilled part of the vow; he had left his roistering ways behind, finding satisfaction in a life far different from anything he had known in town. He could accept that. What he had not counted on was falling in love.

Abruptly he rose, scraping his chair back. Thinking of this did no good. He was tired and hungry and very confused, and he would need time to sort things out. He did love Alana. That was all he knew. What he was going to do about it was another matter. He was well aware of what was due his title, and his position. He very much doubted that his family would accept her.

Deciding to postpone any more thoughts on the subject until he had dined, John headed for the kitchen to retrieve his tray. As he pushed at the green baize door, however, he met resistance. "Oh, bother!" a feminine voice came from the other side. "Do let me through, before I drop this tray."

In spite of all that had he had learned that afternoon, John

TAKE ADVANTAGE OF THIS SPECIAL OFFER,
AVAILABLE *ONLY* TO
ZEBRA REGENCY ROMANCE READERS.

You are a reader who enjoys the very special kind of love story that can only be found in Zebra Regency Romances. You adore the fashionable English settings, the sparkling wit, the captivating intrigue, and the heart-stirring romance that are the hallmarks of each Zebra Regency Romance novel.

Now, you can have these delightful novels delivered right to your door each month and never have to worry about missing a new book. Zebra has made arrangements through its Home Subscription Service for you to preview the three latest Zebra Regency Romances as soon as they are published.

3 **FREE** REGENCIES TO GET STARTED!

To get your subscription started, we will send your first 3 books ABSOLUTELY FREE, as our introductory gift to you. NO OBLIGATION. We're sure that you will enjoy these books so much that you will want to read more of the very best romantic fiction published today.

SUBSCRIBERS SAVE EACH MONTH

Zebra Regency Home Subscribers will save money each month as they enjoy their latest Regencies. As a subscriber you will receive the 3 newest titles to preview FREE for ten days. Each shipment will be at least a $11.97 value (publisher's price). But home subscribers will be billed only $9.90 for all three books. You'll save over $2.00 each month. Of course, if you're not satisfied with any book, just return it for full credit.

FREE HOME DELIVERY

Zebra Home Subscribers get free home delivery. There are never any postage, shipping or handling charges. No hidden charges. What's more, there is no minimum number to buy and you can cancel your subscription at any time. No obligation and no questions asked.

3 FREE BOOKS

TO GET YOUR 3 FREE BOOKS
FILL OUT AND MAIL THE COUPON BELOW

Mail to: Zebra Regency Home Subscription Service
120 Brighton Road
P.O. Box 5214
Clifton, New Jersey 07015-5214

YES! Start my Regency Romance Home Subscription and send me my 3 FREE BOOKS as my introductory gift. Then each month, I'll receive the 3 newest Zebra Regency Romances to preview FREE for ten days. I understand that if I'm not satisfied, I may return them and owe nothing. Otherwise, I'll pay the low members' price of just $9.90 for all 3 books and save over $2.00 off the publisher's price (a $11.97 value). There are no shipping, handling or other hidden charges. I may cancel my subscription at any time and there is no minimum number to buy. In any case, the 3 FREE books are mine to keep regardless of what I decide.

NAME _____

ADDRESS _____ APT NO. _____

CITY _____ STATE _____ ZIP _____

(   )

TELEPHONE _____

SIGNATURE _____ **RG0194**
(if under 18 parent or guardian must sign)

Terms and prices subject to change. Orders subject to acceptance by Zebra Home Subscription Service, Inc.

GET
3 FREE
REGENCY
ROMANCE
NOVELS—
A $11.97
VALUE!

grinned as he stepped back, letting Alana push through the door. "Miss Sterling."

Alana stopped, her eyes growing huge. "John! I—that is, I didn't realize it was you."

"As you see."

"Oh. Well, I'll just be on my way—"

"No, wait." He reached out his hand, detaining her. Her arm felt slender and yet strong under his fingers, with a warmth that seemed to spread through him. "Dine with me tonight."

"I—I'm not sure—"

"Please?" He guided her toward the library. "I've things to tell you."

"Oh?"

"Yes. I may have found a trace of the Folletts."

Her eyes widened even more. "John! Really? Tell me."

"I'll get my tray first." He held the library door open for her. "Go on. I'll be back in a moment."

Alana hesitated, and then walked in. "Oh, very well."

John returned to the library to find Alana sitting, staring ahead dazedly, Camilla's letter in her hand. "You found out something about the Folletts," she said, looking up at him.

"Yes." He set his tray down on the table and gently took the letter from her fingers. "Careful with that. It's quite old, and we don't wish to get it stained."

"Oh. No, of course not. Alfred Carstairs." Her brow wrinkled in a frown he wanted to kiss away. Good God, he must be in love. "I know of a Carstairs family in Yorkshire, where I lived—had a post, but I don't remember their having any connection with this part of the world."

Distant relations of his, he nearly said, but held back in time. "A common enough name."

"Indeed. Oh, but it's a start!" She set down her fork. "We could write to them and find out if they are connected."

"We could." He took a bite of chicken. "And then what?"

"Why, then we'll tell them—good heavens." She sank her head into her hands. "They'll think we've run mad."

"Precisely."

"Unless we don't tell every detail. We could say it's a matter of an inheritance."

"That would be dishonest."

"Well, it is! The crystal heart is an inheritance. So is the vow."

"No." He shook his head. "I'm not pleased about coaxing them here through some misapprehension," he said, and wondered why she suddenly looked so pleased. "We may certainly find out if there's any relation, but I doubt we'd get anyone to come here. Not in time, certainly."

"But does it have to happen here?" She leaned forward, her eyes shining. "All the vow stipulates is the crystal heart and the commitment to true love. It doesn't say where."

"It doesn't seem fitting," he said slowly, thinking it out. Of course, he knew something she didn't. A Follett descendant was at that moment in the house. "It seems as if it should happen here."

"It does, doesn't it," she agreed. "Perhaps they could tell us something about the crystal heart, though."

He nodded. "That is a thought. I wonder," he went on, taking a bite of boiled potato, "if it has to be Sir Gabriel's crystal heart, or if any would do."

"I would think we'd need the original. I'll ask him later."

"Why not now?"

She stared at him. "I doubt he'd appear. He seems to exist only to complicate my life."

"Mine, too. I met him, you know."

Alana set down her water glass so hard that the contents sloshed over the brim. "What? You didn't tell me. When?"

"This afternoon. I have to admit, Alana, I didn't believe you about him."

"I know that. Good heavens! Tell me everything."

"I was in the gallery." John went on with his meal, as if nothing of import had happened. "Apparently he's got impatient with the slowness of things. Suddenly, there he was." John grinned. "Called me a lightweight."

178

"That sounds like him. Good heavens." She gazed off into space. "Then I didn't imagine him."

John's eyes sharpened. "Did you think you had?"

"I did wonder—not that I'm given to such fancies, of course. But, yes, I wondered. It is very strange, after all."

"Quite. Don't you feel as if he's manipulating you?"

"I think he has no choice." Abstractedly she picked up her fork and began eating again. "Tell me everything."

"Very well." John leaned back and narrated the events of the afternoon, omitting, however, several significant pieces of information. Until he knew for a fact that he was descended from Sir Gabriel, he would not share that with her. As far as his feelings for her went—well, that was something he'd deal with in his own good time. Not even a ghost would interfere with that.

"And he never said a word," she said, shaking her head, when he'd finished.

"You've seen him since?"

"Yes. Just before I came down for dinner." She smiled. "Meddling old thing, isn't he?"

"Hush. He'll hear you."

"Oh, no. I made him promise not to spy on me."

"Good." He leaned back, relieved. "When was that?"

To his surprise, Alana turned crimson. "It doesn't signify."

"Tell me." He leaned forward, intrigued now. "When did he promise?"

"John—"

"Alana. Tell me."

"I don't think—"

"Tell me!"

"Oh, very well! The last time you kissed me."

"Ah." He sat back, smiling; she looked everywhere but at him. "So if I were to kiss you again, he wouldn't know."

"Well, you're not, so that hardly matters, does it?"

"Why not?"

"Why not what?"

"Why aren't I going to kiss you again?"

179

She rose, tray in hand. "This has gone far enough."

He rose as well, struck by an urgency he didn't understand. Sir Gabriel was right. One had to go after love, or forever regret it. How Alana earned her living didn't matter so much as who she was, bright, intelligent, honest, and so damned desirable he wanted to take her into his arms right now. "Sir Gabriel did tell me one more thing."

Alana stopped, her back to him, her head turned to the side. "Oh?"

"Yes." He crossed the room and took the tray from her, setting it down on a nearby shelf. "He told me not to let love get away."

"John—"

"If I let you walk out that door without kissing you again, Alana, I don't think I can bear it."

"John, we can't."

His arm slipped about her waist. "Why not?"

"Because it wouldn't be—because we just can't! Oh, do let me go."

"You don't really want me to, do you?" He tilted her chin up with his fingertips, and saw the answer in her eyes. "You don't."

"No. Oh, John—"

"I've waited a long time for this," he said, and at last kissed her.

It was different from the other times. The first kiss had been a kiss of possession; the second, though sweet, of desire. This was a kiss of promise, and as his lips moved over hers, the world opened for him in a way it never had before. In her arms he had found his future. "God, I love you," he said into her hair when he at last released her, and felt her jerk against him in surprise. "Marry me."

180

Ten

For a moment Alana could only stand very still, rooted to the spot. Marry him! It was all she wanted. And yet, how could she? All the objections she had had to the match remained. "John, I'm not sure—"

"Do you love me, Alana?" His hold on her tightened. "Do you think you could learn to love me, even a little?"

"Oh, John, I do!" She threw her arms around his neck, casting her misgivings to the wind. "I do. But marriage—"

"It will work, sweetheart. We're good together, don't you see? Look how we've worked on finding the crystal heart."

"It's not the same as marriage."

"And we can laugh together, too. Remember in the attic, putting on the wigs? I've never met anyone who views the world as you do."

"Nor I you. But, John." She pulled back, searching his face. "Can you support a wife?"

He smiled in a way she didn't quite understand. "I'd manage. You'd never want for anything, sweetheart, I'd see to that."

"John, I—" *I am an heiress,* she wanted to say, but the words caught in her throat. "You love me, even though I have no fortune?"

"Alana, I'd love you even if you had a fortune."

But would he? The chill of reality touched her. "I don't know," she said, and pulled away.

"Alana—"

"I need time to think! I had no idea you felt this way."

His hands were at her shoulders, his lips at the nape of her neck, sending delicious shivers down her spine. "Not even a little?"

"Ohh. I can't think when you do that."

"Good. Don't think. Alana." His hands, firm now, turned her toward him. "I meant everything I said." His eyes were serious. "I want to marry you."

"I need time," she repeated softly, though it was hard. Everything in her urged her to cast herself into his arms, to cry out that yes, she would marry him, and never mind the consequences. But she couldn't. She had spent too many years being sensible, considering everything before she made a decision. "I'm sorry, John, but I do."

"How much time do you need?" he demanded. "Do you want to spend your life always in the employ of others?"

"That is not the question, John." She laid her fingers on his lips. "Money is not the question."

"Then what is? Dash it, Alana, I love you."

She almost gave in, then. She almost threw herself at him, giving him the answer he so desired. What held her back, she never knew afterward. "I know. I love you, too. But this is a big decision, John. You've had time to think about it. Grant me the same privilege."

"Damn it." He glanced away, and then back. "Oh, very well. How much time do you need?"

She calculated rapidly in her mind, figuring how many days it would take for a letter to reach her grandfather, if she decided to tell him, and how much longer after that she would need to convince him. "Until Valentine's Day."

"Valentine's Day! That long?"

"Yes. But appropriate, don't you think?"

"Dash it, not if the answer is 'no'!"

"Shh." She laid her fingers on his lips again. "Think of all the time you'll have to convince me."

His eyes brightened; his arms reached for her. "I say, Alana, that's a capital idea!"

"No." Laughing, she eluded his grasp. "Not tonight, sir. I still have things to see to. And we cannot be seen together too much, else we'll lose our positions."

"Hang our positions!"

"John. Not a very sensible attitude for a man planning to marry."

"I don't want to be sensible. Oh, very well, I won't force you. But I insist upon seeing you at least once a day."

"We still have costumes to find, sir."

"So we do." He smiled down at her. "I do love you."

"And I you." She returned the smile. "But I'd best go."

"One more kiss," he said, and pulled her into his arms.

It was many kisses later before Alana was allowed to leave. She returned her tray to the kitchen, checked on a sleeping Lady Honoria, and then, feeling as if her feet barely touched the ground, returned to her room. From the drawer in her writing table, she withdrew the crystal heart, placing it around her neck. John loved her. It hardly seemed possible, but it was. Someone loved her for herself.

"So," a voice said behind her. "He finally found the courage to propose."

Alana spun around. "You promised not to spy on me!"

"I was not spying on you, madam," Sir Gabriel said in injured tones. "I was spying on him."

"Oh, honestly!"

"I suppose he's a decent enough sort. You could do worse."

Alana picked up a brush and began pulling it through her hair with short, angry strokes. "Not that it's any of your affair. I do wish you'd stop watching us."

"Have you forgotten, madam, that I have other things at stake than your romance?"

"No." Alana lowered the brush, looking for him in the mirror in vain. When she turned, it was to see him standing, hat held before him and shoulders squared. A proud man, was Sir Gabriel, but she could see the sadness in his eyes. "No, and

I assure you I'm doing what I can. Oh!" She dropped the brush and came forward. "Do you know, John may have found where the Folletts went to."

Sir Gabriel inclined his head. "Yes."

"I believe he said something about writing to friends and relations to find out if they know the family."

"Then he didn't tell you."

"Tell me what?"

"That he has already begun doing so."

"No." Alana eyed him, though he wouldn't return her look. She had the oddest feeling he'd been about to say something else. "We were, ah, distracted."

"I remember," he said dryly. "You are going to marry him, then?"

She turned away. "I don't know."

"What? Are you a fool, woman? Would you choose a life of work over a life of your own?"

"I'm not so certain being someone's wife means having a life of one's own," she retorted. "Oh, never mind, you'll never understand that. I told him I needed to think about it, and I do."

"What is there to think about?"

Her hands slashed the air in frustration. "We've been over this! You know there are things I must consider."

"You are making much of this. Are you so certain your grandfather will disapprove?"

"Yes. You don't know him."

"And you do not know—"

"What?" she said, when he didn't go on.

"How he will react."

"What is it you know you are not telling me?"

"Nothing, dear lady. But I think you do both yourself and Mr. Winston a disservice by not revealing who you are."

"And if I do? What if he wants me only for my money?"

"Dear lady." He smiled. "Haven't you faith enough in what is between you?"

"No," she whispered. "It was never enough in the past."

"Trust me on this, ma'am. You need to tell him. You'll not know, else."

"Don't press me. I will tell him when I can."

"When will that be, madam? Time is growing short."

"I have time. Until Valentine's Day."

"Precisely. Valentine's Day. Do not delay too long in your decision, madam, or you may regret it."

"Why does it matter so to you? I won't forget your situation, simply because of mine."

He inclined his head. "Thank you for that. But remember what I said, madam. Do not let love slip away." With that, he faded.

"I hate it when you do that!" she cried. "Must you always have the last word?" Her only answer was silence. "I suppose you must. Oh, bother." She turned back to the mirror, and slowly her frowning visage cleared. John loved her. Whatever her other problems, she had that to hold to. She was loved. There was just one problem. Would she still be loved when she told him the truth?

Sir Gabriel swept into the gallery like an avenging angel, setting up a breeze that stirred the dust in little eddies and that made the maid, who was dusting the picture frames, look up in sudden wide-eyed fright. Ignoring her, he stopped before a portrait, slowly removing his hat and holding it to his chest. His Madeleine. He remembered well when the portrait had been painted, how he had stood behind the artist and teased his wife, until her eyes sparkled and her cheeks were pink. She had been so alive, so vital. Some of the life had been lost in the reproduction he saw before him, but that bothered him not. It was the only way he had seen her in more than a century.

"I do not understand people today," he began, without preamble. "Were you and I so foolish as these two? No, you needn't look at me that way. I know that I was. But at least we loved, Madeleine. At least we knew that." He stared at the portrait, as if by doing so he could bring it to life. "John Winston is our descendant, can you credit that? And when he at last summons the courage to propose, she refuses him. Bah." He began to pace. The maid, feeling the air stir again, glanced around, and then fled, her feather duster falling unheeded. "She's a stubborn wench, Maddy. Much like you. She will not listen to me, no matter what I say. Ah, Maddy." He stopped again in front of the portrait. "I miss you so. If you were here, you could talk to her. If you were here . . ."

His voice trailed off, and he turned sharply away. She wasn't here, and that was his burden. For a moment this evening he had thought he was on the way to being free, until Alana had refused the proposal. For he knew she would, no matter how much she might profess to be thinking the matter over. Someone had hurt her in the past because of her inheritance, and rather badly. She would never tell Winston her true identity, unless—

He turned slowly back to the portrait. "Unless someone does it for her, Maddy? Is that what you would suggest?" His smile grew. "Yes, I thought it might be. Very well. I shall do so." He bowed low. "We shall be together again, madam. I promise you that."

She loved him. John sat in the library, his work neglected, a foolish grin on his face. Alana loved him. Funny, what that meant to him. Where once he would have avoided parson's mousetrap with all his energy, now he positively anticipated it. He could conceive of nothing more satisfying than the life he lived now, a scholarly life, with Alana by his side. Oh, they'd go to London, of course; he hadn't changed that much. And he'd probably capitulate and learn to manage the estates, against the day when he became the marquess. He had, however, found meaning in life again, from his work, and from Alana. No longer was he bored. The future was far too exciting.

The embers of the dying fire flamed suddenly, as at a draft, and then Sir Gabriel stood before him. Even that wasn't enough to jar him from his mood. "Congratulate me, sir. I took your excellent advice, and I am to be married."

"You will not be if you do not take action, sirrah. You are in danger of losing what you most desire."

John frowned at the figure standing before him, looking surprisingly solid. "Miss Sterling loves me."

"So she does, but she does not trust you."

That brought him out of his chair. "I say—"

"I shall give you the chance to prove your trustworthiness by telling you who she really is."

"I beg your pardon?"

"Use this information well, boy, and remember. Love can easily be suffocated."

"I don't know what you are talking about—"

"Miss Sterling is the granddaughter of the Duke of Grafton," he said, and disappeared.

"What? Wait! Come back. You can't say such a thing and then disappear, damn you. What the devil do you mean, she's a duke's granddaughter? Why would she be working here—"

"Excuse me, sir." The butler put his head around the door, which John had not heard open. "Is all well?"

"Yes." John glared toward the fireplace, and then looked back at the butler. "Yes, everything is fine. I was speaking aloud the lines for Lady Pamela's play."

The butler glanced about the room, and frowned. "I see. I shall leave you then, sir. Good night."

"Good night," John answered absently, staring dazedly ahead of him. Good God, this couldn't be right. How could Alana possibly be the granddaughter of a duke? One of the most powerful and wealthy in the land, as well. Such a person would certainly not be earning her living as a companion to elderly ladies. She would instead be in London, easily making an advantageous marriage . . .

Something nagged at the back of his mind. Frowning, John rubbed his aching head, trying to remember. He didn't pay much heed to the marriage mart, didn't care much who was engaged to whom, so long as it wasn't him. There was something he remembered hearing about, though, a rather spectacular end to an engagement, when at a ball a young woman had dashed a cup of punch in her erstwhile fiancé's face. That had caused a scandal that society had not soon forgotten. It had, if he remembered, correctly, been at Grafton House. More to the point, it sounded like something Alana would do.

The thought made him grin, taking him out of his abstraction for a moment. She had a temper, his Alana. He wouldn't want to be on the receiving end when she really got angry. By the same token, however, she didn't lose her temper over trifles. If she were the one he was thinking of, she must have had provocation. Dash it, he wished he'd listened more to the *on-dits* at the time.

What had happened to Grafton's granddaughter after that incident? Racking his brain, John dredged up old memories. She hadn't been seen in society after that, had she? It had been put about that Grafton, enraged, had banished her to his estate in Yorkshire, but other rumors had flown, too. Rumors that Grafton had lost track of the wayward girl, and was searching for her. Dimly he remembered that even he had discussed that very topic one evening over several bottles of wine at the Cocoa Tree. His conclusion then was that he was glad not to be linked with such a hotheaded young miss. Yet here he was now, several years later, in exactly that position, if Alana were indeed who Sir Gabriel said she was.

If she were . . . If so, then their marriage would be eminently suitable, God help him, and any objections his father may have had would be stilled. Not that that worried him anymore, but it was one obstacle removed. For if she wasn't Grafton's granddaughter, still she was very much a lady, in manner and breeding. She would make a splendid marchioness. How she would react when she discovered his real identity was something he didn't want to contemplate just now, though he could easily reproach her as well. The irony of their both disguising themselves wasn't lost on him.

The question remained. Was Alana a duke's granddaughter,

and if so, what should he do about it? He could confront her with it, of course. What then, however? She'd be angry, perhaps even a little hurt. Though he expected she would admit it, one thing he doubted she would do was reconcile with Grafton. She was stubborn; so, he knew from Grafton's friendship with his own father, was the duke. Whatever had caused the estrangement between them, he doubted either would end it, unless prodded to it. The only person who could do so now was him.

John crossed back to the table. This situation couldn't be allowed to go on. If he were finally going to marry, he would do so properly. That meant obtaining Grafton's permission. If in the process he reunited Alana with her grandfather, that was all to the good. She shouldn't be without family. Pulling a sheet of paper toward him, he began to write.

Eleven

Two letters went out from Heart's Ease the following day, one addressed to the Duke of Grafton, the other to the Marchioness of Ware. Both occasioned a good deal of excitement and speculation in the servants' quarters. What could Mr. Winston want with them? Even more intriguing, how did he know them? The servants were well aware of the romance between John and Alana, if their employers were not. This latest development added an element of mystery that intrigued everyone.

Alana knocked briefly on the library door some days later and then came in. "Whew!" she said inelegantly, blowing out her breath and slouching into a chair. "Such a morning as I have had. Nothing would do but that Lady Pamela try on the clothing we found for her costume."

John looked up from his papers, grinning. "They didn't fit."

"Indeed not. Far too small, and not one is pink. She is much put out." She returned the grin. "She is saying people must have been smaller a century ago, and has decided she must have a suitable costume made."

"With less than a week to the masquerade?"

"So the dressmaker said. But nothing will do but that Lady Pamela have her gown. In pink satin, by the way."

"God help us," John groaned.

"Yes, well, we won't have to be there to see it." She rose. "I've been ordered to do one more search of the attic. Will you help me?"

"Certainly." John rose and crossed the room, holding the door open for her. "Though we've gone through everything already."

"I know, but I couldn't very well refuse." She led the way upstairs to the attic, where both stopped, looking about at the jumbled array of trunks. "I don't know what she expects me to find."

"God knows. I'm glad of it, though."

"Why?"

He smiled and bent forward. "Gives me a chance to be alone with you."

"John!" She leaned away from his mouth, hovering a few inches from hers. "Do behave yourself."

"I thought I was," he said, and lowered his head.

"Oh, very well, just one kiss—mmph!" The rest of what she had been about to say was lost as his lips touched hers.

John pulled back. "What were you going to say?"

"Hm?" She looked up at him, her eyes dreamy. "I've no idea," she said, and, hooking her arm about his neck, drew his face back down to hers.

It was a considerable time later when, rumpled and flushed, they at last got down to the work at hand. "I'll be glad to see the end of these," John commented, kneeling and opening a trunk. "Never seen so many clothes in my life."

" 'Tis criminal to keep this locked away like this." Alana held up a gown of green silk, trimmed with yellowed lace. Of the style of 150 years ago, it had a long, pointed waistline, a full skirt, and long, full sleeves of white muslin. "Is this not lovely?"

"If you say so. That color would look well on you. Matches your eyes."

"If I were going to the masquerade—oh, well." Carefully she folded the gown. "A shame it won't be worn."

John stopped her in the act of lifting out another garment,

and turned to her. "If you were going, who would you go as?"

"I've no idea."

"Strange. I'd have expected you to think about it."

"I've no reason to."

"No? To pretend for one night you're someone other than yourself?"

"Why would I want to do that? I'm perfectly content as I am."

"An impoverished gentlewoman, hired to take care of others?"

"What would you be, then?"

"A scholar," he said, promptly. "But a wealthy one."

"Is there any such thing?"

"More than likely."

"Not in my experience."

"There must be people in the aristocracy who enjoy books."

"Name one," she retorted.

"Well—can't seem to think of anyone just now. But that's who I'd be." He lifted out the green silk dress. "In this gown, you could be whatever you wanted. A princess, or a duchess, if that is too exalted for you."

She shot him a look. "A duchess?"

"Why not? Or a duke's daughter, or—"

"This is quite enough of make-believe, sir. I am what I am," she said tartly.

"So you are." He set the green dress aside, frowning a bit. There, he'd given her the chance to tell him who she was, and she hadn't taken it. For that matter, though, why hadn't he told her about himself? Alana was not the only person keeping a secret.

"Well." Alana rose, dusting her hands together. "That is the last of that trunk. I shall just have to tell Lady Pamela we couldn't find anything more."

"Good." John slammed the trunk closed, sending up a cloud of dust that made them both cough. "Before we go."

"What—John!" she exclaimed, as he caught her about the waist.

"Just one more kiss." He kissed her soundly and then stood, holding her close against him. "Would you consider marrying a wealthy scholar, Alana?"

"This isn't a masquerade, John."

"I know. But would you?"

She was quiet for a few moments. "First I'd wish to tell him—"

"Mr. Winston. Miss Sterling. Oh!" The maid who had appeared at the top of the stairs stepped back, her hand to her mouth. "Beggin' your pardon, I'm sorry to be interrupting, but Lady Pamela sent me."

"We were just about to come down." Alana stepped away from John, patting at her hair. "Does Lady Pamela want to see me?"

"Both of you, miss. There's visitors for you."

John and Alana exchanged looks. "For us? But how can there be—who is it?"

"Don't know, miss, but Lady Pamela seemed terribly excited."

"We'd best go, then," John said, touching Alana lightly on the back. "It's time for luncheon, in any event. Where are these visitors, Libby?"

"In the drawing room, sir."

Alana and John exchanged bewildered looks again. Visitors for them, in the drawing room? "Who could it be?"

"I've no idea," Alana murmured. They had descended from the attic and now stood before the drawing room door, Alana brushing futilely at her skirt. "And I'm all over dust."

"You look fine." John reached past her to open the door, aware of the servants who flitted about the hall. Odd. They usually weren't here, this time of day. "After you."

"Thank you." Alana preceded him into the room, and then stopped so short he barely avoided colliding with her. A second later he, too, stopped dead, in shock. The visitors, two

193

gentlemen of advancing years, had risen to greet them. "Grandpapa!" Alana gasped, her face white.

"Father!" John exclaimed at the same time. It made them both stop and look at each other again. "Your grandfather?"

"Your father? But I thought—"

"So here you are, gel," the Duke of Grafton said, cutting across her words. "Well, are you going to stand there all day, or do I have to come to you?"

"I—oh, Grandpapa!" Alana flew across the room, to be enfolded in his arms. She was vaguely aware of the other people in the room, Lady Pamela and Sir Ronald and Miss Valentine; aware also that John had crossed to the other man and was shaking his hand. His father? That, though, was something she would think about when she could take it in. For the moment the only person who existed for her was this stubborn, well-loved old man. "What are you doing here?"

"Came looking for you. If you knew how I'd been searching—" The old man's eyes were moist as he surveyed her. "What are you doing, gel, working as a companion when you know I'd give you anything you want?"

"Grandpapa, it's not about that, and you know it."

"Just fancy!" Lady Pamela cut in. "All this time, we had two members of the aristocracy working here and didn't even know it."

"Two?" Alana looked over to see John standing with the other man. The resemblance told her that they were indeed father and son. "But who—"

"It is ever so exciting. A duke and a marquess, in my house. Naughty of you to play such a prank on me," she said, wagging her finger playfully at Alana.

"A marquess?" Alana looked at John, who had the grace to look embarrassed.

"It was a wager," he said, turning to his father. "To see if I could hold a position for six months. No one here knew."

"One of your more corkbrained schemes. Eh, Grafton?" the marquess said.

"Not as corkbrained as my granddaughter, here. Alana, like

194

to make you known to the Marquess of Ware. Good friend of mine. Oh, and his son, Viscount Kirkwood."

"Viscount!" Alana stared at John. "But you never told me!"

John grinned for the first time since coming into the room. "You never told me, either. I'd say we're even, wouldn't you?"

"I suppose." Alana looked up at her grandfather, her head whirling. "But how did you find me? I thought I'd covered my tracks."

"Yes, want to talk to you about that. Got a letter from young Kirkwood, there."

"And then he wrote to me, to ask me what my son was up to," the marquess said. "First I knew of it."

Alana wasn't listening. "You knew," she said to John.

"Yes," he admitted, "but not for very long."

"You knew!" She pulled away from the duke. "How long were you going to let me go on before you said anything? Or were you enjoying making a fool of me?"

"Alana, it wasn't like that—"

"Oh, wasn't it," she said bitterly.

"Lainie, gel, this isn't the place," the duke began.

"A wager. A wager! Was seducing me part of it?"

"No, dash it, Alana, you should know better than that."

"Why should I? It was all a charade, wasn't it? Everything you said and did, even this!" With a mighty pull, she snatched the crystal heart from her neck, heedless of the red mark it left on her skin. "This is as false as your love."

"Dash it, no! I do love you, Alana."

"No, you don't. You're just like all the rest. You love my money, my position—"

"Damn it, that's not true!"

"Would you have courted me if I really were plain Miss Sterling?"

"Alana," the duke said, sternly. "Enough of this, now."

"Oh, yes, 'tis enough." There were tears in her eyes as she looked at John. "I trusted you, and you lied to me."

"You lied to me, too." John looked up at the ceiling in

195

exasperation. "I only did what I thought was best. I thought your grandfather should know where you are."

"So you wrote to him? Ooh! I cannot believe your nerve! I thought you were different, but you're like all the rest. All you care about is having an aristocratic bride."

"If that's what you truly think of me, then forget I ever asked you to marry me."

"Gladly! Take this back, then," she said, and threw the crystal heart at him.

John dodged, barely avoiding being hit on the cheek by the heart as it flew past. It continued on until it hit the wall with a thump, knocking out plaster and falling into brilliant shards on the floor. Shocked silence filled the room, all eyes on the heart, shattered into a hundred tiny pieces on the oaken boards. "Look what you did," John said into the hush, and Alana ran from the room.

Twelve

"Would you care to tell me more about this wager?" the Marquess of Ware drawled. He was sitting at ease in a chair in the second-best guest bedroom, while his valet unpacked his bags. Across from him John sat, leaning forward, hands clenched between his knees. An hour had passed since he had first seen his father in the drawing room, an hour since the crystal heart had shattered into fragments. He still had not recovered. "Or is it something you're ashamed of?"

"No, nothing like that." John flicked his fingers impatiently and sat back. "It was stupid, I'll grant you that, and if I hadn't been in my cups, I wouldn't have done it. Or if I hadn't been bored," he added, glancing away.

"Bored, is it? It's as I said. You should come home and take up your responsibilities."

"You don't understand."

"What is there to understand? Someday you will come into the title, and unless you're prepared, it will overwhelm you. The land is part of you, John. It's bred in you."

"I'm not like you. That's what you never seem to understand." John rose and began pacing. The marquess watched him and, after a moment, waved his hand at the valet, dismissing him. "You were right about one thing. Several things, actually. London life was beginning to pall on me, and I do

197

need to learn how to run the estates. But I'm no farmer, Father. It's not what I'd do if I had my choice."

"What would you do, then?"

"Exactly what I'm doing now." John sat again, leaning forward in his desire to make his point. "I've learned something about myself these past weeks. I do need to work. But my work, Father. Something to do with books and research. I think," he said, sounding a bit surprised, "I might like to write books."

"Books." The marquess eyed him with distinct disbelief. "Well, it's better than gaming your life away in town, I suppose. Books." He shook his head. "What brought this on? Miss Sterling?"

"No. Well, a little, perhaps. All that time I thought she was exactly who she said she was, and I admired her. Never complained, never wished for what she couldn't have, just made the best of things. I learned a great deal from her. Until I learned—damn it, why couldn't she tell me who she was?"

"How did you find out?"

"I—" Faced with the prospect of telling his eminently reasonable father about Sir Gabriel, John quailed. "It doesn't signify. Why didn't she trust me enough to tell me?"

"Why didn't you trust her enough to tell her the truth?" the marquess said dryly, and went on before John could answer. "Seems to me you both have something to answer for. Any road, you're well out of that match."

John stared at the marquess as he rose and crossed the room. "What do you mean?"

"The girl's flighty. Look what Grafton's had to endure."

"If he hadn't—" John began, and then stopped. What had Alana and her grandfather quarreled about? "He must have done something to drive her away."

The marquess, bending over the washbasin to splash water on his face, straightened. "Only wanted her to make a good match. Damn, I should never have sent Mitchum away. Where's that dratted towel?"

"Here." John handed him a towel, amused in spite of the

situation. "You should try living without servants to do everything for you for a time, Father. Most illuminating."

"Huh." The marquess wiped his face dry. "Fortunately, I don't have to. What do I do with this?"

John took the damp towel and hung it on the washstand. "No, but it's interesting what you learn when you no longer have a title to rely on." John went still. "I wonder if that's why she did it."

"What?"

"Alana. Miss Sterling. I wonder if she tired, too, of being sought after for her money and position."

"Huh. Foolish of her. With all she has, she could make an advantageous marriage. So could you."

"Yes, yes. Is that why she ran away from Grafton?"

"There was some talk of a broken engagement, I understand. Never did quite understand it. True, the young man, young Putnam, I believe it was, wasn't in funds, but his background was impeccable."

"Putnam!" John's face puckered, as if he'd tasted something sour. "The man's a womanizer."

"What has that to say to anything? It would still have been a suitable match."

"But he didn't want Alana. That explains much." Explained her references to men she had known in London; explained why she had run away; explained what she had said about him in the drawing room. Understanding that went a long way toward easing his anger and bewilderment.

"You're well out of it," the marquess repeated. "By the by. Your mother asked me to give you these."

John, sitting again, looked up to see his father holding out a letter and a small, tissue-wrapped object. Something about it jarred his memory. He wasn't really surprised, upon unwrapping the layers of tissue, to find a crystal heart, suspended upon a chain. "For God's sake," he muttered.

"Been in the family for years." The marquess sat across from him, indicating the heart with a nod. "Don't know why she wanted you to have it."

199

"For God's sake," he said again, holding up the chain. So like, and so different from, the one he and Alana had found in the attic. This chain was shining gold, not tarnished silver. As for the heart, it was deep, pure crystal, catching the weak rays of the winter sun and refracting them into tiny rainbows scattered across the oak paneling of the room. John squinted at the clasp, and saw, with a sense of inevitability, that there were initials etched there. "GF" on one side, "MF" on the other. Gabriel Follett and Madeleine Follett. It was the long-missing crystal heart. He was, indeed, a descendant of Sir Gabriel, able to fulfill at last the old vow. The only problem was, Alana wanted nothing to do with him.

"She wants me to bring you home," the marquess said, and John looked up, dazed. "Says she hasn't seen you in months. Unless you want to go on with your wager."

John looked back at the heart, turning on its chain. "No. I've proven to myself I can do it. That's all that matters."

"Good man. We'll go as soon as we can. Damn."

"What?"

"Forgot. Our hostess gave me this."

John took the pink scrap of paper his father held out to him. It was heart-shaped, and on it had been scribbled an invitation to the Valentine's Day masquerade, for the Marquess of Ware and the Viscount Kirkwood. A smile briefly touched his lips. Alana would appreciate this, he thought, before remembering that Alana likely wanted never to speak to him again. "I'm not surprised. She'll want to keep us here as long as she can."

"I'll not stay for this. We'll give our regrets this evening."

"No," John said, so firmly that the marquess looked at him in surprise. "I want to see this through."

"I beg your pardon."

"I'll stay for the masquerade." Valentine's Day. Of course. Nothing would be settled until Valentine's Day. Between now and then, anything could happen; a stubborn young woman could even be persuaded to change her mind. John smiled. He wasn't giving up yet.

Alana closed the door of the best guest bedroom, where her grandfather was staying, behind her, and fled to the sanctuary of her own room. Of course she wouldn't be required to act as a companion any longer, Lady Pamela had told her. Not her, the granddaughter of a duke! It really was too bad of her, not to tell the Valentines who she really was. So Lady Pamela had said, and Grandfather had agreed, drat the man. Oh, she knew things had changed and could never go back as they were. She would, however, have welcomed the distraction of Lady Honoria's tart comments and even, God help her, her complaints.

Her room was a haven. Sinking down at the writing table, Alana massaged her aching temples with her fingers. Oh, what a dreadful coil! She had lied to John; he had lied to her. In that they were both guilty. If that were all that was between them, they could get past it. There was more, though. John knew who she was, had known for some time, apparently. Before he had proposed? It didn't bear thinking about.

Sir Gabriel suddenly materialized before her. "That was not well done of you, madam."

Alana rubbed again at her temples. "Oh, do go away. I've been through quite enough."

"Throwing the heart like that. I've told you, madam. Never toss away love."

"Love. Ha! He doesn't love me."

"By the lord Harry, you are the most pigheaded, stubborn pair it has ever been my misfortune to meet!"

"And what of you?" Alana accused. "When you can tell me that you made no mistakes, then you can give me advice."

"I thought you would profit by my experience." He dropped down to one knee before her. "Marry the man, Alana. You know 'tis what you want."

"I can't. Grandfather doesn't approve of the match."

"What?" Sir Gabriel pulled back. "What is he thinking?"

"Lord knows. It is almost funny. All this time he has been

urging me to marry, and now when I've found someone suitable, he doesn't approve. Ooh!" She rose and stalked about the room, hands balled into fists. "He wants me to return to Yorkshire with him. He says that John has a reputation for wild living—"

"Has he, indeed?"

"Apparently. And because of it, he isn't good enough for me." She spun around. "And the Marquess of Ware apparently doesn't approve of me! You would think he and Grandfather would be at daggers drawn, but they are quite united in this. Ooh! It makes me so angry I could—"

"But you do not wish to marry Mr. Winston, madam."

"It should be my choice! Oh, I don't know what I want anymore." She sank down at the writing table again, massaging her forehead. "Do please go away. I've the most terrible headache."

"I am sorry for it, madam. I will leave you, then."

"Thank you. Do you know," she said, raising her head and catching Sir Gabriel just as he faded, "I don't even know how John knew who I was. We never met in town. Of that I am certain."

Sir Gabriel reappeared. "I, ah, I'm afraid I told him."

Alana stared at him. "You? Why?"

"Because he was being so blasted slow at things! I thought this would hurry him along."

"It certainly did. So that is why he proposed," she said grimly, and looked up. "Or did you tell him after?"

"Afterwards. You were being stubborn, too, my girl. I thought he would confront you, not do what he did." Sir Gabriel shook his head. "I do not understand people today."

"So he didn't know who I was when he proposed," she murmured.

"No. Mind you, he finds you more suitable now."

"Suitable!"

"Of course. The granddaughter of a duke—"

"Oh, get out! I will not be courted for my position."

"Madam, he loves you."

"Not enough, apparently."

"He did the honorable thing, writing to your grandfather."

"Drat him and his stupid sense of honor! Drat all men. I'm tired of the lot of you. Always meddling, always ordering one about—"

"I can see you are upset, madam. I shall leave you, then."

"Upset! Yes, I'm upset. Come back!" She jumped to her feet as Sir Gabriel faded away. "There's more I want to say to you—oh, go, then! I—yes, what is it?" she called, as a knock sounded on her door.

Lady Pamela stepped in. "Oh! I thought perhaps your grandfather was in here with you."

"No, ma'am." Alana composed herself by a great effort. "Is there something I can do for you?"

"Naughty girl, not telling me who you were." Lady Pamela glanced about the room, as if looking for someone else. "I declare, I am quite vexed with you."

"I am sorry, ma'am. There were reasons."

"But it doesn't signify. Imagine! A duke, a marquess, and a viscount at Heart's Ease! My Valentine's Day masquerade will be a stunning success. You will come, won't you?"

Alana shifted from foot to foot. "Ma'am, I don't think—"

"Oh, please, do say you will! I wrote this just for you."

Alana took the pink paper heart Lady Pamela handed her, knowing at once what it was. It was odiously familiar from the long hours she had spent writing invitations. She was not, however, going to be a guest at the masquerade. Not if she could help it. "I shall have to speak with my grandfather, but—"

"A most charming man. He is agreeable, he said, if it is what you want. Do say yes." Lady Pamela laid her hand on Alana's, beaming at her. "Lord Ware and Lord Kirkwood are staying."

"Are they?" Alana said in surprise. And her grandfather had actually agreed to the invitation, as well. Her stomach sank. There was no way she could gracefully refuse.

"Yes. It would be the most romantic thing if we could announce your betrothal that night."

"No! That is, there's no betrothal, ma'am."

"No? Whyever not? You could do much worse, dear Alana. If I may call you so?"

"Yes. My grandfather doesn't approve the match."

"Mercy!" Lady Pamela stared at her. "Well, we shall just have to talk with him, shan't we? In the meantime, have you a costume? I will tell my dressmaker to make you something, if you wish."

"Oh, no, that's not necessary. I should be able to find something in the attic. If you don't mind," she added.

"Oh, no, not at all." Lady Pamela smiled. "I shall let you rest, now, you must be tired after all that excitement! Shall we see you at dinner tonight?"

Alana briefly closed her eyes, and then gave in. There was no way out. "Yes, ma'am."

"Very good." Lady Pamela smiled at her, and went out.

Left alone, Alana again drifted over to the writing table, sinking down upon the chair, the paper heart still in her hand. With sudden energy she crumpled it, tossing it far across the room. Dratted Valentine's Day masquerade! She wished she'd never heard of Heart's Ease, or of Mr. John Charles Winston, Viscount Kirkwood. Never had she dreaded a Valentine's Day more. Everything was ruined, and how it would ever come out right, she didn't know.

Thirteen

"Good morrow, madam."

Alana blinked sleepily, pushing herself up on her elbow in bed and brushing her hair back from her face. "Sir Gabriel?" she said, looking at him across the room, where he sat at her writing table. "What do you here this morning? I've hardly seen you all week."

" 'Tis Valentine's Day."

"Oh, Lord, so it is." She collapsed back onto the pillow and then suddenly sat up again, tucking the coverlet around her shoulders at the gleam in his eyes. "Oh, Sir Gabriel! Your vow—"

"No matter. I had hoped that perhaps you might find happiness." He shrugged. "It seems not meant to be."

"Well, sir, if I were to believe old traditions, you are the first male I've seen today, and so you will be my sweetheart," she teased.

He didn't smile. "I'm not for you, madam. I would not be enough for you."

"You may not exactly be substantial, but you're far more trustworthy than most men I've met." She smiled. "I can depend on you to appear when I least expect it."

"Madam, I believe you're being too harsh on young Kirkwood."

"And I believe that is none of your affair. Would you kindly leave, sir, so I may dress?"

"In a moment." He rose and crossed to her. "You've a costume for this evening?"

"Yes, a dress I found in the attic. Why?"

"I would that you wore this." He pointed toward the bottom of the bed.

For the first time Alana noticed that a gown was spread there. It was the green silk gown she had seen in the attic, but it looked different. The silk was vibrant, bright, no longer faded, while the lace around the neckline was a pristine white. How Sir Gabriel had managed this she didn't know, she thought, reaching out to touch it. "It is beautiful, sir."

"It was my Madeleine's," he said, making her look up sharply. "It would please me greatly if you would wear it."

"I—yes," she said, before she could change her mind. "If it fits, I will."

"I am pleased. I will leave you, then." He turned, and then stopped. "You will be leaving tomorrow."

"Yes." Alana kept her voice steady by a great effort. Tomorrow she and her grandfather would leave. Left behind would be Heart's Ease, and the way of life that had been hers for five years. Left behind would be John.

"I will say goodbye to you, then, madam."

"Oh, no—"

"I fear I will be in no mood to speak to anyone tomorrow."

"Oh, Sir Gabriel." She held out her hand, and then withdrew it. Even if he were near, she couldn't touch him. "Pray don't despair. I shall keep searching for your family, and perhaps next year—"

"I hold out little hope, madam. I do thank you for all you've done."

"Oh, Sir Gabriel."

"Good day, madam." He swept off his hat, and bowed. "And goodbye."

"Sir Gabriel!" she cried, but he had faded from view. He was gone.

Tears prickled at her eyes as she stared at the spot where he had been. Absurd to feel this way, such loss and grief for a man long dead. Oh, if only she had been able to help him! It seemed more than one person would be bereft on this Valentine's Day.

A little while later, dressed for the day, Alana left her room and walked toward the stairs. There, at the landing, she encountered John.

For a moment both looked at each other, and then John nodded. "Good morning, Miss Sterling."

"Good morning, my lord." Alana fell into step beside him going down the stairs, feeling a curious mixture of joy and pain. In the last few days they had hardly seen each other, except at meals; when they had, they had barely spoken. It was sweet relief, and exquisite torture. She prayed he would not renew his protestations of love; she wished that he would.

"You are leaving tomorrow?"

"Yes. And you?" she asked, though she knew the answer.

"Yes." He stopped at the bottom of the stairs and turned to her. "Alana—"

"Oh, there you are, my lord!" Lady Pamela, garbed in a pink morning gown, bustled into the hall. "I know you'll want your breakfast, but when you're done, may I see you about the play? There are some lines I am certain Camilla would never have said."

John shot Alana a look, and she bit back a smile. It really was most ridiculous, this play Lady Pamela insisted on staging, especially since she had removed what both John and Alana thought were the best lines, those brimming with humor. She had replaced them instead with simpering platitudes. What made the situation more humorous was that those lines had been taken directly from either Camilla's journals or letters. John would be happy to be done with this task, Alana thought, and her amusement faded. Once he finished, he would leave. Would she ever see him again?

"Come. We can discuss this over breakfast." Lady Pamela took John's arm and led him toward the dining room, leaving

Alana to follow. As she walked behind them, feeling alone and abandoned and unable to keep her eyes from John, a startling thought came to her. Except for Sir Gabriel, who surely didn't count, John was the first man she had seen today. Was he, against all odds, to be her sweetheart after all?

"This is the damnedest, oddest house I've ever seen," the Duke of Grafton growled that evening, as he escorted Alana into the music room, where the masquerade was to be held. He was not in costume, but wore only a domino and a mask. Alana had had trouble coaxing him to wear even that much. "Damn place is all pink."

"Grandpapa, hush. You promised to behave," she murmured, though privately she agreed. Lady Pamela had outdone herself for this gala night, carrying the decorations to an extreme that Alana could never have imagined. Like many of the other rooms in the house, the music room was painted pink. Lady Pamela, however, had not been content with that. Nearly every inch of the wall was covered with lacy hearts, satin hearts, velvet hearts, of all sizes and all shades of red, from palest pink to deepest burgundy. Festooning the walls, and the gallery above where the musicians played, were garlands of silk roses in pink, red, and white, twined with pink satin ribbons and gilded vines. The chairs were upholstered in crimson velvet; musicians and servants alike suffered in red doublets and white hose; and hanging from a doorway was a porcelain Cupid, all pink and white. It was, so Alana had been told, meant to act as a kissing bough did at Christmastime. There was even a sprig of mistletoe hanging from Cupid's arrow. Alana took one look at that and vowed to keep as far from it as possible.

As startling as all this was, though, what caught all eyes was the trellis, in the far corner of the room. It bloomed with more silk flowers, and in it stood Lady Pamela and Sir Ronald, holding court. She glowed in a gown of bright pink satin, something Alana was convinced the real Camilla would never have worn; poor Sir Ronald looked morose and rotund in the mulberry velvet coat she and John had found in the attic, worn with lace at the cuffs and the full breeches fashionable long ago. Alana felt a spurt of sympathy for him. "I do see what you mean, Grandpapa," she said. "It is a bit much, isn't it?"

"A bit much? This house is a bit much. I'm here only for you, Lainie girl."

"For me!" Alana stared at him. "But I thought you wanted to stay."

"Good Gad, no! Just thought you should have some fun, after working all this time," he mumbled, not looking at her.

Alana stared at him consideringly. "Grandpapa, what are you planning?"

"Are you accusing me of something, girl?"

"I know you." Her eyes narrowed. "I will not marry Kirkwood."

"And I don't want you to. Enough of this, girl. Can't a man want to see his grandchild enjoy herself?"

"You usually don't. You usually have another motive."

"I am hurt, girl, by your low opinion of me. I want only what is best for you."

"Unfortunately we tend to disagree on what that is."

"But you will come home with me now."

"Yes, Grandpapa." Alana smiled. For all her grandfather's gruffness, there was a pleading look in his eyes. "I will come home. So long as you don't pinch at me to marry," she added.

"Harumph. We'll see. Ah, good evening, Ware. What think you of all this?"

The Marquess of Ware, similarly attired in a domino and plain mask, shook his head. "Never seen anything like it. Good evening, Miss Sterling."

Alana curtsied. "Good evening, sir. And—" Her voice died. Behind Lord Ware stalked—Sir Gabriel? But he wouldn't appear here, would he? Yet there he stood, tall, commanding, in a coat of forest green velvet, with his hair carefully arranged in long curls and a huge plumed hat upon his head. His eyes were hidden by his mask, but she knew the gleam in them well. "I—what are you doing here?" she hissed.

"Good evening, Miss Sterling," he said, sweeping off the hat and bowing low. Alana's sense of unreality increased. It wasn't Sir Gabriel's voice; it was John's. "Are you well? You look a trifle pale. Rather as if you'd seen a ghost."

He knew, the wretch! But, good heavens, the resemblance was amazing. Why had she never remarked it before? "Good evening, Lord Kirkwood. 'Tis rather warm in here."

"So it is." John glanced around. "And very pink." For a moment his eyes met hers, and the old companionship, the old sense of sharing secrets that no one else knew, returned. Then he looked away, and the moment was lost.

"Harumph." Grafton was glaring at John. "Contracted any more wagers, Kirkwood?"

"No, sir."

"Harumph. Well, you both look as if you planned your costumes together."

"No," John and Alana said in unison, and then he looked at her more closely. "That is the gown we found in the attic."

"Yes," Alana replied briefly. She had no intention of telling him where she had got it.

"It suits you."

"Thank you, sir. If you'll excuse us, we should make our greetings to our hosts."

"Ours, too. Grafton, there's something I've been meaning to ask you," Lord Ware said, and took the duke's arm. The two men moved off, engaged in conversation, leaving John and Alana alone.

"Well," John said, after a moment. "Shall we, ma'am?"

Alana regarded the arm he held out to her, and then sighed inwardly. She didn't want to touch him; she wanted to touch him so much! "Thank you, sir," she said, and placed her hand on his arm. She was acutely aware of his nearness as they crossed the room, and of the strength of his arm under her hand. Warmth spread through her in tingling waves, an odd feeling, but not unpleasant. If only she could trust him—but she could not go on with that train of thought. It would do no good.

"Why, Miss Sterling," Lady Pamela gushed, when John and Alana reached the trellis. "That is you behind the mask, is it not? And—is it really Lord Kirkwood? Why, Sir Ronald! Does he not look the very image of Sir Gabriel Follett's portrait?" Sir Ronald mumbled something that they took as assent, and she hurried on. "The resemblance is amazing. And Miss Sterling. I see you chose to dress in the style of the time. Like me."

"Yes, ma'am. I had this from the attic."

"How very resourceful of you. But, green, ma'am? On tonight, of all nights?"

"Pink doesn't suit me, ma'am."

"Well, no matter, you both look very well together." Looking up toward the gallery, she waved her hand. Instantly the music the orchestra had been playing ceased, and a waltz began instead. "There. I've asked them to play that just for you. Do go and dance."

They both stared at her in dismay. "Ma'am," John began.

"Lady Pamela, I don't think," Alana protested at the same time.

"Oh, do go!" She beamed at them. " 'Tis only a dance, after all. And pray do not forget my play later."

John and Alana looked helplessly at each other. There was no hope for it. "Miss Sterling?" John said, holding out his hand.

"Thank you, sir." Alana let him lead her out onto the floor, where other couples already waltzed. His arm went about her waist, holding her close. Much too close. "And was this your idea?"

"No. I want this no more than you do."

"Why?" she flared. "Am I so unattractive, then?"

"Dash it, Alana! You make no sense. What do you expect me to say?"

"I don't know," she said, her anger suddenly evaporating. It hadn't been directed at him in any event, but at circumstances. Oh, why couldn't things be different? "Why can't you be more like Sir Gabriel?"

John looked down at her in surprise. "What did you say?"

Alana looked away, feeling her face color. "It is of no moment."

"You wish me to be like a ghost? Is that what you are saying?"

"No." Alana looked up at him. "He has remained true and steadfast to one love for over a century. I admire that."

"He'd little choice."

"If you recall, he did choose his fate," she retorted. "It isn't his fault others aren't so faithful."

"What do you want of me, madam?" he said, sounding so like Sir Gabriel at his most imperious that she blinked. "Do you wish me to be some insubstantial vision that comes and goes according to whim?"

"No! That's not what I'm saying."

"I am a man, Alana. A flesh-and-blood man. Not perfect, not particularly romantic, but a man. I have my faults. But please do not tell me Sir Gabriel was perfect, else he wouldn't have got himself into such a fix."

"Sir Gabriel sees love for what it is. He sees how important it is."

"And I do not?"

"I don't believe so, no, sir."

"Huh. All that I've done, to help him fulfill his vow, even to finding out—"

"What?" Alana said, when he didn't go on.

"Nothing. It doesn't matter, now." She didn't know, he thought. He had never told her he was descended from Sir Gabriel.

"Did you learn more about his descendants? Tell me!"

"I found a clue. Damn it, Alana, Sir Gabriel's waited this long, he can wait another year. I cannot. Don't you know I love you?"

Alana looked away. "I know you think you do."

"I know you were hurt in the past. My father told me," he said, as she looked up at him in surprise. "Do you really think I give a jot for your position? I would have married you before

I knew who you were, and you know it. If you can't get over your damnable pride—"

"I can't trust you!" she cried. "I've seen how you are with other women, flirting with them, and I know of your reputation. How will I ever know if you love me for myself?"

"Dash it, Alana!" He whirled her about in frustration. "Very well, if that is how you feel, I can't change your mind," he said, finally. "But when the crystal heart broke, so did my heart."

"Oh, gammon!"

"I love you, Alana." He gazed down at her, his eyes piercing and intent. "I always will."

Alana stared back at him, wanting to believe him, not daring to. If she did, if she took the chance—but what if he hurt her? She couldn't bear to go through it again.

"The music's ended," a gruff voice said beside her, and she looked up to see her grandfather. "Not done to embrace like this in the middle of a crowded room."

"Oh!" Alana pulled back, her mind whirling. So absorbed had she been in their conversation that she hadn't noticed the dance ending. "How foolish of me."

"Remember what I said," John said, still holding her gaze with his, and raised her hand to his lips. "And remember, it is still Valentine's Day."

Alana snatched her hand back, feeling as if she had been burned. "I—yes," she said, and turned, walking blindly away.

"Impertinent young pup," the duke growled, and Alana snapped out of her thoughts.

"He isn't," she protested. "I think he truly loves me, Grandpapa."

"Harumph. A lightweight like him? How could you ever be certain he doesn't want you for your fortune?"

"He has one of his own, and a title. He doesn't need mine. And he's no lightweight, Grandpapa. He may have come here on a wager, but I've seen him working. I don't know of many other young men who would have set to it as well as he did."

"Harumph. You make him sound a paragon. The man flirts, Lainie."

213

"It's just his way! It means nothing. Why, I've even seen him flirt with Lady Honoria. She loved it, of course."

"Still, don't know if you can trust someone like that. Never know if the flirting's real or not."

"I can trust him. Underneath he's solid and dependable. He's shown that, even though what I asked him to do seemed foolish, and—well, never mind." But he had helped in the search of the crystal heart, even when he'd been convinced that Sir Gabriel didn't exist. She could depend on him. She could trust him. "I love him, Grandpapa."

"Do you, eh?" He peered at her from under bushy brows. "Well, Lainie girl, if it's what you truly want, I won't stand in your way."

"You won't? Oh, Grandpapa!" She started to throw her arms around his neck, and then stopped, arrested by the gleam in his eye. "Why, you old humbug."

"What?" he said, his voice innocent.

"You wanted this all along, didn't you?"

"Well, my dear, I do think it a suitable match."

"Suitable! But you've protested against it all week."

"And you decided in spite of me, eh?" His eyes twinkled. "Do you think I don't know you, Lainie? If I'd pushed this match you would have stood firm against it."

"I—" She stopped. "I would have, wouldn't I?"

"That you would. You always were a stubborn puss."

"John was right. I did let pride get in the way of love," she said wonderingly, and glanced away. Across the room, under the Cupid suspended from the doorway, stood John, bending to kiss Susan Valentine, with every appearance of pleasure. Something snapped inside her. A moment before, he had been professing his love for her. Now he was romancing Miss Valentine. "I was wrong," she said, and moved away.

"Lainie? Where are you going, girl?"

"I am tired of this masquerade, Grandpapa. I am going to go to the library and find some peace." And with that, she turned and fled the room.

Fourteen

"Where is Alana going?" John said, coming up beside the duke at that moment.

"Damned if I know, my boy. One moment she was standing here, perfectly happy, and the next, something set her off." He looked across the room. "Miss Valentine looks lonely, standing under the Cupid. Why not pay her some attention, boy?"

John barely glanced at Susan. "She has been standing there for the better part of five minutes, hoping to attract someone." He grinned. "I've been hiding in the card room."

Grafton laughed. "Good for you, my boy. Don't let Lady Pamela catch you in her snares."

"I've no intention of it. Sir." John's smile faded. "I need to talk with you about something."

"You wish to marry my granddaughter. Very well."

John stared at him. "Just like that? I thought you disapproved the match."

"Oh, no, no. Ware and I discussed it coming here, and we think it's an excellent thing. Knew if we told you two, though, you'd balk."

"For God's sake," John said. "You tricked us."

"Mm, I suppose we did."

"I should be angry." John was grinning again. "I couldn't understand why my father wasn't pushing me to marry." His gaze sharpened. "I have your permission, then, to pay my addresses to your granddaughter?"

"Yes, yes. Go after her, my boy. She said something about going to the library."

"The library? Well, I suppose it's a fitting place. If you'll excuse me, sir," he said, and turned, walking with purposeful strides out of the room. Alana was going to listen to him this time. She had to. His future depended on it.

The library was dark and quiet, just as Alana had hoped it would be. After lighting a taper, she bent to stir the fire into life, and then rose, rubbing her hands together for warmth. Dark, quiet, and cold, and yet she wouldn't return to the life and warmth of the music room unless forced to. Not if it meant watching John make love to other women. Flirting was one thing, kissing quite another. Though she knew she could trust him, deep in her heart a tiny doubt remained. She was no beauty, and she was past her first youth. What could he possibly see in her?

The door opened, and she looked up, gasping in surprise at the figure silhouetted in the doorway. "Sir Gabriel!"

He stepped forward. "No, 'tis only me," he said. John's voice.

"Oh! For a moment I thought—"

"I know what you thought. This damned wig." With a quick gesture he swept the wig from his head and stood there, not a supernatural being, but just John, very alive and very dear. "Will I have to compete with him the rest of my life?"

"No." She turned away to poke at the fire. "What do you here?"

"Your grandfather said you were here. Said something upset you."

"Upset me!" She whirled around. "Of course it upset me. What did you think?"

"What?"

"Oh, don't play the innocent with me! I saw you kissing Susan Valentine."

216

"What? When?"

"Not five minutes ago, under that stupid Cupid in the doorway."

"Good God, it wasn't me! I was with Lady Honoria in the card room."

"What? Then who—"

"Ask her if you don't believe me."

"Then who was kissing her?"

"No one. She has stood under that Cupid all evening, and I've seen no one approach her."

"But I saw—there's no one else here in cavalier dress in that color, and—my God!" She sank into a chair. "Sir Gabriel."

"What?"

"It had to be. No one else would have seen him, only me. That meddling, interfering man—"

"Alana." John knelt before her, his face creased with concern. "Are you quite well?"

The face she raised to him was merry with laughter. "Yes. Oh, John, don't you see? We've been surrounded by a pack of matchmaking old men all week."

John grinned. "And if we have? Is it so bad?"

She looked at him. "No. I—no."

"Alana." He grasped her hands in his. "Sweetheart, I know you were hurt before, and I can't undo that. But can't you forget the past? I have. I've given up my wild ways. Oh, it's true, I was something of a rake in town, but I wasn't happy. I never was. I was always searching for something I could never find. Until I came here, and found you."

"Oh, John." She reached out to lay her hand on his cheek. "And I broke the crystal heart. Your heart."

"No matter. There's another." From his pocket he withdrew the crystal heart, letting it dangle before her from its chain. "The real one."

"John!" Alana reached out for it. "It can't be."

"But it is. See? There are the initials."

" 'GF and MF,' " she read. "Good heavens, this is it! But where did you find it?"

"I didn't. My mother sent it to me. You see, Alana," he smiled, "it appears I'm descended from Sir Gabriel."

"Gammon!"

"No, 'tis true. She wrote me a letter, detailing the ancestry. I imagine she's very curious why I wanted to know."

"You're Sir Gabriel's descendant."

"Yes."

"And you have the crystal heart."

"Yes. And I've given up my roistering ways."

"The conditions to be met, to fulfill the vow."

"Not quite." He clasped the heart about her neck. "I give this to you not because of your fortune, not because of an old vow, but because I love you with all my heart. Will you marry me?"

"Oh, John!" she exclaimed, and cast herself into his arms.

The door from the hall opened. "See? Told you they'd be in here," the duke's voice grumbled, and both he and the marquess came in. "Everything settled between you two?"

"Yes, sir," John said, as manfully as he could, considering he still held Alana close. "Wish us happy. We are to be wed."

"Well, what are you hiding in here for? Come out and let's announce it to everyone."

John and Alana looked at each other. "Shall we?"

Alana fingered the crystal heart. "I think it's appropriate, don't you?"

"Yes. But I warn you, madam, I shall want some time alone with you."

"You will have it, sir," she said lightly, letting him help her to her feet. At the door she stopped, turning and looking into the room where so much of her life had changed. "John!" she gasped, clutching suddenly at his arm.

"What?" he said, looking back, and his eyes widened. "Good God. Is that—"

"Shh." Holding onto each other, they watched as a glow grew in the center of the room. In it stood a dark-haired lady, lovely, smiling, her eyes focused only on the handsome cavalier who approached her. Lady Madeleine and Sir Gabriel, reunited at last, after so many years. She held out her hand; he took it in both of his. The glow strengthened, intensified, until the two people watching had to shield their eyes against it. Then, suddenly, it was gone. The library was empty.

"Good God," John said again. "If I hadn't seen it with my own eyes—"

"They found each other again," Alana said, wonderingly. "Because of us."

"Yes. Because of us. As we have found each other." John glanced one last time into the room, and then took her arm. "Come, my love. They'll be waiting for us."

Alana, too, looked into the room, and felt peace fill her. "Yes," she said, holding onto his arm, and walked away. Behind her was the past. Before her was her future. The legend of the crystal heart had been fulfilled.

Fit for a Prince
by
Anthea Malcolm

One

Alessandra Dudley regarded her brother with exasperation. He was about to make the mistake of his life. "It's barbaric, Simon. What chance do you think such a marriage would have of success?"

"As much chance as any other marriage." Simon settled back in the mahogany Sheraton elbow chair and carefully crossed one well-shaped booted leg over the other. His voice was light, but his jaw was firmly set. From the time he had first learned to put two words together, Simon had looked just so whenever his mind was set on something.

"But you're not in love with her," Alessa protested, voicing the really criminal part of the whole business. "You don't even *know* her."

"Don't work yourself into a state," Simon advised. "I've agreed to meet Charlotte de Chambeau, not to marry her out of hand."

"And when you do meet her?" Alessa demanded. "What then?"

"I get to know her, she gets to know me. If I think she suits, I ask her to marry me. If she thinks I suit, she accepts."

Alessa shuddered. "Don't be provoking, Simon. You can't mean to go about it so coldbloodedly."

"What would you have me do? Pretend undying devotion the moment I clap eyes on her? *That* would be dishonest."

"I'd have you meet a woman and come to care for her and ask her to marry you because you love her," Alessa said, leaning forward in impatience. "That's worked very well for countless people I could name."

There was a moment of silence. Outside the wind came up, rattling the windowpanes. "But I'm not like other people," Simon said quietly. "I'm the Prince di Tassio."

Something in his expression checked any retort Alessa might have made. Simon's words did not stem from arrogance. They were a statement of the life he had been bred to from the cradle. Alessa drew her wool shawl more closely about her shoulders, feeling the chill of the January morning creep into her snug sitting room. Exasperation giving way to concern, she studied her brother across the book-strewn expanse of the sofa table. He was disgustingly handsome. Even looking at him through the clear, unromantic eyes of a sister, Alessa could not but note his fine-boned face, his well-drawn mouth, his dark almond-shaped eyes.

It was not the face of an Englishman. Like her, Simon had inherited the high, Slavic cheekbones of their Russian mother and the dark hair and pale skin of their Savoyard father. But Alessa doubted if her own face had ever held the stamp of duty and authority which had characterized Simon since childhood. The difference between being born a boy and being born a girl, she supposed, feeling at once a sense of relief and a twinge of envy.

But there was a remoteness about Simon which was new, as was the haunted look she sometimes glimpsed lurking at the back of his eyes. He had always been old for his age, but since his return from an extended tour of the Continent a year ago, he had seemed almost frighteningly in command of himself. There were times when Alessa felt she could no longer reach the brother of her childhood. She thought of her own children and vowed, not for the first time, that they would not be burdened as Simon had been.

"It's quite unforgivable of *Maman* to try to arrange your future this way," Alessa said. "You'd think she'd have learned her lesson interfering in my life without meddling in yours as well."

Simon grinned. "Credit me with a little more initiative. When have I ever let *Maman* tell me what to do? It wasn't her idea that I get married. It was mine."

Alessa was taken aback. An arranged marriage seemed much more suited to her mother's aristocratic European notions than to the free-thinking Simon. "Why?" she demanded.

A log fell from the grate and thudded against the fender. Simon got up and went to the fireplace. "Because I've had my fill of being an eligible bachelor," he said, picking up the brass poker and pushing the log back into the fire. "Because I don't much care for living alone. Because there ought to be a Princess di Tassio." Simon replaced the poker and leaned against the white-painted pine mantel. "Because I'd like children."

"Yes, that's another thing—" Alessa broke off, and made a show of smoothing her twilled cashmere skirt, wondering that Simon could speak so calmly when the process of making children was so intoxicatingly delicious. Not for the first time Alessa wondered about her brother's amorous experiences. Simon was too proud to pay a woman for her favors and too honorable to exploit a servant or a tavern wench. But surely there had been women in his life, women he had cared for as he could not yet care for the unknown Charlotte de Chambeau.

"Very wise, Alessa," Simon said, a glint of amusement lightening his eyes. "There are some questions which are out of bounds, even for sisters."

Alessa drummed her fingers against the green-and-ivory chintz of the sofa arm. "Simon, you can't make an arranged marriage."

"You did, and it seems to have worked out very well."

"I was lucky," Alessa protested. She was so in love with her husband that it was hard to remember the awkwardness and formality of the day she had accepted his proposal. She had thought she was marrying Harry Dudley, Earl of Milverton, because it was a prudent and sensible match, but even then she had not been as indifferent as she wanted to believe. "I think I knew how I felt about Harry the day I agreed to be his wife," Alessa told Simon.

"It just took you two years to admit it. Cheer up, perhaps I'll fall in love with Mademoiselle de Chambeau at first sight."

Alessa looked into her brother's eyes and realized what bothered her most about the arrangement. "That's the worst of it, Simon. I don't think you even *want* to fall in love."

For a moment the haunted look was back in Simon's eyes, so vivid that Alessa wanted to put her arms around him, so intense that she knew she did not dare to. Then he retreated behind a cheerful mask. "No sense in quibbling further," he said. "Are you or are you not willing to host a house party here at Moresby so I can meet Charlotte de Chambeau?"

"Oh, very well," Alessa said, slumping back against the sofa cushions with a sigh. "That way I can at least keep my eye on you."

"Your generosity almost overwhelms me." Simon returned to his chair. "Mademoiselle de Chambeau and her aunt will arrive in England in early February."

"So *Maman* said. It seems awfully hurried."

"That can be laid at the door of Charlotte's father. He's a widower, and it seems he hasn't the least idea what to do with his daughter. Now that she's left the convent where she was educated, he wants to see her settled as soon as possible."

Alessa straightened up and punched the cushions into shape. "It had better be a fairly large house party, so your meeting with Charlotte isn't too obvious. As far as the other guests are concerned, we'll just say she's the daughter of *Maman's* old friend the Comte de Chambeau. You wouldn't want to be forced into a betrothal by careless talk."

"I have no intention of being forced into anything," Simon said.

That, Alessa knew, was perfectly true. Somehow, it didn't make her feel any better. "I'll ask old friends who can be counted on to be discreet," she said, going to her writing table to begin making notes. "The Windhams and the Scotts. And perhaps the Melchetts, they always liven things up. We'll need a few single men to round out the numbers. There's Bertram Westcourt, he's always agreeable. He was at Oxford with you, wasn't he?"

"We overlapped for a year or two," Simon said, with a noticeable lack of enthusiasm. "From what I've seen, he's just as witless now as he was then."

"But he's quite charming, and the most amiable guest imaginable." As Alessa searched through sketches and correspondence for a mended pen, her eye fell on a letter from Marianne Stratton, her husband's recently married cousin. "I think I'll ask Marianne and Gerald," she said, recalling the trouble she had read between the much-crossed lines of the letter. "I'm afraid their marriage isn't working out as well as might be hoped."

Alessa expected Simon to make a remark about the perils of marrying for love, but instead he said in a serious tone, "I'm sorry to hear it."

"The truth is, marriage is hellishly difficult, no matter what." Alessa reached for a clean sheet of crested writing paper. *"Maman* will want to be here, of course. I hope she's considered the possibility that you and Mademoiselle de Chambeau may not suit."

"Oh, yes. She made a point of telling me neither she nor Charlotte's father would dream of forcing our hands. After all, times have changed."

Alessa groaned. "It's not funny, Simon."

"On the contrary. Laughter is the only way to respond to *Maman.* I learned that years before you did."

"I'll ask the guests for the second week in February," Alessa said, returning to her notes. "That will put my St. Valentine's Eve ball in the midst of the party."

"Capital," said Simon. "You can use the ball as an excuse for the house party."

"Yes," Alessa agreed, "though it seems a travesty for you

to be arranging this marriage against the background of a holiday for lovers."

Simon refused to rise to the bait. Aware of the sound of high-pitched voices, Alessa turned to the window. Through the mullioned panes, a relic of the original Jacobean house, she glimpsed her husband and children coming back, windblown and disheveled, from a tramp around the grounds. Harry waved, using his other hand to balance their two-year-old daughter, who was perched on his shoulders. Alessa waved back, her spirits lightening as they always did when Harry was about. At the same time she felt a pang of sorrow. There was so much her brother would be missing. "Simon—" she said.

Simon had walked over to the window. He waved to Harry and the children, then turned to Alessa with a look which told her she could not reach him. "See to arranging the house party, Alessa," he said, moving toward the door. "Leave arranging my life to me."

Alessa sighed and returned to her lists. There was nothing more she could say. For the moment.

Having persuaded his sister to go along with his plans, however reluctantly, Simon made his escape from the sitting room. Though he was very fond of his brother-in-law and his nieces and nephews, Simon did not feel like facing Alessa's happy, boisterous family just now. Fortunately, Moresby was a satisfyingly large house.

He was doing the right thing, Simon told himself, striding purposefully down the picture-lined corridor. He was doing the only sensible thing for a man in his position. There were considerations more important than love in making a marriage. If Charlotte de Chambeau was agreeable, there was no reason they could not have a very happy life together.

Simon paused beneath the archway that led to the cool, wainscotted great hall, a room that reeked of tradition. There was a time when he had thought arranged marriages an antiquated institution. But that was before— His mind carefully shied away from the events of the autumn before last. That was before he had seen enough of the world. Before he had fully considered his responsibilities as the Prince di Tassio. Before—

Despite all his best efforts, a memory of warm blue-gray eyes and gleaming chestnut hair, of seductive warmth and heart-wrenching laughter, intruded on his thoughts. That was before he had known Justine.

Justine de Valon settled back against the smooth, silk-covered squabs and told herself it would do no good to be nervous. When she and Charlotte had set sail for England, she had known she would meet Simon, known they would be staying in the same house. She had made her bed and she would have to lie in it.

This singularly inapt comparison brought hot color flooding to Justine's cheeks. She raised her hand to tug the brim of her hat forward, praying the shadowy light in the carriage would hide her blush from Charlotte.

Contrary to her wish, this action seemed to catch Charlotte's attention. But perhaps Charlotte would have spoken anyway. She had been staring out the window for at least two minutes, and two minutes, Justine had learned, was about as much contemplation as Charlotte could manage. "I'm so glad you're here with me, Justine," Charlotte said, speaking in the English she was determined to practice before their arrival at Moresby. "It may be horrid to say so, but I am quite relieved Aunt Mathilde's health did not permit her to travel with me. I am sure she would not have been nearly so sympathetic."

Justine folded her hands in her lap, wondering for the hundredth time if she had been a great fool to agree to be Charlotte's chaperone. She had had so little time to decide. Her late husband's cousin, the Comte de Chambeau, had written to say that his sister was in ill health and he was in urgent need of a female relative to escort Charlotte to England. As Justine was an Englishwoman herself, the comte thought she would suit admirably. He required an answer by the next post.

It was only when Justine had joined Charlotte at Calais, the day before they were to sail, that the preoccupied comte had bothered to mention that the visit to England had been arranged so that Charlotte could meet the Prince di Tassio, a prospective husband.

The mention of Simon's name had thrown Justine into turmoil. Yet it would have been difficult to turn back at the last minute. Besides, given her financial straits, the temporary security of life as Charlotte's chaperone was tempting indeed. She and Simon were both adults. There was no reason they could not be civilized about the meeting.

So Justine had told herself at the inn in Calais. Now, her reasoning seemed more flawed with every mile they drew closer to Moresby.

Charlotte was staring in frowning concentration at the footwarmer. "Isn't there anything more you can tell me about the Prince di Tassio?" she asked, looking up. "He spent over three months in Paris. You must have met him dozens of times."

Justine adjusted the mulberry velvet folds of her pelisse. "It's difficult to make oneself heard at large parties, let alone get to know anyone," she said, suppressing an image of a half-undressed Simon drawing her into his arms in the privacy of her bedchamber. "He always seemed very agreeable." Agreeable? Dear God, what a pallid word to describe the fervent young man who had shown her such tenderness and passion.

"I suppose he will be there to meet us when we arrive." Charlotte reached up to tuck a honey-brown curl beneath the brim of her bonnet. "Is my hair all right? Perhaps I should have worn the violet pelisse."

"The blue looks charming," Justine said, smiling at the younger girl. "So does your hair."

Charlotte frowned again, tugging at her satin-edged collar. "Do you think he will like me, Justine?"

"I'm sure he will," Justine said, feeling a lump rise in her throat. In the past few days she had come to be very fond of Charlotte. She wanted Charlotte to be happy. She wanted Simon to be happy as well. That was why she had sent him away.

"I'm afraid I won't know what to talk to him about," Charlotte said, tracing a pattern with the toe of her terry velvet boot. "Do you suppose he's had a great deal of experience with women?"

Justine choked and brought her hand up to her mouth, feigning a cough to cover her confusion. Simon had not been experienced on that first night, though even then there had been nothing awkward about him. "I couldn't say," she murmured. It was the literal truth. She couldn't possibly discuss Simon's amorous experiences with Charlotte. "But I wouldn't call him a flirt."

"Or a rake?"

"Certainly not," Justine said and then wondered if she had spoken with unnecessary firmness. How many other women had Simon bedded since the end of their liaison? Jealousy stabbed through her, a jealousy she knew she had no right to feel.

"Well," Charlotte said, stroking the fur of the chinchilla muff resting on the seat beside her, "he's bound to have more experience with women than I have with men. I must say, it's ridiculous that anyone thinks a convent can prepare a girl for the world. Anyway, I shan't mind how many mistresses he has, as long as he's discreet."

"I'm sure the prince will not keep mistresses after he is married," Justine assured her. Simon was far too honorable to do so.

"Oh, but I expect him to," Charlotte said with sunny confidence. "That is quite *convenable* in an arranged marriage."

Justine regarded Charlotte with concern. "I know it's difficult to think of such things when you haven't even met, love, but you and the prince may come to genuinely care for each other."

"But I do not wish to fall in love with him," Charlotte said, wrinkling her nose. "All the girls at the convent who were in love were either dreadfully silly or fearfully unhappy. Lucille

231

used to be sick every morning, and in the end she had to go away to the country. I don't think I should like to be in love at all."

"There's no denying it can cause heartache," Justine said, feeling just such a pain in the vicinity of her own heart. "But it can also be quite delightful, particularly with an eligible young man."

"Were you in love with Monsieur de Valon?" Charlotte asked with curiosity.

Justine was silent for a moment, recalling the charming, reckless man Armand de Valon had been when she'd first met him. Eighteen—Charlotte's age—and fresh from the country, she had been dazzled by the handsome French cavalry officer who had made her the Baronne de Valon and swept her off to lead a glamorous life in Paris. It had been at least a year before she'd faced her husband's dreadful improvidence and another year before she'd admitted his infidelity. "When we were married I was very much in love," she told Charlotte.

"And later?" Charlotte persisted.

In all honesty, Justine knew her love for her husband had been effectively killed long before he died fighting a duel with another woman's husband. But she knew a fierce determination to protect Charlotte from the harsher realities of life. "One's feelings change with time," she said. "But I never stopped caring for him. After all, one marries for companionship and affection."

Charlotte giggled. "There are all sorts of people who can provide that. But only a husband can give a woman her own establishment. I made up my mind years ago that I would marry at the first possible opportunity. How else am I to have the freedom to do as I please?"

Justine wondered just what activities Charlotte included under "doing as she pleased." The girl was a bewildering combination of naïveté and worldly wisdom. Despite her own bittersweet marriage, Justine hated to see Charlotte dismiss love out of hand. Surely Simon at least would be sensible enough not to make a marriage without genuine sympathy on both sides. Or would he?

Justine turned toward the window as if by doing so she could banish such thoughts. Simon could take care of himself. She no longer had the right to interest herself in his life.

The sight of the frosted hedgerows reminded Justine that whatever else lay ahead, it was good to be back in England. She must play the hand that had been dealt her and live her life one day at a time, as she had ever since she'd faced widowhood and the mountain of debts Armand had left.

"Something is wrong?" Charlotte asked with concern. "You are worried about leaving the baby, perhaps?"

Justine started. Her sudden intake of breath left a film of condensation on the window glass. Charlotte had unwittingly reminded her of the reason she couldn't continue to simply live life as it came. She no longer had only herself to think of. "Minette will do very well at the inn with her nurse," she said, though she had felt a pang of loss ever since they had driven away from the inn near Moresby village. It was the first time she had been separated from her daughter.

"We should have brought her with us to the house party," Charlotte said. "I am sure Lady Milverton would not have minded if I'd told her you have a ward who is a very young child."

"No," Justine said firmly, "I couldn't have imposed on Lady Milverton like that. It is better this way, Charlotte, believe me." Unwillingly to leave Minette in France, Justine had told Charlotte that the baby was the daughter of a dear friend who had died in childbirth. Charlotte, mercifully, seemed to believe the story. "And it will be better not to speak of it to any of the guests at Moresby, just as we did not to speak of it to your father," Justine added.

"So you keep saying. If the problem is that your friend wasn't married to the baby's father, I do think we're making the most awful fuss about nothing. I am sure the prince and Lady Milverton would understand, and anyway, who would know?"

"Charlotte—" Justine protested in alarm.

"Don't worry, Justine," Charlotte said with a serene smile, "I'll do as you ask. After all, you know a great deal more about such things than I do."

Justine permitted herself a small sigh of relief. There was no reason Simon or anyone else at Moresby should know about Minette. The only people at the house party who would be aware of the child's existence were Charlotte and Cécile, the maid they had brought with them from France. Cécile, who was following in a second carriage with the luggage, was a good-hearted young woman whom Justine felt she could trust. Though Justine knew she was treading on dangerous ground, she told herself that if she just behaved sensibly, all would be well.

The carriage slowed and turned, and there was a crunching sound, as if they were moving onto a gravel drive. Charlotte at once pressed her face against the glass. Turning back to the window as well, Justine glimpsed the weathered stone of lodge gates and the start of a line of lime trees, stark and leafless on this February day.

"We're nearly there," Charlotte said in a bright, strained voice.

"Yes," said Justine, wondering which of them was the more afraid.

Marianne Stratton stared critically into the cheval glass and smoothed the skirt of the striped *gros de Naples* dress she had changed into upon her arrival at Moresby. "Neither Alessa nor Simon has met this French girl who's to arrive today," she said, adjusting the lace collar at her neck.

"Then why the devil has Alessa invited her?" Gerald demanded, appearing in the open doorway of the dressing room which connected their bedchambers.

"Apparently her father is an old friend of Simon and Alessa's mother. But it sounds to me as if someone has match-making in mind." Marianne patted her golden-brown curls and turned to look at her husband. At the sight of him, she gave a little start of surprise. Gerald had dismissed his valet when she'd dismissed her maid, but he was far from finished with his toilet. He wore neither waistcoat nor coat, and though he held a cravat in his hand, the buttons at the neck of his shirt were unfastened, affording a glimpse of springy dark hair. Marianne's stomach clenched, partly with apprehension, partly with something else she could not name.

"Poor Simon," Gerald said. "Nothing like having a bunch of females trying to steer you into matrimony."

"You find matrimony so disagreeable?" Marianne asked before she could stop herself.

"Of course not, m'dear," Gerald said quickly. "Didn't mean anything of the sort."

The excessive solicitude in Gerald's voice only made it worse. If matters had been comfortable between them, they could have laughed about such things. Marianne found her eyes straying again to the open neck of his shirt and then to his snug-fitting, buff-colored pantaloons.

Feeling intensely grateful that Alessa had managed to give them separate bedchambers despite the large number of guests to be accommodated at the house party, Marianne turned back to the mirror. "It's only natural for Simon's family to want to see him settled," she said, making a great show of fumbling with the cord and tassels which fastened her collar. "A man in his position must have an heir." Marianne nearly bit her tongue the moment the words were out of her mouth. Talking of heirs only made it worse.

"But why the devil must they import someone all the way from France?" Gerald demanded. "Plenty of agreeable girls in England."

"Yes, but Simon is almost French himself. That is, he's from Savoy, which is somewhere between France and Italy, though I've never understood exactly where. And for some reason, now they're calling it Sardinia."

"Dash it, Marianne, the fellow went to Oxford. Can't get

much more English than that. Not but what there *is* something a bit foreign about him," Gerald added, in a thoughtful voice.

"I expect it comes of being brought up on the Continent." Disconcertingly aware of her husband's nearness, Marianne moved to the dressing table. "He was eleven before his mother settled in England and married Michael Langley."

"Still don't see why Simon has to marry a frog. Not to say that all French women . . ." Gerald's voice trailed off and he gave an embarrassed cough.

"I'm sure there's nothing as formal as a betrothal yet," Marianne said, hunting through her jewel case for her pearl earrings. "I doubt Simon would agree to marry a girl he had never met. I doubt his mother would agree to it, if it comes to that."

"Always one to make careful decisions, the Princess Sofia," Gerald said, though it sounded as if his mind was on something else.

There was a note in his voice which unnerved Marianne. She retrieved one earring and began to search frantically for its mate. "Alessa told me Princess Sofia isn't expected to arrive at Moresby for a few more days. I expect Simon is relieved not to have to meet Mademoiselle de Chambeau with his mother standing by."

"Very likely. But I'm really not interested in Simon and his Frenchy just now."

Marianne heard her husband crossing the room as he spoke. The sound of his footfalls on the Brussels carpet seemed to reverberate through her. Just as she found the second earring, Gerald's hands closed on her shoulders. "Bound to be a lot of confusion with all the guests arriving," he said, his breath hot against her face. "No harm in staying in our rooms for a bit."

Marianne froze. This was worse than usual. Never before had Gerald approached her in daylight, when she was fully clothed, with her hair just done. In fact, he hadn't approached her at all for over a fortnight. To her own surprise, she had almost begun to miss it. And yet—

Gerald's hand slid down over the carefully arranged collar and cupped her breast. She could feel the hardness between his legs. As he kneaded her breast, a sharp, sweet warmth spread through her, making her body go tight in places she couldn't mention.

Disturbed by her own reaction more than by her husband's nearness, Marianne twisted round and pushed against his chest. "Gerald, we can't. It's the middle of the afternoon."

"Damn it, Marianne——" Gerald drew in his breath, then released her and strode to the chair where he had left his neckcloth.

Marianne felt a pang of loneliness at the loss of his touch. Perhaps she should have agreed. At least he had shown that he still wanted her as a woman. But it would have been so odd, with all that daylight spilling in through the windows. And how ever would she have been able to face Alessa and Simon and the others afterward?

"We should go downstairs soon," she said, smoothing her gown. "Alessa said there would be refreshments in the small saloon. I'm sure more of the guests have arrived by now. I saw Lord Westcourt's carriage from the window just a few minutes ago."

"Westcourt?" Gerald swung round, clenching the cravat in his hand. "You didn't tell me he was coming."

"Didn't I?" Marianne tugged the collar back into place, recalling the way Gerald's hand had felt against her breast. Suddenly she wished she could call him back, but she hadn't the remotest idea of how to do so.

"You know damn well you didn't. If Westcourt thinks he can hang about your skirts here the way he did in London——"

Sometimes it seemed as if Gerald was determined to deny her any enjoyment in life. The thought of Bertram, Viscount Westcourt, who was so charmingly attentive, so solicitous of her welfare, only reminded Marianne of how very different her husband was. Not that in his own way Gerald wasn't as handsome as Lord Westcourt—both men had thick brown hair and pleasing features—but he was not nearly such an understanding and engaging companion. "Don't be vulgar, Gerald. Lord Westcourt would not 'hang about' any woman's skirts, and I would not allow him to do so."

"Humph. I've seen the way that fawning puppy looks at you. When a man looks like that at a married woman, it's plain enough what he's after."

"And how would you know, Gerald?" Marianne demanded, lifting her chin. "From your own experience?"

"If a man's wife so clearly finds him distasteful—" Gerald broke off and stared down at the crumpled cravat in his hand. "Devil take it, it's ruined. I'll have to get a fresh one."

But he hesitated a moment, as if there was something more he wanted to say. Marianne twisted her hands together, hurt and angry, uncertain how to reach him, uncertain if she wanted to do so. The strained silence was broken by the sound of carriage wheels against the flagstones of the forecourt.

Relieved at the interruption, Marianne hurried to the window. Below in the forecourt, framed by the tawny brick of the two projecting wings of the house, a post-chaise was drawn up. Alessa was standing on the stone steps leading to the house, wrapped in a shawl against the February wind. Her husband Harry stood on one side of her and Simon on the other. It must be Charlotte de Chambeau, and they must have had someone waiting at the lodge gates to warn them of her approach.

"They *are* making a fuss about her arrival," Marianne said, momentarily forgetting the tension between her and Gerald.

Gerald joined her at the window, but to her relief he did not speak. The coachman jumped down, lowered the steps, and opened the door of the carriage. There was a moment's delay, and then Mademoiselle de Chambeau emerged, though all that could be seen of her were the top of an expensive-looking bonnet ornamented with flowers, an enormous chinchilla muff, and the skirts of a fur-trimmed dark blue pelisse.

Alessa was descending the steps, followed by Harry and Simon. Charlotte de Chambeau stepped toward them. "She's very small, isn't she?" Marianne said. "Even shorter than I am." Mademoiselle de Chambeau looked as if the top of her head would barely reach Simon's shoulder.

Gerald did not respond. He was looking beyond Charlotte de Chambeau. Marianne followed the direction of his gaze. The coachman was helping another lady to alight, a taller lady, dressed in a pelisse of mulberry-colored velvet, which revealed an enviable figure, and a matching velvet hat. She raised her head for a moment to look up at the house, and Marianne had an impression of large, vivid eyes and chestnut hair which seemed bright even on this gray day.

Marianne looked at Gerald again, aware of a sinking sensation in the pit of her stomach.

Gerald had eyes for no one but the woman in mulberry velvet. "My word," he exclaimed, a note in his voice that Marianne had never heard before. "It's Justine."

Two

Out of the corner of his eye Simon saw that a second woman had descended from the carriage, but his attention was on Charlotte de Chambeau. His first thought was that she could not possibly be eighteen. Or perhaps it was that he had forgot how very young an eighteen-year-old girl could be. Charlotte's fresh face, with its slightly snubbed nose and light smattering of freckles, still held the roundness of youth. Her small stature exaggerated this impression. In her dark pelisse and elegant muff and bonnet, she looked like a little girl dressed up in her mother's clothes.

"Welcome to Morseby, Mademoiselle de Chambeau," Alessa said, holding out her hands. "I am Lady Milverton. My husband, Lord Milverton, and my brother, Simon di Tassio. We are delighted to see you." Alessa squeezed Charlotte's hands, then looked beyond her to the second lady who was waiting beside the carriage. "And this must be your aunt . . . ?"

Simon followed the direction of his sister's gaze. The blood rushed from his head. It could not be she. But he would have known those wide, brilliant eyes and that full-lipped mouth anywhere. Everything—the tilt of her head, the graceful set of her shoulders, the way her gloved hands were loosely clasped together—cried out that this was Justine.

"Oh, no, Lady Milverton," Charlotte said with a laugh, "this isn't my aunt. This is my cousin, the Baronne de Valon."

Something that was suspiciously like joy welled up in Simon's chest. A wave of hot desire swept through his body, followed by a cold burst of fury and a sense that somehow there must be a logical explanation for why his former mistress was standing not ten feet away, a few paces behind the girl who might become his wife.

"Aunt Mathilde's health did not permit her to make the journey, so Madame de Valon agreed to chaperone me instead," Charlotte was explaining. *"Papa* wrote to the Princess Sofia to let you know."

"That accounts for it," Alessa said, with a smile which embraced both Charlotte and Justine. "We don't expect *Maman* to join us for a few more days. And she may not have received the letter yet herself. The post is not always reliable. In any case, I am very glad to welcome you, Madame de Valon."

Simon forced himself to speak past the tightness in his throat. "Madame de Valon and I have met before. In Paris, the autumn before last."

"How charming of you to remember, Prince." Justine stepped forward, close enough now that Simon could see the fine texture of her skin and smell the hyacinth scent that brought back such unbearable memories. Her eyes met his for a moment, and he saw that she darkened her lashes just as he remembered. The message in her gaze was clear: Do not worry, I will say nothing. We can pretend it never happened.

The sensible course, but quite impossible to carry out. Simon felt another stab of anger that she had come to his sister's house, on this, of all occasions. "I trust you have been well, madam," he said, looking into the eyes he would once have sworn owned all his soul. "I have had no news of you since I left Paris." And not for want of trying. Justine had sent his letters back unopened.

"I have been living in the country." Justine's voice was level, but he thought her breathing had quickened slightly.

"Ah," Simon said. "That accounts for it." Beneath the high velvet folds of her pelisse, was her skin as soft and warm as he remembered? Did the hair peeking so decorously out from the brim of her hat still tumble loose over her shoulders with the same glorious abandon?

Simon felt the pressure of Alessa's gaze on him for the briefest moment, but she spoke to her guests. "You must be tired after so many days of travel. I'll show you to your rooms. After you've refreshed yourselves, you can meet the other guests."

A gust of chill wind swept through the forecourt. Two footmen in the green-and-buff Dudley livery were hurrying down the steps to see to the second carriage, which had pulled up with the ladies' luggage. Simon tried to impose some order on his thoughts. Charlotte de Chambeau had come all the way from France to meet him. At the very least, he owed her his undivided attention.

Forcing himself not to look again at Justine, Simon offered Charlotte his arm. "May I escort you into the house, mademoiselle?"

Charlotte perched on the pink velvet chaise longue in the dressing room she shared with Justine and began to unlace her boots. "Thank goodness," she said, reverting to French. "It wasn't as bad as I thought."

Justine carefully removed her hat and placed it on the dressing table. It had been even worse than she'd anticipated. She hadn't expected to feel so sharp a stab of pain or so treacherous a rush of longing.

Simon seemed much older. Looking into his cool eyes, she had felt a wrench of grief for the loss of the idealistic young man she had known. There had been more than surprise in his gaze. She could swear he was angry. He had every right to be angry, of course, especially as her visit had taken him by surprise. But she had convinced herself that in the fourteen months since they had parted, the memory of their last quarrel would have faded and Simon would be grateful to have escaped so lightly from the affair. Now she feared that was not the case. Worse, the thought had given her a moment of satisfaction.

"They all seem quite agreeable," Charlotte said, starting on her second boot. "Lady Milverton is very elegant—that dress she was wearing looked like it came straight from Paris. And Lord Milverton is pleasant, and not at all stuffy."

"And the prince?" Justine asked, her throat dry.

Charlotte stood and began to unfasten her pelisse. "He is quite reserved. And older than I expected."

"He's had a great many burdens in his life." Justine sat at the dressing table and sought refuge in fluffing her hair. "I suspect he was forced to grow up quickly."

"Lucky man," Charlotte said, shrugging out of the pelisse. "There's nothing more odious than being forced to remain a child." She dropped the pelisse on a nearby chair and pulled at the ribbons on her bonnet. "In any case, he doesn't seem at all romantic, so I needn't fear he'll complicate matters by thinking he needs to court me."

Justine smoothed her forehead, suddenly feeling rather old. "I think you can count on him to be honest with you in all matters."

"I do hope so." Charlotte tossed her bonnet after her pelisse and returned to the chaise longue. "I want to be sure we're clear on the terms of our relationship before I make any sort of commitment."

"Surely it's a bit early to be thinking of commitments," Justine said, aware of an unexpected hollowness in her stomach. "You've only just met."

"It's never too early to think of such things." Charlotte flopped back against the embroidered silk cushions, arms folded above her head. "Marriage is the most important decision a woman can make. There's no point in doing it at all if my husband is going to restrict me as much as *Papa* does. I shall be very clear with the prince about the freedoms I expect."

Justine could only applaud Charlotte for wanting her freedom. Perhaps the girl was right to view marriage with clearer eyes than Justine herself had done. Yet for all her matter-of-factness, Charlotte was still innocent in many matters. "You do realize that the prince's expectations of marriage may not be the same as yours," Justine said, turning to face Charlotte directly.

"Oh, I know he will require certain things of me," Charlotte said with confidence. "I will have to run his household and entertain for him. And of course, he will want an heir." She frowned at the plaster ceiling above. "We must come to an understanding about how often he is allowed to visit my bed."

Justine swallowed. "It—it is certainly something to consider."

"Exactly. I know he will have to visit me, at least until I begin increasing, but it would be tiresome to be importuned every night." Charlotte pushed herself up on her elbows. "Is it very dreadful, Justine? What happens between men and women, I mean."

Suddenly the light, silk-hung room seemed unbearably close. Justine tugged at the buttons on her pelisse. Charlotte's question was a perfectly natural one for a girl contemplating marriage. Justine recalled wishing for someone to give her an honest answer to such a question in her own girlhood. Like Charlotte, Justine had lost her mother at an early age. The aunt who had given her a season in London had not spoken of such matters until the night before Justine's wedding, and then only in the vaguest terms.

"In the right circumstances, it isn't dreadful at all," Justine said carefully.

Charlotte looked unconvinced. "The girls at the convent used to tell all sorts of stories. It sounds as if it hurts."

"Well, it can a bit, the first time, but not if the man is gentle." Justine's fingers clenched on the cold metal of the gold buckle at her waist. Armand had not always been gentle. But Simon had. She forced herself to continue unfastening the pelisse, only to remember the feel of Simon's hands as he loosened her clothing.

244

"I got the impression one enjoys it only with a man who isn't one's husband," Charlotte declared.

"That's nonsense. One's married state has—has nothing to do with one's response." Justine kept her voice steady with an effort. She felt a desperate impulse to laugh. It was either that or cry. "It is a matter of one's feelings for the gentleman in question."

"And of his skill?" Charlotte asked with curiosity.

Justine felt a tremor run through her. She could almost feel Simon's fingers trailing against her skin and hear his voice softened to a caress. He might not have been a practiced lover when he first came to her bed, but his fervor had been like nothing she had known before. "If two people"—she started to say "love" and bit back the word—"if two people care for each other, the rest will come."

Charlotte wrinkled her nose. "It sounds as if it's more trouble than it's worth. I don't think I shall bother with it once I've given my husband an heir. Do you think I should wear the white sarcenet or the jonquil silk to dinner?"

"Well?" Alessa asked, settling herself on the sofa in her sitting room. "What do you think of her?"

Simon moved toward the fireplace, reluctant to commit himself to a long discussion by taking a chair. He would have liked to avoid this conversation altogether, but he knew Alessa would pin him down sooner or later, so he had accompanied her to her sitting room when the gathering in the small saloon broke up. "Charlotte seems very agreeable," he said.

"And?" Alessa fixed him with a firm stare.

"And what?" Simon countered. "I've only known the girl for a matter of hours."

"Oh, Simon." Alessa shook her head, her dark eyes clouded with a worry Simon knew was genuine. "There's so much more to it than finding someone agreeable. It may have taken me an unconscionably long time to admit I love Harry, but—" She hesitated, staring down at her hands.

"Yes?" Simon asked. Alessa wasn't making this easy for him. He saw no need to make it easy for her.

Alessa looked up at him. "But I knew from the first that I wanted to bed him."

Simon had a shatteringly clear image of a silk-hung bed in a house in Paris and the ravishing woman lying against the sheets. "You were always impulsive," he told his sister. "I take these things more slowly."

"Then you don't find her attractive?" Alessa demanded.

Attractive? When Justine had been so close by? "Nothing of the sort," Simon said, striving for a cheerful tone. "She's very pretty." This seemed inadequate, so after a moment's pause, he added, "And refreshingly free of pretension."

"Simon, she's a child." Alessa sprang to her feet and moved to join him at the fireplace. "A likable, engaging child."

Simon smiled in spite of himself. "I'd forgotten how young eighteen is."

"I hadn't," Alessa said.

The remembered pain in his sister's eyes reminded Simon of Alessa's unfortunate first betrothal. "Don't worry," he said, laying his hand over hers where it rested on the mantel. "Whatever comes of this, I won't allow Charlotte to be hurt."

Alessa snatched her hand away. "It's not Charlotte I'm worried about. It's you."

Simon laughed. "Your concern is flattering, sister, but I think I can protect myself from likable, engaging girls of eighteen." Besides, no hurt could be as strong as the end of his affair with Justine. He would never allow himself to be so vulnerable again.

Alessa regarded him for a moment, seeing, as she frequently did, far too much. Then she turned and began rearranging the row of Chinese vases which stood upon the mantel. "Madame de Valon seems charming," she said in a conversational tone, "though not the sort of chaperone I would have expected for a girl fresh from a convent."

"What do you mean by that?" Simon demanded, bristling as he had in Paris at any slur upon Justine's character.

246

"Only that she's quite young herself," Alessa said, looking up at him with a perfect counterfeit of innocence. "And obviously she's rather a dashing sort. Gerald seems very taken with her. I gather he knew her in Paris as well."

Jealousy tightened Simon's chest as it had during the gathering in the small saloon when he watched Gerald Stratton hovering behind Justine's chair, an inane look on his face. "Yes, so it seems," Simon said, matching Alessa's tone. "It must have been before I was in Paris."

"His response is understandable, she's quite indecently beautiful. I noticed even Harry looking at her with appreciation. But it can't be easy for Marianne. She was flirting madly with Bertram Westcourt in defense."

"So I saw. I can't believe Marianne has any serious interest in Westcourt."

"Of course not,"Alessa agreed. "She's madly in love with Gerald, though I've never understood why. Whatever Gerald's relationship with Madame de Valon, I do hope he has the sense to leave it in the past."

"I doubt Gerald was ever her lover," Simon said, though he was aware of some sickening fears on this score himself. "She's not—"

"Not that sort of woman?" Alessa asked with a smile. "How very male you sound, Simon. As far as I'm concerned, a widow has a perfect right to lovers. Even a married woman does, if her husband serves her the same way. Did you ever meet the Baron de Valon?"

"No, I believe he died two years or so before I was in Paris." But Simon had heard enough to form an exceedingly low opinion of Justine's husband. He hesitated. Then, because it seemed important that Alessa be sympathetic to Justine, he added, "Armand de Valon was killed in a duel with the husband of another lady."

"Oh, dear," Alessa said with genuine sympathy. "How disagreeable for Madame de Valon. Do you think she was very much in love with him?"

"I've rarely heard her mention his name," Simon said with

perfect truth. "But I doubt her husband's infidelity came as any surprise to her. Apparently Monsieur de Valon was known for his love affairs, his monstrous bills at the tailor's and the bootmaker's, and his disastrous luck at the gaming tables."

"A paragon indeed. I hope he didn't leave his wife in straitened circumstances."

Simon glanced down into the fire. Justine had refused to discuss money, just as she had refused to take any of it from him. She had not even allowed him to give her presents more extravagant than a simple pearl brooch. "I don't know the details," he told Alessa. "She plays cards very well. She's far more skillful at them than her husband was."

"A woman as beautiful as Madame de Valon would have no difficulty finding a man to support her," Alessa said in a thoughtful voice. "But perhaps she's had her fill of marriage."

"Very likely," Simon agreed, his voice carefully stripped of emotion. Certainly Justine had not been interested in marriage with the eager young man who had had the misfortune to fall in love with her.

"Still," Alessa continued, tracing a flower pattern on one of the vases, "a woman doesn't necessarily need to marry to find a man to assist her with her expenses."

"Madame de Valon never took that way out," Simon said firmly. "Men hang about her, and that's given her—"

"An undeserved reputation for amorous dalliance?"

"Yes."

"You seem to know a great deal about her."

Realizing he had been betrayed into saying far more than he intended, Simon drew in upon himself. "Paris isn't so very large. One hears things."

Alessa abandoned the vases and looked him full in the face. "Simon, I've never seen you so transparent. Was Justine de Valon your mistress?"

"You insult her."

"Don't be absurd," Alessa said, laying a hand on his arm. "I'd hardly think the worse of her for caring for my brother.

248

But it must be fiendishly awkward for both of you. Do you want me to—?"

"God give me patience." Simon flung away from his sister and strode to the door. "No, Alessa, I don't want you to do whatever it is you were about to suggest. I don't want you to do anything. If everyone can refrain from interfering, this house party may just possibly be able to proceed in a civilized manner."

"Simon," Alessa said.

There was a note in her voice which forced Simon to turn round. "Yes?"

"Please be careful."

"Don't worry," Simon told her, his voice grimmer than he intended. "Tassios know how to take care of themselves."

Justine hurried across the forecourt, feeling invigorated by the fresh, chill morning air and her ride through the Bedfordshire countryside. And by an hour with Minette. At the memory of her daughter's tiny hand closing about her own, Justine felt herself smile. Minette smiled spontaneously now and babbled all sorts of interesting combinations of sounds, though nothing Justine could yet convince herself was *"Maman."* Just before they'd left France, Minette had rolled over for the first time. Justine hoped her daughter didn't reach another important milestone while she was away at Moresby.

As she pushed open a side door to the house and moved into the dimmer light and staler air of the corridor, Justine forced herself to confront the reality of her situation. Even if Simon and Charlotte did not reach an understanding, sooner or later her duties as a chaperone would come to an end. What was she to do then? Remain in England? The idea had a certain appeal. Since Minette's birth, Justine had felt a yearning for the home of her own childhood. And perhaps the reputation she had acquired in France would not follow her across the Channel. It might be easier to pass Minette off as her ward.

But it was eight years since Justine had lived in England, and there were no friends or relatives to whom she could turn. Her father had died not long after her marriage. She had already decided it would be impossible to turn to her aunt and uncle. They had advised against the marriage to Armand, and it would be difficult for Justine to admit her mistake. More important, she doubted she could convince them that Minette was the daughter of a friend. To tell them the truth was out of the question. They would never understand. Besides, they had two young daughters of their own, now both on the marriage mart. If there was gossip about Minette, if the stories Justine had faced in Paris did reach London, the girls' chances might be affected. No, in good conscience, Justine knew she could not turn to her relatives.

But perhaps the most telling objection of all to remaining in England was the fact that Simon was here. Seeing him again made Justine want to stay, and that in turn made her realize how dangerous such a course might be.

Yet if she returned to France, what then? She could resume her old life in Paris, maintaining a precarious existence with her skill at cards, but that would hardly give Minette a secure future. She could stay in the country in the dilapidated chateau—a farmhouse, really—that her husband had left her. That might do while Minette was a child, but how was she to provide the girl with a dowry and the respectable background she would need to make her way in the world?

On this bleak note, Justine reached the great hall. She was crossing the stone floor to the archway that led to the staircase when a voice arrested her. "Good morning."

The familiar timbre made her shiver. It was Simon. Justine turned round to see him standing in an open doorway, impeccably dressed, as always, a newspaper held in one hand. Her heart seemed to do a mad sort of dance. "Good morning, Prince." She had decided formality would be best between them.

"Out for a morning ride?"

"Yes." Justine was grateful for the shadows in the hall. This was the worst time to find herself facing Simon, with her visit to Minette so fresh in her memory. "The countryside is lovely. I've missed England."

"I've come to think of it as home myself." Simon hesitated a moment. "Could I have a word with you in private? There are things we should discuss."

Had he been watching for her from the window? Last night at dinner they had been seated at opposite ends of the long table, and Simon had made no effort to seek her out later in the drawing room. Justine had given him a wide berth, feeling it should be left to him to decide if they needed to speak alone.

Seeing him in a crowd had been painful enough. A private interview was bound to be wrenching. Steeling herself for what lay ahead, Justine moved to the doorway where he was standing. The skirt of her riding habit brushed against his legs as she passed him. She felt the casual contact run the whole length of her body.

They were in a sitting room done up in shades of yellow, no doubt one of many such chambers at Moresby. It was smaller than Justine would have liked. She moved to an upholstered chair on the opposite side of the room, as far away from Simon as she could contrive. When she had seated herself, she drew a breath and looked up at him, trying to gauge his mood. Was he still angry? It was impossible to tell. He wore the look of detached formality which she had seen him adopt before, but never with her. That he had placed such a barrier between them hurt more than an outburst of rage.

"I'm sorry," she said, wanting to make one thing clear. "It must have been terribly awkward for you, not knowing I was to accompany Charlotte. I assumed the Comte de Chambeau's letter would have reached you before we arrived."

"A natural misapprehension." His tone was neutral and polite.

Justine fidgeted with her riding crop, then forced herself to place it on a nearby table. "I didn't know Charlotte was coming to England in order to meet you until the night before

251

we sailed. By that time it was too late to make other arrangements."

"You needn't concern yourself. I trust we are both equal to the situation." Simon moved to a chair, closer than Justine would have liked. "But I did think we should speak to ensure that there will be no uncomfortable moments later." He folded the newspaper and set it aside. "I take it Charlotte knows nothing of our—past relationship?"

"Good God, what do you take me for?" Justine exclaimed. "I would not speak of it to anyone, and certainly not to her."

"I did not think you would. I only wanted to be sure—" He broke off. For a moment she thought she glimpsed a trace of the old Simon, but the moment was quickly gone. "Do you think Charlotte and I are suited?" he asked, leaning back in his chair.

Justine swallowed. "I think that is a matter for you and Charlotte to decide." She gripped her hands together, her nails digging through the leather of her gloves. "I am very fond of Charlotte and I would like to see her happily settled."

"With me?" Simon's face was unreadable, like that of a card player determined not to betray his hand.

Pain lanced through her, as sharp as that she had felt on the day she sent Simon away. She looked steadily at him. "If that is what you both want."

"Is it what Charlotte wants?"

Justine hesitated, thinking of Charlotte's forthright views on marriage. "Charlotte sees marriage as her passport to independence. But she is very young. I do not want her to be hurt."

"She will not be, if it is in my power to prevent it. I have no wish to cause anyone pain."

The mask was broken and his eyes showed the pain of their own parting. Justine had an impulse to put her arms around him. She clutched the arms of her chair to restrain herself. "Simon—"

"It is a risk of youth." The mask was once again in place.

"You're right, of course. Fortunately, Charlotte seems a sensible girl."

"Yes. But she is very much alone in the world. Her father wants her off his hands and wishes her to be married as soon as possible. I feel responsible for her."

Simon raised his brows. "You fear she will ruin her future by consenting to be my wife?"

"I fear she will decide her future too hastily."

Simon's eyes seemed to grow a little less cold. "I know that Charlotte is young," he said in a gentler voice. "I will try to be careful, for both of us."

"Thank you," Justine said, sincerely grateful.

There was little more to say. Painful as the discussion had been, now that it was at an end, Justine found herself wanting to prolong it. She got to her feet quickly and picked up her riding crop. "I should go up and change for breakfast."

Simon rose. Justine thought he was going to allow her to leave without further conversation, but as she moved past him, he reached out and seized her wrist in a grip that shook her to her soul. "Why did you send me away?"

The words were spoken with raw torment. All the feeling that had been suppressed during their previous exchange now blazed from his eyes. She was so close she could feel the warmth of his breath. "Because it was time."

"I would have married you."

A tremor went through her. She would never forget the day he had asked her to be his wife. His proposal had been so unexpected and so bittersweet. It had meant the world to her that he had asked, but she had known she could not possibly accept him. "You must now be very grateful that you did not," she told him, pulling her hand away from his clasp.

"Had you come to detest marriage so much?" Simon asked, his dark gaze still holding her own. "I would have done everything in my power to make you happy."

"Simon." Almost, Justine yielded to the temptation to lay her hand against his face. "You were young. I was your first woman."

"I loved you," he said in a quiet tone which tore at her heart.

Justine forced herself not to look away. "Young men like you don't marry women like me."

"You think that mattered to me?" he demanded fiercely.

The weight of her years in society pressed down on her shoulders. Some things could not help but matter, even to a man like Simon. "Not then," she said. "But one day you would have known you'd made a mistake."

"You can't—" Simon checked whatever he had been about to say. "Forgive me," he said, his voice carefully controlled. "You should not have to justify your reasons for not wishing to marry me. I will not embarrass you further."

Justine managed to smile. "I trust for the next few weeks we can avoid embarrassing each other."

He smiled in response, a sweet, genuine smile which brought a lump to her throat. "It seems the least we can do."

The smiles faded into a moment of awkward silence. Just as she was about to leave once again, Simon said, "Do you plan to stay in England?"

"I will remain with Charlotte as long as she needs a chaperone," Justine told him, knowing he understood as well as she did that this might mean until Simon and Charlotte were married.

"Of course." He smiled again, but this time the strain showed. "Then there's no more to say, is there?"

Justine thought of all that she longed to tell him. "No," she said. "Nothing at all."

Three

It was Charlotte's idea to take a turn around the room. It was her third evening at Moresby and she had lost all trace of shyness. When the gentlemen rejoined the ladies after dinner, she turned to Simon as a matter of course. She did not beg or simper, nor was she coy about the matter. She asked him straight out if he would join her.

Simon looked down at the soft honey-colored hair of the woman he might ask to be his wife. This directness was her most endearing trait. In fact, it was her only endearing trait. Simon shut his mind firmly against this traitorous thought. There was a great deal to be said for directness in a marriage.

"I do so hate to sit still," Charlotte said. She spoke in French, as she did whenever they were alone. "When I was at the convent, we were forever sitting or standing or walking in straight lines with our eyes looking at the ground. I think the sisters were afraid we might see a man and die of fright."

"Perhaps they were afraid you might see a man and die of joy."

Charlotte stopped abruptly and turned round to face him. "Prince, you are being naughty." She tried to look stern, but her mouth quivered with suppressed laughter. "Or else you are teasing me."

"I would never dream of teasing you," Simon said, with what he hoped was suitable gravity.

"Not that I would mind if you did, for I would only tease you back." Charlotte resumed walking, wielding her fan vigorously. The proper use of a fan, she had told him, was a matter for instruction at the convent. Simon suspected she had embroidered on the sisters' teachings, for there was nothing demure in the way she held the delicate bit of painted ivory. "I would have been very pleased to see a man now and then," she went on, reverting to her earlier comment. "Not that they are particularly beautiful to behold." She gave him an appraising look. "Though I must admit you are pleasant enough to look at," she concluded. "But one can't deny that men are different. And when everything one sees is so tediously the same, day after day, one longs for variety."

"And do I provide sufficient variety?"

"Oh, you do very well. I've never talked so much to a man before, except to *Papa*. Actually, I never talked very much to him. He likes women to listen. So I've not had a great deal of experience, and I'm immensely glad I have you to practice on."

"I'm happy you find me useful" did not seem an appropriate retort, so Simon held his tongue. Charlotte took no notice of his silence. "And it's a very good thing I do," she continued, "for none of the other gentlemen seems inclined to talk to me. Except Lord Milverton, of course—he's very pleasant, but he's much too old, so he doesn't count—and two or three others in the same case. Really, except for you and Viscount Westcourt and Georgiana Dudley's young man, there are scarcely any eligible young men about."

Simon forbore to point out that she had not been invited to Moresby to meet a large number of eligible young men. Only one. He looked back to see Georgiana, Harry's younger sister, in earnest conversation with the man she was to marry in the spring. Georgiana was very much in love. As was Simon's closest friend, Peter Carne, who was now on his wedding journey. Simon felt very much alone. All his friends seemed to be getting married, and all seemed blissfully happy.

He turned back to Charlotte and made a vague gesture that

encompassed the house and the company and the awkward way in which they were thrown together. "I'm sorry. Are you very bored?"

"Bored? No, I don't think so. There's so much to learn. But I did hope that tonight we might have some dancing."

"I'll ask Alessa. If we can find someone to play for us . . ." Charlotte's eyes were suddenly alight. "Oh, yes, the very thing. I know all the steps, but I've never danced with a man before, except our dancing master, and he was too short to be a proper partner, though he was a great dandy. And if we can't find anyone to play the piano, perhaps your sister can bring out the card tables. Justine is very good at cards. She's been teaching me how to remember what cards have been played and how not to give away what I hold in my hand. It's so much more fun when you can win. I adore cards."

This was something Simon had learned about his possible future bride in the past three days. This, and the fact that she was impatient and outspoken and of a generally cheerful disposition. And woefully young. Of course, she would grow up. She could be molded. No, not that, the idea of molding anyone was distasteful. But she needed direction, and Simon was not sure it was a task he wanted to undertake.

They had reached the end of the room. The rose drawing room at Moresby was a long, high-ceilinged chamber. It would do very well for the St. Valentine's Eve ball Alessa was planning in four days' time, but now, with a smaller company gathered at the other end, it served only to heighten his sense of isolation. He was conscious of the chill in this part of the room, the warmth of the fire not reaching so far. "Shall we go back?" he asked, offering Charlotte his arm.

He could see now how the others were arranged. Alessa was seated on a sofa near the fireplace, dispensing coffee and conversation to a cluster of the women guests. Harry, standing a little apart with some of the older men, would be discussing farming or politics. Bertram Westcourt had drawn up a chair beside Marianne. He held an open book in his hand and seemed to be reading aloud. Simon suspected it was poetry.

A number of the other men were gathered around a second sofa on which two women were seated. One was Miss Crosbie, the daughter of one of the neighboring families that had been invited to augment the company that evening. The other was Justine.

"You've noticed it, too?" Charlotte asked. "How they hover around her. She's very attractive, isn't she, for an older woman? Well, she's not so very old, but she's very experienced."

"Experienced? You mean that she's been married." Simon did not want to continue this particular conversation.

"Oh, that. Yes, of course. But she's had lovers, too, don't you think? More than one, I suspect. Watch how she stares into their eyes, as though the man she's addressing is the most important man on earth. She's very good at it. I expect to learn a great deal from her."

"Don't you think—" Simon stopped, aware that he was about to say something that bordered on the priggish. There was really no way to tell your prospective wife that you did not want her to be a copy of your mistress. What an innocent Charlotte was, thinking that she could make herself into a Justine. He didn't want a Justine. He didn't want an experienced woman. He wanted—he wanted a wife. But between that vague requirement and the forthright girl whose hand rested lightly on his arm, there seemed to be only the dimmest connection.

"Think what?" Charlotte prompted him.

"Don't you think we should hurry and ask my sister about the dancing? Lady Windham is an excellent pianist. I'm sure she'd be happy to oblige."

Charlotte turned to him with a radiant face. "Oh, Simon, what is it the English say?" She frowned, seeking to form the English words. "You're a jolly good sort."

It was, Simon thought, some sort of recommendation for husbandhood.

* * *

After a night of fitful sleep, Simon rose early and went for a solitary ride. The evening before had turned from a merely pleasant occasion into a rousing, even raucous success. There had been at least eight couples on the floor, and sometimes more. Charlotte had proved a vigorous dancer, with energy and a sense of rhythm taking the place of lightness and grace. Those belonged to Justine, who, with Charlotte and Marianne, never lacked for partners.

Simon had danced with all the women but Justine, even urging his sister to the floor, but he could not avoid coming face-to-face with Charlotte's cousin, nor avoid her eyes and her rueful smile. He could not help remembering that the first time he had seen her had been on the dance floor, at a party at the Hôtel de Fontenay, and that from that moment on he had seen no one else.

Simon spurred his horse and cleared a hedge that bordered the home farm, his mount's hooves crackling the frozen earth. The hedge was leafless, the trees bare, the sky a dull, uniform gray. The chill in the air was enough to make his teeth ache. But not enough to make him forget.

He could not remember his younger self without pain. He had tried to put the memories behind him; God above, how he had tried. He thought he had succeeded until an ill fortune brought Justine in his path again.

She had been his first woman. The first he had desired, in a more than generally carnal way. The first he had pursued with an intense singleness of purpose, knowing that now it was time, now it was right. The first he had loved.

It had been a heady experience, those months of autumn in a city made magical by her presence. It was the only time in his life Simon had felt truly alive, free of the bonds of family and princehood and obligation, free to pour out his soul into the keeping of this wondrous woman. Justine had been a warm and generous lover, taking him easily into her bed as though she, too, knew how right it was that they should be together.

Simon pulled up his mount and sat perfectly still, willing

the memories to come again. Nothing moved in the bleak winter landscape save his horse's breath and his own, rising visible in the frigid air. A small animal scrabbled in the underbrush. The horse started. Simon gave him a reassuring pat, then set him into an easy canter along the stream that ran a half-mile north of the house.

The memories were not friendly. He tried to recall the way Justine looked when she was tender or amused or drunk with passion, but all he could see was her face on the day she had sent him away. Fool, he had thought it would last forever. He had wanted to marry her, but she had refused him. Simon, she had said, her voice warm and gentle, you don't have to marry me. Women do these things. It doesn't mean . . .

It doesn't mean anything. That's what she should have said. Yes, we've loved one another, but love is no more than temporary pleasure. Didn't you know? Haven't you learned?

Simon turned his horse with a vicious tug at the reins he instantly regretted. Murmuring soothing words to the animal, he set him toward the house. Oh, yes, he'd learned. Justine had completed his education. He'd come back to England knowing who he was and how his life must be lived. And just how far he could trust his own heart.

Simon entered the house thinking of hot coffee and a very large breakfast. A solitary meal, with the newspapers and perhaps Harry for company. But the sound of voices coming from the breakfast parlor told him that most of the company was up and prepared for the day. Simon decided that he was not so very hungry. He did not want to see his sharp-eyed sister. He did not want to see his implacably cheerful Charlotte. He particularly did not want to see Justine.

He turned instead to the morning parlor, a small, quiet room cheerful with sunshine on those days when the sun deigned to appear. He would ring for coffee and forget the papers.

Unfortunately, the parlor was not empty, but its sole occupant seemed in a mood to match his own. Simon was fond of Harry's cousin, Marianne. A restful woman with very little to say on her own account. They would have coffee together and say nothing at all.

"Good morning," Simon said, closing the door behind him. Startled by his voice, Marianne turned to look at him and he saw that her face was washed with tears. He moved quickly to the sofa on which she was sitting. "My dear girl, whatever is the matter?"

"Nothing." She sat up very straight, gulped, and then burst into tears. "But it's so unfair!" Her words were muffled by her hands, which now covered her face.

"I'm sure it is." Simon sat beside her and pressed his handkerchief into her hand. "Why don't you tell me about it?"

Marianne mopped her face, blew her nose, and crumpled the handkerchief into a ball. "Thank you, Simon. I knew you'd understand."

"But I don't, actually. What is it that's so unfair? Was someone unkind?"

"No. No one at all. Only Gerald." The tears threatened again and she mastered them. "My husband."

Simon heard Charlotte's voice telling him that she intended to learn a great deal from Justine's experience and remembered how he had swallowed his retort. Gerald had been pursuing Justine shamelessly the last three days, but there was no way Simon could tell Marianne what he thought of her husband's behavior. He chose his words with caution. "I understand that's a hazard of married life."

"Oh," Marianne said in a small voice.

"Not that Gerald or anyone else has a right to be unkind," Simon said hastily. "Was he scolding you?"

Marianne's face flushed with color. "He was threatening me. What am I supposed to be, his slave? Can't I be allowed to speak to whom I wish? Can't I be allowed to make my own friends? How can he say that I humiliated him? He scarcely speaks to me when we're in company and hasn't much to say when we're alone, but it's perfectly clear what kind of woman he prefers. He was making an absolute ass of himself over her last night. They knew each other in Paris years and years ago, and he seems to think that gives him a right to . . . Well, perhaps they *are* friends, but if he can have a particular friend, why can't I?"

It was the longest speech Simon had ever heard her make. "It's Bertram Westcourt, isn't it?"

"Yes, of course it's Bertram. I mean, Lord Westcourt. He's a thoroughly respectable young man, and he's invited everywhere. We were forever seeing him in London. He has such beautiful manners. And he's so interesting to talk to. Do you know, he actually likes to know what a woman thinks about things. And he's so—" Marianne broke off, suddenly confused.

"Well favored?"

Marianne blushed. "Well, that too. Not that that's important. What I really like about him is his mind."

"Of course," Simon said gravely.

"I count him as one of my dearest friends," Marianne went on. "Or I would, if I were allowed to receive him. Gerald makes the most awful fuss whenever he calls. I don't know why, for there are always dozens of other people about. Of course, there was the time . . . I sometimes think Gerald has a very nasty turn of mind. It's not as if there's anything of that sort between us—between me and Lord Westcourt, I mean. I have always behaved with the greatest propriety, but it would serve Gerald right if I hadn't. Didn't." Marianne fumbled for the handkerchief and blew her nose again. "What's sauce for the goose . . ."

"Quite." Simon could understand infidelity in marriage, though it saddened him to see it. Couples could grow apart. But Marianne and Gerald had been married less than two years. "I'm sure Gerald loves you."

"Love? Gerald loves his possessions. His horses, his carriage, his boots—he's very proud of his boots."

"And his wife. Though I suspect the problem is that your husband sees you as a possession and not as a woman."

Marianne's eyes widened. "Oh, Simon, how clever you are. That's it exactly." She looked down at her hands and twisted her wedding ring round her finger. "But I'm not a very valued possession. Perhaps if I were a different kind of woman . . ."

Simon knew that she was thinking of Justine. There was no comparison between them—Justine was vibrant where Marianne was pallid—but Marianne was very pretty and she was more than Gerald deserved. "You're an attractive woman just as you are, and your husband is a fool if he doesn't see it."

Marianne sighed. "Then I'm afraid he's a fool. Simon—" She colored. "Simon, what is it that men like? In a woman?"

Masses of fire-tinged hair. Wide, blue-gray eyes. A generous mouth. A receptive body. Warmth and tenderness and laughter. Any man would want Justine. But he could hardly say this to Marianne, who was pretty enough in her own way to be anything a man would want if she were not so shy nor so—unawakened. And that must be at least in part her husband's fault. But Simon could not say that, either.

He was struggling for an answer when the door opened and Justine entered the room. Simon stood up at once, his feelings veering wildly between joy and despair. Then he remembered how Justine had smiled at Gerald when they were dancing last night and realized he ought to be angry. He felt his face congeal into an impersonal mask.

"I'm so sorry," Justine said. "I didn't mean to intrude."

"Not at all. I was just leaving." Simon turned to Marianne. "If there's anything I can do, don't hesitate to come to me," he said in a low voice. Then, grateful for his double escape, he went out of the room, leaving the two women behind him.

Justine felt his sudden departure like a slap across the face. They had agreed to be civilized, but Simon wanted nothing to do with her. Not that she should have expected more. She had hurt his pride, and he did not take rejection lightly. She wished for the thousandth time that there had been some other way for them to part.

Marianne Stratton had left the sofa and moved to the window, where she stood looking out at a grove of yew trees. Justine knew that she had interrupted a scene of some emotional intimacy, but she would not embarrass Marianne by leaving suddenly, as though she had noticed it. "I confess I came in here to escape the others for a short time," she said. "I'd forgot how exhausting house parties can be. All that enforced jollity. Perhaps you were seeking a temporary refuge too."

Marianne turned round, surprise on her face. "Oh yes, that's it," she said. "That's it exactly. So tiring."

"But if you'd rather be alone . . ."

"No. Oh no, not at all. I'd be glad of the company." She seemed about to say more, but looked confused and retreated hastily to the sofa. "Won't you sit down?"

Justine selected a chair that did not quite face the sofa. Its placement invited conversation but did not demand it. Marianne seemed to have something on her mind. Justine suspected that it might have to do with Gerald's attentions to herself.

"Madame de Valon," Marianne began.

"Yes?" Justine said after a moment. Gerald's wife was a very pretty young woman, but she was irresolute and obviously unhappy.

"It's so strange. Your being English, I mean. You seem so very French."

Justine smiled. "I've lived abroad for a number of years. But I assure you, I'm English to the core."

"You aren't like anyone I know," Marianne insisted. "Your clothes, your scent, the way you smile, the way you walk and move your hands. I'm sure you've learned a great deal living in France. In Paris." Her voice was wistful.

Justine felt a moment of sympathy for the young woman's vague longings. "I've learned nothing you couldn't learn as well in London," she assured her. "One big city is very like another."

"Oh, but I'm sure that's not true. My husband has always talked about Paris in a way he would never talk about London." Marianne twisted the wedding ring on her finger. "You knew him there, didn't you?"

"Yes, we met occasionally when he was in Paris. That was before he was married," Justine added, hoping that Marianne would understand her message. Gerald had courted her assiduously during his few weeks' stay in the French capital and had been a thorough bore, but none of it had anything to do with his relationship with his wife. Unfortunately, Justine thought, he was pursuing her in the same way at Moresby, and now he was a married man. She would have to be careful, for Marianne's sake as well as her own.

"He admires you tremendously," Marianne said in a determined voice. "Anyone would. You're a very beautiful woman, and you've had a great deal of experience . . . I mean, you've been married, and . . ." She made a vague gesture. "And all that."

Justine forbore to point out that Marianne could also be accounted an experienced woman as far as marriage was concerned. The point, she knew, was in the "all that." The goose. Gerald's wife was trying to say that she had had lovers. Which was true, though it was none of Marianne's affair. Marianne must be screwing up her courage to ask if her husband had been one of them.

But Marianne proved her wrong. In a bright, hurried voice which suggested that she was frightened by her own boldness, she said, "They're so much more civilized about these things in France, aren't they? I mean, they understand that it's quite natural for women to want to choose their friends just as men do. And there's no reason for anyone to get upset if a woman forms a particular attachment to another man. Is there?"

Justine remembered the glow on Marianne's face while Bertram Westcourt was reciting poetry. The poor child was starved for admiration. "I certainly see no reason why a woman should not enjoy conversing with a man other than her husband," Justine said cautiously.

"But it's so much easier for a man, isn't it?" Marianne leaned forward with an air of throwing caution to the winds. "I mean, they can come and go as they please without an escort, and no one thinks twice if they disappear of an evening or don't get home until dawn. Whereas a woman . . . How *do* French women manage these things?"

There was now no mistaking her meaning. But Justine was hardly in a position to counsel Marianne on the unwisdom of taking this particular path. And perhaps it was only a matter of curiosity. "A lady would think twice about calling unescorted on a gentleman," she pointed out. "It invites comment. But there is certainly no reason she cannot receive her friends in her own home."

"But if she wants a private conversation. I mean, her husband might be home in the evening, or he might come home during the course of it."

"Then she would receive her friends in the afternoon. Or in the late morning."

Marianne gave a start of surprise. "In the morning?" She glanced at the window as if to gauge just how much light was entering the room. "I would never have thought . . ."

"It's not uncommon," Justine said, when the silence threatened to grow between them. It was a pity that women were confined to so many kinds of darkness. "A woman may even converse with her husband at such an hour," she added, thinking to expand Marianne's understanding of the marital relation. Perhaps that had something to do with the obvious difficulty she was experiencing with her husband.

"Oh!" Marianne stood up abruptly. "I mean, oh, of course. This has been a most interesting conversation, Madame de Valon. I am so glad we have had this little talk." And without waiting for a reply, she walked quickly to the door and left the room.

Justine sighed. First Charlotte, and now Marianne Stratton. Both such innocents, she thought without censure. She had been innocent herself once. And her young self would have welcomed—not advice, no, never that—but information. She could have avoided some painful surprises. And it would have made her choices easier.

I should set up a school, she thought. Young ladies of quality tutored in avoiding the pitfalls of social intercourse. How

266

to get what you want without incurring censure. Or, all the things your mother would never dream of telling you.

Justine laughed at her own folly. She was older now. And experienced, as both young women had been at pains to point out. And wiser, at least, wise enough to not interfere in the lives of others. She stretched, got to her feet, and moved toward the door. She should see if Charlotte was in need of her company.

The first she knew of the paper on the ground was the harsh whisper of sound as her foot brushed against it. She bent down and picked it up. It was a half-sheet, folded and refolded into a small packet that might fit into one's sleeve. Marianne must have dropped it in her hasty progress across the room.

Justine debated taking it to her. She might welcome having it back. Or she might be embarrassed by having it called to her attention. Or it might not be hers at all. In which case . . . Confessing to a shameless curiosity about her fellow guests, Justine unfolded the note. It must indeed be Marianne's, for though it bore no salutation, it was signed, with a number of flourishes, by her adoring Bertram.

The silly fool. He was proposing a tryst, in of all places the folly at the far end of the grounds. In the dead of winter. Judging from his prose, he could at least supply sufficient heat for both of them. Enough for a stolen kiss or two, though scarcely enough for more. Justine rode every morning to the inn three miles down the road and could testify to the bone-chilling cold of February in Bedfordshire. It would give pause to the most ardent of lovers.

Oh, well, it was hardly her affair. Justine carefully refolded the note and wished she had not given in to the temptation to read it. Tucking it into the bosom of her dress, she left the room and went in search of Marianne. Gerald's wife would be frantic at its disappearance. She would have to find a discreet way to return it to her.

* * *

The men spent the morning outdoors, some on horseback, some on foot. Simon went with Lord Milverton to inspect an improved drainage system of which Milverton was very proud. The women were left to their own devices. Justine sat with Charlotte reviewing fashion plates. Though she had been provided with a substantial wardrobe prior to her visit, Charlotte had decided that her clothes were much too youthful, and though well enough for the country, would never do for London. Justine tried to put a rein on Charlotte's enthusiasm for crimson satin and egret feathers. When Charlotte could not be swayed, she was forced to give her a lesson on the difference between taste and ostentation. To her credit, Charlotte listened with every appearance of taking her mentor's words to heart.

The discussion of fashion drew in some of the other women in the party, including Marianne Stratton, who seemed to have acquired a new sense of purpose since her morning tête-à-tête with Justine. But when the talk turned to servants and children, Charlotte developed a sudden longing for activity. She begged Justine to walk with her in the grounds. They were wilder, she said, and a good deal more exciting than the stiff rows of poplars that had bordered the convent.

Wrapped in warm cloaks, they explored the stream that ran behind the house, then turned to follow a gently sloping piece of ground that led to a ruined building whose white marble columns and broken roof could be glimpsed beyond a stand of hazel trees. Moresby's folly, Lady Milverton had explained, when she'd pointed it out on the day of their arrival, built on the whim of a Milverton wife sometime in the last century. A temple of Venus. Bertram Westcourt had made an appropriate choice for his appointed rendezvous. Justine wondered if Marianne would keep it.

They stopped to look at the view below. "Shall we go down?" Charlotte asked.

"Not today," Justine said, pretending to a weariness she did not feel. "I think it's time we returned to the house."

"You can't be tired already." Charlotte's unbounded energy

made Justine feel far older than her twenty-six years. "Oh, very well," Charlotte continued, falling in step beside her.

They had not gone more than a dozen paces when Charlotte stopped again and pointed to a man striding across the ground in the distance. "Look. Isn't that Sir Gerald? *He's* going toward the folly. If I run down and meet him, perhaps he'll show it to me. He can bring me back to the house later."

"No," Justine said sharply. It *was* Gerald, and in a very few minutes he was going to walk in on his wife's tryst with another man. "Charlotte, you must go to the folly by yourself. I'll head off Sir Gerald."

"But—"

"Lady Stratton may be inside. If she is, and she's not alone, you must send her companion away. Wait with her for a few minutes, then bring her back to the house. If anyone sees you, you've been exploring the folly together."

"Oh." A look of great delight spread across Charlotte's face.

"Don't run. You'll call attention to yourself. But hurry."

Justine gave Charlotte a moment to get away, then turned to intercept Gerald, waving one arm high over her head to catch his attention. "Halloo," she called.

He checked his stride, looked round, then came rapidly toward her. "I'm so glad I found you," Justine said, walking toward him with a pronounced limp. "It's the stupidest thing. I turned my ankle—no, not seriously," she added, seeing the look of alarm on his face. "But I'd be so grateful if you'd give me your arm to help me back to the house."

"My dear Justine." He had progressed to the use of her given name when he was in Paris, though she had told him their acquaintance did not warrant such intimacy. "Of course I'll help you. No, by God, I'll carry you." He came toward her as though he would scoop her up in his arms.

Justine retreated. "No, no, I assure you, it's not necessary."

"Perhaps I'd better look at it." He dropped to one knee and placed his hand on her skirt.

Justine moved back again. "Your arm, Sir Gerald, that's all I want. If I might just lean on you a bit."

Gerald rose reluctantly and held out his arm. "You shouldn't be walking alone."

"But I love being out of doors. As it seems you do yourself."

"We have so much in common." He placed his free hand over the hand she rested on his sleeve. The movement brought him round so that the folly behind them was in his line of sight. "Ho, there's a woman going into that odd little temple. Is that where you were headed?"

"No, I find such things tedious." Justine pressed his arm to turn his attention back to herself.

"By George, so do I. I say, are you all right? Perhaps you should rest a bit. There's a bench over there, behind the privet hedge."

It was a transparent ploy, but it would take them out of sight of the folly. "What a very good idea." Justine allowed Gerald to lead her to the bench, which she found was more secluded than she would have wished. No matter, they would stay for only a few minutes.

"I'm so glad to have this chance to speak to you alone," Gerald said. "There always seem to be so many people about."

They were sitting very close. Justine moved down a little on the bench. "It's a large party. And a very pleasant one, don't you think? Are you looking forward to the St. Valentine's Eve ball?"

"Oh, hang the ball and hang the party. Justine!" Gerald slid closer to her, his thigh pressing her own, and seized her hands in his. "Justine, I adore you!"

Justine laughed. "Hardly that. You may admire me, if you like, but that is all I will permit." She tried to pull her hands away, but he clasped them tighter and drew them against his chest. His face came down to hers. The devil. He was going to kiss her.

Justine turned her head away and felt a moment of intense embarrassment. Two gentlemen of the company had stopped not twenty feet away and were staring at them. One was their host, Lord Milverton. He, at least, would be sensible about the matter. But the other was Simon. His mouth was clamped in an uncompromising line, and there was a deep furrow between his brows. Justine met his gaze and embarrassment turned to despair. He was furious.

Four

Simon knew that Gerald had been paying more than common attention to Justine. He had never thought that Justine would encourage him. But there was no mistaking the position in which they had been found, nor Justine's embarrassment at their presence. Damnation. He had known the woman had lovers. He had at least credited her with taste.

Harry waved cheerfully at the couple and turned away as though he had seen nothing more than two of his guests enjoying the meager sunshine of a February afternoon. Simon followed his brother-in-law, aware of a burning anger in his chest. He had no claim on Justine. What she did with her life was her own affair, not his. But in this case it was. She was hurting Marianne, and Marianne had come to him for help.

He must speak to Justine. The thought of forcing her to confront her own perfidy was immensely satisfying. Or perhaps, Simon admitted, trying to be honest with himself, he merely wanted to be in her company, to open old wounds and revel in the pain her presence caused him.

Simon made his excuses to Harry and went back to the house, where he informed the footman on duty in the hall that he would be in the library and would be grateful if Madame de Valon would meet with him there on her return. He spent the next quarter-hour in a fury of impatience, for once taking no pleasure in the tiers of books that filled the walls up to the high plaster ceiling. Why did she still linger in Gerald's company? The woman was shameless.

He had thought of a dozen ways of beginning the conversation, but when the door opened at last, he could remember none of them. He watched Justine remove her cloak and lay it over a chair. She stood, hands clasped loosely before her, and regarded him with a grave expression. Her color was high, but the cold could account for that. There was no trace of embarrassment on her face, no consciousness of wrongdoing. Her hair, freed of the confines of her hood, fell in glorious abandon about her face. She was shallow and self-seeking, but heaven defend him, she was beautiful.

Simon's anger flared anew. "How could you do it?" he blurted out.

"Do what, Prince?" she said coolly.

She was going to brazen it out. "Gerald Stratton, madam. Or have you forgot the matter so soon?"

"Sir Gerald and I are acquainted. He gave me his arm to return to the house."

"He gave you a good deal more than that. And you welcomed it. I know what I saw."

"You saw what you wished to see. A common failing, but I did not expect it of you. You used to have more discrimination."

"As did you," Simon retorted, stung by her words. "I was once proud to be your—" He broke off. He would not say it.

Justine's face flushed with color. Good. He had at least broken through her reserve. Her breathing quickened and she turned her head away. "Simon, you are a fool. Sir Gerald means nothing to me."

The admission made it worse. She was not in love with Stratton, yet she dallied with him. A meaningless flirtation. Perhaps more than a flirtation, but meaningless nonetheless. Like their own romance. A transitory pleasure that did not engage the heart. Not Justine's heart. "Sir Gerald means something to Marianne," Simon informed her. "God knows why, save that he *is* her husband. Have you forgot that, too? Does the ruin of a marriage lie so lightly on your conscience?"

Justine looked back at him. She opened her mouth to speak, then apparently thought better of it. After a moment, she said, "Sir Gerald has not been a good husband to his wife, but I am not responsible for his behavior. If you wish to complain of it, complain to him. I wish Lady Stratton no harm."

"You have an odd way of showing it, madam."

"If I do, Prince, it is none of your concern. You have no cause to question my behavior. You have no right."

"I have every right—" Simon broke off, aware that he had none at all. "I have every right," he continued in a more temperate tone, "to be concerned about the welfare of a friend."

"Lady Stratton is fortunate in your friendship." Justine turned away and gathered up her cloak. When she reached the door, she looked back at him. "I will govern my behavior as I choose. Good day, Your Excellency."

The door closed behind her with a loud click that had the tone of finality. Simon knew that the cords that had once bound them together were severed at last.

Or they had never existed. The attachment had been all on his side. Justine had played him for a fool. No, if he was honest, he would admit that she had never pretended to feel for him what he had felt for her. She had tried to tell him so, but he had refused to listen. Love was a treacherous companion. It made one deaf and blind.

Simon strode to the window and pushed aside the heavy burgundy drape. It was a bleak day. The final traces of sun had disappeared, but below the window, a few hardy snowdrops defied the absence of warmth and light. Life cried out to be heard. Winter was here, but it bore the possibilities of spring. Simon felt the tide of his anger recede. It was time to forget, time to marry and make children.

The decision taken, Simon felt an immediate lightening of spirit. There was no need to wait. He had decided some weeks since that he should take a wife, and now one was at hand. He left the library and went in search of Charlotte. She was in the small saloon, not alone, as he had hoped, but surrounded by six or seven of the other women guests. Justine was nowhere in sight.

The ladies were about to organize a card table. Simon was welcomed with cries of delight and invited to join them. He declined and reminded Charlotte that he had promised to show her the portrait gallery in the old part of the house. "Now?" Charlotte asked, a frown of exasperation marring her youthful face. Simon remembered that she was very fond of cards.

"If it's inconvenient . . ." he said, his tone making it clear that it would be inconvenient for him if she did not agree. Perhaps she recognized something of his purpose, for she stood up at once and said she would be delighted to go with him.

"You never told me anything about pictures," Charlotte said, as they climbed the broad golden oak stairs. It was an observation, not a complaint.

"If I didn't, I should have. Do you like painting?"

"Not especially."

The light from the mullioned windows on the stairwell fell across Charlotte's face. Simon thought she might grow up to be a rather attractive woman. He smiled at her. "I do, but these aren't particularly good. Mostly generations of Dudleys. Harry's family. No one goes up to the gallery. It's a good place to be quiet."

Charlotte gave him an appraising look. "A good place for us to continue our acquaintance?"

"Yes," Simon said shortly. He did not intend to make a declaration on the stairs and did not want her to force his hand.

They walked in silence to the end of the first-floor corridor, climbed another flight of stairs, and emerged into a long, dark-paneled gallery. Charlotte paused. "Are you going to kiss me?"

Simon was startled out of his preoccupation with the speech he was about to make her. "I wouldn't dream of it." Then, thinking this might sound ungallant, he said, "I wouldn't impose myself on you. Not on such short acquaintance. And even then, not unless . . . Not unless I was sure you wanted me to."

Charlotte gave him a look of gratitude. "That's a relief. I'm not at all sure I'd like it. And I wouldn't know what to say afterward." She looked up at the rows of paintings, scarcely visible in the light that penetrated the gallery. "They're very brown, aren't they?"

It was an apt description. The clothes and background of the subjects were uniformly dark, lightened only by the paler tones of a face and the gilt-painted wood with which the portraits were framed. "There are some chairs further on," Simon said. "We might as well be comfortable."

Charlotte moved toward the pair of carved mahogany chairs which stood underneath the furthest window. "Oh look," she said, "you can see the folly from here." Some secret thought lit her eyes, but she did not choose to share it. She sat down, wrapped her paisley shawl more closely about her shoulders, and looked up at Simon expectantly.

"I hope you aren't too cold," Simon said, aware for the first time that the gallery had no source of heat.

"It doesn't matter. We were always cold in the convent and I'm used to it. Besides, I'm not the least bit sickly."

It was a promising attribute in a wife. "That's good," Simon said. "That is, I'm glad you enjoy good health. For your sake."

Charlotte did not reply. She continued to look at him as though she waited only on his pleasure but wished he would get on with it. Simon hastily took the other chair. He had had no trouble making his feelings known to Justine, who had not expected his proposal. He did not know how to make his intentions clear to Charlotte, who did. "Mademoiselle," he said, "there is something I must say to you."

"Is it about our marriage? It's rather early to be talking of that. I've been here only four days."

"I don't find it too early, at least on my part." Simon leaned toward her as if his nearness would convey the ardor his voice lacked. "You must know that I would be agreeable to the match."

Charlotte lowered her eyes and twisted the ends of her shawl. "And you wish to know if I would be agreeable as well."

It occurred to Simon that he might have offended her modesty. "I won't press you for an answer," he said. "But if you take me in aversion . . . If the idea of being my wife is distasteful to you . . ."

"Oh, no," Charlotte assured him. "If I must be someone's wife, I'm sure you'll do as well as anyone. It's only—" She raised her eyes and took a deep breath. "It's only that I have a great many things to consider."

"I see." Simon did not, but he supposed that Charlotte, who accepted marriage as her fate but was clearly not yet ready to marry anyone, was going to propose a postponement of the day on which they would be wed. Simon was prepared to give her as long as she needed, provided that the matter between them would be settled and he would be irrevocably bound on his course.

"There are matters on which we must agree," Charlotte said. "For instance, I would like to know how many children you require."

Simon stood up abruptly and stared down at her. This was not what he had expected. "I—I haven't thought—I want to have a family. I ought to have a son."

Charlotte smiled. "That's understood."

"Or two," he added quickly. "In case of . . ."

"In case of an accident. Yes." She frowned. "I cannot promise to give you sons."

Simon stared at her, conscious for the first time of how the marital arrangement might appear to her. "I cannot promise to get them on you," he said gently.

"Yes, but I would not wish to be forever increasing. How many children must I bear before we can put a stop to it?"

Simon was not sure how to answer her. "Six?"

277

"If they are all girls, six would be a great many. It would be very tedious to find husbands for all of them."

Simon had not thought through what setting up a nursery entailed. She was right. Six was rather more than he had envisioned. "Four?" he suggested.

"Done," Charlotte said with a triumphant smile.

"Well, yes. If you like. On this matter we are agreed." Simon looked at her closely. "Would you want it included in the marriage contract?"

"I don't see why not. It is of some importance to both of us."

It was, but Simon could not look forward to seeing the most intimate details of their marriage laid out on parchment for the lawyers to peruse. Then it occurred to him that Charlotte, who knew very little about men, might have some fears of the marriage bed. "It won't be necessary to start a family at once," he told her. "I'd be prepared to give you as much time as you need." He stopped, hoping she would take his meaning.

"Oh, no, I'd rather get it over with." She did not add, "and go on to the more interesting pursuits of life," but she might as well have done so. Charlotte had given no sign of maternal feelings. It was understandable. A few months ago she had been treated as a child herself. "Where will we live?" she asked with a greater show of interest.

"I intend to purchase a house in the country." Her face fell, and he quickly added, "But I will also take a house in London."

"That's better." Charlotte's good spirits were restored. "I'm not very fond of the country, having lived so much in it, but I'm sure I will adore London."

"And we must sometimes visit my estates on the Continent. When we do, you may wish to spend some time in France."

"Oh, I don't think so," Charlotte said, tossing the suggestion aside. "When we are in London, may I go to parties?"

"I will certainly be happy to escort you. Within reason,"

he added, not wishing his life to be turned entirely upside down.

"Oh, you need not be forever hanging round my skirts. I intend to have my own friends. And my own carriage and coachman. You will agree to that, won't you?"

It was not the marriage Simon had envisaged, but Charlotte was young, and he supposed he must give her her head. "Provided you choose your friends with discretion—" He broke off, feeling rather pompous. " . . . And do not wager large sums of money, that I will not allow," he continued doggedly, "and do not neglect our children—I do not see why you should not have the freedom to see whom you like."

"I am not stupid, Prince. I will never give you cause for embarrassment, and I will be in all things discreet. Just as I expect you will be discreet about your mistresses."

"I do not intend to keep a mistress," Simon said, with a good deal of heat.

"Well, I certainly hope you will," Charlotte retorted. "I would not want you to be forever visiting my bed. After our family is complete, I see no reason for you to visit my bed at all."

Simon wondered where she had acquired her ideas of marriage. Then he wondered if Justine had been filling her head with this cynical nonsense. "Husbands and wives frequently enjoy each other's company," he pointed out.

"Not the husbands and wives with whom I am acquainted."

"I don't know what experience of marriage you have had, mademoiselle, but I know several couples who are quite in love. My sister, for example. She married for sensible reasons and in time became very attached to Harry."

"Yes, Lady Milverton does seem fond of her husband." Charlotte thought about it for a bit. "So you are saying that in marriage, love may come later?"

"Affection, certainly. And perhaps even desire."

"Oh, I think not," Charlotte said hastily. "I wouldn't expect anything like that between us."

He had shocked her. She had spoken so knowingly of the

marital relation, but she was a child at heart—blessedly free of romantic illusions about love, but knowing nothing of the wonder that can develop between a man and a woman. He would have to be very gentle with her. "I would not want to force you," he said, seeking to ease her anxieties on this score.

"I understand my duty, Prince. We will have two sons, or four children in all. But after that, you will make other arrangements for your pleasure."

Simon realized he had not thought much of what kind of marriage he might be making. If he had thought of it at all, he had assumed it would be something like Alessa's. A sensible match, sensibly agreed to, but with growing affection and some sort of mutual passion. If the fates were kind, they might even come to love each other. "I would hope, mademoiselle, that we would be friends. There would be little reason for us to marry otherwise."

"Oh, there might be many reasons," Charlotte replied, "but you are quite right, it would not be at all agreeable."

"We might in time become more than friends."

Charlotte gave him a considering look. "You are saying you may have desires. You also said you would not force them on me."

"Not unless you have desires, too."

"I don't expect I will. But then, I know very little of such things."

Simon felt he had won a concession of sorts. "We are agreed, then?"

"Yes, we are agreed." Charlotte sighed. "I am so glad that is over. Now we can talk of more important matters. I suppose you have a great deal of money."

It was Simon's turn to be shocked. He took refuge in formality. "Sufficient, mademoiselle, to keep you in comfort."

"I was sure you did, or *Papa* would never have agreed to my coming to England, no matter how old and well connected your family is. *Papa* thinks a great deal of money."

The turn of the discussion was making Simon uncomfortable. "Surely the details can be worked out in the marriage settlement."

"Yes, of course. I only wish to know if you will make me an allowance. To spend as I please. I do not want a husband who is forever complaining about the price of my bonnets."

After the difficult passage he had just negotiated, Simon was relieved to have something so simple to settle. "You will certainly have your own allowance. It will be a generous one, but you must learn to live within it."

Charlotte gave him a brilliant smile. "Oh, I will. And I may keep Cécile as my lady's maid?"

Simon agreed. He further agreed to a minimum of two footmen, a sufficient number of parlormaids, a day and a night nurse for the children, and a cook imported from France. To his surprise, Charlotte did not ask to be married in her native country. London, she said, would do very well, though she would like to return to France after the wedding to show off her new clothes and newly married state to her friends. She did not mention her father.

They had been in the gallery the better part of an hour. Charlotte was buoyant. Simon felt drained. He was relieved that his future was now arranged, but he felt oddly depressed. He escorted Charlotte back to the newer portion of the house, wondering at his contrary feelings. It was as sensible a match as one could hope for. What more had he expected? He looked down at the soft mouth and determined chin of the woman he was going to make his wife. She had been honest with him, he could not fault her for that. There would be no misunderstandings between them. And no mystery. That was it. To his chagrin, Simon had to admit that he had hoped for a touch of romance.

Justine fastened the skirt of her riding habit, cursing her fingers for their clumsiness. A pox on all men. Bertram Westcourt, for his silly infatuation, which was likely to ruin Marianne Stratton. Gerald, for being such an egotistical fool. How could the man believe she found him attractive? And Simon, who willfully misunderstood everything. He ought to have known her better.

Her sudden access of anger had at least brought her out of the swamp of self-pity into which Simon had thrown her. She had spent the past hour sitting on the windowseat in her bed-chamber, grateful for the chill blasts of air that crept through the cracks around the window frame. She had thought she and Simon could at least be civil to each other. Instead, he had turned stupid and vengeful, wrapping himself in his tattered pride.

It would have been so easy to explain why she was found in that ridiculous position with Gerald, but only at the cost of exposing Marianne's secret. She would not have explained to Simon in any case. It would have been an admission that he had some claim on her. And that he did not.

Justine retrieved her riding boots from the wardrobe and sat down at her dressing table to tug them on. She should have rung for Cécile, but she would not risk having the girl see her ravaged face. If it would not mean abandoning Charlotte, she would leave the house for good. At least she could leave it for an hour. She had seen Minette only that morning, but she would go to her again and let the child's warmth and innocence remind her of what was important and what was not. Simon's anger was unpleasant, but of no great moment. Minette's future was.

Her boots on, Justine picked up a hairbrush and pulled it through her tangled hair, scowling at her reflection. She was distracted by a light scratching at the door. "Come in," she called, quickly composing her features and turning to face her visitor.

Charlotte entered the room. "Oh," she said, disappointment evident in her voice. "You're going riding."

"Yes, but I have time to talk." Justine had not seen her young charge since that morning, when she had sent her off to the folly to warn Marianne that her husband was coming her way. Of course, Charlotte would want to talk about it. She wondered that it had taken her so long to do so. "Did you find Lady Stratton?" Justine asked.

"No. She had not come at all." Charlotte sat down on the bed and folded her hands in her lap. Her color was high and there was an air of suppressed excitement in her manner.

Justine smiled. For a convent-bred girl, it had been a singular adventure. "Was Lord Westcourt there?"

"Oh, yes," said Charlotte, with the air of someone whose train of thought has been interrupted. "I told him we were out walking and I wanted to see the folly, but you were too tired to accompany me."

"Actually, I had turned my ankle. Sir Gerald was kind enough to see me back to the house."

"You're so clever, Justine."

"But you were clever, too, not letting Lord Westcourt know that we knew of his appointment with Lady Stratton."

"Oh, I would never have done that," Charlotte said, her air of distraction gone. "Men are forever having their own way. We women must help one another if we are to have any freedom at all. And it turned out very well. Lord Westcourt was disappointed when he saw who I was, but he hid it very well. He showed me all over the folly and then he told me of his travels on the Continent. He says I absolutely must see Italy. He is a most engaging young man. We talked for the longest time. And then he walked back to the house with me. Part of the way back," she amended. "I told him it might look odd if we were seen coming in together."

Charlotte was becoming all too adept at intrigue. It occurred to Justine that she had been remiss in leaving her alone in a situation that might give rise to comment. "No one saw you, then?"

"Not a soul. Not that it would have mattered if they had. Oh, Justine, I have something very important to tell you. The prince and I have come to an agreement."

Justine felt a painful constriction in her chest. She had known that it would come, but she had not expected it so soon. Her face was stiff with the effort to not cry out in protest. "An agreement?" she said. "You mean that you are be-trothed?"

"Yes. I'm telling no one but you. We won't announce it just yet, not till the St. Valentine's Eve ball. You would have been so proud of me, Justine. I did not give him an answer at once, not until I knew that the marriage would be arranged to my satisfaction. We are to have a house in London and I will have two footmen and keep my own carriage and come and go as I please. I will have a generous allowance—though I must learn to keep within it, the prince says—and I may have what friends I choose, as long as I do not embarrass him. On my part, I will give him children. He wants an heir and another son, in case something happens to the first. But if we have only one boy, or nothing but girls, I may stop after four children. And after that, he will not come to my bed at all." Charlotte frowned, as though remembering some part of her conversation with Simon. "Unless I want him to. The prince says that I might, but I don't think it very likely." Char-lotte's face brightened. "So you see that for a husband, he will not be much of a bother."

A bother. Justine winced. Oh, Simon, this isn't like you. This isn't the wife you need. "When will the marriage take place?" she asked, struggling to keep her voice composed.

"Not till the summer. The lawyers will take forever to ar-range things, and besides, the prince has agreed that I may have a season in London before I become a married woman. So you and I will have several months in London together and go to three parties every single night. Justine, tell me the truth. Don't you think I have done very well for myself?"

She had. If Charlotte's goal was to have her own estab-lishment and as much independence as was possible for a woman, she had done very well. Justine told her so. And if Simon's goal was to have a family and a wife of impeccable lineage, he had done well, too, though she did not think he would be happy.

But who was she to say what would make him happy? Char-lotte, with a clear-sighted purpose she would not have expected of her, had told him exactly what kind of a marriage they would have, and Simon—perhaps she did not know him as well as she had thought. Simon had accepted Charlotte's terms.

Justine congratulated Charlotte again, then excused herself and made for the stable. Tears threatened to choke her. She had known that it was long since over between them. She had not known how deeply it would hurt. She had not known how much she loved him still.

Two men saw Justine ride off. Gerald had thought he was alone, but a flicker of movement on his left caused him to turn his head. It was Simon di Tassio. He had apparently just come round a clump of trees near the path that led from the stable to the main drive.

Gerald raised his hand in acknowledgment of the meeting. "Tassio. Well met. Came out to smoke a cigar." Gerald had, in fact, come out because he had got a glimpse of Justine slipping out of the house, but it wouldn't do to say so. He patted his coat. "Drat, I must have left my case in my room. Afraid I can't offer you one."

Simon waved the apology aside. "No matter. I don't smoke."

Not smoke? He was an odd one, Alessa's precious brother. Polite and well spoken, you could give him that, but kept to himself. Danced attendance on Justine's protégée, Mademoiselle de Chambeau. Of course, that was expected of him. It was why the little French girl had been invited. A sweet child, but too inexperienced for Gerald's taste.

The clatter of hooves on gravel sent both men's attention to the figure cantering down the drive. Damnation. If Simon hadn't put in an appearance, Gerald might have managed to intercept Justine. As it was, he'd have to take what pleasure he could in the sight of her nicely rounded bottom bouncing suggestively in the saddle.

Gerald gave voice to his thought. "Superb seat, that woman

has. As much at home in the saddle as she is on the dance floor."

"Madame de Valon is an accomplished woman."

Accomplished, yes. Gerald thought she must be just as skillful in bed. The thought made him grow hot. Not like his pretty little Marianne, who cringed and went tight all over whenever he tried to touch her. What the devil was a man to do?

"You knew her in Paris, didn't you?" The matter was a sore point with Gerald. He had prided himself on his prior acquaintance with Justine giving him some advantage in relation to the other men of the party, but Simon had apparently known her as well.

"Yes, we met a number of times when I was there," Simon said. "The year before last."

Gerald calculated the months. "I was there then myself. Just after the new year. Before I met Marianne."

"Ah. That accounts for the reason we did not meet. I was in Paris in the autumn."

"Just so. Splendid city."

"Yes, splendid," Simon agreed.

Gerald felt an insane rush of jealousy. Had Simon been Justine's lover? There were stories enough about the Baron de Valon's lovely young widow, though Gerald had never been able to pin them down. Certainly Justine had refused to allow him any intimacies beyond kissing her hand. Not that there was any question that she liked him. Why, even today she had sought him out with a cock-and-bull story about turning her ankle—no sign of that when he had seen her running out of the house just a quarter-hour ago—and had leaned on him very prettily and might even have let him kiss her, if Simon and Harry had not chanced by.

"She rides every day," Gerald said, not caring whether or not it looked odd that he had noticed, "but usually in the morning. I wonder where she goes."

"Perhaps she likes the exercise." Simon was still staring down the drive. Justine had disappeared.

286

"My man said her horse has been seen at the inn that lies two or three miles beyond Moresby."

Simon turned on him sharply, giving Gerald a look that made him wonder if indeed he had cause to be jealous. No, surely not now, when the prince was courting Mademoiselle de Chambeau. But perhaps in the past. Gerald knew well that one did not easily forget Justine de Valon.

Simon moved a few steps away from the other man, hoping to put an end to the conversation. He had gone for a solitary walk to think about his new status as a betrothed man and had not expected to see Justine. Nor had he expected to encounter the man who had been embracing her that morning. Gerald's presence roused him to fresh fury, tempered by the realization that Justine, wherever she was bound, was not riding to meet Marianne's husband.

It was small comfort. Gerald boasted continually of his acquaintance with Justine before his marriage. Had the man been her lover before she had taken Simon to her bed? And who had warmed her bed after? "There are a number of reasons she might stop at the Crown," Simon said, trying to think of what they might be.

"Her horse has been seen there more than once," Gerald insisted. "Deuced odd."

"Then I suggest you ask her. Though I think the lady is entitled to some privacy."

Gerald had the grace to blush. "Quite so."

Simon turned toward the house and Gerald fell in beside him. Simon was intensely conscious of the other man, aware that they were bound together by their suspicions. For it *was* odd. The Crown was a small inn on the edge of Moresby village. It boasted no comfort that would draw a guest of Moresby. Then why was Justine riding there? And whom was she meeting?

They were a fine pair, he and Gerald Stratton. One a married man and one newly betrothed, both obsessed with a woman who wanted neither of them. For Simon now wondered if he had misconstrued that scene in the garden. Justine might be Gerald's flirt, but Gerald was not privy to her secrets.

This conclusion did something to lift Simon's spirits. They were dashed again when the men came in sight of the house. A carriage was drawn up before the steps, a dark green carriage that Simon knew all too well. His mother had arrived at Moresby.

Five

The Princess Sofia, widow of the Savoyard Prince di Tassio, now wife of the English commoner Michael Langley, considered her words. She was seated in a small sitting room done up in her favorite shade of blue. A tea tray was before her, her son was on the sofa beside her, and Alessa had had the good sense to leave them alone.

She had had all too little time with Simon of late, and she feared she had some cause for concern. "I am very glad to see you," Sofia said, brushing his hand lightly. "Though you look a shade distressed. Is anything the matter?"

"I am not fond of large house parties, *Maman*. Some of the guests try one's patience."

"That is why the parties are large, so one can lessen the impact of the disagreeable people. Would you like another cup of tea?"

"No more, thank you. And you must admit that the situation with Mademoiselle de Chambeau has been difficult. I would have preferred to meet her more quietly."

"If you had, and you found the girl not to your liking, you would have found it far more awkward. Believe me, Simon, I know what I'm doing." Her son stirred restively beside her. "I had a letter from the Comte de Chambeau to inform me of her departure," she went on, seeking to reclaim his attention. "It seems she was not accompanied by her aunt."

"No, by Madame de Valon. Her husband was a distant relation of the comte."

Sofia watched her son closely. The moment was crucial. She knew that Simon had had a liaison with the widowed Justine de Valon a year or more ago. A friend in Paris had written to tell her of the relationship, and at the time, Sofia had applauded it. Simon had not been one to take his pleasure wherever he might find it. Indeed, Sofia had feared he might avoid pleasure altogether and was thus much relieved to learn that he had found a woman who would initiate him into the mysteries of love. But Simon's manner on returning from the Continent did not suggest that the experience had been wholly liberating. It would be a pity if he had taken the affair seriously.

"I have not met Madame de Valon," Sofia said. "I understand she is rather young."

Simon stood up and walked a few steps away, then turned to face her, hands clasped behind his back. "She has been a more than adequate chaperone."

Sofia gave it up. If Simon would not talk, she must approach the woman herself. "What do you think of her?" she asked after a moment.

"Madame de Valon?" Simon looked startled.

"Mademoiselle de Chambeau."

"A charming girl."

"You're being provoking, Simon. Do you like her?"

"We became betrothed this afternoon."

There were few situations Sofia was not prepared to handle. This was one of them. She opened her mouth to speak, but could not find the words. Her consternation must have showed in her face, for Simon had the temerity to smile at her. The wretch. He was enjoying her discomfiture.

"We will not announce it for a few days. What is the matter, *Maman?* I thought you agreed that it was time for me to marry. Do you think I should have waited for you to give me your approval? The decision is mine alone. I know what I'm doing."

It did not please Sofia to have her own words flung back in her face. Simon had always resisted her persuasion, but now, she realized, he was wholly beyond her control. She made a wry face, then accepted the inevitable. "I am surprised that it has happened so soon, that is all. I take it you find her an agreeable young woman."

Simon chose to misunderstand her. "We have come to an agreement in all important particulars. House, carriage, servants, her allowance—"

"You sound as though you are buying a horse."

He raised his brows. "Surely these are matters that must be considered. Mademoiselle de Chambeau was most anxious that they be settled before she gave me an answer."

"Bah! These matters are food for the lawyers, not a young girl's concern. Does she find you attractive?"

"As much as any man, she tells me."

Sofia frowned. Indifference was not a promising basis for a lifetime together. "She is prepared for marriage?"

"For a young woman, there is no other honorable estate. And she is eager to have her own establishment."

"She understands that she must give you children."

"Four, *Maman*. That is the number we have agreed on. She does not wish to be forever increasing."

This was a position with which Sofia had some sympathy, but she found it indelicate that Mademoiselle de Chambeau should have bargained about the matter with her son. It did not augur well for the joys of the marriage bed. Sofia chose her next words with care. "What of you, Simon? Do you find her . . ."

He smiled. "She is well favored, *Maman*. There will be no difficulties on that score. She will provide me with children, and I will give her the life that she desires. We have struck a reasonable bargain."

It was too much for Sofia. She thought of her own happiness with Michael, her second husband. "But what of affection? What of common interests and mutual respect?"

"Did you feel affection for my father, madam?"

"Don't you dare fling my past in my face." Sofia's first marriage had been arranged by her parents and had brought her nothing but distress. "Men are free to choose. Women are not."

"I am free, *Maman*," he said coldly. "And I have chosen."

Sofia summoned a smile. She had smiled at worse disasters. "I am sure you have chosen well, Simon. I only wish you to be happy. Come, it is time I met your Mademoiselle de Chambeau. Will you bring her to me?"

Simon nodded and left the room, leaving Sofia to reflect on the folly of having mentioned the Comte de Chambeau's daughter in the first place. Still, Simon had asked her if she knew of a suitable bride. He was determined to wed, and wed he would, no matter how undesirable his choice. At least the girl was young and malleable.

But she knew her son. Simon was not happy. He had gone into his retreating posture, where reason or cajolery or anger could not reach him. Sofia was privy enough to the gossip of the *ton* to know that Simon had had no entanglements since his return from the Continent. Perhaps the problem lay there, with what had happened in Paris. The idiot. Had he been foolish enough to fall in love with his first mistress?

She waited for Simon's return in an agony of impatience. So much depended on the girl, on what might be made of her. When the door opened, she rose quickly and walked toward it, holding out her hands to Simon's future bride. "My dear, I am so happy to meet you."

The girl was small, much smaller than she had expected. Her complexion was good, her features regular, save for a little retroussé nose. Her hair, a soft golden brown, was caught up with a ribbon and allowed to fall streaming down her back. She was well proportioned, with a figure that showed promise of a pleasing fullness.

Charlotte curtsied prettily. "I am honored to meet you, Princess. My father sends you greetings."

"How kind," Sofia murmured, sure that the comte, a bad-tempered old man without a social grace to his name, had done nothing of the kind. "Come sit beside me and let us become better acquainted. Simon, you may leave us."

"I think not, *Maman.*"

Sofia raised her brows and stared at him. Her son stared back. Sofia retreated to the sofa, reminding herself that she would have many occasions to talk to the girl by herself.

Simon handed Charlotte to a chair nearby and sat down beside her. The girl had a determined walk, but she sat quietly enough, her hands in her lap, her eyes modestly downcast. "I understand you are to be my daughter-in-law," Sofia said.

"If it pleases you, madame."

Sofia looked pointedly at her son. "If it pleases Simon. And you as well."

Charlotte looked up, her face alight. She had very pretty eyes, brown with flecks of gold. "Oh, it pleases me very much, Princess. I am happy to have my future settled, and on such generous terms. The prince will be—" She broke off, looking confused.

"A complaisant husband?"

Simon frowned. The frown was echoed on Charlotte's face. "Please, madame, I am not sure what that means."

Sofia summoned a smile she did not feel. "A husband who will strive to please you."

"Oh, I hope so." After a moment Charlotte added, "Of course, I will strive to please him as well."

"That augers well for your mutual comfort."

"Yes, it does, doesn't it?" Charlotte said with enthusiasm, quite forgetting her demure demeanor. "We have talked very frankly about it and agreed that I shall not live in his pocket nor he in mine." She smiled at her future husband. "The prince has been most agreeable. I am sure he is the kindest man I know."

"A high recommendation." Sofia thought of her earlier words to Simon. He had dismissed them, but perhaps they would mean something to Mademoiselle de Chambeau. "I hope that your marriage will be based on mutual respect and affection."

"Respect?" Charlotte looked surprised, then lowered her eyes. "But of course I will respect my husband. He is a man, and therefore worthy of regard." She might have been reciting out of a book.

"And affection?" Sofia prompted.

Charlotte blushed. "I imagine that will come with time. One is bound to become fond of a person who treats one with kindness."

It did not sound like the marriage Sofia had wished for her son. Perhaps he saw more possibilities in the girl than she did. She glanced at Simon. He was smiling at his intended bride, but the smile did not reach his eyes. "When is the wedding to be?" Sofia asked.

"Oh, not too soon," Charlotte said quickly. "The lawyers must draw up documents, and we must have a house and other things. Besides, the prince has promised me that I may have a season in London first."

"How very wise," Sofia said. "To give yourselves time to become better acquainted." At least Simon did not propose to marry the girl out of hand. Perhaps the match would prove better than she feared. But Sofia could not help feeling that it would not.

The message was brought to Justine just as she was going upstairs to change for dinner. The Princess Sofia would be grateful if Madame de Valon would spare her a few minutes of her time. She could be found in her dressing room.

An inquiry to the footman who brought her the note gave her directions to the room in question. Justine made her way upstairs, thinking of what she must say. She had no doubt about the reason for the summons. Simon had taken Charlotte to meet his mother shortly after her arrival, but it was natural that the princess would want further information about the young woman to whom her son was now betrothed.

The suite the princess and her husband occupied on their visits to Moresby was a few doors beyond the rooms given to Justine and Charlotte. Justine scratched on the middle door, received permission to enter, and pushed open the door.

It was a delightful room, done in the same shades as the blue saloon. The princess, who had been seated at her dressing table, rose at once. "Madame de Valon? How charming of you to come so promptly." She gestured to a pair of blue-and-white chintz-covered chairs before the fireplace. "Please sit down."

Justine settled in one of the chairs, grateful for the warmth of the brisk wood fire crackling in the grate. The princess seated herself in the other. She was wearing a dressing gown of sea-green silk that intensified the color of her eyes. Her bright gold hair showed not the faintest trace of gray. She looked much too young to be Simon's mother. "How may I help you, madame?" Justine asked.

"It is not help I seek," the princess said with a rueful smile, "but information. Or perhaps reassurance. A mother's prerogative, you understand. I have just learned that my son and Mademoiselle de Chambeau have reached an understanding. Did you know . . ."

"Charlotte told me earlier this afternoon. I gather the matter had just been arranged."

"It happened very quickly. How long have they known each other? Four days? I would have expected an acquaintance of some weeks." The princess leaned forward, her manner confiding. "Tell me, madame, what do you think of the match?"

Justine could not share her reservations about the marriage without revealing that she knew Simon far better than she should. Besides, she owed her loyalty to Charlotte, who was clearly pleased with her decision to become Simon's wife. She chose her words with care. "Charlotte is a sweet-tempered girl, and quite unspoiled. She knows little of the world as yet. She is barely out of the convent."

"She knows quite enough to have negotiated matters that should be the province of her father and his lawyers. And some that should not be negotiated at all." The princess pursed her mouth in an expression of distaste. "She has even got my son to agree to a limitation of her family responsibilities."

Justine felt obliged to come to Charlotte's defense. "She is very young. She has had no mother to guide her, and her father is not—not a sympathetic person. Her visit to England has given her a taste of freedom, and she is impatient to try her wings. She will settle in time, and she is amenable to guidance."

"Perhaps," the princess said, giving voice to Justine's own reservations. "The young woman seems very determined."

"But inexperienced. She is eager to learn."

"As long as it does not interfere—"

"With her independence, yes. Once she has had a taste of it, it will seem less precious to her," Justine added, with more assurance than she felt.

The princess made a dismissive motion with her heavily ringed hands. "We shall see. She is Simon's choice, and I must be content. Though I confess I would feel better if he showed more enthusiasm for the match. My son, I fear, is not a happy man."

Justine turned her head and looked into the flames, hoping to hide the tears that threatened to disgrace her before the princess. Her own unhappiness she could bear. But to have Simon turn away from joy, to have him choose to make a marriage with a woman who did not care for him, was infinitely worse. "Perhaps he feels the weight of his responsibilities," she said carefully. The tears were now at bay and she could once more face the princess.

"He always has. But his mood is not generally somber." The princess shrugged, making her gauzy wrap flutter about her shoulders. "I am perhaps making too much of our encounter. I cannot always hold my tongue, and it brings out his stubborn side. Yet it has occurred to me— Madame, may I speak frankly?"

Justine looked at her in surprise. She had assumed the interview had come to an end.

The princess took her silence for assent. "You knew my son in Paris."

Justine stiffened, scenting danger. "We were acquainted," she said in a colorless voice.

The princess laughed. "Come, we are women. There must be no false delicacy between us. It is said that you were lovers. Is that true?"

Justine could deny it, but she did not know the princess's source of information. And why should she deny it? There was nothing of which she need be ashamed. "It is true," she acknowledged.

"I am glad you are honest. Understand, I do not criticize you for the liaison. On the contrary, I am grateful that you gave Simon the experience . . ." The princess made a vague gesture that encompassed all the wonder and passion and pain that accompanied such an affair. "But Simon feels things intensely. I knew when he returned to England that something of the sort had occurred, and I wondered then if he had taken it more seriously than he ought. Then today, when he spoke of you, I thought perhaps some feeling for you still remained. At least your presence would have reawakened his earlier pain."

The fact that she might be right did not lessen Justine's resentment at the princess's words. "Madame, I did not know that the prince and I would meet when I agreed to come to England. I have no designs on your son. I would not resume our liaison even if he wished it, which I assure you he does not. He has been embarrassed by my presence in this house, as I have. Whatever feeling he once had for me is long since dead. Indeed, he has been incensed by what he is pleased to call my attempts to ruin the marriage of Lord Milverton's cousin."

"The accusation is, of course, unjust."

It was a statement, but Justine could hear the underlying question. She would not dignify it with an answer. She folded her hands in her lap to still their trembling and tried to keep her voice light. "So you see that I am no longer an object of the prince's desire."

The princess watched her for a moment. "You are right to be angry at my son's words. You are a beautiful woman, madame, but beauty exacts its price. One cannot always avoid a man's attentions, and people adore gossiping about those they have cause to envy. And a widow is always considered fair game." The princess paused as though considering her next words. "You were much talked about in Paris, you know. Simon has probably heard the stories and taken them literally, as men so often do."

Justine turned her head to look at the princess. There was no censure in her face or voice. But neither was there denial that the stories might have some basis in truth. The princess did not blame Justine de Valon, but she would remind her of the world's opinion.

"I do not wish to pry," the princess went on, "but there is one question that I must ask you. Not out of vulgar curiosity, you understand, but because your answer may affect us both."

Justine gave an icy nod, though she burned with indignation. The princess wanted to know if she loved Simon. Well, she did. Foolishly, desperately, and hopelessly, but it was no one's business but her own. The denial formed on her lips.

"You retired to the country a year ago," the princess said. "It is rumored that you had a child."

Justine hid her shock and dismay as best she could. So much for her efforts to be discreet. "I do not think—" she began.

"That I have any right to ask. Of course," the princess agreed. "But I must know. Is Simon the father?"

"No," said Justine without thinking.

"Ah, I see." The princess seemed to dismiss the question of the child's parentage. "Is it a boy or a girl?" she asked with every evidence of interest, one woman to another.

"A girl," Justine admitted, and then wished that she had not.

"Charming. You have left her in France?"

In for a penny . . . There was no reason now to not answer the further question. "She is with me, madame. That is, with her nurse. They stay at an inn on the outskirts of Moresby village. I go to see her daily, but I do not think my visits have been remarked."

Justine was rewarded for this touch of defiance by a look of horror on the princess's face. "Mademoiselle de Chambeau," she whispered.

"Believes her to be my ward, the child of a dear friend who died at her birth. Charlotte had no qualms about her accompanying us and I believe has given her presence no thought since we arrived at Moresby."

The princess rose from her chair, clearly agitated. She turned and looked down at Justine as though she were a puzzle she could not quite master. "I will not ask you again who fathered your child. No, do not deny that it was Simon. You have the same stubborn pride as my son, and you will say only what you wish me to hear. But if it is true . . . If the girl is my granddaughter, I want to provide for her."

Justine felt a great welling of resentment against this woman who insisted on intruding in her life. "If it were true, I would take nothing from you."

"Don't be a fool. I know the straits in which your husband left you. You have more than yourself to consider. Your daughter's future is at stake. It will be difficult enough in any case. I can make it easier."

Justine got to her feet. She was taller than the princess by a few inches, and the difference gave her a sense of control. "If I admit that my daughter is your grandchild. I have heard you, madame. I admit no such thing."

"Very well. I will say no more about the matter. I think in any case it is best if Simon does not know. If the child is of an age where he might raise questions about its parentage . . . You understand, he is in an odd mood, and may not choose to be reasonable."

Justine felt her face grow warm. "I would never want the prince to know. You can be assured of my silence. And Charlotte's. Despite her artless chatter, she knows how to be discreet."

"She is a sensible girl. I trust you will be as well." The princess looked at her a moment, then seemed to come to a decision. "Mademoiselle de Chambeau has told me she wishes to have a season in London before her marriage. I think she should stay with me during this time. She will then be under my protection, and she will have no further need of a companion. It would be wise for you and the child to return to France. Not to mince the matter, it would be best for you to cut short your visit to Moresby. For the sake of Simon's peace of mind."

The princess's demand brought Justine up short. For all the pain of these last days, the thought of making the final break with Simon was too wrenching to contemplate. "I promised Charlotte's father that I would stay with her until her marriage." Justine knew it was a futile protest. She could not possibly install herself under the princess's roof for the several months before the wedding, not with Simon in and out of the house every day.

"I will write to the comte and make things right." The princess stood very straight and her face was without any trace of softness. "If you return to France— *When* you return to France, I will see that you are provided for for the next year. Not because of the child, but because you are a woman of spirit and I appreciate your frankness in this difficult situation. And because I am grateful for your past favors to my son."

The words slashed Justine like a whip. "I will take nothing," she whispered. Then, unable to say more, she turned away and fled the room.

Justine stood trembling outside the dressing room door. The princess had stripped her bare, leaving her without a shred of self-respect. Whore, that was all the pretty words amounted to. A whore who had served her purpose and must now be bought off because she had grown inconvenient. The words made a mockery of everything that had been between Simon and herself. For a brief time they had loved one another. For an even briefer time she had allowed herself to believe in that love. Its fruit lay in a cradle three miles off. And for her daughter's sake, and the sake of the man she could not stop loving, she must turn tail and flee to France, abandoning the hope of a better life in her native land.

Well, a pox on the princess and a pox on her son and—no, not on Charlotte, she wished Charlotte well. Justine lifted her chin and straightened her back and started down the corridor. Three steps brought her face-to-face with Simon.

He stopped abruptly, his eyes going to the door by which she had been standing. "You've been with my mother."

Justine caught her breath. "The princess wanted to know how Charlotte stood in my estimation," she said after a moment, pleased that she was at least in control of her voice. "I told her Charlotte is a most amiable girl and I wish you happiness in your marriage. May I repeat my wishes now, Prince? I have not been able to offer you my congratulations."

Simon refused to play the game. "Is that all?" he asked, with an unexpected show of concern. "She did not make it awkward for you?"

There was no reason he should not know. It would arm him against his mother's intrusion. "She knows about us, Simon," Justine said quietly. "She was not upset. She only wanted to be assured that it was over between us. I told her that it was."

The lines in his face deepened, a sign of his anger. They were standing very close, so close that she could feel his heat and remember the smoothness of his skin when it was sheened with sweat. Memory threatened to engulf her and she moved a step away. He did not seem to notice. "She had no right . . ." he began.

"There is no problem," Justine said, moving aside as though to pass him. "The princess and I understand each other. If you wish to avoid her interference, I suggest you show more enthusiasm for your coming marriage when you are in her company."

Simon swore under his breath. "Damnation!" He looked

once more at Justine. "And you? Do you share my mother's qualms?"

"I am concerned only for Charlotte. She seems quite happy in the match. Good day, Prince."

Justine walked rapidly down the hall to the sanctuary of her room. The door to the adjoining dressing room was open, and she heard the sound of voices and youthful laughter. Moving to the door, she saw Charlotte seated at the dressing table. Marianne Stratton stood behind her with comb and brush, attempting to do up Charlotte's hair.

Charlotte swung round, dislodging a lock of hair and several hairpins. "Oh, there you are. Don't you think this is an improvement? I always look so dreadfully young. I was complaining about it, and Marianne said she would help prepare me for London."

Marianne lifted the lock and jabbed more pins into place. "There."

Charlotte looked in the mirror, a look of delight on her face. Her gaze went to the reflection of Marianne in the glass. "Why, we look just alike," she said. She stood up and put her arm around Marianne's waist.

They were indeed much alike, though Charlotte was the shorter by an inch or so. But their hair, done now in an identical style, was the same shade of golden brown, and their soft-lipped faces both showed the roundness of youth.

"But my clothes will never do." Charlotte pointed to the gowns strewn on every available surface. "They are so—so insipid. Marianne will introduce me to her dressmaker in London, but till then . . ." Charlotte's shoulders sagged. "But Marianne has promised to dress me for the ball. Surely we can contrive something."

"That is very kind of you, Lady Stratton," Justine said. Marianne looked prettier and far more animated than she had during their exchange that morning. It occurred to Justine that Gerald was not Marianne's only problem. She might be lonely. "I'm sure you will contrive something suitable."

302

"Oh, suitable," Charlotte exclaimed. "I would far rather be dashing."

"You're too young to be dashing," Justine said, feeling old beyond her years.

"I'm too short," Charlotte said in a mournful voice.

Justine caught sight of an open rouge pot on the dressing table. "And you're too young to have need of rouge."

"Oh, Justine, please. Just a little. In the evening."

Justine could not resist her pleading. She remembered her own youth far too well. She smiled at Charlotte. "Don't tell your father."

She returned to her room, closing the door on the young women's animated chatter. Her temples were beginning to throb, a reaction to her interview with the princess. She flung herself on the bed and pressed her hands against them. She would have to return to France. It was the only honorable thing to do. But not on the princess's terms. She would not give her the satisfaction of admitting that Minette was Simon's daughter. That secret, at least, was her own. Nor could she accept the charity the princess had offered her at the end of their interview.

Yet how were they to live, she and Minette? A life of genteel poverty was all that she could offer her daughter. Unless she became the expensive whore the princess thought her. That was unthinkable. Perhaps she should swallow her pride and accept the princess's offer. She was trapped, if not by poverty, then by shame.

One thing was clear. She would not go to London with Charlotte. And she must contrive to leave Moresby as soon as it could be done without causing comment. She would go after the ball. She would not abandon Charlotte till then. But once it was over and Charlotte's engagement was announced, there would be no more reason for her to remain at Moresby.

Six

As the first sweet, haunting notes of a waltz filled the rose drawing room, Simon was aware of a leaden sensation in the pit of his stomach. Alessa always did her best to create a romantic setting for her St. Valentine's Eve ball, but this year she had outdone herself. Streamers of red and pink ribbon and white lace ran from the chandeliers to the four corners of the room, caught up with velvet roses. A trifle gaudy, perhaps, but they blended with the rose silk wall hangings. In the soft candlelight the effect was one of lightness and charm. The color of the ribbons and roses was reflected by the crystals in the chandeliers and by the mellowed gold and silver of the candelabra that had been gathered up from all over Moresby and placed about the room.

A noble effort on Alessa's part, Simon thought, considering her opinion of his betrothal. Perhaps she thought he and Charlotte needed all the romance they could get. Alessa had even chosen to begin the ball with a waltz, a dance for lovers, rather than a quadrille. This particular waltz was a favorite of hers, Simon knew, one she often danced with Harry.

Simon glanced down at his betrothed. Charlotte's gaze was fixed somewhere beyond his shoulder, so that he found himself looking at the top of her head. She was wearing her hair differently tonight, in an elaborate arrangement of curls similar to the style Marianne affected. From this angle she looked remarkably like Marianne, for both woman had chosen to wear white dresses sashed in red for the evening.

"You're very quiet, Simon. I thought one was supposed to make polite conversation when one danced." Charlotte smiled up at him. Her eyes were bright and there was a hint of rouge on her cheeks. She was looking remarkably pretty, Simon thought, with the detached affection with which he might have noted the same thing about Alessa or one of his nieces.

"I beg your pardon," he said. "What would you like to talk about?"

"Oh, anything will do," Charlotte said, her gaze straying about the room. "What is one supposed to talk about?"

"I believe," Simon said carefully, "that the waltz is viewed as an excellent opportunity for flirtation."

Charlotte stared at him with an expression of distaste. *"Must* we?"

"I think betrothed couples are exempt if they wish it," Simon told her, keeping a straight face. "Married couples certainly are."

"That's a relief. I wouldn't even know how to flirt." Her brows drew together. "Can you flirt, Simon? I don't believe I've ever seen you do so."

Simon was growing used to such questions from Charlotte. Had he flirted with Justine in Paris? he wondered. Hardly. From the first, his feelings had been too intense for anything so lighthearted. Nor had Justine flirted with him. She had been unfailingly honest—in sharp contrast, Simon thought, to her playful behavior with Gerald Stratton and the other men present tonight.

"I wouldn't say flirting is one of my chief accomplishments," Simon told his betrothed truthfully. Then, thinking he should not brush Charlotte's interest aside, he added, "But if you like, I'll endeavor to improve myself."

"Oh, you needn't bother on my account," Charlotte assured him. "I'm having much too much fun to put my mind to flirting. This is my first ball, you know. Is it very like the entertainments in London?"

Simon looked around the room, noting the hectic, exuberant atmosphere. Alessa had managed to round up a number of young people from the neighboring houses. Everyone seemed bent on snatching as much pleasure as possible from the midst of winter. "It's less formal," he said. "And not quite as crowded."

"Do you think my dress is all right?"

Simon glanced at the dress again. It seemed more sophisticated than the gowns Charlotte usually wore, perhaps because she had pulled the sleeves down to the edge of her shoulders. She had very pretty shoulders, but the sight left him unmoved. "You look charming," he told her.

Charlotte frowned intently. "I was afraid white would seem horribly old-fashioned, but Marianne says it is always becoming. I do want to look my best for the betrothal announcement. Oh, dear." She cast a quick look around. "Do you think anyone heard me?"

"I doubt it," Simon assured her. "In any case, it scarcely matters now. They'll all know soon enough." He was aware again of the sick feeling in the pit of his stomach. By the end of the evening, he would have committed himself to Charlotte in front of the hundred or so people gathered in Alessa's reception rooms. He had already committed himself, of course. Having offered for Charlotte, he could not in honor draw back. Nor did he want to, he told himself firmly. Marriage to Charlotte might not be everything he had once hoped for, but they could learn to deal very well together.

As he twirled Charlotte around, Simon caught sight of Harry and Alessa waltzing together, close enough to cause talk, had they not been husband and wife. Not far off, Georgiana—whom Simon had frequently heard disdain all forms of sentimentality—was gazing adoringly into the eyes of her betrothed. Looking further about the room, Simon saw his former governess, Fiona Carne, dancing with her husband every bit as closely as Harry and Alessa. Simon's throat tightened. Fiona and Gideon seemed as much in love as they had when they'd married over ten years ago. And yet, Simon reminded himself, there had been a good deal of hurt between them before they'd finally found happiness.

A glimpse of Justine's chestnut hair, shining in the candlelight as she whirled around the room with one of the guests, reminded Simon of all the reasons he was marrying Charlotte.

"Justine looks lovely tonight, doesn't she?" Charlotte said, following the direction of his gaze.

Justine, in a gold-colored gossamer dress which seemed to float as she moved and revealed entirely too much of her figure, made Simon's body grow hot and his senses swim unnervingly. "Not as lovely as you," he told Charlotte, the lie sounding hollow to his own ears.

"It's sweet of you to say so," Charlotte said, in a cheerful voice, "but I know I can't compete with Justine. Not yet, anyway. I was going to model myself on her when I went to London, but I see now that my height and coloring are too different. The same is true of Lady Milverton. I think I shall model myself on Marianne instead. We are much more alike."

Simon breathed a sigh of relief. The prospect of a wife who modeled herself on his mistress was too horrible to contemplate.

"Do you think Marianne is very much attached to Lord Westcourt?" Charlotte asked. She was now looking to the other side of the room, where, Simon saw, Marianne was waltzing rather madly with Bertram. He felt a stirring of alarm.

"They've been friends for some time," Simon told Charlotte.

"Oh, Lord Westcourt is terribly in love with her," Charlotte said, as if everyone knew it, which, Simon reflected, was probably true. "He has been telling me all about it."

"All about what?" Simon asked, looking sharply at his fiancée.

"His feelings for Marianne. He says he had to confide in someone, and I expect he hoped I'd tell Marianne how he feels."

"And did you?" Simon asked, not sure what to make of this new development.

"Yes, most of it, except the parts that were too silly to bear repeating."

Simon frowned. Marianne could easily get in over her head. If only Justine had had the decency not to toy with Gerald, there might be some hope of salvaging the Strattons' marriage. Anger cut through Simon, and he knew it was not only on Marianne's account. He pulled Charlotte closer into his arms. She smelled of violets. A sweet scent, but not potent.

"Simon, you're going to leave a mark on my dress," Charlotte protested.

"I'm sorry." Simon at once relaxed his hold. He thought of Justine, who refused to stay away from a man like Gerald, so clearly her inferior in spirit and wit; of Marianne, whose love for her husband drove her into another man's arms; and of Charlotte, who longed for sophistication, but had no taste for romance. He wondered if he would ever understand women.

"I am so glad I have a chance to practice at a large entertainment before we go to London," Charlotte said. "I own I am a little nervous about London, especially as Justine will not be there to advise me—"

Simon looked down at her in surprise. "Surely Justine is to remain with you until the wedding," he said, betrayed into using Justine's given name.

"That was the arrangement," Charlotte agreed, not seeming to notice this slip. "But now Justine says that as I will be staying with the Princess Sofia, I will not have need of another chaperone."

Simon knew he ought to be relieved. To have Justine living under his mother's roof, to have to see her daily, to squire her and Charlotte about London, to prepare for the wedding with her close by, could only be painful. Besides, for Marianne's sake, the sooner Justine got away from Gerald, the better. But instead of a surge of relief, Simon felt a stab of worry. He recalled his encounter with Justine after her interview with his mother. Had *Maman* said something to her? Worry gave way to anger. Whatever his quarrel with Justine, his mother had no right to tell her what to do.

When the dance came to an end and Charlotte was claimed by a new partner, Simon went in search of Sofia, determined to get at the truth of the matter. But he found his mother in the adjoining cardroom, making one at a game of five-card loo. Simon resisted the impulse to drag her away from the game. The last thing he wanted was a public scene. If he had been sensible, he would have waited until the ball was over before seeking his mother out at all. Where Justine was concerned, he still found it impossible to behave sensibly.

The sight of the baize-covered card tables reminded Simon of evenings in Paris when he had seen Justine play cards with devastating skill. Though she had never admitted it, he suspected her card playing had as much to do with her need for money as with her enjoyment of the game. She was not a wealthy woman. The security of her position as Charlotte's chaperone must mean a great deal to her. If his mother had driven her away—

Biting back a curse, Simon left the relative quiet and order of the cardroom for the noise and confusion of the ballroom. A country dance had just ended and partners were being chosen for new sets. Simon knew he should dance with Charlotte again before the end of the evening, but that could wait, perhaps until after their betrothal was announced. Charlotte seemed to have no desire for his company at present. She was surrounded by half a dozen young men and had apparently changed her mind about flirting. Perhaps, Simon thought, she viewed it differently when her fiancé wasn't involved.

Justine was also in the midst of a crowd of ardent gentlemen. Simon looked away from the sight of her smiling up at one of them and found himself staring at Marianne, who had retired to the edge of the dance floor and was receiving the attentions not only of Bertram, but of three other men as well.

"Simon. Just the person I wanted to see."

At the sound of the warm voice, Simon turned around with pleasure and relief to smile at his former governess. Fiona was wearing a dark green dress which set off her pale gold hair. When he was a boy, he had thought she was the most beautiful woman in the world. He had continued to think so until he met Justine. Simon pushed aside this unwelcome thought. In addition to being elegantly beautiful, Fiona was one of the few women whom he had always been able to count on to behave with utter sanity.

Unfortunately, Simon thought, as he looked into Fiona's clear gray eyes, she shared Alessa's ability to see more than he wished. But unlike his sister, Fiona did not ask awkward questions. "Can I persuade you to help me find a glass of champagne?" she said, after the slightest pause. "Gideon's talking politics. I'll be lucky if I can reclaim him before the party breaks up."

"Of course," Simon said, offering her his arm. "There are footmen circling about with trays, but with this crowd, the champagne's bound to have gone flat. Let's try the refreshment room."

They escaped the press of the ballroom and crossed the hall to the small saloon where refreshments were laid out. Fiona spoke lightly about the latest escapades of her two young daughters, and the excitement of her stepdaughter, who was attending the ball for the first time. Simon was grateful for the innocuous conversation. Though Fiona's house, Sundon, was less than an hour from Moresby, he had not seen her since the start of the house party. She knew the reason for Charlotte's visit, but she did not know of the betrothal. Simon found himself reluctant to tell her. There was too much he didn't want to discuss.

Fiona regarded Simon with concern as he negotiated a path through the crowd around the refreshment tables. A month ago, when Charlotte de Chambeau's visit was first proposed, Alessa had driven over to Sundon and informed Fiona that Simon was about to ruin his life. Fiona had been concerned by the prospect of Simon making an arranged marriage, but years of being a governess, stepmother, and mother had taught her not to interfere. Simon had always been able to take care of himself. Yet seeing him now, Fiona felt a wave of alarm. Simon had always taken his responsibilities seriously, but tonight he looked as if he had the weight of the world on his shoulders. Most worrying of all, she had never seen him appear less sure of himself.

"Here we go. Guaranteed fresh from a newly opened bottle." Simon emerged from the crowd carrying two glasses. "Princely authority does have its uses. So does being the hostess's brother."

Fiona smiled. "Do you think princely authority could extend to finding somewhere quiet to sit down?" she asked, taking one of the chilled glasses.

This last was no easy task, but Simon led the way to a cushioned bench set in an alcove opening off the corridor, far enough removed from the main reception rooms to be relatively free of traffic. Fiona settled her silk skirts and sought for a way to allow Simon to talk without boxing him into a corner. "We had a letter from Peter yesterday," she said. Her stepson Peter, now on his honeymoon, had been Simon's closest friend since boyhood. "He sounds blissfully happy, almost to the point of incoherence."

"I had a letter last week," Simon said. "Judging by its tone, it's a good thing he and Radka decided to stay in England for their wedding journey."

"Very true," Fiona agreed. "There's little point in exploring the Continent when they only have eyes for each other."

Simon was silent for a moment, staring at his hands. Fiona wondered if he was thinking how he might spend his own wedding journey. "I've often envied Peter for loving Radka so completely all these years," Simon said, suddenly looking up at her. "I don't think he's looked at another woman since he was seventeen."

Fiona had never before heard Simon express jealousy of his friend. Not for the first time, she wondered if Simon had ever been in love. He was almost like a son to her and there were so many things she couldn't ask him. "Most people aren't so fortunate," she said. "Finding the right person at all is difficult enough, let alone finding him or her the first time one falls in love."

Simon gave a wry smile. "You think it's as simple as finding the right person?"

"I don't think it's simple at all," Fiona said truthfully. Her own marriage, though happy, had certainly taken work. "Marriage is difficult for everyone. But being in love helps."

"Does it? In some cases it would seem only to complicate matters."

Fiona took a sip of champagne, hiding her frown behind the glass. This was not the Simon who had been so worried when his sister made a marriage of convenience, who had seemed to understand Alessa and Harry's real feelings for each other before they did themselves. Whatever Simon's romantic experiences, they must have been painfully bitter.

"It's more difficult for you than for Peter," Fiona said. "So much is expected of a Tassio." She smoothed a wrinkle from one of her gloves, wondering how to gracefully introduce the subject of the girl Simon might make his wife. "It must be difficult for Mademoiselle de Chambeau as well," she added. "Women have less freedom in these matters than men."

"Damn it, Fiona." Simon brought his hand down hard on the gilded wood of the bench. "It's bad enough that I have *Maman* and Alessa trying to tell me what to do. Don't you start, too. It's my life."

"Yes," Fiona agreed, pleased that he was at least expressing honest emotion, "it is. Be sure you can live with the decisions you make."

Simon twisted the heavy wrought-gold Tassio ring he wore on his left hand. "You don't think it's a good match." It was a statement, not a question.

"I have no idea whether it's a good match or not," said Fiona, who had had only a brief glimpse of Charlotte de Chambeau. "But you're clearly not in love. And who would expect it after a week's acquaintance?"

Simon stared at the marble-topped table on the opposite side of the corridor. "This meeting wasn't arranged for Charlotte and me to fall in love," he said, an uncharacteristically harsh note in his voice. "We can't all be like Peter, true to our first love forever."

Fiona reached up to touch her jade necklace, an early Valentine's Day gift from her husband. Her fingers clenched over the smooth beads. She was convinced the "first love" Simon spoke of was someone very specific.

The sound of footsteps and low-voiced conversation echoed down the corridor. A young couple passed by, the man's dark-coated arm draped intimately about the waist of the woman's pale blue dress.

"Marrying for love may not always be wise," Fiona said, when the couple had passed from earshot. "But Mademoiselle de Chambeau seems very young. And you seem very unhappy."

Simon fixed her with a hard stare. Fiona was reminded that the strong-willed boy who had once been her pupil was now an even stronger-willed man. "I know what I'm about," he said.

"I'm sure you'll do very well, whatever you choose," Fiona said, laying a hand on his arm. "I've always trusted you to make the right decision."

Simon gave the ghost of a smile. "How typical, Fiona. That's an infinitely greater burden than telling me what to do." He covered her fingers with his own. His dark eyes held a vulnerability she had not seen since he'd come back from the Continent. "I trust you will have no cause to doubt your faith in me. I should have told you sooner. I have asked Charlotte to be my wife. Our betrothal is to be announced tonight."

Fiona drew a breath, forced a smile to her lips, and said the only thing possible to say. "Then I wish you very happy. I hope I have not been dreadfully impertinent."

"You said nothing I didn't already know." Simon's mouth twisted with self-mockery. "No one can accuse me of not going into this with my eyes open."

"Then you're more fortunate than some." Fiona sought refuge in smoothing back a strand of hair to mask a sickening feeling of worry. Simon was right. He was going into marriage with a clear-eyed view of the future. But he did not expect the future to bring him happiness.

Justine accepted a glass of champagne from a young man whose name she could not remember and gave him what she hoped was a dazzling smile. She was determined to make it clear to Simon, his mother, and anyone else who was interested that she had no designs on the Prince di Tassio.

"You must go in to supper with me, Madame de Valon, I insist." The young man who had brought her the champagne pressed her hand with unnecessary ardor. Groans and a flurry of protest went up from the half-dozen other gentlemen gathered around the chair where she was sitting. Justine sipped the champagne, beginning to wish she had not been quite so determined to prove her independence of Simon.

Gerald Stratton's voice rose above the sounds of protest. "See here, Kingston, Madame de Valon is going in to supper with me, and there's an end to it."

Kingston, that was the name of the man with the champagne glass. Justine's relief at having acquired this information gave way to worry as Kingston got to his feet to face Gerald. They were evenly matched. Kingston was a good five years younger, but Gerald was at least two inches taller. Both men looked as if they had experience with their fives.

"So you keep saying, Stratton," Kingston declared. "But I haven't heard Madame de Valon agree to let you escort her."

"You must forgive me, gentlemen," Justine said, seeking to head off a scene. "I've been much too busy enjoying myself to give any thought to supper."

Gerald seemed to take no notice of her. "Madame de Valon and I are old friends," he told Kingston.

"I had hoped Madame de Valon would go in to supper with me," ventured Mr. Crosbie, who had a kind face and charming manners. "But surely it is something a lady may be allowed to decide for herself."

"Whomever she chooses, it seems plain it isn't going to be you, Stratton," Kingston informed Gerald with relish.

Justine set her champagne glass down quickly, cursing Mr. Kingston's tongue. Gerald drew a breath of outrage and grabbed hold of Kingston's lapels. Before matters could escalate further, someone hidden by the crowd grasped Gerald by the shoulders.

"Easy there, Stratton. Looks as if you could do with some coffee." The tone was pleasant but implacable. The voice was Simon's.

"See here, Tassio—" Gerald began, twisting around.

"Let's talk about it outside, shall we?" Simon said, in a tone that brooked no compromise.

Justine got to her feet to see Simon and Gerald facing each other while a bewildered Kingston looked on along with the other men. Gerald was angry and belligerent, his pride hurt. His temper would only worsen if Simon took him away. Simon was more than equal to the situation, Justine knew, but he should not have to spend his betrothal ball dealing with such unpleasantness. This was her problem.

"Sir Gerald and I were just about to take a turn about the room," she said, walking forward. "Please excuse us, Your Excellency."

Simon met her gaze for a moment, the concern in his eyes giving way to a look of cold disgust. Don't be a fool, Justine wanted to say, do you think I really want to spend time with this stupid man? Do you think I could possibly feel anything for him like what I felt for you? Do you think I could feel it for anyone else? But she bit the words back. If Simon thought her a shameless flirt who did not take her love affairs seriously, so much the better for all of them.

"I see. I did not understand the situation, madam. Pray forgive me." Simon made her a slight bow and stepped away from Gerald.

The taste of despair bitter in her mouth, Justine smiled at the other men and took Gerald's arm. Gerald gave her a smile of immense satisfaction. "Arrogant young puppy, Tassio," he murmured as they moved away from the others. "To think I was actually afraid you were in love with the fellow."

"Don't be silly," Justine said, her voice sharper than she intended.

Gerald stopped walking abruptly, staring across the room as if transfixed. Justine followed the direction of his gaze and saw Marianne Stratton and Bertram Westcourt seated side by side on a small settee. As she watched, Bertram seized Marianne's hand and lifted it to his lips. Marianne cast a quick glance around the room, but did not pull her hand away.

Gerald sucked in his breath, his hand tightening painfully on Justine's arm. Then he turned and smiled down at her with what seemed to Justine to be grim determination. "Think we might manage to find a place to be private, m'dear?"

Justine had no desire to be alone with Gerald. On the other hand, it would be preferable to a public scene. Grateful for the tour Lady Milverton had given her of Moresby, Justine led Gerald out of the ballroom and across the hall to an antechamber opening off the small saloon. As she had hoped, it was unoccupied. The lamps were lit, but there was no fire and the air felt unexpectedly chilly after the heat of the crowded ballroom. Just as well. She needed all the help she could get to cool down Sir Gerald.

"My darling." Gerald kicked the door shut and pulled her into his arms before she could move away. His gloved hands were sticky. His mouth was wet as it sought her own. Justine had never thought the taste of champagne could make her gag so violently.

"You forget yourself, Sir Gerald." She struggled to get her arms free and pushed hard against his chest.

Gerald drew a breath, as if the wind had been knocked out of him. "But I love you."

Justine stepped away from him and tugged her sleeves back into place. "I fear I cannot return the sentiment."

"You weren't so particular in Paris, if the stories are true," Gerald protested, looking at her in bewilderment.

Justine winced inwardly. "You should never listen to stories."

"You can't go on being that chit's chaperone forever," Gerald pointed out, taking a step toward her. "I could set you up in a house. We could—"

"Do you think I would be any man's mistress, let alone yours?" Justine demanded. She had resisted that path ever since her husband's death. She would not live off any man, even—especially—Simon.

"It isn't like that," Gerald insisted, sounding as if he really meant it.

"How else can it be?" Justine asked, retreating to the safety of the fireplace, where the poker was handy if the need for it arose. "You're married."

"Married?" Gerald gave a harsh laugh. "My wife doesn't take fidelity seriously. Why should I?"

The bitterness in his tone brought Justine up short. She considered him for a moment, recalling his reaction to the glimpse of his wife and Lord Westcourt, and made a startling discovery. "I don't think you really want me at all, Sir Gerald."

"Not want you?" Gerald took another step forward, though he seemed more purposeful than ardent. "What nonsense—"

Justine put up a hand to forestall him. "It's not nonsense at all," she said, feeling much more cordial toward him. "How could you want me when you're so obviously in love with your wife?"

Her words checked him as her gesture could not. For a moment she glimpsed a raw pain in his eyes which she understood all too well. "My wife doesn't want me," he said in a flat voice.

"Has she said so?"

"She doesn't need to. She cringes when I touch her."

Justine had a clear memory of her own wedding night. Armand had at least been a practiced lover, if not always a thoughtful one. Judging by Gerald's kisses, he was considerably less skilled. Justine suspected he stood in crying need of some womanly advice. Deciding the poker might not be necessary after all, she moved to a brocade sofa, wondering how to put the matter delicately. "Sit down, Sir Gerald."

As soon as Gerald seated himself beside her, Justine regretted choosing the sofa. Chairs would have been much safer. But Gerald sat a foot away and made no effort to touch her. His ardor seemed to have given way to black depression.

Justine spread her fan open in her lap and stared fixedly at the painted silk. She had never had such a discussion with any man, let alone one she knew so little. "You have not been married long, have you?" she asked.

"Two years this summer," Gerald muttered, looking at the floor.

"Your wife is quite young," Justine said. "I imagine she feels shy."

"Shy?" Gerald raised his head and stared at her. "With *me?* I'm her husband."

Justine choked. "Marriage vows do not turn a girl into an experienced woman," she pointed out, keeping her voice steady.

"No, of course not. Didn't mean anything of the kind. That is—" Gerald looked away, color creeping above the high starched points of his shirt.

"I think," Justine continued, relieved Gerald found the scene even more awkward than she did herself, "that you should hold your wife more."

"Devil take it, woman, I can barely get near her," Gerald protested, stung out of his embarrassment.

"I don't just mean with—with amorous intent," Justine told him, plunging forward with determination. "Be gentle with her. Show her how precious you think she is."

"But I've tried—" Gerald broke off with a frown, as if mulling over his behavior in the bedroom.

"Kiss her," Justine said, pressing up her advantage. "Be romantic. Let her grow comfortable before you try anything more."

"But she's not—"

"And when you desire more," Justine persisted, "move slowly. These things can take longer for women than for men. Think of her pleasure, not your own."

Gerald's frown gave way to a thoughtful expression. "You think—"

"I think you will find Lady Stratton is far more responsive than you expect," Justine told him. "Before long you will find that you can take your pleasure together."

Gerald stared at his hands, a smile beginning to spread across his face. Then the smile was abruptly wiped away. "Marianne doesn't love me. You saw the way she was looking at Westcourt."

"Perhaps she was trying to make you jealous," Justine suggested.

Gerald looked at her in surprise, as if such a thing had never occurred to him. He shook his head. "That's nonsense."

"Is it?" Justine asked gently. "Haven't you been trying to make her jealous by paying court to me?"

Gerald opened his mouth to protest, then shut it again, a look of stunned realization on his face. For a moment, he sat stock still. Then he let out a whoop of joy and gave Justine an exuberant hug.

"You look quite ferocious, Simon." With a whisper of rose velvet and a waft of well-blended scent, Alessa emerged beside Simon on the edge of the dance floor. "What's the matter?"

Simon drew a breath and smiled at his sister. He could hardly admit that he was angry because the image of Justine walking through the crowd on Gerald's arm was burned in his memory. "Isn't battling my way through large crowds and shouting to make myself heard over the babble reason enough?" he asked.

"Rubbish," Alessa told him. "You've coped with far worse in London with the best goodwill in the world." She laid a hand on his arm and drew him into a recess formed by a pier table and a marble pedestal bearing a bust of some long-gone

Dudley. "Not having qualms about the betrothal, are you?" she asked softly.

"A bit late now, if I was," Simon said, keeping his voice light.

"We could delay the announcement," Alessa suggested. Her eyes were dark with worry. Simon had seen just such a look on her face whenever her children tried anything she thought risky.

Touched, he brushed his fingers against her cheek. "It wouldn't make any difference, 'Lessa. I'm committed."

Alessa smiled at the use of her nursery name, though her eyes remained serious. "I understand Madame de Valon may be going back to Paris earlier than expected."

"Charlotte mentioned it," Simon agreed, with what he thought was a very good show of unconcern.

"I thought you might be relieved," Alessa said. "You look rather sick."

"It's hardly my concern," Simon told her. "Madame de Valon is her own mistress."

"I'm so glad you recognize that," Alessa said with a smile. "These past days you've been acting as if you were afraid she was someone else's." Before Simon could respond, Alessa slipped away from him and struck up a conversation with Rachel Melchett.

Just a few more weeks, Simon told himself grimly, and the house party would be over. At least in London he had his own rooms. That he would soon be sharing a house with Charlotte he pushed to the back of his mind. Charlotte, at least, would not interfere in his life. It was part of their agreement.

The thought of Charlotte reminded Simon that he had been absent from her side for longer than might seem appropriate on the night their betrothal was to be announced. He set off in search of her, but as he moved through the crowd, his arm was suddenly seized in a feverish grip.

For a fraction of a second, Simon thought it was his betrothed. Then he realized that the woman before him was an inch or so taller. "Simon," Marianne breathed, "you must advise me. It's so dreadful. I don't know what to do."

"What's happened?" Simon asked, pulling her toward the

320

meager privacy afforded by the windows which ran along the back wall.

"Gerald is a beast." Marianne twisted her gloved hands together. "Only yesterday he read me the most horrid lecture about Lord Westcourt, and tonight he's spent the entire evening looking down Madame de Valon's dress. They left the ballroom together just now."

Simon felt his fists clench. He had not known Justine had been so brazen as to slip off with Stratton in the midst of the ball. "Perhaps they went to the refreshment room," he suggested. It was the charitable explanation, though he was feeling anything but charitable.

Marianne sniffed. "Madame de Valon has had men bringing her refreshments all evening—and Gerald looked as if he had more than champagne on his mind. Oh, Simon, I don't know what to do."

"About Gerald?" Simon asked, thinking a knock in the teeth would answer very nicely.

"No, about Lord Westcourt. He wants me to meet him in the conservatory at eleven-thirty. He's asked me to meet him before and I never have, but this time it would serve Gerald right, so perhaps . . . Do you think I should?"

Simon drew a breath, trying to push aside his own jealousy. Marianne was on the verge of doing something very silly. They could not possibly talk about it in the ballroom. "Let's go somewhere quiet," he said, offering her his arm. "I could do with a few minutes of escape myself."

Marianne seemed relieved at the prospect of a tête-à-tête. Simon led her out of the ballroom and across the hall. The antechamber next to the small saloon was not usually opened for parties, but Alessa kept the lamps lit in case any of the family needed a place to escape.

Wondering what on earth he was to say to Marianne, Simon opened the door to find his former mistress in the arms of Marianne's husband.

Seven

The ballroom was insufferably hot. Or perhaps it was the champagne. Charlotte was not used to champagne. *Papa* allowed her a sip or two on special occasions, but until her arrival at Moresby, she had never had as much as an entire glass. And never as many glasses as tonight, when the trays filled with glasses of the sparkling liquid seemed to rival the brilliance of the glittering chandeliers.

Charlotte loved the look of champagne, the bubbles rising in the golden wine. She loved the way it felt when she drank it, the delicious tickling in her nose. She was even getting used to its taste.

But there was no denying that she felt the least bit unsteady on her feet. She excused herself abruptly from the knot of young men with whom she had been surrounded ever since her waltz with Simon and made her way to the edge of the ballroom. She looked back at the swirling movement of the dance, thinking that flirting was after all not so very hard. One looked down, fluttered one's fan, then looked up abruptly at whichever man one had chosen as the object of flirtation, widening one's eyes ever so slightly as though the sight of him filled one with sudden wonder and admiration. It worked excessively well. Charlotte had brought a blush to more than one cheek this evening and had elicited a variety of strangled comments such as "You have beautiful eyes" and "Oh, I say."

Charlotte giggled, looked round to see if she had been over-heard, and nearly collided with a footman carrying one of the ever-present trays of champagne-filled glasses. He recovered with great skill and begged her pardon. Charlotte giggled again, then curtsied and begged his. She made her way into the hall, reviewing her behavior. What on earth had she been about? One did not curtsy to footmen. Thinking she had best concentrate on her walking, she moved carefully down the hall. She would go upstairs and sit in the room Lady Milver-ton had set aside for the ladies who wished to retire momen-tarily from the press of the ballroom. A splash of cold water on her face would work wonders.

She reached the foot of the staircase and looked up. Two elegantly gowned women stood at the head of the stairs, pre-paring to return to the ballroom. Charlotte did not recognize the elder of the two. The other was unfortunately the Princess Sofia.

Charlotte was not equal to the encounter. She turned abruptly and made her way through the maze of rooms that would lead her eventually to the conservatory.

The decision was made without thought but came, Charlotte realized, from some primitive instinct of self-preservation. The princess would not approve of her future daughter-in-law wan-dering about the house in such an unstable condition. Char-lotte had best not be seen until she had greater command of her head and her feet.

The conservatory, at least, would be dark and quiet, two qualities that at the moment had everything to recommend them. It might even be cooler than the overheated ballroom. Charlotte slowed her pace, was careful about opening doors and closing them quietly behind her, and finally reached her goal.

The conservatory doors were open. The lamp that hung from the domed glass ceiling of the entryway was lit, shedding a greenish glow on the white marble of the woman who stood on a pedestal directly beneath. Odd that the statue should be green. The color must come from the reflected light of the

323

vines that climbed up the entryway walls and festooned the dome and dipped below it. Charlotte looked up, then wished she hadn't. She rested her forehead against the cool surface of the statue. The woman, some kind of goddess, sported an improbable pair of wings. A chaste goddess, for her hands rested modestly over her breast and her lower parts were covered with a knotted drapery, beginning at the last possible point beneath her hips—another inch would have been disastrous.

The marble soothed her. Feeling somewhat better, Charlotte moved forward and came to the stairs that led down into the conservatory proper. There were five steps, she remembered, and she took them carefully, counting as she went. There were no lights beyond, but the entryway light would enable her to see enough to find one of the benches that were placed conveniently around the conservatory. Charlotte loved the room, a place of sudden turns and hidden alcoves, filled with hundreds of plants and flowers, most of whose names she did not know.

The damp scent of foliage and earth deepened as she moved further into the room. She walked slowly, letting her eyes adjust to the darkness. It was not so very dark after all. A few lamps had been placed on the ground, illuminating the paths between the trees and shrubs but leaving everything washed of color. It was another world. It was blissfully peaceful.

Another two steps and the peace was shattered. Charlotte was conscious of a rush of air and then of a man's voice, harsh with emotion, crying, "Oh, my dearest love!" The next instant she was swept into a surprisingly strong pair of arms. Her hands, thrown up to ward off the assault, were crushed against a hard chest. The scent of a man filled her senses. It was not unpleasant—a mixture of a spicy odor and a faint smell of sweat. More pleasant than the scent of *Papa,* who had a dry mustiness about him, or Père Dubos, who always smelled vaguely of candles and incense.

Then scent was washed away by sensation. The man's lips, soft and hard at once, were covering her mouth. It must be a very passionate kiss, though she had nothing against which to compare it, save the prince's restrained salute that had sealed their betrothal. This was far more interesting. She opened her mouth slightly, the better to experience this passion, and felt a shock of surprise and dismay as a warm tongue slid between her lips.

It was, she decided after a moment, rather agreeable. Her hands feeling cramped, she pulled them free of his chest. Then, not knowing what else to do with them, she wrapped them around his neck.

The sight of Justine in Gerald's arms made Simon sick with fury. He would tear those illicit lovers apart. He would beat Gerald to a senseless pulp and leave him prostrate before her feet. Better, he would leave him dead. Never again would Justine shame herself—and him—by engaging in such a despicable liaison.

Beside him, Marianne gave a faint moan. Simon had forgot her entirely. His fury receded and he turned to give her support. But she eluded his arm and without a word ran out of the room. Leaving the wanton couple to do what they would, Simon ran after her.

Marianne had had a fearful shock and must not be left alone. At the entrance to the ballroom, Simon caught a glimpse of a white dress. He followed, but could not find her in the crowded room. He would have sworn that the women at the ball were dressed in colors of every hue, but now half of them seemed to be wearing white.

Simon pushed his way through the throng, avoiding conversation when he could, exchanging a few words when he must. "If you're looking for Mademoiselle de Chambeau," an excited young man told him, "she went upstairs eons ago. And she's promised me the next dance. It's deucedly unfair." Simon thought of asking him if he had seen Lady Stratton, but decided against calling attention to Marianne. "Women," he said, shaking his head in commiseration. He smiled and pushed on.

He was being carried along on a wave of outrage and anxiety. After five minutes he stopped and began to think. Marianne would want to avoid the ballroom at all costs. She would seek somewhere private to tend her wounds. Unless . . .

Simon turned abruptly and hurried out of the ballroom. Damnation. He should have thought of it at once. She was going to meet Bertram Westcourt.

The conservatory was dark. Simon paused in the dimly lit entryway and pulled out his watch. Twenty past eleven. With luck, Marianne had not yet arrived and he could get Bertram out of the way. He ran down the steps and paused to get his bearings. No one was in sight, but surely he had heard a sound. He listened carefully and it came again—a breath, a sigh, a soft moan, he could not tell which.

It was enough. Simon strode purposefully toward the source of the sound, turned a corner, and saw them, two figures wound tightly together, the man's dark head bent, the woman's hair of a lighter hue. Simon recognized the distinctive knot of curls that Marianne affected. Her dress was white and her sash was of a darker shade that he knew in proper light would be red.

He was late, but not too late for action. With a roar of outrage, Simon sprang forward and pulled the entwined couple apart. The woman gave a cry and stumbled backward. Simon ignored her. His attention was all on the man, who stood now with his mouth open, dazed with shock and unfulfilled passion, his hands still raised to hold the woman he had been embracing.

With all the pent-up fury and anguish of the past week Simon took careful aim and struck a blow to Bertram's jaw.

At the same moment Marianne screamed and Bertram, distracted, moved his head. The jab should have knocked him out. As it was, it left him lying on the ground, stunned but fully conscious. Marianne flung herself upon him and tenderly raised his head against her breast. Then, in a most uncharacteristic blaze of fury, she turned to Simon. "You beast!"

The voice was not Marianne's. Simon leaned down and peered at the woman's face. Good God, it was Charlotte.

"Simon?" Charlotte seemed equally startled. "Oh, Simon, how could you? We had an agreement."

Bertram struggled to sit up. He looked from Simon to Charlotte. "Agreement?"

"Yes, we're going to be married," Charlotte said, in a voice she might have used to describe a change in the weather.

"Oh, my God." Bertram rubbed his jaw tenderly.

"It's quite all right," Charlotte said brightly. "We're going to lead separate lives."

This was almost too much for Simon. By rights he should break the engagement here and now—the thought gave him an intoxicating sense of freedom—but he could not. Charlotte was being silly out of reason, but it was not her fault. In the dim light of the conservatory, he had mistaken her for Marianne. It was obvious that Bertram had as well.

Still, Charlotte might have struggled just a little in his arms. They would have to have a serious talk about her behavior. Unless she had not been surprised at Bertram's embrace and the encounter had been planned. Simon pushed the thought away. Marianne had been quite clear about the proposed assignation, and even Bertram would not be witless enough to make appointments with two women at the same time.

"It was a mistake," Bertram said, looking up at Simon. "I didn't know she was Mademoiselle de Chambeau. I thought she was—" He broke off, apparently realizing he was about to be ungallant. "But I have offered her an unpardonable insult. I am quite prepared to give you satisfaction."

Simon suppressed an absurd desire to laugh. "Don't be an ass," he said. He gave Bertram his hand and pulled him to his feet, then turned and gave his hand to Charlotte. She stood unsteadily and would not look at him. "Are you all right?" he asked with sudden concern.

Charlotte's dress was crumpled. A lock of hair had been

disarranged in the tussle and fell over her face. She made a futile attempt to pin it up, then abandoned the effort, her eyes filled with despair. "Oh, Simon," she wailed, "I think I am going to be unwell."

Alarmed, Simon put his arm around her waist and led her further into the reaches of the conservatory. When they were out of sight, he helped her to a bench.

"I'm so very sorry," she said. Then his faithless young wife-to-be, the future mother of his children, bent her head over her knees and was thoroughly sick.

Marianne fled from the antechamber into the ballroom as though the light and noise and crowds of people would blot out the image of her husband in the arms of Madame de Valon. How could Gerald humiliate her so, in the middle of the evening, at a large entertainment? True, the door had been closed, but anyone might have seen them. She and Simon had.

She had forgot about Simon. Dear Simon, he had tried so hard to be kind. Marianne paused at the edge of the dance floor and wielded her fan vigorously. It was dreadfully hot and she was breathing in unbecoming gasps. She must get hold of herself and think what she must do next. She was strongly tempted to run upstairs to her room and fling herself on the bed and shriek and throw things. But she never threw anything, though she was often tempted to do so, and besides, someone might hear her.

Marianne moved slowly along the edge of the dance floor, her eyes downcast to discourage any attempts at conversation. What she ought to do is march right back and confront Gerald with his perfidious behavior. But she could not bring herself to face that woman, and—she had to admit it—she was a coward and Gerald always managed to put her in the wrong.

The wrong. That was it. If Gerald accused her of all sorts of nameless trespasses, then she would trespass in deed. She snapped her fan closed with sudden decision. Her husband might not want her, but Lord Westcourt did. She would go to Bertram. Now, if she could only find the conservatory.

Marianne, her eyes no longer downcast, moved toward one of the two double doors that led out of the ballroom and found herself suddenly besieged by people. There was a tall young man, not nearly as nice as Bertram, to whom she was promised for the next set, and two others who also wished to engage her to dance. Marianne had not had two seasons in London for nothing, and though she was burning with impatience, she turned them all away very nicely and left them reasonably satisfied. She hurried on, only to be stopped by an elderly woman in a gray satin dress and an elaborate lace cap who claimed to be a friend of her mother's. Marianne answered an interminable series of questions, some of them quite impertinent—how could she be increasing when Gerald never came near her—murmured unintelligible replies, and at last made her escape.

The hall was cool. She looked around, trying to remember the way to the conservatory. Moresby was an old house and had been much rebuilt, with rooms and passages added at the whim of its various occupants. She stepped behind a pillar to avoid a footman who might offer to help her and tried to form an image of the arrangement of rooms on the ground floor. She took two wrong turnings before she finally reached her destination, out of breath and not a little agitated.

And all the time she was thinking of two men. Bertram, dear sweet Bertram who understood her as no other man ever had. And Gerald, who had taken a lover and thereby given her every right to take one of her own.

Marianne walked through the doorway into the conservatory. It was like stepping into another world. And so it was, for after tonight she would never be the same again. No longer a chaste, modest wife, but a woman of the world, like Madame de Valon. The thought gave her the courage to cross the entryway and descend the steps. She stopped, letting her eyes adjust to the darkened room. What had Bertram said? An alcove, around the corner to the left.

She felt suffocated, as though she had run a great distance and could not breathe. A hard pulse was throbbing in her neck. She stayed irresolute at the foot of the steps. Then she remembered the sight of that woman crushed in Gerald's arms. The image gave her resolution and she hurried forward, turning left as directed.

And he was there, standing before an enormous palm, his hair falling over his eyes. The dear boy, how distraught she had made him. "Bertram," she whispered. She ran forward and flung her arms around his neck. "Dear Bertram," she said, her voice muffled against his neckcloth, "how foolish I have been. But I am here. I am yours."

His arms went about her, though not as tightly as she wished. He drew his head back and looked down at her as though not sure of what he would find. "It *is* you," he said with some surprise.

"Who else would it be?"

He looked at her uncertainly. Why didn't he kiss her? He was so respectful, so shy. She pulled his head down and stood on tiptoe to bring her mouth to his. His arms tightened then and he kissed her in earnest. Marianne felt a sudden cramping in the region of her heart, but whether it was joy or sadness she could no longer tell.

The moment was abruptly shattered. Marianne heard a howl of rage and in the next instant she was flung cruelly aside. She stumbled and fell to her knees. Above her Bertram was staring open-mouthed at the man who was hurling himself toward him. There was a blur of movement. Marianne caught a glimpse of white and of a large object raised above their attacker's head. Then the man was laid out, stunned, on the floor. Marianne peered at his face and shrieked. "Gerald!"

Justine hurried forward. She and Gerald had looked everywhere for Marianne and had come in desperation to the conservatory. Gerald had insisted that she would be with Westcourt and he had been right. But there were two women in white. Marianne was on the ground, cradling her husband's head in her lap. The other—now, why wasn't she surprised?—was Charlotte, still holding the heavy potted plant with which she had struck Gerald on the head.

Charlotte was staring at Gerald with a look of horror. Justine relieved her of the pot and pulled her aside. Even in the dim light of the conservatory the girl looked deathly pale. There was a faint sour smell about her which suggested that she had recently been sick. "Is he dead?" Charlotte whispered.

Bertram shook his head in dismay. "Oh, Lord, I'm sorry. I'm so sorry."

"Gerald." Marianne shook her husband's head. "Gerald, do wake up."

"I didn't mean to hurt him," Charlotte said. "But I couldn't let him knock Bertram down again."

Marianne's startled gaze went to Bertram. She seemed to have entirely forgot the man she had been kissing enthusiastically a few moments before. Then she turned to Charlotte. "Bertram? But he wasn't knocked down at all. It was Gerald you hit. Charlotte, if he doesn't recover, I will never forgive you."

"I will never forgive myself." Charlotte escaped Justine's restraining arm and knelt beside the unconscious man.

Justine was so caught up in the scene on the ground that she did not see Simon until he appeared abruptly at her side. "For God's sake," he said in a furious whisper. "Can't you leave them alone? Both of them. Haven't you done enough harm?"

"There's a lot to be said for being a widow," Charlotte was saying, "once you're out of that horrid black." She looked back at her companion. "Justine can do exactly as she pleases."

Marianne followed the direction of Charlotte's glance and gave a cry of outrage. She was about to speak, but at that moment Gerald uttered a pitiful moan. "Oh, my darling," Marianne cried, stroking his forehead.

Gerald looked up and saw Charlotte, who was also hovering above him. "Marianne?"

"*I'm* Marianne," his wife informed him. There was a distinct lessening of softness in her manner.

Gerald shifted his head. The movement must have brought him pain, for he groaned. He turned his eyes toward Bertram, who had retreated as far as he was able. "That was the devil of a blow. Unfair. I was the injured party."

"I didn't hit you," Bertram protested.

"Something hit me." Gerald struggled to a sitting position and felt his head. "From behind." He seemed confused.

"*I* hit you," Charlotte said firmly. "I couldn't let you hit Bertram. You had to be stopped."

Gerald looked at her with indignation. "*They* had to be stopped."

Simon continued to stare at Justine as though he would force an answer from her lips. Justine ignored him. She drew Charlotte to her feet and took her a little way apart. In her present state, Charlotte could not be held responsible for her words.

Gerald had turned to his wife. "How could you go to that man?"

"I'm so sorry," Bertram said again, his hands clutching his hair.

"How could you run off with that woman?" Marianne's voice was filled with indignation. "In a public place, just a step away from the ballroom. Anyone could have seen you. Is that why you brought her here?" She pointed an accusing finger at Justine, "So you could have more privacy for your intrigues? Why not take her upstairs to your bed and be done with it."

Simon was again at Justine's side. "Leave, I beg you. I'll take care of Charlotte."

Justine pushed Charlotte in his arms. She could not let Marianne's accusation pass, and Gerald seemed incapable of coherent speech. "Lady Stratton," she said, "it was not like that at all."

"That's right," said Gerald. "Not at all."

Marianne ignored her husband. "I *saw* you," she said, her

voice quivering with indignation. "Do you deny that my husband was holding you on the sofa in a most unseemly manner? Do you deny that ever since our arrival he has run at your heels, slavering over you like a fox with a chicken?"

Simon left Charlotte to her own devices and walked forward. "It doesn't matter any more, Marianne. Madame de Valon is leaving England. Tomorrow, I trust."

It was Justine's turn to be furious. "I agree, Lady Stratton, ever since I have been in this house your husband has made a profound nuisance of himself. But tonight I understood why. He was trying to make you jealous."

"He was kissing you."

"It was gratitude," Gerald said. "Justine was explaining my duties as a husband."

Simon looked sharply at Justine.

Charlotte gave a whoop of delight and ran up. "Oh, Justine, you were? You must tell me all about it."

"I'm truly sorry," said Bertram.

"And I see that I must amend my behavior," Gerald continued, with the air of one making a handsome apology. "Can't have you running off with other fellows for satisfaction." Gerald struggled to his feet, then gave his hand to Marianne. "And speaking of satisfaction . . ."

Bertram threw back his shoulders. "You've treated your wife abominably, Stratton. But I had no right to be kissing her."

Charlotte laid her head on Justine's shoulder. "He kisses beautifully. I felt it all the way down to my toes."

"Bertram," Marianne said, "you didn't!"

"I thought she was you."

"It was the champagne," Charlotte explained. "I had to get out of the ballroom and I knew the conservatory would be quiet, and the next thing I knew, I was in his arms." She closed her eyes. "It was delicious."

"Two women." Gerald shook his head.

"I'm quite prepared to meet you on the field of honor," Bertram said, his voice resolute. "After I've met the prince."

"The prince?"

"Yes, they're betrothed. I've offered him satisfaction as well."

"Which I've refused," Simon said in a firm voice. "You'd best refuse as well, Stratton."

"He was kissing my wife!"

"I was kissing *him*," Marianne said. "It was a kiss of gratitude."

"Gratitude?" Gerald could barely contain his outrage.

"Yes, Gerald." Marianne's voice had a note of steel that Justine had never heard before. "You'd do well to remember it."

"Just why— No, never mind. It's not important." Gerald lifted his wife's hand and placed a tender kiss upon her palm. "Come, my love. Let me take you back to the ballroom." He slipped his arm around her waist. "Unless you're tired. We could go straight upstairs."

"Later, Gerald. Mr. Spence is waiting to dance with me."

"Hang Mr. Spence! If you dance with anyone, it will be with your husband."

Marianne broke free and turned to face him. "And there will be no nonsense about fighting a duel?"

Gerald took a deep breath. "No. I promise."

Marianne linked her arm with his. A smile lit her face. "Perhaps I do not want to dance after all."

They walked off together. "Poor Bertram," Charlotte said. "Now he doesn't have anyone."

Justine suddenly felt very tired. Simon was looking at her, his eyes black and intense. He seemed bewildered and uncertain. She looked away, unable to bear his scrutiny. "Come," she said to Charlotte, "I'll take you upstairs and put your dress and hair to rights."

She moved slowly toward the entryway with Charlotte, black leafy shadows rising high above them. "Oh, Justine, I'm so confused." Charlotte's voice was filled with tears. "I don't think I want to marry Simon."

"I've made a bloody mess of things, haven't I?" Bertram said, when the women had disappeared from sight.

The words echoed Simon's feelings exactly. "We both have."

"I never realized she actually cared for the fellow. Or that he was anything but indifferent to her. I was wrong about a lot of things."

As was he, Simon realized. His pain at losing Justine had made him blind to what was before his eyes. He had been all too ready to condemn her. In his eagerness to sever their connection he was little better than Gerald, seeking out a woman—any woman—to whom he could bind himself. He had misjudged Justine. He had been grossly unfair to Charlotte. And equally untrue to himself.

"The thing is," Bertram said, "you can't stop loving them, can you?"

Simon walked further into the conservatory, Bertram by his side. They reached the windows at its end. Light spilling through the carelessly drawn ballroom drapes made shafts of brightness across the winter grass, broken by the shadows of leafless branches. "No, you can't," Simon said. He had always loved Justine. He loved her still, beyond reason, with a certainty that swept all obstacles aside. But it had taken tonight's madness to make him see it.

Bertram turned suddenly to face Simon. "See here, Tassio. About Mademoiselle de Chambeau. She's a charming girl and easy to talk to, but I never meant . . . that is, I'm sorry about kissing her. Well, not sorry, exactly. It was deucedly pleasant, but I never would have if I'd realized . . . And then I thought she was someone else. But if it hadn't been for me, she wouldn't be so confused now, and . . . and things would be right between you."

Could he ever make things right? Simon wondered, scarcely hearing Bertram's words. He had treated Justine abominably. It was his jealousy and his wounded pride, but that was no excuse. "I'll go to her," he said. "I'll make her understand." He would tell Justine again how much he cared for her. He would wed her, if she would have him. And if she refused him again, he would at least not deny his love. Not to her, nor himself, nor the whole world.

"Oh, will you?" Bertram said. "It wasn't her fault at all. She was upset by what I did, I'm sure she was. And then, seeing Stratton laid out cold on the ground after she'd bashed him with the pot . . ."

Simon stared at Bertram as though he had come from another world. "You mean Charlotte?"

"Of course I mean Charlotte. I mean Mademoiselle de Chambeau."

"Yes, I'll speak to her, too," Simon said, realizing that he would have to do so before he could approach Justine.

"Tell her I'm sorry," Bertram said, a mournful note in his voice. "Tell her she'll never have to see me again. Tell her I'll leave Moresby tomorrow."

"Don't be twice an ass." Simon put his hand on the other man's shoulder. "Go back to the ballroom, Westcourt. Find a pretty unattached woman—there must be a dozen of them about—and ask her to dance."

Bertram gave him a half-hearted smile and walked away. Simon looked after him for a moment. Somewhere in the house he heard a clock strike midnight. It was the start of a new day. St. Valentine's Day. A day for lovers. Determined to learn his fate, Simon, too, left the room. Before he could seek out the woman he loved, he had to find out whether or not he was still betrothed.

Eight

The quiet in the family sitting room was broken by the gentle crackling of the wood fire. The clean scent of pine filled the air, a welcome change from the smell of perfumes and scented candles in the reception rooms during the ball. Simon settled into the comfortably worn damask of a high-backed chair, a glass of whisky cradled between his hands. It was a family custom to gather here after an entertainment when all the guests had either departed or retired to their rooms.

Usually, they spent a good hour discussing the high and low points of the evening. But tonight could hardly be called usual. After he'd left the conservatory, Simon had found Charlotte, subdued but seemingly quite sober. She was very sorry, she told him, but she feared she wasn't ready to marry anyone yet. Would he mind terribly releasing her from their betrothal?

As gravely as he could, Simon had assured her that he would respect her wishes in the matter. Feeling drunk on relief and elation, he had informed his family that the betrothal was at an end. Discussion had been impossible in the midst of the ball, just as it had been impossible for Simon to seek out Justine.

When the family were finally alone, Georgiana stayed only long enough to give Simon a quick hug. Sofia kissed Alessa, congratulated her on the ball, and went up to her room without

337

mentioning Charlotte. Michael gave Simon a look of sympathy and followed. Harry pressed Simon's arm and took himself off as well, leaving Simon alone with Alessa. Simon wasn't sure whether he was grateful to his brother-in-law or angry with him.

"On the whole," Alessa said, regarding Simon over her gold-rimmed teacup, "I'd say you look relieved."

Talking about Charlotte with his sister, Simon discovered, was not nearly so difficult, now that he and Charlotte were no longer betrothed. "Charlotte's much too young to be ready for marriage," he said. "If I hadn't been so pigheaded, I'd have seen that from the first."

"A handsome admission." Alessa set down her cup. *Maman* still means to take Charlotte to London. She says Charlotte has distinct possibilities, but that she requires some firm guidance."

Simon smiled. *Maman* is being remarkably restrained. All she said to me was that she assumed Charlotte and I were doing what was best for both of us. For once, she was absolutely right."

"I think she's been worried about you. I know Fiona was. She absolutely refused to discuss the betrothal with me, which must mean she was afraid she'd be betrayed into admitting her doubts." Alessa removed her pearl-and-diamond earrings and began to massage her earlobes. "Does Madame de Valon still mean to return to France?" she asked with a fair attempt at an idle tone.

Though Simon took a sip of whisky, the heat coursing through his body had nothing to do with the drink. "I don't know," he said. "Why don't you ask her?"

Alessa looked directly at him. "If you let her get away, you're a fool."

"Are you suggesting I resume an illicit liaison under your roof?" Simon asked, gauging his sister's reaction.

Alessa continued to look at him. "If you like. But that's not what I had in mind."

Simon's fingers clenched around the cold crystal of the

glass. "She may not want me," he said, in a light tone that was belied by the sickening sense of dread coiled within him.

"*She's* a fool if she doesn't," Alessa said.

Simon grinned in spite of himself. "That's a truly handsome admission, sister mine."

Alessa smiled back. Then her face grew serious. "It's a risk, Simon. But without such risks, life is nothing." She stood, the earrings in one hand, and shook out her skirt. "If I say anything more, you'll think I'm impertinent. And if I don't go to bed, I'll never manage to get up and have breakfast with my children."

Simon accompanied his sister upstairs, but Alessa made no further effort at conversation, for which he was grateful. Life seemed at once too wondrous and too terrifying for him to attempt anything as mundane as casual talk.

At the head of the stairs, Alessa gave him a kiss on the cheek, then went into her room. The sound of Harry's voice and Alessa's answering laughter spilled into the corridor before the door swung shut. Simon remained where he was, his hand clenched on the carved wolf which ornamented the newel post. The impulse to go to Justine's chamber, hammer on her door, and insist that she marry him at the earliest possible opportunity was almost overmastering. He took a step forward, then checked himself. Justine would probably be with Charlotte, who after the events of the evening would almost certainly want to talk. He had waited over a year. What were a few more hours?

An eternity. He returned to his room and undressed, but found himself unable to sleep. He spent the night in an armchair by the windows, watching the sky lighten with agonizing slowness. A sense of freedom made him lightheaded. The knowledge that he knew exactly what he wanted intoxicated him. Yet underneath it all was a gnawing fear. Justine had refused him once. Why should it be different now?

He recalled his last glimpse of her in the conservatory. He would swear she was not wholly indifferent to him. But there was the matter of her mysterious visits to the inn in Moresby village. Had she been having secret rendezvous with one of the guests? Or with some other man? It didn't matter, Simon tried to tell himself. If she would marry him, they would forget the past. But would Justine want to?

When he could stand it no longer, Simon dressed and started downstairs. Justine rode early in the morning. He would intercept her before she left the house. He would ask her nothing about the reasons for her rides unless she chose to tell him.

He paused on the half-landing and glanced out the window. Through the blur of condensation on the glass, he glimpsed a woman in russet galloping out of the stable yard. Even before he wiped the glass clear he knew it was Justine. His stomach clenched. There was no help for it. He had to follow her. That he might find himself confronting her lover he knew full well. But he also knew that he wanted her more than anything in the world. And Alessa was right. Life was nothing without risk.

Justine turned her horse into the yard of the Crown. The early morning air was damp against her skin and the wind tugged at her hat and the skirt of her riding habit. She knew she ought to feel happier than she did. Last night, Charlotte and Simon had been on the verge of trapping themselves in a loveless marriage, and Marianne and Gerald's marriage had been on the verge of collapse. Now, Charlotte would go to London, where she would have a chance to grow up and try her wings and eventually meet a young man with whom she could be happy. Simon would have time to recover from his determination to marry for convenience. Before too long, no doubt, he would meet a young woman with whom he could truly fall in love. Even the Strattons' marriage seemed miraculously mended.

All had turned out far better than Justine had dreamed possible a few short hours ago. So why this heavy feeling in her heart?

She knew the answer, of course: because as soon as could be decently contrived, she should leave Moresby and return to France. And if she had a scrap of honor or sense, she would never see Simon again.

Justine pulled up on the reins. The inn was quiet, with little to disturb the gray mist hanging over the building. The mail had not yet arrived and there were no carriages drawn up in the yard. Rob, a young stableboy with whom Justine had grown friendly, hurried over to take the reins of her horse. As Justine accepted his hand and slid from the mare's back, she heard the sound of hooves against the cobblestones. She turned to see a familiar dark brown horse. She raised her eyes further and found herself looking at Simon.

Justine was aware of the labored breaths of her horse. Or perhaps what she felt was her own trembling. She could think of only one reason why Simon would have followed her here. He had learned about Minette.

Simon swung down from his horse and handed the reins to Rob along with a handful of coins. Rob cast an inquiring glance at Justine, as if to be sure she really wanted to be left alone with this stranger. Justine was grateful for his loyalty, but she nodded. If Simon knew about Minette, she would have to face him sooner or later.

She and Simon stood listening to the retreating hoofbeats and footsteps. Simon's eyes were dark and intense, as they had been last night in the conservatory, but he did not seem angry. There was a kind of tautly strung excitement about him which surprised her.

The stable door creaked shut and they were alone in an island of mist and silence. Justine drew a breath, knowing she owed him an explanation. "Simon—"

"No. Listen to me first." Simon crossed to her in two strides and seized both her hands. The warmth of his clasp sent a shock of longing through her. The heat in his eyes made her dizzy. "I love you," he said. "I loved you in Paris, and I love you now. There's no other woman for me. I don't think there ever could be."

Justine stared up at him, caught by the force of his gaze, stunned by the sweetness of his words. It was a moment before she trusted herself to speak. Joy could so easily betray her into saying the wrong thing. Had learning about Minette somehow prompted Simon to make this declaration? No, his eyes were telling her he had thoughts for no one but her. With a start of surprise, Justine realized he didn't know about Minette at all. "Is that why you followed me here?" she asked. "To tell me this?"

Simon's hands tightened about her own. "I couldn't wait any longer."

Oh, dear God, it was true. Simon was here before her, saying the words she had never thought to hear from him again. The pain was more than she could bear. Justine wrenched her hands from his clasp. "I won't be your mistress, Simon."

Simon regarded her with surprise and what seemed very like indignation. "Good God, Justine, I don't want a mistress. This time I won't settle for anything less than marriage."

The wind had come up, swirling the mist around them, but not as wildly as the thoughts tumbled in her head. "You can't," she blurted out. "You can't marry me."

"I'm a Tassio," Simon retorted. "I can do what I please." He started to reach for her again, then checked himself, as if to say he would not use that weapon to win her.

"It's because of Charlotte," Justine said, speaking quickly, before her thoughts could run away with her. "Even though it wasn't a love match, you're bound to be hurt, but in time—"

"Hurt?" Simon gave a shout of laughter. "I've never been so relieved in my life." He stood looking at her for a moment with an expression in his eyes that took her breath away. "I was a fool not to insist on marrying you in Paris," he said softly.

"You were too young." Justine folded her arms in front of her, fighting the impulse to rush into his arms.

Simon shook his head. "I've never been young."

Justine drew a shuddering in breath. She couldn't allow her-

342

self to believe in what he was offering her. "You don't know why I came to the Crown," she told him.

A shadow seemed to flicker across Simon's face. "It doesn't matter," he said with determination. "We can put the past behind us."

Hysterical laughter rose in Justine's throat. "That's just it, Simon. I can't. The past will always be with me."

Simon laid a hand on her arm. "Don't be afraid," he said, his eyes gentle.

"I'm not afraid." Justine gave way to impulse and placed her fingers over his own. "It's the way things are."

As she looked into his eyes, Justine made her decision. Simon had come to her with his soul stripped bare. Whatever else was possible between them, she could at least be as honest as he. Without speaking, she took his hand and drew him toward the inn.

She could feel Simon's tension as they crossed the yard. Did he think he was going to be confronted with a rival? It was no good trying to explain. The situation would speak for itself soon enough.

The maidservant sweeping the floor in the entry hall nodded to Justine, used to her visits. Justine led Simon up the narrow stairs to the room she had taken at the back of the inn, removed from the noise of the street, with as much sun as was possible in Bedfordshire in February. Emilie, Minette's nurse, got to her feet when Justine opened the door. A country girl from near Justine's château, Emilie had recently suffered the humiliation of an out-of-wedlock pregnancy and then the grief of losing her baby. She had been pleased at the chance to escape to England as Minette's wetnurse.

At the sight of Simon, Emilie's smile of greeting faded to a look of surprise. She dropped a quick curtsy and glanced at Justine.

"It's all right, Emilie," Justine told the girl. "Go and have some breakfast."

The cradle the innkeeper's wife had given them stood near the windows, partly concealed by a table and armchair. Justine didn't think Simon had seen it yet. When the door closed behind Emilie, Justine motioned Simon to follow her. She did not look back, but she heard the check in his footsteps when the cradle came into view. There was a moment of absolute quiet. Then she felt him come to stand beside her.

Minette was asleep, her fingers curled against the bed-clothes, her lashes resting against her soft skin. Justine raised her eyes from the cradle and forced herself to look at Simon. "This is my daughter, Minette."

Simon continued to look at the cradle. Justine could feel the weight of the silence pressing in upon her. "I remember when Alastair was born," Simon said, after a long moment. "Alessa's eldest. I'd say your daughter is less than six months old."

Justine held herself very still. "She'll be five months at the end of February."

Simon turned to her at last. Justine wasn't sure what she had expected. Anger perhaps, or disbelief. Certainly surprise. Instead, his face held a look of sheer wonder. "She's ours, isn't she?" he said.

Unable to speak, Justine nodded.

"I wish you'd told me," Simon said gently. There was no censure in his tone. "A child needs a father."

"I didn't know until after you'd left. And I didn't want—"

"To make demands." Simon's mouth twisted in a wry grimace. "My darling, I'm so very sorry," he said, brushing his fingers against her cheek. "What you must have been through. I should have wondered—I thought we'd been careful—"

"We had." Justine managed a shaky smile. "Accidents happen."

Simon regarded her with concern. "You must have cursed me for leaving you in such a state."

"No," Justine said quickly. "When I got over the shock, I was glad. I knew it would be awkward, but I wanted—" *Some part of you.* But if she said that, she would admit the strength of her feelings for him, and then she would have no defenses left.

Simon looked back at Minette. "She's beautiful. With Alessa's children I didn't quite realize . . . It's miraculous, isn't it? That we could create something so—"

"Perfect." This time Justine smiled involuntarily. She hadn't realized how much it would mean to her to be able to share such a simple moment with her baby's father.

"Yes." Simon looked down at Minette a moment longer, then turned to Justine with decision. "This changes things. I said I should have married you in Paris. Now it's obvious that I did. We've been married for at least fifteen months."

Justine stared at him. "Don't be absurd," she protested.

"I'm being practical. We have to think of Minette's future."

"Good God," Justine exclaimed, "do you imagine I've thought of anything else these past months? But we can't—"

"These things can be arranged," Simon said. "I'm the Prince di Tassio."

Justine put a hand to her head, which had begun to spin wildly. "It's a lovely quixotic gesture, Simon, but how on earth would you explain why you proposed to Charlotte when you already have a wife?"

Simon grinned. He almost seemed to be enjoying himself. "No one knows but the family and Charlotte herself," he pointed out. "And Bertram, I suppose, but I'll have a word with him. My family can be counted on to keep quiet, and Charlotte will be agreeable." The smile left his eyes. He looked at her with utter seriousness. "We can have marriage on any terms you want, Justine, but don't refuse me. I don't want our child to grow up without a name."

Justine swallowed. All her fears for Minette were reflected in Simon's eyes. Her heart raced wildly. She couldn't— "I don't want you to marry me because of Minette," she said, the words torn from her throat.

"God give me patience." Simon gripped her by the shoulders. "Haven't I made my feelings clear? I asked you to be my wife before I knew Minette existed. I'm not a child. I haven't been coerced or blackmailed or bewitched—well, possibly bewitched, but it's an enchantment from which I have no wish to be released. I love you, Justine."

A dozen protests rose in her throat, but she could not form them into words. Simon's eyes seemed to see into her soul, past any lies she could utter. For the first time she let herself truly consider a future as his wife. Happiness surged through her, robbing her of breath and the power of speech.

"Just promise you'll never send me away again," Simon said, his voice ragged.

"Oh, Simon." Tears stung Justine's eyelids. "I don't think I could. You're so infernally stubborn."

His breath left him on a shuddering sigh. He pulled her tight against him, his hands sinking into her hair. A sound between a laugh and a sob escaped her lips as she pulled his head down to her own. His mouth tasted of relief and joy, of remembered happiness and future promises. She clung tightly to him, qualms and fears swept aside by the sureness of his touch and the rightness of the feel of his arms around her.

A cry from Minette was perhaps the only thing that could have restored her to sanity. Simon released her at once. Justine drew back, giddy with happiness, her hair spilling around her face, her hat slipping to one side, and lifted her daughter into her arms. Scarcely able to believe it was real, she glanced up at Simon.

What she saw in his eyes banished any doubts. Justine smoothed Minette's hair and looked from her baby to her baby's father. "Would you like to hold your daughter, Simon?"

The mist had begun to clear and a fitful sun streamed through the windows of Sofia's dressing room. Simon closed the door firmly behind him and moved toward the table near the fireplace where his mother was sitting.

Sofia set down her cup of chocolate and looked at him as if trying to judge the reason he had insisted on this early-morning conference. It was over two hours since Simon and Justine had returned from the Crown, but Simon knew his

346

mother considered ten-thirty a ridiculously early hour to rise after a night of dancing.

"If it's about Charlotte," Sofia said, pouring a second cup of chocolate, "I think that has all been arranged very satisfactorily."

"It isn't about Charlotte." Simon pulled out one of the chintz-covered chairs and seated himself. "It's about Madame de Valon."

Sofia handed the cup across the table to him, her eyes wary. "I understand she means to return to France."

"On the contrary." Simon pushed aside the chocolate. He had no taste for it at the best of times. "She is staying in England. With me."

Simon watched with satisfaction as the words registered in the depths of his mother's green eyes. Her finely arched brows drew together. "You can't seriously mean to marry the woman."

"Not exactly." Simon smiled at his mother with the greatest good will. Nothing could dim his happiness. "Justine has been my wife for over a year. We have a daughter who is almost five months old."

The color drained from Sofia's face. "She told you."

"About the birth of my child?" Simon said gently. "I have known all along. My wife and I have no secrets from each other."

Sofia stared at him for a long moment. "Do you imagine you can get away with this?" she demanded.

"Why not?" Simon countered. "You've taught me that few will question the word of a Tassio."

"Don't be impertinent, Simon." Sofia drummed her fingers on the tabletop. "You're doing it for the child, of course. I understand your sense of obligation. But there's no need—"

"There's every need," Simon said, before his mother could offer an unpardonable insult to Justine. "I have a duty to my daughter. And I can't live without her mother."

Sofia's eyes widened. She released her breath in a sigh of resignation or acknowledgment. Then she settled back in her chair and took a fortifying sip of chocolate. "I take it you have thought of a reason why the marriage has been kept secret?"

"You were unalterably opposed to it," Simon informed his mother, pleased to have won his first objective. "Justine's pregnancy was difficult and we did not want to risk a confrontation with the family until after the baby was born."

Sofia pursed her lips, as if giving the story honest consideration. "That," she pointed out, "does not explain why you brought Madame de Valon to your sister's house not as your wife but as the chaperone of a young girl to whom you were paying court."

"Oh, Charlotte's all right," Simon assured her. "Justine and I have already had a talk with her. She thinks the whole thing is very romantic and she'll do anything to help. Fortunately, the betrothal was never public and Charlotte and I have hardly been behaving like lovers."

Sofia was almost betrayed into a smile. Then her eyes narrowed. "None of this explains why you did not present your wife at Moresby as—as the Princess di Tassio." There was the slightest catch to her voice on this last. She had been the Princess di Tassio for many years.

"I wanted you to have a chance to get to know Justine before you learned of the marriage," Simon told her. "Now that you have met, you understand what a truly remarkable woman she is and how lucky I am to have won her. You have no further objections to the marriage."

"I see." Sofia regarded him for a moment. "Do I have any choice in the matter?"

"Naturally." Simon fixed her with a hard stare. "You can choose to see your granddaughter branded a bastard. I don't recommend it. I'll never forgive you, I doubt that Alessa will, and I imagine Michael won't think too highly of you, either."

Sofia added some more chocolate to her cup and stirred it with careful precision. "There's no need to be so theatrical, Simon. I have no wish to see any child hurt, and certainly not your own. If you have decided to make Madame de Valon

348

your wife, it will be best for everyone if the marriage is believed to have taken place before the birth of the child. You will of course wish to have a—a second ceremony?"

"Of course. The first marriage took place in France. Justine says she will not feel properly married until we have a wedding in England with our families present."

"Ah." Sofia smiled. "Yes, that should answer. There will be talk, of course, but you can brazen it out. By the time the child is grown, I doubt anyone will remember."

"Precisely." Simon looked at his mother with affection. He had never felt so in charity with her. But because he wanted her to do more than accept the marriage, he added, "I love Justine, *Maman*. I was mad even to think of marrying anyone else."

Before Sofia could respond, there was a knock at the door. It was Alessa. "I hope you've settled it all," she said, sweeping confidently into the room. "I've brought Justine and Minette."

Simon got to his feet and looked sharply at his sister. He wasn't at all sure this was the time to introduce their mother to Minette. Alessa smiled at him with sunny confidence as if to say, "I know what I'm doing, I've been coping with *Maman* longer than you have."

Justine followed Alessa into the room. She had changed from her riding habit into a dress of a soft fawn-colored material which seemed to make her hair glow even more richly than usual. The pearl brooch Simon had given her in Paris was pinned to her bosom. Minette was cradled in her arms, her head peeking out from folds of blanket.

Simon met Justine's gaze. For a moment the world was reduced to just the three of them. He crossed the room, touched the baby's head lightly, and put his arm around Justine. Together they could face anything. And yet— For all her faults, Sofia was his mother, and life would be much more pleasant if she could treat this marriage with more than resignation.

Sofia got to her feet, smoothed the skirt of her dressing gown with care, and looked at Justine. "I understand you are my daughter-in-law. I hope you will forgive me for not acknowledging you sooner. It was too bad of Simon to keep his marriage from me."

Simon felt some of the tension leave Justine's body. She met Sofia's gaze directly. "There have been too many secrets on all sides, Princess."

It seemed to Simon that some sort of silent acknowledgment passed between the two women. But Sofia made no move to come forward and look at the baby.

"Do come and see Minette, *Maman,*" Alessa said. "She's quite enchanting. And she most definitely has the Tassio mouth."

Sofia glanced at her daughter, as if to say she understood that Alessa was trying to play upon her sentimentality. Then, with the slightest shrug of her shoulders, Sofia moved toward Simon and Justine. "Another grandchild," she said, her voice light, though her face softened as she looked down at Minette. "You're right, Alessa. Definitely the Tassio mouth."

Simon sent his sister a look of gratitude, then turned to the magnificent woman who would soon be his wife. Her mouth curved in a smile that was only for him. Simon tightened his arm around her. He no longer felt old. He was eternally young.